The House of Returned Echoes

THE HOUSE OF RETURNED ECHOES

ARNOŠT LUSTIG

Translated from the Czech by Josef Lustig

NORTHWESTERN UNIVERSITY PRESS

Evanston, Illinois

Northwestern University Press
Evanston, Illinois 60208–4210

"The Echo" appeared in a slightly different version in *New England
Review* 15, no. 3 (summer 1993): 99–142.

Printed in the United States of America

10 9 8 7 6 5 4 3 2 1

ISBN 0-8101-1858-0 (cloth)
ISBN 0-8101-1859-9 (paper)

Library of Congress Cataloging-in-Publication Data

Lustig, Arnošt.
[Dům vrácené ozvěny. English]
The house of returned echoes / Arnošt Lustig.
p. cm.
ISBN 0-8101-1858-0 (cloth) — ISBN 0-8101-1859-9 (pbk.)
I. Title.
PG5038.L85 D8613 2001
891.8'6354—dc21

2001000568

Thanks to the National Endowment for the Arts.

And to friends who helped: JoAnn Margaret Cooper,

Jessica Friedman-Blackman, James Mitchell,

Charles Larson, and Rob Scott.

My God! Before we were created I was nothing, and
now that I am created, I am as much as if I had not
been created: dust am I during my life, all the more
after I die.
Behold! Here I stand before Thee like a vessel, full
of shame and degradation. Thy will be done, Oh Lord,
my God and God of my fathers, that I may sin no more,
and where I have sinned before Thee, forgive through
your abundant mercy, but not through pains and evil
sicknesses.

*—Prayers for Ordinary Days, Sabbaths and Holy Days as
well as for the Day of Atonement*

I make with you this day a covenant
which declares that never again
shall I bring a flood into the world
and that I shall not suddenly obliterate all the lives,
as I have done this time.
So long as the earth remains the earth,
night and day will alternate,
summer and winter, warm and cool,
the time of sowing and reaping,
but never shall I bring about a flood again.
The rainbow which you see in the sky
is a visible sign of this covenant.
Whenever I behold it,
I shall recall my promise,
which I have given.

—Genesis 9:10–12

✿

Contents

Preface

The House of Returned Echoes is a book about my father, who died in the gas chambers of Auschwitz at the end of September 1944. When I went on a journey around the world in 1965, I took the manuscript with me. I wrote in hotel rooms while in Persia, India, and China; in Ceylon, Tokyo, and Hanoi; and, finally, in San Francisco and New York. Before departing from New York for San Juan, Puerto Rico, with the airline tickets for Madrid, Paris, and my return to Prague, I left my car, borrowed from an émigré friend, unattended for a moment. When I returned, the car was opened and the suitcase with my manuscript was gone.

A representative from Prague said that he suspected the American Secret Service; the American police said they suspected the Secret Police of the other side. No one has ever located the suitcase. I rewrote the book from an earlier draft. I had the feeling that, in a sense, one completes the writing of a book before he touches the paper. Everything came back to me—it is easier to return a lost book to paper than to return to earth the lost people one writes about. This, then, is the story surrounding *The House of Returned Echoes.* It is the story of a man for whom family was the reason for his creation, for which he struggled against fate. In his case, this fate was Germany, the Nazis, and the struggle for dignity. It is a story about the times he confronted—like a ship's pilot setting out to sea in a coracle without oars.

It is also a story about a man who, like many others, believed until the end that the Nazis would not go through with their threats because he himself could never carry out such things on anyone—or admit that someone might be happy in the midst of others' misfortunes. He relied on what is called civilization and its laws, instead of relying on the instinct which says that man is his own devil and that he who does not defend himself perishes. He was one of the twelve million killed in the camps of World War II. In the same way that all people are identical, and yet unique like their fingerprints, this is a story, then, of a man and his family and the other people close to them. Or, we can say that they all are inspiration, mixing truth and fantasy, as in any fiction. But down at the bottom lies the reality—the Final Solution, which the Nazis planned, created, and mobilized.

It was said that zyklon-B, which the Germans used for exterminating people in Auschwitz-Birkenau, had the bitter smell of almonds. Perhaps. It seemed to me that while writing, no matter where I was, I was breathing it—as if it were still in the air—that I am still breathing it, every night and each day. It transformed living people into dead ones, hope into despair, usefulness into futility. I hoped to write an honest book.

The House of Returned Echoes

FAMILY

From Helena's notes:

In the night, Papa dreamed that for the first time, Grandpa Ferdinand, who stole horses, took him along. They rode together to the market and on the way back bought coffee, grapes, fruit, and lots of other good things. Papa smiled about it in the morning at breakfast. Did Grandpa Ferdinand really steal and sell horses? Isn't that only a family legend that Papa perpetuates so that we don't feel too small or too important? I have never yet guessed where Papa was going with it. He tells the story as if he were laughing at something inside himself. With his peaceful blue eyes, he seems like he could embrace all the people in the whole world and drink coffee at the same time. It's too bad that I never got to meet Grandpa Ferdinand. He died when Papa was fourteen.

"You have to learn how to be born," Emil Ludvig said. "Isn't it a wonderful thing to breathe the fresh air to your heart's content?"

"The most important thing is to start on the right foot," Anna replied. "Let's go, then, so we'll be back in time. How long do you want to stay there?"

"Why do you think about the end before you even get started?" Emil asked, smiling.

Life is a question of practicality, he thought. It's clear what escaped me. I need money. There's nothing new under the sun, as Anna always says. Where'll I get it without stealing?

Emil sometimes thought about the fact that even the most ordinary people play many roles in their lives. In his mind, he stood in front of a mirror: he saw himself as a breadwinner, businessman, and husband; friend, relative, brother-in-law, and uncle; and, at various other times in his life, son, student, soldier, and shop assistant. He was reminded of the way he'd sometimes slipped out of one role and then had to return to it later, and how at other times, certain roles merged and became, or were, mutually exclusive of one another. A man had to cue himself as to when to take on a role with the curtain up: to say "yes" in one role, "no" in another, and "maybe" in yet another. Sometimes he had to appear to play one role and talk as if he were playing a second, while in reality, he was playing a third.

Emil laughed at his own ludicrous thoughts. For the moment, he was lucky in at least one role: even though he sometimes had to be on the run all day, away from home, he always made it home and never had to spend the night anywhere else. I'm like a swallow—gone all day but always coming home at night to rest, he thought to himself.

He managed to maintain his carefree ways—that helped him. He didn't bother much about the role of housekeeper and doctor. (Anna outdid him in those arenas, anyway. She believed in the generic healing power of garlic, even if the smell forced you to hold your nose.) He took delight in his children, Richard and Helena. He wondered which roles in his life he had yet to play and to what depths a person might stoop for his family. He knew that there was one role he'd have to play in a little while, but he didn't yet know quite what it would be. He only knew what he wanted from it. Subconsciously, he asked himself if he was up to it. He knew that a person wants to stand his ground in all his ventures, especially if they are witnessed by people who matter to him.

It was a clear winter day. The snow had been swept off the sidewalks, but the rooftops were still white with the painless weight. Emil looked over at the children, Helena and Richard. They hadn't a clue about his troubles, which fit with the way Anna blew them out of proportion. It was good; one day they would have enough troubles of their own. It occurred to him that they were still a young family with the very best still ahead of them. The thing was to not let anything worry them. Money is only money, after all; the important thing is still to be young and to have enough strength to do everything. (Unfortunately, he added to himself, for *everything*.)

"Papa, why do people kill animals?" asked Richard.

"The last thing I would kill is an animal," replied Emil. "Why did you think of that?"

"You didn't answer me," Richard objected.

"I don't like to talk about killing," Emil said.

That morning he had read in the newspaper how a tiger at the Busch circus had killed a keeper with a swipe of its paw to the skull, which had burst like a hazelnut. They had been to the circus last Sunday. The newest attraction was the hypnotist. He chose a woman from the audience and conjured up in her memories of her parents she'd forgotten. Had her parents beaten her? Yes, they had, the woman said.

"It isn't that easy to kill," Emil added.

"Are you going to talk about killing?" interjected Anna. "If so, I don't want to listen."

"Killing always comes last," Emil stated. He felt an echo inside of the lightheartedness that revives the energy and the inexperience of youth. If carefree ways or frivolity meant youth, he couldn't complain; he felt young. It was as if one half of a man could already be the head of a family and the other half still be in the realm of youth, which believes in success and in miracles big and small and which trusts almost everything or everyone else, except himself. Wasn't it part of lightheartedness to believe that most people had their opinions but only he could really see?

Kralovska Avenue led straight as an arrow from their shop at number 137. There was a barbershop next to the vacant lot where a post office was to be built; on the other side was a marriage bureau with big photographs of happy couples in the window. The Balek and Cezare di Carlo Company, importers of southern fruit and delicatessen, sat in the same block next to a cutlery shop, which had an advertisement in the window beside a picture of forks for the American movie *Ali Baba and the Forty Thieves*.

The lower part of the shop in the building where Uncle Arthur lived was rented to a hardware store. Every winter—this one too—they had a display of heaters without prices listed: the slow-burning American stove, the Musgraves Original; Belgian radiators for factories or warehouses; German heating pistons with fireproof glass; and fake English fireplaces.

Emil Ludvig, holding Anna by the hand, stopped in front of the display. He studied the heaters to see which one, if he had the money, would best suit their shop on Kralovska Avenue. (Every winter Anna's hands got frozen.)

They had already passed the vacant lots left by condemned, demolished buildings. (He didn't like empty spaces.) He could see his own reflection in the window case. He was wearing a new coat; he buttoned it up. After the third fitting, the tailor on Kralovska Avenue had taken two of his assistants out to the sidewalk to demonstrate that a man has to know how to walk in a fine suit. ("You look like the president of a bank, Mr. Ludvig, it's only the truth," he'd said.) Emil wasn't the largest of men, and it made him feel bigger when he dressed well and walked upright. He couldn't explain it to anyone (and he didn't try), not even to himself. There was a little touch of vanity in it, but everyone likes to look his best in front of others.

The tailor had become famous in the neighborhood for his stolen, state-owned Zeiss telescope. Since the fall, he'd been peeking in on the honeymoon of the music teacher who lived above the cleaner's on the first floor of the building across the street. The teacher would wake up this, his second wife, in the morning by kissing her on her stomach, and once she awoke, he would put a mug of coffee and her morning roll right on her bare skin. If anyone in the Mercury pub claimed that some men were afraid of women, including their own wives, that didn't apply to the music teacher.

"I'm thinking about Arthur," Anna said. She was wondering where Emil had gotten his carefree spirit or his sometimes almost out-of-place happiness. Where did his energy come from? (She should have been asking herself, at least, this last question.) Her thoughts led to their relatives.

How could someone be amazed by someone and curse them at the same time? Anna asked herself. You have to learn how to get along with relatives. Her mother had taught her that. As far as relatives were concerned, the maxims "Silence is golden" and "silver speech" applied. Everybody loves a winner, but if you're unlucky, don't pay attention to the score. Last time Arthur put it better: The war between men and women was the only war where enemies happily slept together in the same bed. Arthur also liked to talk about the tailor's observation escapades. No one had yet stolen a telescope from the state which could look at what he really wanted to see.

"I wouldn't want to tell anyone twice how they're supposed to behave on a visit," Anna reminded the children. "That applies to Papa too. It would be sad if I have to repeat this again at Arthur's."

They stopped at the landing in the mezzanine. Anna glanced at Helen and Richard. Emil admired the little cherubs with their rounded stone rumps set into semicircular hollows. The walls of the stairwell were papered with Dutch windmills.

Emil Ludvig rang the bell. The noise sounded like lead buckshot hitting a tin bowl.

"Next time around I want to be born as an Arthur," Emil exhaled. (He thought of the remark Arthur had made the last time they'd visited, that the happiest man in the world was the one satisfied with himself and who didn't need anybody else. There's not many of those and never will be, he said to himself.)

"Oh, it's you," Aunt Martha called out through the open door. She squinted a bit; her blue eyes were extremely nearsighted. She wore the same gold wire-rimmed glasses as Emil: 20/300 in her left eye, 20/500 in her right. "We were expecting you last Sunday."

"Well, here's our guests," Arthur sang out. "Who do these beautiful children belong to?"

"How goes it, Arthur?" asked Emil. "What's new?"

"A couple of people died in the business; one of them was a big competitor of mine. He shouldn't have pushed himself so hard. Where've you all been that you didn't show up last Sunday?"

Arthur was all smiles. He had raven-black hair and thick eyebrows of the same color. A Christmas tree stood in the corner of the living room. All kinds of scents and smells mingled throughout the flat. Double curtains of (already yellowing) white silk and faded red velvet hung in the windows.

"It smells like a forest in here," Emil said. "If you had bought a bigger tree, you would've had to make a hole in the ceiling to the flat upstairs. Who lives up there anyhow?"

"Some big shot from a failed bank," Arthur replied. "He fought at the Piave River, like you. Got a leg wound like you too—the only difference is that he got rich from it."

The Piave was a place and time far in Emil's past, but a person never forgets what he went through, heard, saw, or did. Arthur had touched a nerve. Sometimes, you're lucky if you were born a hundred or a thousand kilometers away from where you would have been if it had occurred to some ancestor to wander a little farther or a little less far. He wasn't saying that he would be happy to have a grave someday that somebody could take care of as the two of them and Richard (and Helen and Anna) took care of Grandpa Ferdinand's resting place. You have a different view of death when you're close to it and another one from far away.

If it didn't prolong the life of the dead, it did prolong the memory of their life—of what had been the best in them. Emil's father, Ferdinand, had died when Emil was fourteen; afterward, he'd taken care of his mother and Martha, though sometimes they'd also looked after him. It was a pity, for whatever reason, that Ferdinand had drunk himself to death. It was ironic that Ferdinand had drunk to his children's health so often that in the end, he'd left them all alone.

Richard pondered what his father wasn't saying, and all of a sud-

11

den, the same thought occurred to Emil too. (Did telepathy run in the family?) Arthur had always earned more than they had, no matter what he did; there was probably no point in competing with him. Maybe a person needed someone else to compete with. (From time to time it seemed to Richard that his father thought of Arthur as a rival, so he could prove, by someone he knew well, that he was equal to if not better than him.) Emil Ludvig fought with his suppliers and deliverymen just like Arthur Pick, who had already gotten rid of his own sole proprietorship. Like Uncle Arthur, Emil hated rent and tax-due dates. But Papa could have been a soldier in a split second— which was something Uncle Arthur probably never could do. Papa's shop, which they had gotten from the owner as part of Anna's dowry shortly after the wedding, was a mixed cornucopia, as Uncle Munk had once said. Papa's tribulations didn't get him any contacts, like Mr. Tanzer, Dr. Mautner, and Mr. Neuman from the shop on Primatorska.

It wouldn't be right to talk with Papa about it—here, especially. Richard sensed what his father worried about—even if he probably didn't want to admit it.

"We haven't been to the forest for ten years," Martha said.

Anna and the children sat down. The coal heater glowed in the corner.

Arthur smiled. His nose curved deeply. He knocked on the wooden arm of his chair with the knuckle of his ring finger.

Several Venetian mirrors hung in the apartment. They were placed so that Arthur could see himself from all sides.

"I just can't tear myself away from a mirror," Arthur said.

"The older you get, the more vain you get," Martha stated.

"I don't want to cheat myself out of something nice to look at," Arthur replied.

Anna thought to herself that Arthur would be happiest if he could climb into the mirror itself. What he'd really like to do was to get so close that he could go right through it so he could be certain that nothing had escaped his notice. The mirrors were expensive, and when the family was still alive, Arthur's mother would always remark how much they'd paid for them. Once in a while, Arthur would joke that his mother had been so thrifty that his father had had to tear her holey nightgowns off her. She was known to wear one for ten years before she wore it out beyond any hope of mending. His father would shout that he didn't want a wife wearing a nightgown with holes next to him in bed. He would always tell her that he earned enough in his business to buy her ten of the most beautiful lace nightgowns if she wanted them, but Arthur's mother would still buy only one of the cheapest kind, and soon it, too, had holes. She always said that no money—not even his—grew on trees. Anna was frugal, too, but not to that degree. Arthur took after his father in that he couldn't bear holes in women's lingerie. He insisted that Martha buy only the best for herself and Susanna. When Martha said that to her, this was throwing money away on foolishness, he would tell her that rich enough for him was being able to afford a single hard-boiled egg every day. Arthur's mother had always defended herself, saying she liked holey nightgowns. His father would then ask her, shouting, whether she liked holey underwear too—and then pull them off her. That made her laugh, but she was nervous when he did it with little Arthur watching them. She answered that, no, she didn't like holey underwear, but that she didn't want to end up like Arthur's grandfather had—having to gradually sell off their crystal lamps and Persian carpets, along with his wife's white mink and gold ring with the two diamonds, as well as the big, black piano that no one was allowed to put anything on top of. Those were the years when Johann Strauss composed his famous opera, *Die Fledermaus.* "Go right now and buy new underwear and nightgowns!" he bellowed. "If you insist," she replied. "Today . . . *now!*" his father had yelled.

Arthur always told stories when the subject of family and ancestors came up. His father had been the most cautious person in the family. He didn't believe that the days when someone would throw them out of where they'd settled were long gone. On the contrary, he was convinced that the entire world hated them and would keep on hating them, and that just around the corner, hordes were getting ready to burst in on them without any warning. Arthur's father had made sure that every family member had a valid passport at all times, along with at least twenty gold pieces with the portrait of Emperor Franz Joseph or Empress Maria Theresa on them.

Arthur always liked to say his father had taught him that waiting until the last moment to get your passport was a fateful mistake, even if you never took a step away from your home your entire life until you died in your sleep in bed.

Emil always laughed a little bit at his brother-in-law, but Anna agreed that one never could ever really know what might happen. Her parents had also been cautious and suspicious, even if it wasn't a catastrophe for them if a passport fell out-of-date. And, she pointed out to Emil, no matter whose portrait was on them, twenty gold coins would certainly do them good at the moment.

Sometimes Arthur would say that nobody was going to inherit a thing from him—just the way no one had inherited anything on the death of his father.

Arthur appreciated Anna, Emil, and the children's admiring looks at the tree. He rapped the knuckles of his left hand on the wall where a mounted picture, complete with text, hung above the menorah. It read:

FROM THE HASIDIC PRIMER

The devout can learn three things from a child and seven from a thief in the service of the Lord. From a child one can learn:

1. Always be happy.
2. Never sit idly.
3. Cry for everything you want.

From a thief one can learn:

1. Work at night.
2. If you do not get what you want one night, try again the next.
3. Love your coworkers and brethren as thieves themselves care for one another.
4. Risk your life for something small.
5. Don't place too great a value on things you risked your life for but sell stolen things for a fraction of their original price.
6. Refrain from any sort of torture and beating and abide as you are, even unto the end.
7. Believe your work has value and don't desire to change it for another.

"Interesting," Emil said.

"A person should learn from everything that's got a lesson in it," Arthur said, smiling. "I'm not prejudiced against anything."

Anna cleared her throat.

"Coffee?" Arthur asked.

Arthur Pick had been a long-faithful patron of the Ascherman café and the Sklipek and Nizza pubs, where he played cards for sums both big and small. He went to Ascherman's for his spiritual nourishment and had picked up a thing or two about occult philosophy and the cabala along the way. He'd gotten caught up in the subject of "volatile sparks shooting out from under the blows of a hammer" and in primeval worlds which were flawed and therefore dying. The way things looked now, he didn't give the present world much of a chance. Was evil secondary to good? He would have liked some proof of that. It would be wonderful if all temptations were really only a test. It would only split his head apart, racking his brains from morning until night about where the world and humanity were rushing when most of the time "the good suffer and the sinful live it up." Nor did he try to hide it by preferring the company of sinners. What he enjoyed about the ancient teachings that he called "the superstition and prejudice of our ancestors" were the questions they posed about man and woman. What fascinated him was the assertion that a man's and a woman's souls formed a whole that was separated only throughout man's earthly existence, the body, for only a short time. Arthur liked imagining how that which formed a unit of day and night in the next world could be connected only momentarily on earth. He claimed there were 124 kinds of positions lovers and couples could choose from. To be safe, he ventured into discussion of this area only with Emil. Anna wouldn't like most of them—of that he was sure. It occurred to him that he hadn't been to the café with Emil for some time now. Emil hadn't been allowing himself a lot of time for fun and rest lately.

As long as he was on the topic of coffee, Ascherman's had the best. Thus, in time, he began connecting coffee with the cabala and dessert with bits of occult philosophy. He sat through debates over the misuses of magic and admitted that probably no one would ever get to the bottom of things. He would have been happy to apply some of that magic to cards but relied instead on his good memory, logic, and the ability to count who held what in his hand and then guess what they were up to. He believed that not even the blackest magic could help where the mind failed. He thought the same thing about the art

15

of judging what people wanted from him. He depended on his sixth sense for that. A pathway of the soul certainly had to exist, or else a person couldn't know what someone else wanted from him ahead of time and thus wouldn't be able to prepare himself for it. It was strange how people want someone to help them out—from loans to some kind of redemption. It was all part of the same thing.

"You know the one where the man asks his wife what he should do with the furniture when she dies?"

He tightened the belt of his robe. He was the one who laughed loudest at his own jokes. Emil crossed his legs. Originally Arthur had had a textile shop downstairs in the building where the hardware store now stood, but eventually he'd let it go. Arthur really had a nose for some things: he could hear the grass growing even before it started to sprout. Now he alternated between representing a wine distributor and, in the slow season, selling shoe polish. People have always liked to drink and always will.

Hector-Hugo was lying on the worn, bearskin rug, licking Arthur's slippers. The children noticed that the dog didn't have a single tooth left. He could have also used a bath and a brushing. (Richard had knocked out one of the dog's teeth a year ago when they were wrestling over a tennis ball.)

"This year, for the first time, we'll be alone over the holidays," Arthur said. "Susanna's staying in the convent."

"I miss her," Martha said. "We shouldn't have sent her so far away."

"Our poor little girl," Arthur responded.

He looked over at her picture in the silver frame next to the Venetian mirror: she was wearing a silk scarf edged in white lace.

"Doesn't it worry you that Italy's still got its fingers in the war in Africa?" Emil asked.

"The older I get, the more people get on my nerves," Arthur replied.

"You're not that old yet, Arthur," Anna said.

"And what about Helena?" Arthur asked. "You already look like a little dancer."

"Thank you," Helena replied. She blushed. Whenever they came for a visit, Helena studied Susanna in the brown-tinted photograph. She imagined her cousin in the surroundings of the Italian convent, like a clock standing in front of a silver mirror. She searched quietly in the picture for something it would never reveal.

"What's she doing there?" Richard asked.

"She's taking German, English, French, and Italian," Arthur replied.

"That must cost a little bit," Emil said.

"Don't even ask how much," Arthur said, smiling.

"In a roundabout way, Arthur likes to make a big deal about matters he doesn't agree with," Martha said. "I don't like discussing money."

"I'm happy to play second fiddle," Arthur stated.

"Susanna writes that trains in Italy arrive and depart on time—right on schedule."

"Her hair sure is long and pretty done-up for a convent," Emil pointed out.

"She's got style," Arthur agreed. "She's not there as a nun, Emil."

"Maybe they'll convert her," Martha said.

"Indubitably," Arthur responded.

He took pleasure in the word: "indubitably." Somehow, he felt it made him more important. Richard gazed through the crack to the next room where Susanna's brass bed stood. His parents had promised him one just like it. He felt Helena poking him in the ribs.

"Arthur called her yesterday," Martha related. "He went to the main post office."

"I warned her to watch out for the older professors," Arthur said.

"And he puts out money for that," Martha complained. "They're the most expensive conversations I've ever heard of."

"How could the professors be dangerous to her?" Anna asked.

"They're philanderers," Arthur stated.

"Could you hear her clearly?" Emil asked.

"As if she were standing next to me," Arthur replied.

Aunt Martha was wearing her charm necklace. The little animals and stones and rods clinked together whenever she moved. Some were red or green, orange and blue. She thought the little animals on her necklace were laughing; Arthur had already given up trying to convince her otherwise—it just got on his nerves.

Along with others, Arthur Pick had the idiosyncrasy of sometimes visiting the zoo at night. He was friends with a doctor and the wildcat keeper there. He played cards with them in the Ascherman café or at the Sklipek pub on Rybna Street. After the pubs had closed for the night, if the three men were still in the mood, they'd end up at the zoo. That's how Arthur knew what the eyes of a tiger, a lion, or a hyena looked like at night—as he would make his way past the cages with a flashlight in his hand—or those of a parrot, an owl, or an oriole. He could go around to the cages and recognize the eyes of a boa constrictor, a stag, or a fox. He could identify—just like a zoologist—the green eyes of a doe, the yellow of a fox, the red of a crocodile, and know that orange eyes meant a jaguar. He could tell whether the animal was a cat or a wolf by whether the eyes moved up and down or in a straight line when the animal paced in its cage at night. They all had a good time: Uncle Arthur, the doctor, and the keeper. Sometimes they went to look at the apes. Uncle Arthur had promised Richard that he would take him to the zoo at night for his birthday so he would know what he didn't yet know and see what only a few people got a chance to see.

Last time, Emil had asked his brother-in-law what he got out of going to the zoo at night.

"Some animals," said Arthur, "have an odd reflection of all colors in their eyes because of the refraction of the light rays at night. They seem like living diamonds, emeralds, and rubies. You don't have to be a detective to know an animal by its eyes—that's old hat for a hunter. At night, a hunter can guess what animal's in front of him by its eyes alone—even before he's actually seen it. The ocelot and the fox have the same eyes, even though the fox lives in the forests of Bohemia and the ocelot in South America, but each moves differently. Foxes are like dogs—they run fast with small jumps. So, in a larger cage anyone can tell whether it's a fox or a dog by watching it jump. Cats are cautious animals. They walk or run steadily, carefully, and directly. Deer and snakes have green eyes. But a snake moves slowly on the ground or in a tree while a deer is fast. The eyes of nocturnal animals give off incredible rays, but it would be hard to find the same beauty in a hen's or a rooster's eyes—even in the middle of the night."

"Grandpa Ferdinand used to say that horses' eyes reflect a pale, red light at night," Emil added.

"Yes, Martha was telling me that your father was interested in animals' eyes too," Arthur said.

Richard studied Arthur's enormous, pointy nose. The light from the window hit it, illuminating it so that it was lit from one side and dark on the other. Sometimes Arthur acted like he had ants in his pants. Instead of sitting still, he would go from place to place like a commander always seeking the best vantage point. In Richard's eyes, Papa seemed mild mannered in comparison to the inadvertent roughness of Uncle Arthur. There was a bit of gambler's hesitancy in his uncle. He sensed the competition between the two men. It wasn't that they openly opposed each other or had or wanted to actually voice it—there was a second invisible language which flowed between them, incomprehensible, perplexing, and sometimes cowardly, because it was the two-faced, nameless language of adults.

Helena contemplated possible matches Susanna might make. It already looked like Uncle Arthur wouldn't be pleased with anyone. How would it turn out? Helena wondered to herself. Was it true that not even the very best bridegroom was good enough for a father? Who would Susanna find someday? She thought of the romantic glow of love which envelops a woman far before she first touches a man. She thought of the moment when a girl first feels the touch of a man's lips. Her first kiss. What would be first for Susanna—would she kiss a man or would he kiss her first? Which? Where? When? She thought about Papa kissing Mama for the first time. Finally, she thought about the half of a woman a man marries and the half of a man that marries a woman.

Aunt Martha showed Helena and Richard a collection of gold and silver coins. She explained to Helena that they had sent Susanna to the convent for schooling so that one day she wouldn't be troubled by the things that were always troubling their people a little bit. She kept looking at the Christmas tree as she spoke. The best thing was to adjust oneself, she said. Blend in. Not emphasize the differences. Theirs was the first generation to escape catastrophe. Don't be different, that was it, Martha thought. Assimilate. Susanna was already one step ahead in that area. Martha unconsciously glanced back at the tree in the corner again.

Then she announced that she would fix a snack. "Arthur, will you have sardines with us?" she asked. She put the coins away.

Uncle Arthur sat down at the piano. Hector-Hugo growled quietly.

Helena pondered who'd sent Susanna roses in Italy. She imagined a wedding in white with a dress as white as first snowflakes, a king's horse, or the stars in the middle of the night. Was a girl's soul white? Are the shadows of the soul also light, or are they dark, as they are outdoors? Helena tried to guess if her cousin had already met her true love. In the meantime, Richard watched the turtledoves fly over the table and settle on the cupboard.

Uncle Arthur played the "Baths of Hercules" on the piano in the guest room. As he played, he examined his brown face in the raised piano top. He looked like the Don Carlos he'd seen twenty-five years ago with Martha at the Prague German theater.

"That's nice to listen to," Emil said. He was thinking what Arthur would say to loaning him some money. He tried to fix a number. Two thousand? Four? He needed thirteen thousand, but that was too much to ask for. He would be happy with even a thousand, given the dire straits he was in. It wasn't pleasant to always be in debt. "Who taught you to play like that?"

"Talent," Arthur responded. "I have a connection: a German firm for shoe polish—it's imitation stuff, but who cares for the money? Too bad that you're not in the business, Emil. Ersatz, not ersatz. Someday they'll figure out how to make kids from ersatz."

Arthur could tell what was coming—it was in the air—it was written on Emil's face. He knew his family. Of course, relatives asking for loans didn't leave him breathless. It wasn't the first time, nor the last. It was even a little flattering, if unpleasant.

"I'd like to be less dependent," Emil stated. "I don't feel like going in for a sacrifice. Everyone's struggling with his own crisis. It seems like it's the prerace trials. And everybody's looking at you like you're at the Olympics."

"Have Martha's eyes gotten any better?" he asked. "Arthur, I'd like to bring up kind of a delicate subject."

Arthur stopped playing. He pulled open the lid of a beige box, took out a Cuban cigar, and offered one to Emil. He clipped both of the cigar ends and lit them. The room became wrapped in smoke.

"I didn't know who I could turn to," Emil started. "You're the closest ones to us. It's about some immediate expenses. I've had some unforeseeable outlays again."

Arthur took a puff and exhaled the smoke. Anna was glad she was at the window. "We all live in a world of illusion," he said. And then: "Children, you can talk out loud—you don't have to whisper."

"Unfortunately they're not merely illusions, but bills, rent—every expense must be covered," Emil said.

Was it Arthur's cautiousness? His jumpiness? Hesitation? Or was he playing for time to reconsider? Emil couldn't afford to get angry. He knew that much himself.

"By the way," said Arthur, "Did you know they're playing *Pancho Villa* at the World Theater? I know how you like anything to do with horses and the people on them, besides what they eat. Someday you'll have to tell me what the difference is between an Arabian and a thoroughbred. Have you seen it?"

"Not yet," answered Emil. Was Arthur changing the subject?

"They're playing *Five Weeks in a Balloon* at the Humanity. We went yesterday with Martha. I haven't seen anything as good for a long time."

His face was veiled in smoke. He knew what Emil was displeased about. Truthfully, he didn't like it, either.

"I'm holding on to my line of business. I still think it's not a bad one," said Emil. "It just has to get over a bad spell. Things will pick up again in spring. The winter is short, people run out of money over the holidays, and nobody has ever gotten rich from IOUs. Everything I have is tied up in stock. I've got to twist people's arms just to get them into the store. I stopped new shipments, but I still have to pay for the old ones. I could repay everything to you in the spring, Arthur—summer, at the latest. But I need a little shot in the arm . . . a little time. The best medicine is money. No worries on a full stomach. I almost wish I was that far along already, but one shouldn't wish for time to speed up. I don't want to take advantage of you. Like I say—you can trust me: you're family. If I want to keep people coming in to buy during the winter, the shop has to have a face-lift—everything is shot."

Then he fell silent. What kind of mood was Arthur in? How much would he be able to say about the troubles he knew were causing similar problems for Arthur?

"I'm glad you're doing well, Arthur."

Arthur looked like he was his own butler. He watched his cigar burning from the distance of his elbow. He could blow five smoke rings in a row.

"Do you want advice, Emil?"

"I won't turn it away, Arthur."

The corners of Arthur's mouth dropped a little.

"It's only a question of short-term credit for this season," Emil quickly added.

"To borrow money is just as unpleasant as lending it," Arthur said. He smiled and immediately added, "Blood isn't water."

That sounded vague. It could mean yes just as easily as it could no. Arthur wrinkled his forehead. It was hard to say no to a relative. It would be foolish to expect that he would get everything back— even if so, who knew how long it would take? Perhaps Emil would be an exception, he thought. We'll see—or maybe we won't. He examined what might happen if he let his brother-in-law leave empty-handed. It was just a thought—a fraction of a thought; another possibility. It also occurred to him whether Emil was asking for enough, because then he would be getting into something that would need more investment to get back the first loan. . . . It was true, the times were hard. He saw how people, like Emil, who had small stores were going under. Some things don't have a definition, like love, for example—or anti-Semitism. But everyone knows what and how they feel even without a direct definition. Money, of course, had its own definition.

Arthur calculated to himself how much he'd lent to people he'd never seen come back. He wrinkled his forehead again. There certainly were people who believed that it was possible to jump an abyss in two leaps. Did it make sense to explain to them that you can only jump once? He smiled for the third time.

Once, while visiting Susanna in Italy, Arthur went swimming in the ocean and learned about tides: how the waves could roll over a swimmer if he didn't know what he was doing, if they didn't topple him just by themselves. Arthur had been almost totally swamped for a little while (luckily he'd had enough air in his lungs), and though he didn't dare go down deep, it was enough for him to feel the weight of the ocean pull him down: the water, the dark, and as he touched the bottom, the sand, stones, and death. For a couple of seconds he'd had the feeling that he'd never get out from the whirlpools and undercurrents of the waves, but he did—a wave propelled him clear out of the darkness into the sun where he was able to breathe and he felt that he had done well to be born so that nothing could so easily humble him. After a moment, he was flirting with the local Italian beauties again.

He looked at Emil and wondered how much Emil could probably have saved from his business. He knew from his own experience; savings aren't much or are worth nothing if luck turns its back on you. You start borrowing from savings to invest and then find you're running out of money altogether.

Emil said, "So many people have lost work or gone bankrupt that my head spins during the day, and at night sometimes I can't sleep."

"It won't be so bad, Emil; it's been worse already, don't you think?"

"I don't know why I feel it concerns me when other people lose their livelihoods."

"These are tough times, that's all, Emil, but luckily it's never that way for everyone."

"Sometimes I feel guilty about something I didn't do," Emil said more quietly.

"You're getting out of it honorably."

That sounded promising, Emil thought to himself.

"I'm doing what I can," he said.

"It's a question of personal ability. It's yesterday's successes that you can lean on. Haven't we both been successful most of the time?" His smile, which he didn't stop, was like a gambler's.

"As long as it doesn't go from bad to worse."

And then Emil added, "I believed I'd get myself out from under more quickly, Arthur." He couldn't explain how or what. How long had it been since he'd stopped paying insurance, which Arthur was so proud of?

"Isn't it ridiculous that there are still places in this world where equality is the rule because people don't own anything?" Arthur asked.

"Where is that, pray tell?" asked Martha.

"In the Sahara," Arthur answered. "They don't have levels of society, or classes; they only have minor differences from one another.

They don't attach any importance to property. No one would ever be higher in their eyes for something he owned which another person didn't."

Arthur looked at Emil. He smoothed his thick, dark eyebrows. It seemed like he was hypnotizing Emil. Emil remembered the hypnotist from the Busch circus. After the performance someone had said that hypnotizing people into remembering how their parents abused them was inadmissible and against the law. Most of the time they were fake experiences, fake memories—not real at all, just some aberration—a possibility that never really took place, or sometimes just a mistaken fear.

"What do you want to do?"

"I don't want to bother you with details, Arthur."

"Who needs them?" intoned Arthur. "As my grandfather used to say, money isn't everything, but without it you look like a fool."

Martha looked at her husband with her nearsighted eyes.

"Why aren't you saying anything?"

Arthur smiled into Martha's eyes.

The deeper meaning, except that their father needed money, escaped Richard. With the coins already put away, Martha went to fix the refreshments.

From the window, Anna gazed down at the street. She bit her lip.

"The main thing is, how much?" Arthur asked. He looked at his signet ring. Suddenly, he turned his palm around so that it couldn't be seen. His gaze fell on Hector-Hugo. "Were you ever lucky enough to watch a cat closely as it falls, Emil?" Arthur asked. "It always lands on all fours. First, a cat orients herself—you need a head and eyes for that. Then she sets her front paws in case the ground comes sooner than she expects, and in between, if she's still got the time and the space, she arches her back—then, she curves her spine and drops like a furry parachute. She takes the fall in phases. When she's coming down she lets all the parts of her body absorb the fall, including her tail—that serves as a rudder, so that it will be the softest possible landing."

"I'd like to know how to land on all fours," said Emil, smiling. It seemed to him that that was enough to say in front of the children. The question of how much remained up in the air. How much should he ask for? A thousand? Two? Ten? He wrinkled his forehead, slanted his eyes, thought, and finally didn't mention any amount. Should he leave it up to Arthur to decide how much he could lend?

"Only if we understand each other," added Arthur.

He put his hand on Helena's shoulder and pulled her to him. "Two and a half thousand years ago the king of Babylon, Nebuchadnezzar, built his city to make it the most famous in the world—something like New York, today. And where is it now?"

"We're going to study Babylon next semester, after the holidays," Helena said.

"Well, then, you'll have a head start," Arthur said, smiling. Then he added, "No one is going to hurry to pay you back when they owe you money. The only people who hurry are the ones that have to pay at the table. Wouldn't you rather come into the firm and sell shoe polish, Emil?"

"Emil thinks ours isn't a bad business, Arthur," Anna replied. "We've already invested a lot of time and money—you can't imagine."

"I'm not saying that it's a lost cause . . . only, how long do you want to wait?"

"We're not that old yet," joked Emil. He really did feel that they were still young, but sometimes he didn't feel like it was any relief. Or was it just the opposite? It was all just experience to be clever next time. And it was true that you have to pay for everything.

"It's a German firm, Arthur," Anna added in response to Arthur's offer.

"Business is business. Money has no nationality—or conscience."

"I hope that your money does," Emil said with a smile. "And mine too."

"Business is like the army for the Germans," Arthur said. "They have what Germans call *Auftrasfuhrung*: delegating authority so that everyone who wants to serve gets his chance."

"Two people in our building have lost their jobs," Emil said.

"A person shouldn't be sentimental when it comes to business," said Arthur. "It doesn't matter if you sell wine, textiles, or shoe polish. And in the end that applies almost just the same to who's doing the selling and who's buying. The important thing is turnover. The debt and credit columns. If you're not stealing money from anybody, then you're fine. You don't look like you're going bankrupt, Emil. Your coat says that you're still a man with money enough."

"I have to know what you can pay back. I'll let it roll around my head."

"That's the most I wanted to hear, Arthur," Emil said. "In one year we'll be beyond the worst."

Chirping could be heard from the kitchen. Arthur's hesitation was torturing Anna. If there was a God in heaven, let it not turn out poorly for Emil. (*Thy sun shall not set, thy moon shall not hide.*) Cantor Mario Schapira had praised her for praying well last Friday. It was only unpleasant for Arthur that suddenly they'd torn him from his own troubles to worry about their problems. He didn't like it when someone else relied on his money.

"Money is the best engine on earth," he added. "Blood comes only after. People can think up *perpetuum mobile* on it, cars on gas, on blood, or on electricity, on air, old paper, or water, but nothing will ever beat money for an engine. You'll get yours."

He winked his left eye slyly. His thick black eyebrows made it more emphatic.

"I knew I would," said Emil. He turned red. The blood rushed throughout his body. He didn't know how much, but he knew he'd get something, at least to pull the thorn from his foot. He felt a pleasant heat at his temples. He knew he had won. He only didn't know how much. It didn't matter. It would have been embarrassing to leave without getting anything—especially for Anna and the children's sake.

"If I said that textiles and haberdasheries were on their way out today, I'm not referring to your abilities, Emil. It's about everything *zu grund.* I gave up on the trade so I wouldn't throw good money out the window. Take a good look around: what do you want to sell? I don't want to cheat my people either. I never have enough for them."

It recalled Susanna's picture and spirit into the room. It was only hesitation on the other side of the matter, just like agreement and disagreement—already only an echo.

He looked at the picture of Susanna in her grayish beige dress. The canaries screeched in the kitchen.

"You shouldn't blaspheme, Arthur," Martha said.

"I like to blaspheme," he answered. "Even if it's only at sports."

Martha was ready with the refreshments. She took out a silver tray and flatware: spoons, forks, hors d'oeuvre forks with jade tops for picking up rolled anchovies.

Arthur touched up his brilliantined hair. "I wouldn't say that you're not worth a little money. If it would help, you can have six— no, three—months. No interest, of course. Then I have to pay for Susanna's stay for the second half of the year. I am not a bank, and if something happens, I don't want it to say 'Arthur.' That's enough about money now." His voice dropped. He hadn't said either how much it was going to be. Maybe he hadn't decided yet. "By the way, Martha doesn't need to know about this," he added.

"It's a big favor, Arthur," Anna said.

"I'm happy we can stick together," Arthur replied.

"You'll see it back before the post office is built," Emil reassured him. "You don't have to worry."

"Isn't it warm here?" Arthur asked. "How much? A thousand?"

"I was thinking two, Arthur."

"Two?"

"What do you think?"

"I'd rather not think about it. What about fifteen hundred?"

"Fifteen hundred is fine."

"Done."

"Done."

"But don't thank me."

"Thanks."

Aunt Martha and Helena brought in the tea along with bread and butter and a dish of sardines. There was coffee in the pot. Richard held on to Hector-Hugo so Helena wouldn't be startled and drop it. His hands had gotten scratched up by Martha's cat. She had probably overheard something from the conversation.

Martha measured the distance between her husband's generosity and extravagance; she feared how much it revealed about her own thriftiness (to the point of miserliness). Carrying the tray with the refreshments, Martha was bothered by her rheumatism in both hands. Sometimes it was an unpleasant pain, and she was able to keep it to herself only with difficulty. Arthur's lightheartedness, extravagance, and generosity touched on that too; he had promised her medicine made from Chinese tigers. Somewhere in a café he had heard that it was the best cure for fevers, rheumatism, and hardening of the arteries. At least the money would stay in the family, she thought to herself, and offered Anna, Emil, and the children a piece of cake.

While Arthur inconspicuously counted out the hundreds in a drawer of the writing table, Martha and the children watched the feeding fish. She didn't have an inkling of the transaction taking place: Anna hadn't missed a thing. Arthur gave Emil a roll of banknotes and he slipped it into his pocket without counting it.

"I like animals," Martha said. "Arthur promised me two new white mice next month."

"I sure am nice to Martha," said Arthur, smiling. "We all want it better—to have a little more comfort." He had to have liked both Martha and the animals to put up with them.

"And you know, white mice are very cute," Martha stated. "Bred so well like that."

A little later, Emil and Anna were alone again.

"So it turned out well," Emil said.

"It would have been unhappy if it hadn't," Anna replied.

On the stairs as they were leaving, in the hallway with the wallpaper, Emil realized that the familiar smell of wilted flowers, a tinge of peeling color and the old paint underneath, didn't bother him anymore. Their noses were still full of the turtledoves, little fish, the dog, and sardines. Somehow Emil could not associate Hector-Hugo with the old story about the sailor killed in a typhoon and his faithful, old dog who kept waiting for him in vain. Arthur was on firm ground with both feet and did business with a German firm; he probably wouldn't have lent him the money if he hadn't been. And, he had lent it to him on only his blue eyes and his word of honor. He hadn't asked for paper, with signatures, an affidavit, or seals. Arthur could be— whatever—he wasn't completely bad.

"Button up well," Anna said to Helena and Richard. "You too, Emil."

"The biggest tree, the biggest dog, the biggest piano," she continued. "A daughter in a convent in Italy. The only thing they're lacking is well-bred white mice, and maybe they can deny how they came to be born."

Emil whistled the melody "O Maria" he'd learned at the Italian front. I still have my luck. The old man upstairs likes me.

The air was cold and refreshing. Emil pressed Anna's hand. He felt for his wallet in the back pocket where he had the money, photographs of the children and Anna, and a picture postcard of Helena in a rose-colored taffeta dress. He tried to think about what he would do with the money. Before they got home, the fog started rolling in.

"Richard's growing out of his shoes again," Anna said. "He grows like a weed . . . but don't even think of going out and buying him a new pair tomorrow."

Emil Ludvig felt Anna's warm, moist hand. Flowing from it was energy to be built upon; tenderness which soothed his soul. Shoes, Richard, Helena. A shop of textile goods. The winter season. He straightened himself as in his army days on the Piave River when the general made them march in formation.

At the sweetshop, Emil bought pastries. He had them wrapped up in a silk paper package. He gave one to Richard; Helena said that she would eat hers after dinner.

"It will make me sick," Richard protested.

"Don't you want to be stronger? Then have one, quick."

Richard covered up his mouth. Emil gave him a little slap with his free hand. "Well, I'm not going to force you to eat cake with cream."

"I don't feel like it."

Anna gave them both a reproachful look.

"There was a time when I really wanted to become a professional soldier," Emil said after a while. "A uniform, a steady salary, respect— and the self-confidence of a man who can protect himself along with those who can't. It took me longer to decide than you'd probably think. Two hundred years ago, a colonel would buy his own regiment and would approve what his soldiers ate and who they would marry."

He took Richard by the other hand. They stopped at the turnstiles. The train cars shook. The way home, he thought to himself, is always shorter than when you first go out. Why? It is only an illusion, but somehow true.

The train pulled a couple of cars with coal, then probably another two dozen, and on the end a double car, like a brother and a sister, empty express wagons. The train whistled. It was a calling to which no one ever expected an answer. The last wagon was already lost in the mist. Regular rumbling could be heard on the railroad tracks; an unrepeatable sound you inscribe into your memory. The cars on the train were of all ages and origins—old, older, and the oldest kind, long out of fashion—but still useful and, most important, mobile, with numbers and signs with codes, the place of destination and the originating station, Austrian, German, French, English, Italian, and Hungarian along with two modern coaches with big windows and curtains. As Emil gazed at the train and its cars—personal and freight, open or closed cattle cars, or oil tanks—he thought of everything he had escaped and what he wanted to come out of well and how the things of the world were arranged in an incessant, confusing, soothing, or animal movement; and how luck comes and goes, how it worked, because everyone always, even before he's out of diapers, struggles with misfortune a little bit. That belonged to the structure of the world. The train took beauty and ugliness away with it at the same time, left them behind so a person could choose for himself.

As he watched the train disappearing into the mist with its whistle fading away, Emil recalled how he had wanted to move to America when he was a young man. When someone is at the peak of his strength and things at the very least go his way, he wants to leave conflict as far behind for the hope each person has at the price of daring to start over again from scratch. To stretch out one's hand as far as it can reach to catch hold of an unknown potential.

The train reminded Emil of distant places that had once attracted him, but no longer. As soon as a person settles down, distances take on new dimensions. Instead of going after them, it seemed like they came to him, even if in the shape of Australian, Canadian, or North American apples, Italian chestnuts, Turkish or Greek figs, and sometimes only with Hungarian peppers or spices from Afghanistan or Ceylon tea. He was hungry (for Anna's dinner), and Italian mortadella popped into his mind (on soft sliced bread with a little mustard and mayonnaise and strips of tomato).

"I've never envied anybody," said Emil. "We have what we need—we don't lack for anything."

"What a character you are," Anna said.

"Envy is like an already rusty weapon: it doesn't do anything for you. It's not going to protect you from anything."

They passed closed stores, two of which were in bankruptcy. Without Arthur Pick's money, they could have been the third. He tried to suppress a slight feeling of insecurity.

They got to their house, number 137. The winter shine on the spherical gas tank on the hill above the new gasworks was already dull. Trains whistled from the train station a little way down to Primatorska. Smoke rose from the soap factory, even though it was Sunday. Brass-band music drifted from the Mercury. The metal shutters of the corner shop and three display windows were closed up; they looked like a giant washboard. The cold wind blew against them. The sign above the entrance to the building proclaimed the name of Emil Ludvig. Everything was in its place. Kralovska Avenue. The cutlery shop, the tailor's, the barber and the butcher's, the cleaners, the little nursery school, and the vacant lot where the new post office would be built. The vacant lot looked full of promise with its piles of sand, the hollowed-out earth, the puddles and the snow, the rough mess, ancient materials from which human hands would mold a post office.

Emil couldn't stop thinking if only it were a few months later. He had gotten the loan. It filled the gap that felt like a defeat, which men don't talk about but which they see. He had the feeling of a person who had gone through a crisis. He didn't have to think so much about distant worries which hadn't touched him yet. The general crisis had been lifted—at least for a couple of days. Could he hear the grass growing, like Arthur sometimes said? No guts, no glory. He'd gotten the money. He had secured himself and their livelihood for the coming season, at least, which meant he also had secured the family. When had he first been overcome by the suspicion that his carefree life had come to an end for reasons which didn't include him? He put the thought out of his mind for the evening. You have to know how to be happy from what there is and not be afraid of what could be. He wouldn't think about it anymore. It was Sunday.

At the bottom of his soul he felt a humility he had not imagined before. Was it a person's fault for what he didn't have, and rightly so if he sometimes had more than he needed? He knew there was no point in dragging it around with him like a weight. It could be the other way around; Arthur would know how to get him out of the mess. Whoever gives quickly gives twice.

Emil trusted his conscience. Why did he always need more help than Arthur? Was he sure he didn't envy anyone? He was back at the questions to which he could maybe find an answer if he would think them through to the end. It was like a race he ran in the air; whenever he almost caught up to himself, he would run away again. It was possible that a person took one breath and for a little while was amazed by himself and then for a little while hated himself. How was it possible that love and loathing went hand in hand? Cautiousness and the ability to calculate, to scheme. Didn't he think he was more competent—already today? He would be happy to throw his bigheartedness and forgiveness in the face of the world—including Arthur Pick's—until he won, succeeded, and put his days of weakness behind him. He could imagine himself as two people where one chases the other and at the same time runs away, like they don't want to have anything in common. He felt a pang, which he easily brushed aside. Was that really me? If a clean conscience isn't enough for me, what's left? Suddenly he smiled. I am not as defenseless as I look. I still know how to jump. And it occurred to him that as long as a man was able to manage it, he was happiest inside, with himself, surrounded by his family. He was speaking with his family without using words. But the voicelessness disturbed him.

Richard, who had all of a sudden broken away and run to their house, was waiting for his father and the rest of the family, so they could go up together. Emil Ludvig was singing "La Trieste." He garbled the Italian; it would be lost in a chorus but not in a solo; but no one would understand anyway: "*La Trieste fina tzara o la kytara . . . que belle finne. . . . De Trieste fin a Zara . . . amor, amor, amor . . .*"

From Helena's notes:

Mama is pretty and robust; she has a beautiful face, beautiful soft, moist skin, and dark black hair. I saw a photograph taken when she was just eighteen years old. In the picture, she is serious, thoughtful, and beautiful. I can understand how Papa just smiles when he looks at her. Mama said that when she saw Papa for the first time, on his birthday, September 11, an electric current swept her whole body from stem to stern and took her breath away.

I feel like I'm changed. I feel what I never felt before. I understand what I never understood before. Mountains, the earth, and rivers. Blood. Body. Instincts from so long ago that I feel older than the oldest star and at the same time like a new star that is being born this very moment. I am a little afraid, but something is also relieved. My small breasts and empty stomach overflow like a river after a storm. I felt my connection to the earth; like that of a mother and water and the sunlight and the crops. My blood is flowing. It tells me what will one day come.

I feel what takes away childhood; things that you can't hold on to. Images. Sadness is making a space for that which creates a "woman" out of me.

Mother smiled. She repeated Father's words that everything in life is a circle. Her eyes told me: Welcome to adulthood, ripeness, womanhood. Welcome, healthy and strong by our blood, by your new self-confidence, by our pain for what will come.

I have to admit that Mama is not that elegant when she goes shopping. (She is only pretty and strict.) She is never satisfied with the original price. She just won't pay it — unless it's for the doctor. She'd rather go to eight shops and compare prices before choosing the best one, until she finds the highest quality for the lowest price. This is in contrast to Papa, who would never haggle over a price; he just pays it. That drives Mama crazy. She only holds her tongue and doesn't tell Papa that he's nuts or something, to keep the peace for the sake of us kids. (She probably wouldn't consider herself normal or responsible if she didn't bargain with the shopkeepers.) She says that there is almost no one else in the building who lets money be taken from his pockets as easily as Papa. Hard times taught Mother that. She already knows what it was to be without money, with empty cupboards. That would never happen to Papa, but maybe I'm wrong. Mama finds herself the cheapest haircutters, shoe stores, and repairmen. Most of the time she gets her hands on things for half the price. Is it because she's from the country? Or is it the nature you're born with or what life teaches you? Dad believes rather that a high price means also the highest quality. Both follow their own rules, some openly, others are internal and not made clear but will be in time. (It'll all come out in the wash, like Aunt Martha says.) I'd rather go shopping with Papa, but I learn more with Mother. There's no such thing as a firm price for Mother. She knows it from the shop, when poor customers come in and she has to guess how much she can charge for something so that she can sell it and not take a loss and how much they can pay so they don't go broke, because they don't have any more money. I'm not very happy about that either.

I would definitely want my life to be elegant, like my older cousin, Susanna Pick.

Last night, Father cried out in his sleep. He woke us all up, including Richard. In the morning, he said that he'd had a patriotic dream. At first the Czech police protected him, but then they threatened him. He ended up being wrapped in a blanket by someone; enormous strong hands were holding him. They lifted him up to take him somewhere, and he wanted to yell, but he couldn't until finally a terrible scream — the one we heard — burst from him and woke us up. It woke Papa, too, but nobody mentioned anything to him until he started talking about it himself.

I dreamed once again that I was going to school; we were given some homework, and I copied it from a classmate. All of a sudden, the classmate was twenty years older. She reproached me for not recognizing her and forgetting that she had been kind enough to let me copy her homework in the past. She had changed a great deal: her red hair was now straw colored and cut like a boy's. I tried to tell her I hadn't forgotten her and not to take it that way.

Are bizarre dreams a reflection of anxiety that we suppress during the day? Is it some kind of hidden mirror in which we see things from their flip side through their other potentiality? We all read Sigmund Freud, but even though I read it very thoroughly and I have remained objective, in the final analysis, I didn't learn that much from him and I have to explain things myself. Why do we dream? Why is the night something like a sea that a person enters like a diver, sometimes so deep that it makes one dizzy?

"For God's sake," Emil said on Sunday. "After all, not everyone is descended from royal stock." He thought about taking the family out to a garden restaurant, to Pelc-Tyrolka, but Anna would not discuss it. Why should they spend so much money if she could cook as good a meal at home for a quarter of the price?

"I'm not taking it away from you. Please, if you insist on it, you've got royal blood. Levy-Kohen—rabbis, maybe kings, even though it was a long time ago. How can anyone help it?"

Emil's voice was as playful as when he was still a boy, or as when he'd flown on a horse to meet the wind, full of that vitality which has no name, just the sheer joy, the prerogative of youth, that lasts for a couple of seconds when one is in balance with the stars, rivers, or birds. The immortality of youth. The never-ending confidence of youth—Emil still had lots of youthful energy. On Sundays, Emil was a model of calm and spiritual peace. He felt within himself something perhaps stronger than death; something he'd taken away from the First World War along with his visions and memories of the Piave River.

He sometimes thought about how a person must make choices in life, like a juggler catching three or four balls in one hand and tossing them into the air at the same time: he rarely gets applause for it—most of the time, he ends up having to clap for himself in his mind. Sometimes a person can't even tell the difference between good and better, worse and worst, Emil thought. The world moves faster and faster, and sometimes, life seems like a race against itself. The Germans call it zeitgeist, spirit of the times. Who knows what it really is or isn't? Everything crumbles before a person's eyes: truth, half-truths, lies, and worse than lies; publicity, politics, film, history; a demagoguery which, the louder it gets, the more it assumes that people will swallow it. Sometimes less is more, Emil told himself. What was once fun often becomes a bore. In the end, a person doesn't know his own mind. He needs to collect more experiences to be able to say that he really knows the ropes. The world changes so quickly that before a person can chew what he's bitten off, the future has become the past. The wonder from the First World War wasn't sweetened by the memory of those who died through gassing and the massacres on the Marne. Maturity is as inconspicuously plucked from youth as a butterfly that came into the world as a caterpillar emerges from a cocoon; a man only turns around and before he knows it, old age has caught him by the throat—not literally, maybe, but now life seemed faster and more rushed. In the end, if a person has the time to die in peace, he can still enjoy life, Emil thought to himself with a smile. He used to say *I think, therefore I am,* the way the philosophy textbook from school said. Now he could state either *I eat, therefore I am* or *I hurry, therefore I am.* Maybe people once lived a profound life, but now it was the other way around, that the more dangerous life is, the faster it goes. He felt as though the world and life were a spiderweb being rent apart in front of his eyes—but that also proved that even tatters were still capable of living. Maybe modern life meant to plan less and accept whatever came more. At least it blurred the boundaries between individualities so that a person could make his own way. As long as I have options, I don't have any right to complain, he thought. In the final analysis, when life was at the point where the juggler's act throws the ball with one hand and catches it with the other, it was also in that way that one's life resembles a ball at a fair, dancing and jumping above the small fountain with holiday sharpshooters firing at him with air guns from behind the colored paper flowers in front of the witnesses of their Sunday heroism. A person must be philosopher, clown, and juggler all at the same time.

Sunday wasn't over. The day was split between either going with Richard to Dablice to the waterworks near the cemetery to lay a couple of stones on Grandfather Ferdinand's grave or working by himself at home, which included hunting down bedbugs. One would think that this would diminish their multitudes, but unfortunately it didn't. Nothing had been a sure thing for a long time now. He probably wouldn't force Helena to read *War and Peace* in a week. He himself was content with a new best-seller; it now satisfied him just to read the love verses the way it had once satisfied him to be Anna's lover. Who knew what a person should desire or what was perhaps better doubtful than irrefutable?

Fortunately, what a person can't exactly figure out he can fill in with his imagination. No one can stop anyone from dreaming, creating, or imagining. Maybe the faith of tomorrow is not to believe anything. Sometimes it's better to exchange fantasy for irony—it's more genuine. But what would be moral tomorrow if it were possible to doubt everything today?

"That's just what's sad," Anna said.

Emil was always the first to welcome the spring with a cleaning and an accounting: at night he sorted out how much he still owed, how much he had repaid, how he was doing. (It was not surprising that sometimes he woke up out of sorts; no one would suspect dire thoughts behind that smile of his.)

"Don't be ridiculous," Helena said. "Where are clergy and kings—and where is our family?"

Without a doubt, Helena was the one who knew the most about general history in the family, though Mama and Papa had prettied it up in various places. Why not? Nobody took anything away from anyone else by doing so. Was she really descended from a royal family? They had been royalty only during those times when they still walked around the desert from oasis to oasis, put up tents, took them apart again, and grazed sheep. That was when they were still far from becoming a nation with a written history, laws, and a single God as opposed to many little gods and idols whose history (up to yesterday or the day before) could be tallied back two thousand or twenty-five hundred years. Maybe it had been easier to become a king in those days. Helena was more interested in when it had been less cruel to stay alive among others because they were tough and merciless, when survival in the desert and the wasteland was at stake. What had it really been like? At a time when water was precious and the sun beat down mercilessly, every shepherd in sandals could proclaim himself king around a well. Anna's point of view was simple: it was sufficient for someone simply to proclaim himself king to be one. There were, perhaps, two conceptions of history: one was her mother's, the other the technical secondary school's. Did her mother actually believe that the world began (as it is said in the Old Testament) six thousand years ago?

Helena looked at her mother. Because Anna had gained a little weight this winter, she actually looked robust. Perhaps she had a bit more energy and drive than Papa did. Helena had already developed a clear picture of her family: Papa often lived in illusions, but when it came to the long-gone past, neither he nor Mama was without illusion. Papa often forgot what Mama always remembered. Papa believed that a person was born to be happy—a theory which Mama vigorously shot down. Papa chased one ambition after another; like night trading off with day, he robbed Peter to pay Paul. While Papa leaped between various desires that concerned all the members of his family, obsessed in his own unobtrusive way, Mama kept her feet on the ground mending strangers' clothes with her sewing machine. Papa liked to forget—Mama almost never did. Wasn't it beautiful that she, Richard, her mother, and her father were living in a civilized time when cultural achievements meant more than weapons of stone and iron, of a flush toilet in contrast to a hole in the rock, of a modern shower in contrast to a small waterfall near a lake? Nowadays one didn't have to concern oneself with defending oneself and one's family against the incursions of savages or hostile soldiers, from Assyrians to Romans (as had already been covered in the first three chapters at school). Then, one's most powerful instinct, that of survival, came just before the instinct to eat and stave off hunger. Soon, one didn't have to kill or be killed, so that one could continue to tear the pages off the calendar each day. Later came man's third strongest instinct— to multiply. It might not be necessary to revel in the arms and might of the old kings. Laws were enough to open one to a life without the worry of survival. The laws by which people live today take care of them so that they do not have to fend for daily survival as they did a thousand years ago, with spears, boulders, and slings.

Didn't Aristotle say that education was beautiful and fills a person with a pleasure similar to love? She would not dare to quote this at home, but could, perhaps, to Susanna if she were here. There are those who would prefer education to wealth. What could be more inspiring than the technical high school?

Emil did not let himself be disturbed, but, coincidentally, he shared some of the same thoughts as Helena. Every once in a while he peeped into her textbooks, but only in passing and secretly. In his white cotton nightgown with rolled-up sleeves and his canvas trousers which he had brought from the Great War, he took apart the individual sideboards of the king-size beds, the face and the bottom of the cot, and leaned them against the wall. At one time, he'd set off for the war as a rookie; in four years he'd worked up to a recruiter with three stars. "Mr. Recruiter, come here, Mr. Recruiter, go there," they would say. Every year he was awarded with a distinction, but there was one promotion he might not have received because they'd retreated and left all the military papers behind as well as the armaments and equipment. He'd made it from Prague all the way to Italy. No one would have to tell him anything about Italy ever again. Italy was the most beautiful anarchy man had achieved, even though—as Susanna, Arthur, and Mussolini said unanimously—the trains there ran on time now. He'd made it from Italy back to Prague, and that must count for something. He recalled too many faces who had missed their return leg of the journey on this globe. In time, Emil's war memories became a symbol of something that only his mandolin could express; in its tones, every melody sweetened a touch, and manliness seemed a little more manly regardless of time. But nothing could erase, at least from Emil's mind, what he had achieved and realized as a soldier. This included how disagreeable it was to kill someone you didn't even know and never had seen before—a father of a family like his, or sons of fathers like himself, or brothers, even friends. Still, it was better than being killed by an unknown man who might be equally as blue eyed, fair haired, and with a tummy as nicely rounded as his, who'd been sent to fight just because he'd outgrown boys' clothes when war was declared. In a war, people get killed who have nothing against one another besides being on opposite sides, both of which might turn out to be wrong ones. If a man managed to hate his invisible opponent, he might be better off. That was not Emil's case. It was interesting simply to let it go through his mind, even when he took the bed apart and hunted for bedbugs. Who was born to kill in the twentieth century, for God's sake? he thought. Maybe the last war had been a mistake. Every war seemed to be a mistake after a while. The good thing about the military was that he learned to get up early and quickly, do everything fast when it was necessary, and get along with people.

"Not even a kindhearted person could caress such a deluge of bed-bugs," Emil proclaimed. He thought about a carpenter, a classmate who'd made the furniture for him and Anna after they'd gotten married. He'd been a villager like his father, a friend of Emil's father. When Emil's father had come back to his native village after twenty-five years of prison, a classmate he'd once fought against, who was now an innkeeper, served him. Time had washed away the distinction between the victor and the vanquished. They could have taken over each other's roles. The thought grew within Emil: human behavior is sometimes driven by strange forces and events. It was high time that it changed due to the will of the people instead. He felt how distant the war was. A Jew wouldn't give a nickel for anything that happened yesterday, he smiled to himself. The war had lost its meaning: blood, laughter, tears, closed councils, attacks, and retreats. Then he added, "There's a sea of bedbugs here. Where do these beasts come from?"

"You shouldn't exaggerate," Anna said.

She was ashamed of the bedbug nests, as if they were her fault, but at the same time, she reconciled herself to them. All the houses in the neighborhood, the apartments, hallways, and warehouses had bed-bugs. They spread faster than people. People could only get rid of some; they could not exterminate them all. Emil knew what to do with them, but something about them reminded him of the war, though he couldn't say why. He chose Sundays, the day of rest (as a rule, every other Sunday), to deal with them.

The melody of a religious song reached their ears from the court-yard. The words were about the unfaithful Judas, what he had done and who he betrayed, the aspen tree, and then a repeated refrain. He knew it well; they'd sung the song at the neighbor's every year for many years now. He could recite it by heart.

"You bastards! One of you will betray me." Emil summed it up quickly.

Some Catholic songs were okay, Emil thought but didn't say out loud. How many times already had Easter brought to his mind the week that begins with a great selling period and ends with a discount for almost everyone? They'd been singing the same worn-out songs for twenty centuries. For twenty centuries the church bells pealed to remind everyone who crucified whom—but who'd really cruci-fied whom? No wonder it caused horrible aftereffects. They should stop doing it, mainly because it wasn't the truth. It couldn't be compared to teachings of forgiveness, which had no statute of limitations attached to them. What good was it? The will of the world was strange, sometimes too.

Surely Anna would prefer him hunting for and destroying the bedbugs at night so that no one could see. Such a small creature but so impossible to get rid of.

"So for right now, just forget about the garden restaurant at Pelc-Tyrolka and overpriced lunches on Sunday," Anna declared.

Emil had known for a long time, without being reminded of it, that Anna did not respect Sundays or Christian holidays, although she acted like she did.

It was both ridiculous and enjoyable to imagine that you were from a royal family, especially when it wasn't possible to prove. Besides, literally everyone who was from the Levy or Kohen line, as was Anna, could claim they were of royal blood. The family was either of the rabbinate or royalty, which a long time ago probably made little or no difference. At the same time, he was proud that Anna conducted herself that way in the shop and at her sewing machine, as though a little bit of the shine from her rabbinical family had rubbed off on him as well.

Their kitchen had looked like a workshop for several months now. Anna sewed relentlessly so that they could repay the money they'd borrowed from Uncle Arthur sooner. Mr. Husserle was their best customer: he paid right away. When, unlike Richard, Helena showed him to the door, he'd give her pocket money (which Helena then turned over to her mother, along with the money from the satisfied bill). Karla was a good customer too. It was a shame that she didn't have more money to buy what she needed. She wasn't picky, but she also didn't always pay up. Anna learned to put collars on blouses from her: sometimes they turned out a little crooked, but Karla didn't complain. Karla had bought a new dress for herself for Easter as well as an apron and material which she had made into a gardening outfit with big pockets sewed on for her little girl.

Richard didn't involve himself when Mother sent Helena to deliver Mr. Husserle's shirts and handkerchiefs to him, but he thought about the naked girl he'd seen in Mr. Husserle's apartment and what Mr. Husserle had probably whispered to her. When Karla came into the kitchen, he tried to slip away. The two of them had an accounting between them that Karla knew nothing about—the same with the coachman. When Karla did bring money to pay, he had to restrain himself from telling his mother she ought to wash her hands after touching it. (Karla came into the store with her little girl and his mother would praise how clean and well behaved little Karla was. When would she be going to school? "Time goes by so fast that before you turn around you've got debts over your ears and instead of nursery school you're thinking about dancing classes," his mother would say.)

"Would you all like to go see *A Hundred Men and a Girl* with Deanna Durbin at the movies this afternoon?" Emil asked. "They're showing it at the Anchor."

Even though Emil didn't go to synagogue with Anna (who never missed a service if she could avoid it), it made sense to him that God existed. Besides God, who else was there that a fellow was obligated to kneel before? It seemed fitting to him that one was not to kneel before any person—even the president of a republic or the emperor of the greatest empire, but he preferred going to the movies with Anna over praying with her.

When Emil and Martha were still small, the Anezka Hruzova affair had been the hot topic of talk in town. She had allegedly been murdered in Polna (which was about seven-tenths Jewish) for ritual reasons by Leopold Hilzner, a lazy cobbler, vagabond, and drunkard. The incident had ruffled all the settled feathers even though it was interesting to note that Hilzner preferred to drink beer or rum in his tea with his brother by candlelight in the town pub than the virgin blood of some Christian girl in a thick, poisoned forest in the dark of the night. It always seemed strange to Emil that for two hundred years, the holy inquisition had burned, tortured, and forced hundreds of people into giving false confessions in the name of love, compassion, and humility. Not a single heretic would escape punishment, which served as a warning to others. Even though they'd been registered, case by case, into thick volumes, the actual, exact number was never published anywhere. He imagined the face of the man around whom a religion had originated as his own face, or Mr. Winternitz's, his competitor's, face, or Mr. Husserle's or Arthur's. What would have happened if the Romans had just let him preach what he preached? What would or wouldn't it have led to?

Emil smiled for the third time. He crushed a fat bedbug. The melody from the courtyard rose persistently to the back porch and through the window to them in the apartment. A spot from the bedbug remained on the wall. What had things come to back then? Could they have turned out another way? Probably yes, but differently. Most everything probably had many possibilities besides the basic good or bad, better or worse, worse or very worst.

"You told us you'd show us the house where you were born," Anna said.

Emil continued to crush the bedbugs and their eggs. If one day it was possible, as it probably never would be, he would destroy all the bedbug eggs, and then he could dedicate Sunday afternoon to doing something useful, like going over English vocabulary with Helena or taking Richard for a walk to the cemetery to visit his parents' graves more often than only once or twice a month—but it was a never-ending battle. In his mind, each bedbug told him, *You send me to the fire, to the chimney, between your thumb and finger, and for that I'll suck your blood, Anna's blood, your children's blood; it's pointless.* It was both blissful and distressing to hunt down bedbugs in your own apartment. One couldn't call them exactly the most attractive bugs, either. It was probably possible even to bar bedbugs from the list of those things that give one pleasure just because they are truly ugly.

Emil glanced in the passageway between the kitchen and the bedroom. Everywhere on the walls hung the horse pictures he had painted last year (all thirteen of them). The wall could not hold another picture.

When Emil ignored their present state, the beds looked like they'd come from a salon primarily because of their width, length, and age. If he placed his thoughts of the past wrongs onto the scales of a balance against the bedbugs, the bedbugs would win. The beds are an important thing, just like the table at which they eat and the chairs on which they sit: decent dishes, cutlery, underwear, and clothes. But even more valuable than the clothes in which a man can look good is the man himself. It occurred to him that looking after one's family was one of life's most gratifying pleasures. A person could build a house, a boat, a wall, or a tower, but the proudest creator was the creator of a family. The family was the strongest projection of his will, the best of what he had been capable of. It was the basic source of his balance, his highest plane. It made him happy even to think of his family.

"I'd be interested to know the name of the composer who lived in the building where you were born," Anna said again, so the children would disengage themselves from Emil's endeavor. "Emil, didn't you hear me?"

"Which composer lived there? The one who composed the violin sonatas that were played by famous people like Jascha Heifetz."

"Yeah, tell us how he composed for Paganini as well," Anna said, smiling.

"He composed chamber music," Emil said. "Do you know that French generals had to host their lower-ranking officers at their own dinner tables? Quite a few generals came under the hammer that way. The French king, Louis, prohibited these tables to serve the general corps. That was Louis the Fourteenth. Do you know anything about that, Helena?"

"Yes. He said, 'I am the state,'" she answered.

Next to Emil, Anna couldn't think about serious things—for instance, thinking about who honored or did not honor *her* Easter. (As if the first and last of our fellow countrymen were not the first and last to hear the voice of the only God on Mount Sinai.) It was not that long ago, after all, that everyone could forget it or put on a forgetful face to make themselves look like they had forgotten it. Why, then, was she afraid of contempt for something that no one bore responsibility for?

Emil sang loud enough for the children to hear, and Anna made another face. He sang a hackneyed song about Judas in his tortured Italian, the way he'd remembered hearing it sung during the war.

To avoid aggravation and squabbles with Emil, Anna committed the sin connected with the regulation of permitted and forbidden foods. She could bake a leg of pork with her eyes closed but redeemed herself by trying not to touch the meat (only with her hands as little as possible) and had never swallowed a morsel of it in her life. She salted and spiced the meat by estimating its size. The pork leg looked marvelous turning on the spit—it smelled just as good.

Emil had shown Anna the world. For their honeymoon he'd taken her to Vienna. The children liked to listen to those stories. Anna did not tell them that she'd wanted to go all the way to Italy, like Susanna, but only made it as far as Innsbruck, where Emil was told he was not allowed to leave the territory of his domicile because his taxes had not been paid. He did not boast of that to Anna and her family when he arrived to introduce himself. They remained in Vienna that much longer. Emil took her to a theater to see *Die Fledermaus*. She had never seen anything as cheerful. There was not a single dull moment from beginning to end. Once, she became dizzy. At the station, Emil brought her a beer. "Have a drink," he urged her. It was her first beer. She had had just enough time to get apprenticed, and then suddenly she was preparing for her wedding. She cried at night because she knew that the carefree years of life were ending, but she was happy at the same time: signed, sealed, and delivered. In Vienna they went to cafés, to Am Graben, to the theater and cabarets. Soon, Anna stopped crying during the night. She'd forgotten a great deal but not those days when life was beautiful. She was glad to be in Prague but never stopped missing the old home.

Emil had wanted his first child to be a little girl, and when it was, he brought his wife a bouquet of blue roses. She did not let herself be dissuaded that they may have only appeared that way because she was happy; in her memory, the roses remained blue. Anna had no milk, but she breast-fed anyway and got tuberculosis. Emil couldn't believe that a woman with such beautiful breasts could get tuberculosis. Then Richard was born, and Emil played an old Italian fisherman's song day and night, sang merrily, and recited the most indecent rhymes. When Anna would make herself up and it seemed too much for Emil, he sometimes would send her home to wash it off while he waited with the children in front of the house. For years she wore her ocher-yellow wedding suit and red shoes with semihigh heels so that she would not be taller than Emil.

Her grandfather, who was said to be the smartest of the family, quipped about her honeymoon, "He who marries a baron's daughter will dine like a baron." He liked Emil Ludvig. He looked to him at first sight like a man *aus guter burgerlichen Familie*. Emil brought gifts for everyone and did not forget Grandpa. They held their wedding on Sunday, the twenty-third of August 1923, a beautiful, sunny day she had spent a long time waiting for. Emil gave her a large lacquered purse of raven-black leather with white, red, and pink roses. When people asked her how she met Emil, she just laughed and blushed.

Emil also laughed because they met through a classified advertisement which Anna's younger brother, Frantisek, had placed in the newspaper and Grandpa had paid for. She preferred to tell no one about the advertisement. She was a little ashamed about it but did not know why. Later, she invented a version in which Emil had met her brother Karl in Prague, and the brother invited him to come over and become acquainted with her. But more than that, she heard the echo of the questions every woman asks herself before her wedding night: What will be expected of me? What will he presume I already know? What will I do?

Why does nearly every woman think that the man already knows more than a woman can catch up on before the wedding night? She wished for more time. She prayed to her one God to give her strength, understanding, and the maturity not to appear too inexperienced.

"The composer in the house that I was born in had a son who became a music teacher like his father," Emil said, interrupting the singing. "He thought teaching was a joy and an obligation. If it wasn't for him, I might not even know how to strum the mandolin. And that would be a misfortune."

Anna made clear with her expression: What doesn't he consider to be a misfortune? What might men—big children—think about what is expected of them?

"He stayed in the Dolomites. He got it in the chest at the Piave."

"If you're so fond of teachers, why don't you ever go ask about the children at school instead of always leaving it up to me?" Anna asked. "As if I didn't have enough to do. Don't you want to put these beds back together now?"

"I hope you don't want to argue on a Sunday," Emil said. "You should sleep at night, not sew. I won't let you continue to do so much sewing."

"That would be too sad," Anna said. It was true that she worked all day and at night too. She was afraid that her tuberculosis might return.

She looked at him like a man who, if he does not lie, at least exaggerates. The judge, their neighbor, had a record player and played himself Catholic songs with a mixed choir. They sounded nice. They were different than the worn-out song about Judas; there was something all encompassing in the singing. It was a concerto for the entire apartment house.

"My blood is too precious for me to let myself be eaten by some flat brown beast," Emil said.

"Tell us about Kunigunda," Richard pleaded.

"I won't permit it," Anna said.

She basted the meat. Her cooking and her kitchen were a match for any garden restaurant at Pelc-Tyrolka; she would be crazy to let Emil go to restaurants.

Emil burned the bugs over a candle, which sizzled and choked on its own flame. During the day, the little flame of the candle did not look menacing, but white and transparent. Only when the fat, little insects' bodies sizzled did they know Emil had won his battle with them.

"As Arthur says, either kill or be killed," Emil recalled.

Anna would have rathered that Emil play his mandolin. It carried the energy, sense, and patina of times past. Emil knew an Italian song about how the day burned low and the night arrived, and the night burned low and the day arrived. She liked that one.

"Richard's stealing the sugar," Helena said.

"Now, Richard," Anna reproached him.

In the retired railroad worker's home down in the courtyard, old Kubr's family roasted coffee. His daughter, Lida, had pneumonia. The scent reminded Emil of Grandpa Ferdinand, Solferino, and the generations which had died in their beds.

"How come they didn't send her to the sanitorium?" Emil asked. "She definitely isn't in the young landlord's favor." Emil saw how Richard took advantage of the feud between Anna and himself by furtively eating away at the sugar. Emil thought the boy might actually need it . . . except that Anna had other ideas about what the sugar was needed for.

Richard stood by the window through which he sometimes climbed when Anna chased him with a wooden kitchen spoon in her hand. He climbed like a bug, not actually on the glass, but on the thin frames. Anna became horror stricken at the thought that he would break the windowpanes and cut himself, so Richard easily escaped through the opened window above to the back porch. Climbing windows was as much a skill as riding on truck axles. He was as light as a fly. He was fearless and had never cut himself yet. Anna felt faint just thinking about it. He did not have to do it now, even though he had five sugar cubes in his pocket already.

"Take a look at the garage roof," he said. "They aren't there anymore. The young landlord sold the budgies to some Frenchman."

"Little Helena, how do you say 'lady' in English?"

"'Lady,'" Helena said. "It's spelled l-a-d-y."

Emil recited something between a prayer and a rhyme: "Thanks very much, my dear goat, that you have so sped, that the Lordie's up in heaven that giveth us bread . . ."

Helena blushed.

The kitchen smelled of freshly baked bread. Anna had learned to bake from her mother, who'd learned it from her mother many years before. They knew how to bake their own bread from good wheat flour, and sometimes from several different kinds of flour, so that the family would have better nourishment. Bread represented the past to them, its inclusions and exclusions, isolation, separations and reunions.

From the beginning of time, bread has been the best thing that a person could have, Anna thought. She did not have to say it or think it—it showed in her every movement. It was in the mixing of the bread, the preparation of the yeast, the thickening and leavening of the dough, and the baking and cutting of the bread. It was sufficient for her to look at the round-shaped loaf on the table. It was present in the smell of the bread throughout the apartment. When she thought of good and evil, bread was not only a necessity, but the most basic food. In bread, there was the essence of man, his work, his labors, and God. It made her beautiful, the same way praying in the local Liben synagogue made her beautiful, or looking at the red and gold wooden crown above the altar, or the scrolls of the Ten Commandments, or the excerpt from the five books of Moses. As long as she could bake bread, she would feel safe in the family circle in their apartment. She baked the bread until it was golden. She knew Richard loved the crusts, but Emil saw beyond that: he understood that the baked bread meant family, life, goodness, safety.

Besides rye bread, on Fridays she baked challah, the Jewish bread made with white flour. It was one of the few Hebrew and Yiddish words that Anna knew. Challah, too, filled the apartment with its aroma. Sometimes Anna baked both kinds of bread, brother and sister loaves, man and woman, two breads—the Czech bread and the Jewish bread—two joys. If someone asked Anna by chance, "What is beauty? What is the hope or stability or meaning of all things?" she would look at blue skies, at the freshly baked bread, or at her husband and two small children.

Anna went to the Crested Lark or to Vinegar Street for flour. The neighborhood, Tanner Street and Leather Street, used to be the ghetto in the Liben quarter.

"Don't we have any more wine to give to Richard for his anemia?" Emil asked.

"There would be some if you hadn't drunk it up," Anna said.

Emil blew out what remained of the candle. The wine was called Perla Narentica, and Doctor Mahrer had prescribed it for Richard. It was sold bottled in two sizes: one for eleven and one for fourteen crowns.

"Buy a bottle," Emil said. "At least the eleven-crown size."

"We'll see," Anna said.

"Richard," Anna said, "what did you do in religion class that made Mr. Schapira look at me as if he were offended?"

"I asked whether we had a devil," Richard answered.

"How did it occur to you to ask that?"

"He was talking about the evil spirit of the Lord," Richard said, "but he didn't explain it."

Anna gave up questioning Richard. She'd only wanted to know why they'd sent a comment home about him. Had they written home about anyone else besides him? Zdenek Pick? What had they written about Zdenek Pick?

"You boys are two of a kind," Anna remarked.

"I, too, would be interested to know how you arrived at that question," Emil said.

"Because they were talking about it in a lesson about another religion," Richard said. "During the break, the guys were saying that the hair on his forehead glowed at night, like a cat's eyes at night. Or that he can look like a gorilla. When a girl combs her hair secretly at night in front of a mirror, or just looks at herself in the mirror at night, she'll meet the devil in her bed. Whoever is a lefty must work three days a year for the devil. If you sneeze on a Sunday, you'll meet with the devil. Praying at night is praying to the devil. The devil isn't alone. He has a wife and children. When the dawn and night or the sun and rain meet, you can hear them and what they're brewing. And, no one can meet the devil on a Friday because they're stacking wood in hell." Finally, he added, "Somebody's daddy told them that the Jews kill their children to sacrifice them to the devil. I punched him in the teeth. I doubt he'll say it again."

"That's a lot of trash," Emil said.

"Mommy asked me, so I'm answering," Richard defended himself. "Also, seeing a white and a black horse together means seeing the devil. Killing a cat means fighting with the devil too."

"You shouldn't talk of the devil, lest you invite him in," Anna said. "How come you remember such things?"

She pulled out a cupboard drawer where she kept wooden spoons. Emil made a mental note about what Richard had said about slugging someone with his fist; Richard knew that he would get a fifty-heller piece for it at a more suitable moment. Father rewarded him secretly for that kind of self-defense; Mother did not like it at all.

In that moment, Richard felt how a son's joy in his father resembled and differed from others, like the time Daddy had bought a pair of skis on sale one winter and watched him dash down the snow all the way to the fence, coming to a stop with a stem christie, looking as if he had been skiing for years, like Cousin Susanna in Italy. Or the joy of cutting school sometimes and going to the river to skim stones on water. The feeling was warm, like an invisible gas that inflates a balloon before it rises.

"What else did you talk about?" Anna wanted to know.

"Why God made Eve from one of Adam's ribs."

"Why he made her out of a rib?"

"If he had made her out of a head, she would have been too proud; if he had made her out of an eye, she would have been too inquisitive; and if he had made her out of a piece of ham, she would have been too indecent. The rib is a neutral bone."

"Is that what you're studying in religion class?" Anna asked. She nearly had the wooden kitchen spoon out of the drawer.

Richard made a quick sidestep toward the window. Helena covered her mouth with the palm of her hand.

"Emil, I tell you it's almost better when you take them to the cemetery," Anna said. "I bought sugar yesterday and where is it now? Whichever of you is hungry can eat bread until you're full. The sugar costs six-thirty."

Emil avoided glancing at Anna or Richard. He directed his attention to his pictures of horses. He had been drawing postal horses during the past year. He did not have the urge to draw the cubes and cones on which the shadow falls from the top, the bottom, or the left.

He folded up the cots.

"Richard, could you hold the sideboards for me?" Emil asked. And to Anna, "The grocer greets me apprehensively, as if he didn't really want to."

"He may be angry with us for shopping at the co-op," Anna said. "Just what kind of a person are you, Emil?"

"How can I drive straight if one says to the left, and the other to the right?" Emil said. "You all must let me drive the way I'm driving. I already know how to drive."

The last bed-folding ritual came to pass. Emil pulled out the dresser drawer. He glanced over the old shells of shrapnel, cartridges of fifteen, eighteen, and twenty-eight caliber. They reminded him of the experience when a cannon pulls the horses and the crew into an abyss with it on a completely clear and bright night. The sizzling of meat supplemented the sensation. Emil pushed in the drawer and dusted the horse portraits. Their backs shone; he had painted them well. He took down the imperial post office gray horse to hammer the nail head in deeper. He stiffened the backing of the gray horse with plywood from a cigar box.

Richard read cards for Helena to predict if she would get married and wed in white.

"Daddy likes to narrate novels, but he will have to stop for today," Anna said. "We're ready to eat now."

"A roast," Emil said. "We're not such proletarians to deny ourselves."

"Just what we need," Anna said. All there was to be done now was to send Richard to get beer and instruct him not to drink it but to bring it back quickly so it would still be foamy.

They heard the doorbell ring. "Who could that be?" Emil inquired. "It's a Sunday."

Sunday was certainly a visiting day—but not at the hour of high noon.

"Who's ringing the doorbell?" Anna inquired.

It occurred to Anna that it could be Zdenek Pick's father, who didn't want his son to be friends with Richard because, as he put it, they did not have the best influence on each other. Some Jewish families were careful about their children's company. With the non-Jewish parents it was simpler, because like Anna and Emil, they had no time for children on a workday. (Yesterday, Richard told Anna that some of the boys had taken lard from their homes and greased their scooters and handmade carts with it in order to race down the Prazacka hill and the steep road by the reform school.)

Was the visitor some insurance representative for whom no time and day were sacred?

The meat of the roast leg, dumplings, and sauerkraut, which exuded the winey flavor of vinegar, sent pleasant smells wafting throughout the kitchen.

Emil put the mandolin away on the divan. The waxed cover was cracked into thousands of small squares. He tucked his shirt into his trousers, pulled them up, and then combed his hair with the palm of his hand. He looked at himself in the kitchen mirror. He was presentable. He went to open the door.

In the doorway was an unknown man.

"I'm from Germany," the guest introduced himself in bad Czech, and added in German, "Here, I have a document from the community, stating where I can search for our people." He pointed to the paper on which, listed alphabetically, the name Ludvig was written next to the names Mahrer and Tanzer. He looked like he had come on foot from far away.

"Some of the addresses I bought at the stock exchange in the Ascherman café for three crowns."

Sonya Vackova was in the corridor collecting water into a small jar in order to clean it.

Emil observed that the stranger's shoes were worn down. His coat was unbuttoned, worn out, and shabby. Emil noticed the torn lining.

"And what can I do for you?" Emil asked. "Come inside, so you won't be standing in the corridor."

Simultaneously, he gave Richard money for two half-liter mugs of beer. In German, Anna urged the stranger to take off his things and sit down. The stranger looked around the kitchen for a place to put his coat. Emil hung it up for him above the trunk with spare down comforters. We need these, he said to himself, at the same time thinking of the stranger. It was not difficult to see that the stranger needed them too.

After five minutes, Richard returned with the beer, and Anna said, "Please have a meal with us. If you don't eat the meat from the leg, I can make dumplings and eggs for you." The family did not look at him as suspiciously as before. He had surprised them and caught them off guard. He'd be visiting the Mahrers and the Tanzers after his visit to them. Anna thought of every lost Jewish soul that would find itself in the west instead of in the east, the south, or the north, dispersed to some corner of the world without it being his or her own fault or intention. One moment was enough to awaken what had lain dormant inside her; something that each one carried somewhere, deep inside, so that its very awakening is terrifying without even knowing the shape the fear had taken. Was it an old terror, maybe only the echo of terrors already experienced a long time ago? Did she perhaps hear the grass growing? A cold shiver ran up and down her spine. She kept her lips together so no one would know what she was thinking. Was it just a childish fear which would pass like an icy wind? She didn't have to dig far back into her memory to recall that sometimes her mother or father heard the voices of the long since dead, expelled or beaten, people who had been robbed and had their rights taken away. It was probably never all that far away from her. Maybe it was in inherited memory, something passed down from generation to generation, to all the unknown people who'd lived before her and had found themselves away from the places where they'd grown up, just like this man who'd come today. It was not hard to see those unknown souls, or just their echoes, in him; a frozen haze that resembled crowds without names—a face with a fate that touched her. Everything that had happened to them could very well happen to her. She didn't want to see such people as a crowd, like so many trees in the forest, unless she could see them singly, one tree at a time. It was simplistic, but she couldn't afford to be naive. She was allowed to be modest, but not blind or deaf, to close her eyes if on the contrary it was necessary to open them up again to see and listen, to hear. She heard something crashing about in her head that she would rather not know about. Was it a curse, or would it stop anything to act as though nothing was happening when the something that was being called forth in her was so terrifying? Wouldn't it catch up with those who, in the past, had turned their backs to it? Hadn't the ancestors always been on the run from it their entire lives? Even before she'd looked at him for very long, the figure of the guest burned itself into her memory. It overwhelmed her with an unpleasant suspicion whose source she hadn't fathomed only a little while ago. The moment was enough for her to sense worry, fear, the premonition of something that she'd rather she didn't know. It had to have been an old, but powerful, echo that would never be silent in some people. The times that were coming didn't look like something meant only to scare them—what terrified her was something else.

"Make yourself at home," Emil encouraged him. "Little Helena, bring the chair from the bedroom."

Helena dragged Grandpa Ferdinand's fancy chair into the kitchen.

"Yes," Anna repeated. The stranger reminded her of someone from the Moravian house she'd lived in when she had been little and where she had not wanted to eat the chicks because she had played with them.

"Thank you," the guest said. They put the first plate and cutlery in front of him.

The guest's name was Joachym Luxemburg. Next to their name on the list was a remark: "knock." Mr. Luxemburg may have overlooked it. His eyes had circles under them, as if he had gone to sleep late or risen early. When he took off his hat, his hair proved to be thin around the crown of his head. He tidied it with a sweaty hand. It was possible he had become sweaty because he had walked either too long or too fast. His teeth were not straight by any stretch of the imagination, and in any event, he did not have many. They could see that each time he opened his mouth.

The smell of the roast pork suddenly made them feel a little awkward. Mr. Luxemburg said he ate everything, of course, but did not want to impose. He was fleeing from faraway Berlin. Fortunately, they had confined him there for only a short time, though they'd beaten him and told him they'd hold nothing against him if he would quickly find where the carpenter had left a hole and disappear. They had told him that to a certain extent their interests were the same as his: namely his stay on German soil. It had nothing to do with who had been born where. New times had new requirements. It would be best, they had told him, to bid farewell first to Germany and later to Europe. In this respect, he could rely on their support. Their foundation for this was the law protecting German blood and honor.

Mr. Luxemburg smiled and said he hoped he wasn't forcing the conversation on them or hadn't made it appear that he'd let himself become depressed by it. His pants legs were odd; he looked like a man who'd been on a strict diet and had lost over half his body weight before he'd had a chance to get to a tailor to have his pants taken in. The entire time he'd been without work he'd lifted weights to keep fit. Now it was coming in handy because he was often on his feet for hours at a time. He didn't say that he looked like a soldier who'd climbed out of the trenches and caught the first bullet of the war; that way, he'd already lost the battle. Instead, he'd become a beggar with zeal in his limbs. What was a fellow supposed to do when everything he'd done turned out to be full of flaws? Where was the sense of it anymore, and if there still was sense, where was there any dignity? He didn't want to give away how impoverished he really was. A year ago he wouldn't have said it could happen to him.

"I went to register at the Military Office for the Wehrmacht. I regarded it as my obligation. I was not accepted because of my racial origin," he said.

Anna said that it was sad when a person had to leave the country where he had been born and the house he had called home. She couldn't envision it happening to her.

Before they sat down, Emil had taken ten crowns, put them inside an envelope, and handed it to Anna. Anna passed it inconspicuously to Mr. Luxemburg; it was a lot of money for her even if it probably wasn't much for Mr. Luxemburg. Emil was again touched by something intangible. Something which had already lingered in the air for some time. Something he'd spoken about with Arthur: say the word "Germany" and it resounds with "army" and "Hitler"; something he couldn't or didn't want to touch himself; something which created an invisible barrier behind the comfortable life which they led in spite of all obstacles. He felt his guest's fear but didn't want it to show.

"We've heard some things, but who would believe them?" Emil said.

"Who'd want to do things like that?" Anna asked.

"They'd have to have strong stomachs," Emil added. With his eyes he conveyed that people with such stomachs must also have difficulties with other body organs including hearts and minds. He would wait to discuss that with Arthur. He tried to appear as though he hadn't been caught off guard and regretted that he had only washed up for lunch but had not changed into a suit. Luckily, he had on a clean shirt and pants.

Mr. Luxemburg only mentioned offhand how there were signs in every shop window and at every streetlight in Germany—not offering goods or inviting people to bars, circuses, or to some unseen curiosity, but announcing new anti-Semitic regulations. On November 12, 1938, a huge sign was put up at the bus station for its thirty-first birthday: Jews were no longer allowed in any sports facilities. Elsewhere, another sign stated that Jews were no longer allowed to operate independent workshops. They announced somewhere that Jewish authors were barred from any kind of writing about the territory of Germany. Signs appeared on almost every block, at every bus stop, every streetcar (there were probably eighty signs in all), forbidding "non-Aryans" almost everything except breathing the common air: Jewish children were not allowed to play on German playgrounds with German, non-Jewish children; Jewish smokers could no longer buy cigarettes, cigars, or tobacco; Jewish doctors could no longer treat German patients or continue practicing in their specialties. It had started as early as 1933, but now it had reached a peak. The year 1938 had definitely not been a good year. Now they were also saying that non-Aryans would no longer be allowed to buy soap or razors or shaving cream, not to mention to use public libraries. Jewish judges had already been taken off the bench, the way Jews had been removed from public service or from their posts as clerks in German offices.

Amid his talk he only added that he didn't wish it on them here. Perhaps it wouldn't happen. How long had it been since he'd eaten an egg or drank fresh milk? They didn't like Jews in Germany, he said. Why? He would be happier if it were based on something reasonable which would let him deal with it inside.

"I used to think before that anything that happens has two sides to it, but now I know that it's not like that. There are afflictions that have no reason. There's only one reason and only the devil could explain it."

He stopped himself. He probably didn't want to talk about the devil during Sunday lunch. There was no need to state that the meal was delicious.

"I never thought that some people could base their entire lives on lies," he said as if he were apologizing, "but they can. What the German Reich is based on at this time is nothing but lie after lie."

He sensed what was escaping Emil, his wife, and his children—what hadn't crawled under their skins like it had gotten under his. He sighed but suppressed it so that it didn't appear as though he were complaining.

"Who doesn't lie today or have to deal with lies?" Emil stated so the conversation would not be left only up to Mr. Luxemburg.

The émigré had sad, blue, Jewish eyes. He didn't have to quote the chief rabbi in Berlin, Dr. Baeck, that "a thousand-year history of German Jews has come to an end." Four-fifths of Jews there had been for a liberal Germany, but Hitler and his party were aware that there was not much left to Jews except for attempting to survive and negotiate their way out of their unpleasant state. Thousands and maybe tens of thousands of German Jewish families were in direct danger. Was it only German jealousy, weakness, and envy that fed the loathing, the hatred, and the cruelty toward Jews? What could the Jews have done on their part to have brought this on?

His blue eyes faded. Something drowned in them that he didn't want to talk about: panic, escapes, suicides, the waning will to live to outlast the Nazis and Hitler, the hundreds of thousands of jobs and opportunities that had been lost. Jewish communities had been thrown together into flocks so that the German wolf could more easily devour them. Regulations by the government and city administration, ploys, frauds, lies, and fear were surefire means for the Nazis to frighten the defenseless—German and Jew alike. Tens of thousands of people like him had been left without property and with nothing but their bare skins and the hope that one day they would be able to return. As a country, Germany was steeped in the blood of many Jewish refugees, and it didn't do much for them in other countries, either. A thousand years suddenly foundered like a house of cards. Mr. Luxemburg was coming out of the darkness. Were they leaning on their pride, which didn't have anything to lean on itself? What remained of pride that was riddled by fear like moth-eaten wool dresses? Germany no longer was a safe harbor for Jewish boats like Mr. Luxemburg. After leaving Germany, Mr. Luxemburg often thought about the two types of death a person met with but didn't dare speak about: one way was the Nazis' way and the other way was that of the individual. He didn't want anybody to sentence him in advance for it. The thoughts that Mr. Luxemburg left unstated probably didn't cheer him up much. His blue eyes gave him away by their moist gaze, though he tried to keep them placid so that he wouldn't alarm his hosts.

Emil said that he was glad Mr. Luxemburg had succeeded in leaving (and that he liked the food). Fortunately, Mr. Luxemburg was still single and had left only his parents and other relatives in Germany. His parents were considering emigrating to Palestine. Mr. Göring would be glad to see them go there, even if only two percent of the six hundred thousand German Jews had registered as Zionists. Unfortunately, the English, who held the keys to the lock, were admitting only wealthy people into their country.

The Nazis ran the country in the same way people had done it for thousands of years, by the difference between good and evil, not to mention justice and injustice. They didn't believe that freedom and democracy were the best things a person could work toward and for which he had already sacrificed so much. The Gestapo had accused him of being one of those who had abused the demand for freedom for everybody; there wasn't a society that existed where everyone could be free. As he'd said, he had been lucky to get out of the Gestapo office with his skin.

He took a clipping from a newspaper and read: "Whenever anyone shouts about historical necessity in order to pass an injustice onto the innocent, it cannot end well." (It sounded very ominous in German to Richard and Helena.)

Mr. Luxemburg then stated, "A distant cousin of my mother's said this: 'Freedom only for active participants in the government, or only for members of the party, however many they may be, is not freedom.

Freedom, the one and only, at this time and for always, is freedom only for those who think otherwise.'" He put the clipping back into his pocket.

Anna asked the guest if he enjoyed the food. He had; everyone had enjoyed the meal. Feed the beast well, Emil thought, but how can one enjoy a meal when he has great worries and many of them? It appears he's got a very perceptive cousin, though.

"A man goes to bed at home one evening and in the morning wakes up to find that he has become an emigrant—and on top of that, he is supposed to be delighted with his misfortunes. You have a nice place here—really homey—it's good to feel at home," the visitor said. A zest and a loathing for life alternated in his eyes. One could smell it the way one smelled the onions and garlic Anna had added to season the meat.

Anna ate only dumplings with sauerkraut; it may have crossed the guest's mind that he had received her portion of the meat. Anna blushed. It also occurred to Emil that Mr. Luxemburg might be embellishing the facts in order to get more money and addresses. It was only a fraction of a thought; he knew right away that it was untrue and unfair. The thought also flitted through his mind that a person feels guilty for his thoughts later on. Why did he search for solace in something that made a bigger sacrifice of itself than it deserved to? Was it like the stock exchange at the Ascherman café? Maybe they didn't really sell addresses for three crowns there to poor souls like Mr. Luxemburg.

"Maybe people went crazy for a little while but now they'll straighten up," Emil said.

"People?" Mr. Luxemburg asked. He didn't have to say that the riffraff who had devoured everything didn't have to work hard at it. "They are blaming us for preposterous offenses and crimes, for what we commandeered from them, and for the fact that we're forcing our way into something that should be exclusively German—as if we didn't exist there already."

Mr. Luxemburg spoke about the worst of the three laws that had been adopted at Nuremberg: the law for the protection of German honor and blood. To some people, murder is an integral part of the law—whoever defends Germany and advances it sanctions killing.

It seemed to Emil that the Germans had invaded Mr. Luxemburg's apartment and his life as though they didn't need keys; he had to compare that with the way they were living. He had the impression he was reading a double newspaper touting the world from two different angles: the first would supplement the second, and the second would, perhaps, fill the first. However, they had the good fortune to be living here.

"Many people have left, but even more are unable to," Mr. Luxemburg said. "Nobody wants them. There are fifty-five million unemployed in Europe. Many people still believe in and trust Germany. It is so difficult to believe that so many things have changed nearly overnight. Inside, even though I know what's good for me, I tend to believe what I want or need to, never trusting what I'm uncomfortable believing."

" . . . and the courts?" Emil then asked.

"They are murderers," Mr. Luxemburg said. "It's funny that people can't accept that others could do things they would be incapable of doing themselves. Perhaps we overestimate civilization, expecting that which we must defend ourselves against will resolve automatically."

Emil smiled. "It's like the English and soccer . . . the English believe they're the best in the world and don't let anyone refute it. What they can't do, nobody else can do either."

The lunch saddened and angered Emil. "People cling to what helped them through long years of work: chairs that they sit on and a table at which they eat; clothing in the closet for the winter and for all the seasons. I hope that these things will help you again—only it probably won't be the same as home—or perhaps you can work out a new home. I can assure you that you will like it here in Bohemia. Not long ago, the head of the country was a philosopher, a university professor. He was a brave man, they say. Unfortunately, he died, but at a very old age. I doubt that what is going on in Germany can happen here."

"Sometimes it's even sad to talk about the weather," the emigrant said.

"One shouldn't speak about unpleasant affairs during lunch," Anna said.

She was immediately startled by the thought that the guest wouldn't take it well. After that, Mr. Luxemburg did indeed speak less. If he said something, he tried to do it quietly to sound all the more modest.

Emil translated a few of the things the emigrant had said for Richard: "The main thing is that he got out. He wants to keep going farther. I am assuring him that nothing like that can happen here. He aches in all his joints and bones. He says that sometimes he would like to be something other than what he was born as, what he has done, and what he has become. Maybe it makes him a little bigger or smaller," Emil added. He smiled. He felt that his confidence had grown a little. Was it because of the thought they were in a better place themselves since the guest had it so bad? He turned to Mr. Luxemburg.

"Mr. Vacek, one of the neighbors from the other side of the building, also keeps an eye on the organizations in Germany—like you say they are going. I don't know if they would succeed here. Meanwhile, he looks like five circumcised men in one. His wife is German, but a good woman."

He had wanted to change his guest's thoughts to happier ones but had ended up only sounding ridiculous. He hoped that Anna wouldn't comment how lame he was.

Emil went to get a coat from the closet and offered it to Mr. Luxemburg in place of his torn one. Suddenly he felt a little like Uncle Arthur; he wasn't sure exactly why. After all, he did not need two coats when someone else who was so troubled he didn't know where to turn had such a worn and wrinkled one. The coat was a little tight on the guest and the sleeves a little too long.

"I can imagine what it means to lose your home," Emil said. "I wouldn't want to be in your shoes."

"I hope you never are," the guest said. "Even if the borders seem to be moving and none of them seem safe enough. It would be good if at least the rivers and mountains guaranteed every country safety like in the old days. People are quickly losing what it took them so long to attain. The worst thing is that Germany is acting as though it wants to protect us from ourselves. It's not possible to get out— it's only possible to remain. Either you stay and they'll destroy you or you leave and you'll be without money, work, friends—everything; even your very being is in trouble. They're making fun of what was untouchable yesterday. It rings in my ears every day. I hear the ones that leaving wasn't enough for. Nobody acts like they're listening as they still did a year or two ago, but they don't hear that. The signals that the Reich leadership is giving people like me are unmistakable. Everybody ignores our voices. They want to terrify us by certain words and cover up what they're planning to do. We will probably never understand each other. They're killing Jewish children," he added.

"Surely not," Emil said.

"They are torturing people in the camps."

"I'd be more likely to believe that," Emil admitted.

"Eat up, children," Anna said.

"Let's wait and see," Emil said. "It's not all over yet."

All at once it struck him that the world in which he lived, just like the life he'd always lived with his family, had changed. It was like the falling of hailstones under which not only the roof was creaking, but also the foundations of the structure upon which he'd based his entire existence. He had to learn to accept everything like some juggler in an invisible circus. They were the highest ideals along with the lowest plans and aims or thoughts, the past and the present and the future, like the clasped hands of a three-armed ancient Indian beauty he'd seen pictures of at the museum. Sometimes it was truth and sometimes a lie, and sometimes it swung from fairness to apathy and back again and he had to choose, but he still didn't know what he was doing most of the time. Was it a modern world that he'd been born into? He felt as though he was living a life that led him from small to large but at the same time limped in a gray zone in which it was impossible to distinguish good from bad, right from wrong, and from honorable to not quite honorable to downright dishonorable; at least you couldn't do it at first glance without thinking about it first. The important thing was that it be legal, and a person didn't get into trouble with the law, with rules, with the world as it once was, and how he still wanted it to be. It was more of a standpoint than reality as he understood it. Maybe it happened to everyone who gets older, supports a family, or wants to accomplish something and finds out that it's not so easy. Maybe he was too sensitive, and other people live in the same reality without wondering about it so much.

He thought to himself, I'm still up to it, and he looked at Mr. Joachym Luxemburg. What would I do if I were in his shoes? How would I act if those things were happening here and now? It was a feeling, rather than a clear understanding, but he knew somewhere deep in his heart a change had occurred here as well, without being able to estimate how much it affected him and how far it had gone, and in what direction and circumstances his life would lead from smaller to bigger. How big could it end up being? He glimpsed—by some premonition—the shadow in his soul.

Mr. Luxemburg thanked Anna for the coat; it fit him well. He promised that he would call them soon. He was getting ready to go to the West and was only saving up some money for the trip. Then he thanked them again for lunch, the coat, and the pleasant company. For the first time, he smiled. Nobody—perhaps not even the big shots—had had such food in Germany for a long time. Anna told him to step out of the apartment on his good leg.

In the apartment building they could hear singing: somebody had left to sing at the church. One set of troubles had begun long ago, but new ones were just beginning. Hopefully, everything will turn out well for everyone, Anna thought to herself.

Emil had uneasy dreams that night. He dreamed that Arthur cheated on Martha, who reproached him and said she'd made a mistake by marrying a whoremonger. The dream's echo rested in that word as he awoke. He couldn't get it out of his mind. Someone in the street, it may have been Karla, shouted, "Don't push me, fatso. Nobody can do anything to me I don't want them to." People returned from a religious procession.

Spring streamed into the apartment through an open window. The hill with the steel gas sphere shone in the night. The shadows from the arches of the fire escape ladders gripped the sphere like a hoop through which the stars and the moon were mirrored. They became tangled in the room on the green leaves of the rubber plant and asparagus ferns.

Emil tossed and turned in his bed, even after Anna came in to lie down. All at once, the children suddenly did not seem so small to him. It made him regret something, but he did not know why. They were little for such a short time. They had grown up faster than he wanted them to. Was it better that way in the end? He would have liked to know what it was all coming to. Well, probably no one could know that.

THE BUYING OF TIME

From Helena's notes:

Cousin Susanna has returned from Italy. We've already gotten together a few times. I didn't think we'd get close so quickly. I like listening to her. She's happiest when I ask questions so she can answer me, but she also likes to hear about my life in school, boys, girls, Jewish society, and about how many non-Jewish societies I still manage to make it to. She complained that Uncle Arthur opens up her letters and reads them. It's a revolting, disgusting habit. If it isn't punishable, it's still a crime — an invasion of privacy, an encroachment into what is acceptably sacred. Uncle Arthur probably can't help himself from sticking his nose into other people's business, but Susanna and Uncle Arthur are certainly not "other people" to each other. I know that my papa would never do that to me, but on the other hand, few people write to me. It's a pity.

I try to be open with Susanna, but I haven't told her about Alfred Flexner yet. Should there be limitations on honesty?

I read there's a certain group of Eskimos who sacrifice pieces of flesh from their own bodies to save their children. It reminded me a little of Papa. I think about if I were a mother and my children didn't have anything to eat, I would sacrifice a piece of my own flesh.

3

The night before his morning meeting with Arthur, Emil Ludvig dreamed that his brother-in-law had gotten him a job and then asked him what little gift he had bought him. It was embarrassing for Emil to have no gift. Later on, toward morning, he also dreamed about applying for a job, but first he had to fill out a questionnaire. The questionnaire had twelve parts, each with three subsections that had to be filled out in Czech, German, and a third language he didn't know and had never heard of before. What kind of language could it have been?

To get the job, he had to create something that no applicant before him had ever created. Instead of writing out his experiences down to the last detail, one after another, he was supposed to write them in a parable. What was so strange about that? Perhaps he could use the one about a girl (for example, like Lida Kubrova) who did not know what to do about all the injustice that exists in the world. The form the parable took was, after all, up to him—this would be clear sailing. He opted to choose a more neutral type of girl—the kind of girl one could find on the street these days by the dozens. He had to state his identification number. The girl appeared. Under her arm, where other girls carry a purse or an umbrella, was a copy of *Spanish in a Thousand Words,* but she also had a revolver in her pocket. "Either the destitute will defend themselves or they will be destitute forever. If it were one person, it would have been enough to lock him up or kill him," she said. After all, Lida Kubrova had died of tuberculosis, and her mother had died of lung cancer when Lida was young. Was this not his parable, in fact? Under the heading "education," he put down that lately he only read newspapers. He used to read books, but nowadays he didn't have time. He read "Indian Rubber" and "The Green

Wig" and other old Czech legends, especially the Czech and Jewish tales from Prague, like the ones about Golem and about Rabbi Loewe from neighboring Maisel Street. These days there was more suspense in the newspapers than in the stories writers used to invent. Just this morning they'd written in the *Express* about Freemasons conspiring with their helpers from the East to take over the world.

They sentenced Emil to death for what he had written in the questionnaire. The sentence was to be carried out immediately, in the courtyard of the Ungelt house where he would sometimes buy flowers for Anna and fruits for the children. In the dream, they'd stuck a contraption on his head that resembled a helmet made from a hairdresser's dryer. Before they sent him tumbling into a pit, two long steel needles would shoot out from the sides of the contraption and pierce the sentenced man's brain. Somebody said that it would not be painful. Policemen held him up by his armpits near the edge of the shaft, but Emil jumped before they could put the helmet on him. He flew downward for a long time but landed gently as if he had only taken a step. At the bottom, a corridor led to an office where military judges in German uniforms sat. They said that he should not rejoice in vain because nothing would save him ever again. He only wanted to ask if he were being punished for what he had written on the questionnaire. The lady registrar resembled Erna Vackova from the apartment next door, with her pointy breasts and white teeth. She gave him his documents to read. He did not know that the authorities had been keeping so many written documents on him. They were yellow silk papers with a carbon copy title page; he recognized his own handwriting. The lady clerk asked him where he had received the decoration for courage. She found out by reading the documents that Emil Ludvig had participated with Richard in a May Day parade; by chance, those with whom they marched had chanted, "Out with the Jews." What had he gone to find there—or was Emil Ludvig claiming it was all a mistake? The mounted police broke up the parade; both he and Richard had been hit with nightsticks. Was Emil Ludvig a recruiter? What about the three small stars on the reddish-yellow epaulets? Had he joined when he was seventeen in the third year of the war? Was he glad Austria had lost? The dream ended with laughter.

Anna, in turn, dreamed she had received a silver suit from her relatives in the Promised Land. They were all supposed to drive to the port, board a steamship, and emigrate, but she had forgotten the silver suit at home. They had to go back to get it, but when they got there, the building was surrounded by soldiers in frog-green uniforms, and by the Gestapo as well. The ship sailed without them. A man from the Gestapo consoled them by telling them not to be sorry, because even though the ship had left without them, it would not receive permission to land anyway.

In Germany, thirty thousand people a year hung themselves, jumped out of windows, shot themselves, or poisoned themselves with pills or gas. It did not pay to look into such matters before they happened. As they'd written yesterday in the *Flag:* "It is only an element of natural selection."

The newspapers brought news about euthanasia—mercy killings. Was it in the interest of the child, the parents, the society, to kill a child born with incurable defects? Was it also wrong to artificially extend the lives of the incurably ill or crippled?

Emil shook off the restless night and met Arthur at the Ascherman café on Dlouha Street. Arthur was decked out as if for Monte Carlo; he had on an evening suit, thickly waxed hair, a worn, black diplomat, and a white silk shawl. He was already waiting for Emil.

"They want to transport all our people to the colonies," Emil said.

"Would you like a nice cup of coffee, while we can still get it?" Arthur asked.

"Perhaps we should have sent our children to England, Arthur, but Anna didn't want to, and I'm happiest with the family together."

He had a feeling he couldn't share with anyone that he'd miss every train and would watch as the last car left before his very eyes. He'd made every decision that could change or improve something too late. He felt everything slipping away from him; his fingers were too weak and his arms too short to keep it from happening. What about the family? He was responsible for them. He did not feel fully up to such responsibility. It frightened him. As Arthur used to say, *It's an avalanche.* How did he plan to stop it with only his two bare hands? He caught himself daydreaming that the avalanche stopped by itself. He would have liked to stick to his own rules. Was it all a tragic comedy, as Arthur claimed?

Arthur ordered a cup of coffee and a glass of water for both of them. He asked the waitress what kind of pastry was available. Arthur had promised Emil he would still be able to secure a job for him, thanks to his connection with a German firm. He didn't have a single gray hair yet, and he was proud of it. He glanced at his watch. They had two more hours before the meeting. It was better to kill time in a café than at home or in the street, Arthur thought. These days, they rob our people in the street. It was enough just to have the look of southern origin. He still preferred to be conspicuous than to go unnoticed. The Jewish coffeehouse suited him. (Aren't all coffeehouses Jewish in their own way?)

Arthur watched the nineteen-year-old Aryan lady confectioner's calves as she carried little pastry baskets filled with meringue around the billiards lounge. Most ingredients were ersatz by now, but for some reason they still had coffee—a Colombian blend—from their old reserves. It was amazing that no German authorities had confiscated it for the army yet. "We'll keep serving it as long as we've got it," the waitress declared.

Before Emil arrived, Arthur had been writing love letters to a girl for his colleague, Irving Egon Kahn, a traveling salesman whose parents had returned to Prague from America in the early 1930s during the Great Depression. He sold rubber goods and fixatives. At this point, Arthur had written five letters in reserve. He compared them to a game of chess. He had to know the way he would move in order to anticipate his opponent's move. (All he really knew about Kahn's girlfriend had been revealed to him by chance on a tinted, retouched photograph.)

The Ascherman café was like an island unto itself. It had been a Jewish café even before the war, but now it catered exclusively to Jews since other coffeehouses had signs up—JEWS NOT ALLOWED—and couldn't serve them.

"Sometimes somebody ought to bend me over his knee and slap me on the behind," Arthur remarked, smiling. He looked at the waitress with appreciation.

"Once I dreamed about this waitress. She was a water nymph. She told me in the dream, 'When children look at me, I lie down on my belly. For gentlemen like you, Mr. Pick, I lie on my back.'"

Then Emil said, "The generals won't let Hitler have the kind of war he'd like to have. Just look at it, Arthur—everything is falling apart in front of our eyes, and it's still part of a whole. Countless agreements engraved in stone, no engraving, no agreements—everything that has an extraordinary meaning has none at the same time. Do you want it to make sense? Maybe you don't. That's our world—my life and yours, of the living and the dead and of everyone who has yet to die. It's a fruitful power which bears no fruit, the empire of a divine light in which the human body and soul wander and rise to higher levels from self to self. All for one and one for all—protect yourself with your own fists as best you can. Everything tears us apart and brings us together—like getting dirty and clean—except you don't know in what order. You can label it the earth's gravity or a cosmic law if you like. Did you know that a person can be reincarnated as an animal or even an insect because of the sins he committed in this life? Hitler latched on to that idea—he claims that we're insects. From the way Ascherman's café sometimes looks, maybe we are. But he probably doesn't have a clue that he stole the idea from the cabala."

"Maybe we're already something other than what we used to be but we aren't aware of it yet," Arthur replied. "Do you think that we live in a real or only a made-up world? The only problem is that I don't have any idea who made up this world so that I can prove him a liar. A little more decoration wouldn't hurt me and, as I see it, wouldn't hurt anyone else either. Everything is disintegrating into tiny pieces like a glass door that someone banged his head into and shards of glass are scattered everywhere. You can only visualize it as a glass door if you have a strong enough imagination. Something got off the track somewhere—maybe just the meaning of good and evil. In a little while it won't be clear to me what's up or down, left or right, anymore. I can tell you how it's going to end up, Emil: not only will you soon not believe anything or anybody, you won't believe yourself either—not what you hear, see, or even what you say. It's not a question of truth or objectivity or fairness. There's already a barrier between our truth and Hitler's. There's nothing that would bind all people, like religion or a unified morality did, not so long ago. We're all out for ourselves. No one even wants to have anything to do with anybody else anymore. But you can believe this—as long as it doesn't end up that their fairy tales are refuted by new fairy tales, it can't end up well for us. I'd like to know how and what I'm living for right now."

In the game room, the vice chairman of the Jewish Religious Community, whose wife had poisoned herself with coal gas, played poker. A Wehrmacht unit marched through on Long Street, past the Hotel Bristol.

In regard to the lady confectioner, Arthur told Emil, "It's rumored that she does all her bookkeeping wearing only her underwear and writes love letters completely in the raw—it's said she claims she can't think right with her clothes on—God's honest truth. She carries on her love correspondence dressed only in her birthday suit."

The lady confectioner was also said to have had a relationship with a Gestapo major and to be a quarter hybrid; she would be hanged after the war. Now, her pedigree brought her higher tips and even greater courtesy that was indistinguishable from caution. Was that not being said about many a beauty who had married a half-Jew, and sometimes about women without their husbands, whom the Gestapo had taken away—always at night, so as not to disturb the populace? They came here to find out something, at least, since they had been told nothing by the Gestapo.

Even the officials of the Jewish Religious Community were said to have contacts with the Gestapo, and neither the Gestapo nor the Jewish Religious Community minded, it seemed. The estimation of both rose even in the eyes of those for whom it could not have sunk lower.

"You're looking wonderful," Arthur said to the lady confectioner.

"I hope so, I'm trying to. Thanks—you as well," she replied.

"But of course," Arthur agreed. "We're men in our prime." And then he said to Emil, "I mean that seriously, by the way. After all, aren't we in our best years?" He eyed the lady confectioner as he spoke. "You know, you could be a Teutonic idol," he said.

"This morning I saw a rat sitting here on the stairs by the back door," the lady confectioner said.

"That's a good sign," Arthur answered. "Your house won't get burned, nor will your ship sink."

"I'm not worried about people like you," she said. She was said to be ill; her disease was a secret.

Arthur thought to himself that her type of woman would likely poison with strychnine any man who had been weak in bed. He said to Emil, "She'd probably like my hairy chest. I'm real hairy all over, including my fingers (and he displayed them to Emil). Finally he said, "I wouldn't bet too much money that she isn't one of those women who blame a man for sleeping with her or for going all nine yards—or maybe she'd blame you for getting you to make her go the distance."

Here was the Jewish world in all its dimensions: the shuffling members of the army who had been trapped but refused to admit it; the members of the Central Zionist Union; the representatives of rabbinical trends; the members of the outlawed Social Democrats and the illegal Communist Party; the candidates for failed revolution (but who knew what was yet in store); the Jewish athletes; the experts on Old Testament scrolls, connoisseurs of the Talmud, the scholars; crack physicists and authorities in medicine, history, anthropology, and eugenics, over whom, until yesterday, all universities would have fought, and for whom some learned society on some continent, as yet unaffected by Germany, would have sent an expensive first-class ticket for the *Titanic*.

One café encompassed the representatives of the Funeral Brotherhood, Chevra Kadisha, who made Prague famous, and the cousin of Rabbi Loewe, the creator of Golem, whose younger brother from Moravia had become the head rabbi after the older brother seemed too clever for his office. The other rabbi's relatives were said to have moved to America and settled in management of a calculating machine firm in New York—and how the Gestapo knew about it and if, by chance, it was true. And of course, there were also the representatives of the Jewish underground, a fabric woven out of Jewish flesh and blood, the cells of dissent opposed to Nazi Germany, the Orthodox and freethinkers, the proponents of purely Czech Jewish thought and those of purely German Jewish thought, just like the purely Jewish thought, just like the purely Hungarian, Romanian, and so on, or all and every modesty or haughtiness of the purely Jewish thought, the Jewish racists, cabalists, extremists whose little God's name was Jabotinsky—from the crib makers to the casket makers. The café was a point of intersection for Jewish Europe in accordance with the common era. There might already be deportations in the air, but for the time being, nobody was taking them seriously. In Arthur's judgment, life meant searching for valves and points of departure despite everything.

"You'll never be mistaken claiming that hope is a good breakfast but a bad dinner," Arthur said, "or that the best horse is the one that carries you home."

Then he said, "I like nothing better than writing love letters. You may yet meet Irving Egon Kahn . . . he's supposed to come pick up the letters. I'm willing to donate my precious time to whomever deserves it. I really want to get him together with her—from their first meeting all the way to the wedding."

"Shouldn't we go now?"

"We've got an hour at least." And then he said, "I heard that Hitler had a Jewish doctor."

"That's just it. I don't want to be done away with, Arthur."

While Emil deliberated about how to secure reserves of food, clothing, and whatever could be scraped together, Arthur penned letters.

"I'm not immensely pleased that it's a German company," Emil said. He thought about his family. What would they say about this? He could talk it over with individual members of the family even though they weren't there—he heard their voices (along with his own voice) in his mind. His family was like one big heart that beat in quadruplicate before ringing as one like an invisible bell.

"Don't be ridiculous, Emil. To some extent, all companies are German now. It has nothing to do with the army—with the war either. Besides that, for us, nothing is certain. If you don't take it, Emil, somebody else will be glad to. At least you won't end up winding hemp in a makeshift workshop. Germany has done business with half of Europe."

Arthur continued, "Everybody likes some things better than others. Still, as I see it, only the histories of states and shysters, not to mention out-and-out crooks, are being written. What you or I do, few people will notice. Who'd notice the two of us—you or me, Emil?"

Emil watched Arthur get his letters ready for posting. "We've mailed the first," Arthur said. He got ready to let Emil read what he had written. The café was noisy. "Coffee," the headwaiter said to someone behind them, "stimulates the heart, activity, energy. But when the reserves run out, we'll be drinking ersatz."

"It looks like coffee and tastes a little like coffee, too, perhaps, but just about as well as a wig resembles hair and dentures resemble teeth," Arthur said.

"Better something than nothing," the headwaiter added. "One can comb a wig and bite with dentures."

"Review this for me, Emil," Arthur asked. "If you were a woman, would you respond?

"It's a strange time," Arthur then said suddenly.

"Perhaps it doesn't work up there as well as we thought," Emil said.

"It's the helplessness that's getting on your nerves. I know it well."

"Helplessness or defenselessness, Arthur. I wish I had a rifle."

"Blood's not water, Arthur. Some things a person has to decide for himself. I want to imagine—on my own—after another five or ten years of this, Arthur . . . if you follow my drift . . . so that I can look back with a clean conscience."

"Are you insinuating that I couldn't?" Arthur retorted. Then he immediately added, "People are made of rubber, Emil. And some would prefer to be like a balloon so they can hide when necessary and blow up when their moment comes."

Someone was telling the headwaiter that during the Great War people in Austria were so hungry they ate mice. Supposedly, in Jerusalem many eras ago, mothers ate their own children for the same reason.

"People have to have strong stomachs to want to talk about such things," Arthur complained.

"People like you will find a thousand excuses for everything," said the waitress without stopping. (Considering that she was twenty-five percent Jewish, she certainly looked mighty Aryan.)

Arthur then confessed that he'd dreamed about the lady confectioner. He remembered what he'd dreamed vividly; it had been very memorable: she did everything to him that she could see in his eyes he wanted her to do. Then she'd said, "Men are like small children. The thing they'd like to do most of all is suck a woman's breasts. There's only one way to do that to a man. Maybe it's not exactly milk, but as far as sustenance is concerned, it's not too far off—except that your milk, even when it's white or yellowish like whipped cream or runny butter, isn't milk but blood. You feed me your blood. I thank you for that. At the very least I won't have weak blood myself. And my stomach probably won't growl as much afterward. How long has it been since you were with a woman?" "Are you telling me that I'm giving you blood?" Arthur asked her in his dream. "It could be worse. I don't have anything better to give than my blood anymore." He imagined through what means the lady confectioner attracted her suitors and the way she tamed a man. She had already lived through more than one spree, more than one fit of excess. Had she been referring to his blood but thinking about her own? Her pillow was covered with it. He couldn't tell whose blood it really was—it was in his hair, everywhere.

"You have a colossal imagination," Emil stammered.

"I've got a big everything," Arthur admitted. "Sometimes I dream about girls and other times about cards. My father and your father played craps, but they didn't make any big killings. Grandpa was the opposite. But I believe in one thing, Emil: people have a stronger gift of premonition in bed than when they're running around chasing business all day. I learned to take dreams for what they don't say rather than what they say literally. I'll bet that ninety percent of what I dream turns out just the opposite of how I dreamed it, if it happens at all."

"I don't know," Emil said.

Arthur's dreams didn't have to make for reality in that regard, Emil thought to himself, glancing at Arthur's preoccupied face. Was he dreaming with his eyes open?

"Do you know what Martha was telling me, Emil? When you were little, your parents placed a milk bottle with a nipple, a fairy-tale book, and a pack of cards in front of you. They wanted to see which you would choose. You chose the bottle with the nipple. They may not have placed anything in front of me; but if they had, I'd have chosen the cards—I like colorful pictures. I learned to read from cards."

Emil read Arthur's second letter for Irving Egon Kahn: *Dear Luisa, I didn't think you'd remember me. Your answer has encouraged me. The words I am writing to you fill my heart: I love you. That is our mutual sin.*

In Arthur's judgment, the problem with women was not being able to live without them or with them. What a man wants, a woman *gives.* Either she gives it out of love or because he pays her for it with security, services, money, or she gives it to him as a reward. But she always gives it as if she, herself, were not taking anything in return.

Whores, virgins, sluts, and even saints were connected by their unshakable conviction that they could do whatever they wanted to with their bodies and nobody could use them without their consent. An unconditional "yes" one day might be an equally unconditional (though unexplained) "no" the next. What was more distressing was the truth of it, that sooner or later every man reached that stopping point with every woman. It was the rare woman who was an exception to the rule. In front of Emil, the unknown Luisa suddenly appeared, more than a spirit, but still less than a real woman. Was this how Arthur killed time? In two, three days, the unknown woman would be reading the letter. Without remorse, Arthur enveloped a strange man's emotions like a spider envelops a fly, and all for the ridiculous satisfaction of having won for his colleague something he was unable to have himself. Luisa. Who was she? Did she have an influential father or grandfather, perhaps? Was she pretty? Did she have a dowry? Arthur made a boyish face that, with his waxed hair, made him look like Mephistopheles. Arthur imagined himself in the place of Irving Egon Kahn and wrote how he would sit by the window and whisper to the stars. To count a hundred stars meant finding what one has lost or has not yet had. *I was committed to someone else. I saw her tormented by the path she had chosen, waiting for my encouragement as wilted grass waits for spring rain. I did not manage to break the illusion and lost a woman friend. And then I found out that she was engaged. Everything was comedy and flirtation. Things which a girl should remain distant from. . . .*

Arthur entered the spirit of a life not his own, as if it were. There may have been more in him than that which asked for liberty and expression, even if it should have been a lie.

"A lying offspring grows well," Arthur smiled.

"You've got fantasy," Emil acknowledged.

"I've heard that tune before, mister. If you bite your finger as a child, you'll be a good liar as an adult," Arthur said. "Before you came here I got inspiration from the signs in the coffee grounds. A snake's likeness is an enemy. A square in the coffee grounds is a casket." There was melancholy in his eyes and an intensity that revealed his energy. He reminded his daughter, Susanna, of an Italian gangster. No one could stay angry at him for long. Arthur managed to convince everyone that swindling, large or small, was as much a part of daily life as breathing. Only fools would be cross with him on that account. In a world where each day brings lies and more fraudulent deeds, to do so would be denying life itself. Arthur could work it so that even people that he swindled would ask him for a pardon in advance.

The letter continued: *So foolish, you'll say, why is he writing me? Why shouldn't you know the truth? When you smiled at me on the street, I floated to the clouds. Did the smile mean anything to you? Do you smile like that at everyone? Could you reciprocate my feelings? May I hope? Once more, I beg you for a photograph.*

"I want him to appear afraid of a refusal. He's betting all on one card—the banker." (In reality, he admired women for all of that—and not common, anonymous women either. In his mind was the image he had, a symbol of a woman and a girl with first and last names and addresses that Arthur had an excellent memory for.)

"Is he going to win or lose?" Emil asked with a smile.

"Receiving a letter, passing joy," Arthur replied with a smirk.

"You don't have a pact with the devil?"

"Sometimes I'd be glad to." He still added to the letter the question why love could not be without pain and why it must be heart-rending. To crush the soul, to besmirch, to humiliate, to disappoint, and so on and so forth. And desire whispered into the deaf night, into the waft which caressed him while he feverishly thought of Luisa. Would Luisa tread underfoot? He had nothing to offer her besides a flaming ear and the verses: *From your lips I could drink joy and draw the strength of your eyes for the struggle. . . . Yours, Egon.*

Didn't everybody arm themselves with hypocrisy or illusion for others or for themselves? Emil thought. The wrinkles in Arthur's forehead became accentuated in the light and his dark olive skin grooved in his expressive ruddy cheeks, his bushy eyebrows, a black rainbow above his eyes. Once he'd told Emil that a man such as himself was a prisoner of his own impulses. Were they stronger than Arthur's cautiousness? Stronger than his fear of betrayal? Sometimes it was painful for Emil that his sister, Martha, was Arthur's wife. If not, he would have probably found out a lot more interesting things about Arthur. He would do whatever occurred to him—that's what "strong impulses" were. Regret and contrition always came after—well, sometimes.

"I like doing it for him," Arthur said. "I had to take pains to do a better job on letter number three than two, and to leave possibilities for numbers four and five, and in six I'd like to see them signed, sealed, and delivered."

In letter number three, Arthur emphasized, in the name of Irving Egon Kahn, that he respected sincerity in a girl most of all. Why? That she must figure out for herself. Just as silence is sometimes more eloquent than words, sometimes an innuendo makes a better impression than shoveling out the truth. If she'd only send him a photograph, he would send Luisa his own in return. He swooned with feeling the heat of Luisa's breath at a distance, bowing to her lips with a twig of red coral, where it was only a small step for him to the shine of pearls. Only the rambling of a car in the street returned him to reality. Some people shouted on the street. (It could be heard through the window.)

"That photograph is anonymous," Arthur said. "I need to get a fix on it—an idea. It's amazing what a person can conjure up: at first, it's just a thought, and then it materializes in reality. Give me a touched-up photograph and I'll move the earth."

"You didn't tell me it wasn't her picture."

"So, I play around a little."

"That's some kind of playing, I must say."

"And did you ask me if it was her picture?" Arthur asked. "You could have guessed it." He had a great ability to imagine. Maybe it was his best quality, he said.

"Is it possible that you've never seen her, Arthur?"

"Just like no one knows what awaits him, Emil."

"It's on a knife's edge."

In numbers four and five, Arthur, still representing Irving Egon Kahn, professed his love for Luisa progressively more. He hadn't gotten a letter for a long time; he'd been worried he'd insulted her with something Arthur had composed earlier. Her features were dissolving, but in her he had found a sanctuary to escape from the day's dreariness. Would she enter the sanctuary with him? But for that, Arthur still had to wait for her response. Then a verse again: *From the sludge of life's whirl where he'd risen to the stars, he who had broken the slave's shackles entrusted his pain to distance. . . . Yours, Egon.*

In number five, he just wanted to be sincere. He let Luisa know that she was not the first one to whom he had written such things.

The first one had betrayed an eighteen-year-old's confidence, the second had died, Luisa was the third.

He sent his heart. Would she accept it? He wrote about his inclinations toward art, but he had to be content with business. Three, many say, is a lucky number. In a way, wasn't business an art? Not only poets were artists. Didn't one have to have a gift to be good at business? Therefore, weren't businessmen also artists? He had torn away from his parents. He was incapable of thinking the old way, as they did. Arthur wrote about the forest's singing, where every tree sang its melody. Now he traveled, selling rubber and glues. Not for Luisa, but for himself. He wrote: *I'm the inauspicious little owl of the night's gloom, wandering through the sparkling night restlessly. . . . Yours, Egon.*

"Since the war, I've had trouble with my kidneys and my left eardrum," Emil said. "My left side has never been as lucky as the right. On the right side, I fall asleep like a prince. I can hear that it's as bad as a stock exchange in here, but only from the right side. Shouldn't we go now?"

"We've still got time, Emil. Since I turned over the store keys to the clerks from the Anglobank, I've had lots of time. I'm my own master. No curtains up or down. I don't have to smile at people; I'd sooner slap a few of them. Don't worry. I know you'd like to have it behind you. I'm also counting on you paying me. But we can't jump. We must proceed step-by-step, Emil."

"I like to keep my word to Germans."

"Who isn't a thief, a crook, or a liar at times, Emil, even against his will? Why not call a spade a spade? It's a question of obligations. I feel that a phase of life is already behind us. There's no sense in lying. I never lie and won't lie. Look at Mr. Sternschuss who was in competition with me for sixteen years and you for eighteen. He sometimes kept his word and sometimes didn't. He always got us, even if only by a paltry nickel or dime. But in turn he's had to wear a wig since he was five. We didn't. He rose to the highest level for no earthly reason. I'm living my day. An ant doesn't ask himself whether it makes sense and he doesn't stumble over fallen logs left in his way either. Too bad I don't have enough money to say to you: Emil, don't worry about it."

The lady confectioner brought more coffee and pastry shells filled with mousse. Arthur Pick put on his sunglasses. The confectioner left to serve the gamblers who were playing cards.

"I prefer to write letters for Irving Egon Kahn. That Luisa is practically waiting in bed for him, Emil." There was an echo of his old carefree ways in his voice. No one can hide his nature. It's like a cork floating on the surface of the sea. How you were born is how you'll probably die someday.

The billiards lounge was now full; many guests conversed standing up. In the game room were the vice chairmen of the Jewish Religious Committee. They looked like an advertisement for a trip to Australia—the gentlemen Neuman, Lieben, Fischl—and from the synagogue, Mr. Mario Schapira. Mr. Tanzer wore knee breeches. They all knew more, had more reliable information than Havas's press agency.

Mr. Tanzer looked like he'd lost sixty pounds. His skin lay in folds on his face and he seemed to be constantly sweating.

"I certainly wouldn't want to lose as much weight as Mr. Tanzer," Arthur said. "I heard he got his daughter engaged to some Australian or Argentinean just to get her a visa. It's almost as if they'd sold the girl; she couldn't be a day older than your Richard. Of course, with daughters it's a different accounting." Then he added, "Hector-Hugo is getting older. He no longer eats the oatmeal that Martha makes especially for him in the morning. He's got angina pectoris."

"Poor thing," Emil said.

"What's going to be left, in the end, of all of yesterday's beauty, Emil?" Arthur asked ambiguously.

He added, "Not even Susanna is in a hurry to appreciate and acknowledge. Last year's tree, last year's clothing, last year's stay in an Italian monastery, that's all in the past. Everyone, even in a family, is more interested in what's coming. What's going to happen tomorrow."

"Shouldn't we be going now?"

"The Nazis are said to have discovered underground stores crammed with goods under the Lublin ghetto, and they confiscated everything," Arthur pointed out. "They'd been complaining for years how small and tight and ready to burst Germany was, but it seems now that everything the army has had the time to confiscate fits into it without any trouble at all."

"I haven't drawn a card yet," they heard Leon Blum mutter. "I want to win my money back first." Then he said, "Hitler envies Jews their 'chosenness'—their singular loyalty to only one God. He wants to be a demigod if he can't be a god—but he wants to be the only one." Finally Emil and Arthur heard him say, "Pass." He had the voice of a ventriloquist and the expression of a man who was losing the money that had been given to his wife as a dowry by her mother.

Arthur said, "As my granddad used to say while playing cards, what lies down doesn't run. What you draw once you let lie."

Until just a month ago, Sigfried Sternkopf had lived in a mixed marriage and with his two adult daughters, before his wife moved out with the daughters to her sister's. They demanded that Mr. Sternkopf renounce them and made reference to an illegitimate father who had had a relationship with Mrs. Sternkopf, a non-Aryan mother, nine months before they were born. They had German fiancés. They let him know, privately, that he was a *pechvogel,* a bad-luck charm.

"A man's and a woman's desire is over after the first ecstasy," Arthur said to Emil.

In front of Arthur's acquaintance's house, Emil said, "The German officers I used to know attended first-rate military schools."

On the stairs, Arthur said to his brother-in-law, "He may want five percent from you on top of the commission. But if you try, you can settle on three and a half percent."

"My name is Ernst Kantner," Arthur's acquaintance then said. "I represent the Munich central office in Prague, under the title of a civilian inspector. We are a judicious company. This is not my first European location, and I am certain that we shall reach an agreement. No one yet has complained about me."

"I hope we're on time," Arthur replied.

Mr. Kantner glanced at his watch and smiled. "Punctuality is the virtue of virtues. I, too, never miss an appointment."

Arthur looked at him and Mr. Kantner added with the same smile, "Death always keeps his word to everyone."

"I prefer the punctuality of those still alive," Arthur said.

"Nothing is as expensive as war," Mr. Kantner said. "And perhaps nothing can be more unpredictable; who knows how things will develop on all fronts?"

Mr. Kantner praised the Prague weather. It was not as changeable as in Munich, although both were close, just a stone's throw away, actually. It couldn't be denied that the two countries were that close to each other—Germany and Bohemia, that is. He always spoke of Germany first. Many people from Germany had found a home here as colonists; they had had the opportunity to grow into the land over a thousand years, although they kept their native tongue all that time as well. One didn't lose the language of one's birth, even if one were to neglect it for a certain period of time. That concerned the mutual contacts between both countries. People should be glad to change the place of their activity; it is good that way. It wasn't just a matter of personal taste—there was something more to it, Mr. Kantner said. After a little while, Mrs. Hannalore Kantner put the snack on the table.

They discussed business: the possibilities of buying and selling leather products—all leather products, Mr. Kantner emphasized, and fur products of every kind. For imagination's sake, one could say they included everything from slippers and leather hats, gloves, briefcases, bags, saddles, and horsewhips; everything to the word and letter— literally everything leather. Mr. Kantner smiled while his eyes remained as serious as the words uttered remained light.

Emil Ludvig smiled. To include horsewhips on the list of leather goods presumed having a good sense of humor. For a moment he wanted to reject the rumors that spread not only from the Ascherman café. Mr. Kantner disproved them with his superior knowledge of Germany; the things being said about Germany could not be true under any government because Germany was just too cultured and civilized for such things. Anyone with personal German contacts knew about their obsession with cleanliness, orderliness, respect for written and unwritten laws, for order that makes chaos into tidiness, the respect for work and industriousness, as if the greatest entertainment for Germans was work. Business has beneficial effects. It connects unknown people, making them modest because no one can furnish themselves with everything. Business abolishes borders. It joins countries as well as people. It's commerce more than governments that loosens the straitjacket, that makes the world a more just place in which everyone has a little of what only some might have otherwise had.

Pastries from the large Frankfurt am Main bakery sat on little plates on the table. Arthur paid attention to the pastries and the lady of the house, Hannalore Kantner.

Mr. Kantner smiled without parting his lips. His face took on a military appearance, but maybe only Emil Ludvig thought so. Wasn't Mr. Kantner's civilian courtesy nearly military at times? He looked kindly and attentively. He missed nothing, and it seemed he was a person who did not measure people to himself, but more as what one might have been. He would not likely expect a fish to fly or a bird to swim. Unlike Emil, his wishes were not the father of his thoughts. A business cooperation is the most important cooperation of all, Mr. Kantner felt. He took only one pastry. He ate with a strictly closed mouth. He kept a napkin at hand. Arthur used his napkin, which had embroidered blossoms. Mr. Kantner commented on the diverse possibilities and approaches to doing business. He smiled; maybe he discovered what he said aloud—that a person could not measure a country only by its citizens and its citizens by their country.

"It's not always that easy for everybody," Arthur said. One had to wonder whether he really meant it as a compliment.

"Our military offices are constantly worrying where to get enough shoes, pants, and jackets—and not just for the army," Mr. Kantner said. "We're at our wits' end. As far as the machines go, all that's necessary is for one screw to fall out and all of our efforts will come to nothing. I myself sometimes worry how to manage all of it."

Emil Ludvig thought about everything that was being said, including that which would never be said. According to Arthur, some things would remain taboo. It's a social custom to leave some subjects undiscussed. One of the subjects was so-called nationality and race. Though it's obvious that it's not the same thing for all Germans, we'll have to develop a thick skin. "There's nothing more important for business than stability," he said.

Mr. Kantner showed himself to be educated, clever, and wise. A civilized country with a thousand-year-old culture appreciates balance, calm, the working masses, the turning wheels of factories, men and women in the fields, in the stores, and so on.

"The main thing is the goods," Mr. Kantner said. "We're almost hostages to the market and to our orders and claims. Better that way than the other way around. I think about what decides the value of things."

Emil Ludvig committed himself to five percent without reluctance, even though Arthur pretended to be glum about it. That they understood. They drank black coffee from a white pot with little painted rose blossoms. Emil looked a bit like Mr. Kantner; blue eyes, fair hair parted on the side. Doing business with a German firm didn't mean he'd made a pact with the devil. Mr. Kantner did not keep secret the motives that lay at the heart of all German businessmen—to obtain the greatest amount of scarce goods. It did not make sense to keep it a secret—every businessman knew it quite well. The goods existed somewhere; elsewhere they did not. It was the task of business to pass them from one hand to the other. It was the substance of his work. The protectorates of Bohemia and Moravia were some of the best supplied and equipped territories and, for Germany, business with such a base was more important than it might seem at first sight.

Mr. Kantner asked Emil if he had any children. When Emil said "two," Mr. Kantner went into the next room and returned, handing Emil alligator wallets for Anna and each of the children, with a red fifty-crown note in each.

"Isn't it too much?" Emil inquired.

"Don't your people say that we win people over with gifts and lose them with a trifle?" Mr. Kantner smiled.

"Thank you," Emil said.

"So, five percent, to be sure," Mr. Kantner said. "Think it over."

"Certainly," Emil answered.

"I'll introduce you to my people you'll be dealing with."

Mr. Kantner poured wine out of a bottle with a label on it that depicted a river flowing around a high hill, a castle, and two towers.

They went to the Anglobank. After a while, Emil held in his hand his first new money, an advance on his first commission. Although he had done nothing yet, it was the mark of Mr. Ernst Kantner's company's trust. He passed half to Arthur. Arthur counted the banknotes.

"Seven, Emil. Well, I'm beginning to like it." It was half of Emil's debt. "Between us, Emil, Mr. Kantner won't be that bad off with you either. At one time they called me 'sir' in this bank, 'And your account, Mr. Arthur Pick.' Then I was still trying to convince Martha's family and Susanna that she would never have to scrub floors. But now it appears that we're all quite close to the floor. I hope none of our people who will taste it get water in their knees from kneeling." Arthur laughed, but in his peculiar way, like an actor, or as if someone besides Emil were looking at him. "The army affairs are one thing, the business is another. What, in the end, can scare businessmen off? Maybe my clever daughter Susanna is right when she measures success and failure by failure. She claims we are entering into a phase which no one will be too proud of. Are we still going to stop for a while at the café?"

"Do you want to, Arthur?"

"I promised the confectioner."

"I can go with you."

"As you wish, Emil."

"Would you mind if I walk with you, Arthur?"

Emil still felt strange, like when he'd borrowed the money from Arthur, even though he wasn't sure why. Nevertheless, he felt good. After all, where could one go and not feel guilty?

In a while they were on Long Street in front of the café. Arthur held himself up in his double-breasted suit with a shirt of pure silk and a black, almost funereal, tie. Emil felt something like vertigo, a feeling that had always come when he was more successful than he expected. He may have been born under a lucky star after all; otherwise, it would not have been possible.

The well-known cries came out of the café in which, it occurred to Emil, some people scream whenever and to whatever place fate blows them, although one can tell in advance what reasons they have for shouting. It was the same as in the morning. But, for an instant, the long street appeared like an iceberg on which the afternoon sun shone.

Emil did not feel like going to the café, back to the rumors about deportations and the other face of Germany. Things they had discussed earlier at Mr. Kantner's and his buyer's—the talk about all types of leather goods, including riding whips—flashed through his mind. Certainly one could view that, as with everything, from two entirely different ends. Yes as well as no. Each yes has an embryo of no, and each no an embryo of yes. He wanted a glass of water.

"Give my regards to Luisa," Emil smiled.

It struck him that he might really have had a stroke of luck in the midst of so many people's misfortunes. Should he complain now that good luck met him once again?

He was going to walk back home but convinced himself he could afford a taxi. The city seemed so friendly to him. For one person something is dirt, for another person, purity. That's how it goes. He thought about Mr. Ernst Kantner, about Arthur and Martha, about his family. Was it nonsense to claim that being German is a trait? One general at the Piave resembled Mr. Kantner. He had a round face, a cleanly shaven complexion, and fair hair with a part. That was the general who let three hundred Russians carrying white rags crawl out of the trenches and be shot.

It was nice what Mr. Kantner had said about Samson and Delilah. In the morning at the café, someone claimed that Hitler had a Jewish grandfather from somewhere in Graz, Austria. If it was the truth, one could expect he would not let his "Jew beaters" go to extremes. Someone was said to be paying remittance to his grandmother. Also, one more important general, a certain Mr. Milch, was reputed to have had a Jewish grandmother in Germany, though they recognized his Aryan origin. Who was a Jew and who was not would be decided by the superiors if it came down to it. Hadn't it always been like that? It never touched everyone. Many people could afford to be neutral, although it might not accrue to their honor in the end, either. Definitely they were not and might not be able to be against one race, one tribe, one kind. Was life an angelic privilege paid for by a devilish price, as Arthur claimed? Except for flashes of a truce, life means always struggling for one's survival, working, providing for a family. There are no sublime or great things. Nobility comes only in flashes. He rested against the seat of the taxi and watched the car overtake the streetcars. A lot of it depended on how and where one was born. The city and the people reminded him of a stormy river or sea; he swam and struggled, fought with the waves.

He paid for the cab, got off a ways from the building on Royal Avenue, and rode the rest—one stop—in a streetcar. When he was young, no obstacle had seemed insurmountable.

He decided to bring home open-faced sandwiches from Mr. Balek and Cezare di Carlo's southern fruit import, which, of course, was no longer being imported, although Italy and Germany were hand in glove with each other. Mr. Balek served him without asking the customary small questions about how Emil and the family were doing. The thought about his dreams the night before, about written documents, about the trial and the shaft, about the departure of a ship and the silver suit from Anna's dream, came back to him. Then he contemplated sending Richard to an apprenticeship at Jungman's Square—they would be in the same business, leather. Helena could study privately. There were many, many Jewish teachers without employment. Anna could finally rest up. He whistled melodies from *Trieste.*

Earlier in the day, someone had read an article at the café that said catastrophic times are the best for Jewish talent. He glanced back at the silver gas sphere. He hurried. He looked forward to being at home. He had gained employment and time. The wind tore up the remainder of the poster from the *Pancho Villa* film that had not played for a long time. In the Mahrer dance school, Mrs. Mahrer banged out a mazurka on the piano keys. Karla was reputed to have danced naked in the back room of the Mercury in front of the officers. The innkeeper's wife refused to draw the beer. Emil entered the sealed-off store where the proprietors no longer called him sir. He heard the colonial goods salesman's son arguing—his father had bought uniforms for them but had forgotten to bring the daggers along. He sent them to the cutler's; they objected, wanting to make forks into daggers, not knives. One could hear the water by the aqueduct flowing into a cast-iron shell. The police supposedly did not allow people to attend Lida Kubrova's funeral.

Emil Ludvig felt how he had lined himself up in the course of life, which he had avoided at the same time. Arthur had always done the maximum for him. Did Arthur recognize that with all his help, he had surpassed him? It was like the olden times when they puffed themselves up and exaggerated about how much money each earned.

Anna waited for him at the sewing machine. The apartment had been tidied up. The linoleum glistened.

"So, here I am." He passed the gifts to Anna and the children. He did not have to talk too much or redundantly regarding the gifts of Mr. Ernst Kantner. The small gifts spoke about his generosity, which seemed suspicious to Anna, but lately everything seemed suspicious to her.

"What was it like?" she asked. "Speak. What was it like?"

"Like I'd killed a rich woman—and lived to tell the tale."

"That would be too sad." She disliked talking about killing. If she didn't have to, she would never even kill a fly. Even so, there was a lot of talking about killing. It was better sometimes not to watch or to hear.

"Everything has come off, once again, as I wanted. We're lucky. I hope it's not the luck of the devil." He embraced Anna. He held the children by their shoulders. The safety of a family surrounded him; even if it wasn't just safety, it was something that one, in spite of the world, feels good about if only for being among his kind.

"You knew how to marry, I must say," Emil said. He thought about what joy will do for a person and about what it takes to create joy for others. He already knew from experience that it was only an echo of thoughts about misfortune. Joy and misfortune were like two sisters. People learn to live with this. He learned to live with it too.

"I didn't even dare to suggest that," Anna said.

"Didn't you hear me saying that you knew how to choose who to marry?" Emil laughed.

Emil Ludvig played "Oh Maria" on the mandolin after dinner, along with about a half dozen songs from *Trieste,* which he sang to his own lyrics.

From Helena's notes:

Susanna said the Germans still have two faces in Bohemia, but that it won't be long before they have only one face.

HOPE

From Helena's notes:

I woke up in the middle of the night. I felt as though someone was looking at me. Father sat down next to me. Then he got up and left on tiptoe. He didn't sleep. I didn't sleep either. Mother slept so that she would be fresh when she had to face the sewing machine again. Richard wasn't taking anything seriously. Why worry about things anyway?

Whispering in the middle of the night, Uncle Frank told Mother: "Beggars can't be choosers."

※

4

Emil Ludvig went into the house in front of the railroad station, which seemed the safest. Had anyone seen him? Probably not. There was, after all, a war going on. He was alone. He removed his yellow star and stuck it in his pocket, complete with the safety pin so that in an emergency he could quickly fasten it on again. Nobody had seen him. Good. He would be elated to be cured of this constant fear, this anguish, which had settled on him like some disease. Emil straightened his jacket. It was indeed a good thing that the yellow star with the word "Jude" printed on it with the points and the black German lettering (reminding one of German medieval spires) was not a corrosive substance and left no traces. At the same time, it was the kind of acid that ate a hole in your breast: fortunately, an invisible one.

The station was plastered over with red-and-black posters with public notices. Some of them were attached to wood or to hard board. One of them was in the hallway where he now stood. The radio system played martial music: it announced German victories. If the Third Reich could win the war on the basis of its marching music, the war would have long been over. The fifes and drums took the lead: they were playing the song "The March against England." It was almost a good thing that he didn't know anyone here. Even those people a person does know are really only reflections of the image that we have of them. That is why people prefer simple images to people and then expand those simple images to apply to all people. Then it causes them no pain to see all people of one kind as one and the same person: all for one and one for all—with no differences—from now until the end of time. This applied to him more than to anyone else. Didn't Mr. Jandourek at the Mercury restaurant say that he could have a few

Jewish friends with whom he could have a conversation, *but with all of them?* He couldn't be expected to accept them all, could he? The rest, he admitted, didn't apply to just his Jewish friends (because it was probably better to break it off right now anyway, and the sooner the better if one didn't want to risk his own hide), but it also applied to a few other races and groups, like gypsies and blacks, which were some of them, but by no means inclusive.

Emil looked out through the blinds into the hallway. The radio system called out again:

First notice. According to the Zentralstelle fur jüdische Auswanderung Prag, all persons who, according to paragraph 6 of this summons, are subject to the Reich's protectorate in Czechoslovakia and Moravia on July 21, 1939, are identified as Jews and have not yet carried out their registrations must do so immediately. If these persons live within the confines of the Jewish sections of Prague, they must immediately report to the appropriate division of City Hall, Phillip of Monte Street, number 15, second floor. If the persons in question live in other outlying Jewish sections, they must register at their nearest Community Emigration Department. Any refusal to register will be prosecuted to the fullest extent of the law, even to death.

To death? Emil Ludvig asked himself. He shouldn't doubt it. It wasn't only his life at stake here. This also concerned the lives of his family.

The trip was nice enough, even if he was nervous some of the time. He still enjoyed train travel: the motion and the lightness of the smells, which meant something else for him after each trip, yet they still meant the same thing, the rocking of the locomotive, the sound of the wheels on the rail connectors, the houses, the fields, the rivers, the lakes and ponds, and the telegraph poles. Trains always mean travel and destinations, whatever destination there might be, where you are trying to end up. It is always from somewhere to somewhere. The trip itself is like a promise, and if you have chosen the destination yourself, rarely can anything go wrong. Who would choose to take a trip into danger? He liked to travel by train. He even enjoyed the trip now. It reminded him of something. It brought out memories.

Who knows from which ancestor one gets one's nature? Emil Ludvig thought, as the train rattled on, putting him to sleep. He held on to the sole thought he'd had the entire trip, but despite racking his brains, he was unable to locate in his mind any grandfathers or grandmothers who might safeguard the family, either now or as a last resort. Was there not even a single ancestor? Not even one, he answered himself. Perhaps once there was someone, but I don't know about it.

He continued to muse. Blue eyes and fair hair? That I have. We shall see. Why isn't the old adage "Live and let live" enough anymore? I'm complaining now, he reprimanded himself.

Finally the train stopped; Emil Ludvig stepped off. He went straight to the notary; he would go to the church only if necessary.

The notary was new. He made reference to the fact that the books Emil wanted to look at were buried somewhere in the bottoms of boxes, but if it was that important and if he insisted on it, Emil would have to wait four hours for the notary's assistant to clean the dust off them before they could be brought into the office.

While he waited, Emil found out whose well had dried up or who had discovered a new well in the village, who was involved in a dispute and about what. Sometimes all it took was the digging of a little path in a field to provoke passions strong enough to cause the murder of a brother or a father and the like.

The notary did what he could. None of the names Emil Ludvig searched for could be found in the old books. He did not have to remind the notary that finding the name of even one controversial grandmother would be helpful to him. He also didn't say that even one grandmother of non-Jewish origin meant a hope for a new birth certificate. With that, as with the start of an avalanche, he could roll his first snowball, packing everything else onto it heavily enough so that no one could stop it. Then their current circumstances would become a whole new ball game. The notary smiled. That was why he was a notary; he understood why people came to him. Emil went back in his thoughts to a time when conversion in this country meant saving one's life; he wished that the notary could read his mind.

"As far as purity of origin is concerned, it is in your favor that nobody is in the books," the notary said.

"I traveled here just to be certain."

"I hope that you are certain. Each certainty is better than the reverse, of course."

"That is why I came," Emil Ludvig repeated. "But if I'm not mistaken, these books aren't the only source of records, are they?"

"What do you mean, 'only source'? We're not a town. Still, I get your drift," the notary said; one could see by his face that he did not understand. "I am sorry."

"I was afraid of that," Emil Ludvig replied, as if all fear had already left him.

Of course, the notary knew about all the decrees—everyone knew about them—but he did not say anything, and Emil Ludvig did not see any of the public notices in his office. Was he waiting for Emil Ludvig to say something more? What else might he be expecting? The regulations were too strict. It was better not to singe his fingers. Who knew when and who might unexpectedly pass by? Then everyone might spill whatever he knew—and what then? Who could know for sure today what kind of blood ran in his veins when the third generation of his family had blue eyes and fair hair and spoke in the language of the country where he was born?

"I am sorry," the notary said again. "May I call for the books to be returned now?"

"Thank you, anyhow. Best regards," Emil Ludvig said.

He left, turning around to see if he could see the notary in the window, and then walked toward the church at the other end of the village. Moments later, he was standing in front of a house and annexed church. Behind him, autumn had entered into a large garden with apple and plum trees. The bright afternoon sun shone high above Emil's head.

From the outside, the church looked like a mill with a large garden. It occurred to Emil that sooner or later, during services or over ale in the village pub, both the parish priest and the notary would exchange information about him. On one end of the scale lay beer and a few words—on the other end lay his fate. He suddenly felt naked. After all, it was only logical that what he had been unable to document at the notary he would also try to verify at the church. Why at the church, of all places? Because, he answered himself, just because—and he searched for the ambiguity or the emphasis that the word "church" contained.

Nobody answered Emil's knock. He heard the distant sounds of a village funeral. It was all over for somebody. Everything was now behind him. Wasn't there even a caretaker here? Did the parish priest manage the household by himself? Emil Ludvig decided to wait for the priest on an oak bench under a thin arbor grown over with last year's Virginia creeper. The barking of village mongrels invaded the music. They might have smelled a bitch in heat across the entire length of the village, Emil Ludvig thought. A beautiful waltz, played by the village band in the slow tempo of the funeral procession, sounded quietly along with the autumn wind, the rustling murmur of the pine forests, and the rippling of the pond's blue water where the parish garden ended. It was quiet here even with all the sounds. He recalled how he and Richard had seen the Archbishop of Kromeriz's bed. It had had silk-covered posters reaching toward heaven.

Emil Ludvig looked at his shoes covered with dust from the walk from the train and from the notary office. He arranged his coat. He breathed the autumn air and looked at the fields, into the forests, and at the ground which remains after people are no longer. The trees grew tall, their crowns rocked with the wind. The earth and trees were stronger than a human being. The earth and trees had no race; papers did not convert them from their faith. They would not search for loopholes in these papers, nor new connections to blue eyes and fair complexions. It's not a time to live and let live. (What had Mr. Kantner said about mixed marriages?)

The apple trees were painstakingly tended, as were the plums. Everything at the church breathed quiet and peace—even the dust on the road, the stones out of which the stairs had been made, the well and its windlass.

Suddenly Emil Ludvig was filled with a strange calm. Maybe it is the calm of the living dead, he thought. He listened to the funeral waltz and imagined that the oldest man or woman of the village had died, or a sick child whom the physicians were unable to help, or a girl who had met with an accident. As always, the next day, the music would change its rhythm. Just as the musicians now played the funeral waltz, tomorrow they would play for a wedding or a new villager's birth. In the air, Emil felt a dream about people and the world, a vision of freedom, equality, justice for all, lack of harm, pain, and injustice—all in the direction of the wind. Maybe it was more like a permanent dream (unlike when a person wakes up to remember for a long time before he forgets what he dreamed) than fleeting reality. It held within it the hope that makes a place for everything to improve, or for the bad to become even worse. Emil was reluctant to think more about it. With the scent of the pine trees, moss, and wood of the houses and the stench of the water in the pond with its tinge of fishy smells, the funeral music sounded sweet, as if it were connected with something else. One could hear the melody of the waltz come near for a while, then die away again.

Suddenly Emil Ludvig forgot why he'd come here. He went back through his life almost from the start. He thought about those things he'd done well, as if one interval of his life was ending this very moment and another was just beginning. He felt himself connected differently to this country than before—a thousand years back, through the blood and breath of unknown families that no one could trace in any book. They were contained in the earth and the trees and the moss, like a fragrance contained in the wind, in the moisture in water, or in the warmth of a sunbeam. The trees carry their breath in their leaves; the soil is made fertile by their flesh, bones, and blood. Their hands had given shape to the gardens, to the fields, to the houses, to the paintings in the apartments, to the furniture, to the candle holders and the candles. Hundreds and thousands of families who enriched the earth as the earth enriched them because they worked and lived here, and because a person cannot give much more than living and dreaming and working. All of them were ordinary, insignificant people—a chain, a relay, of men, women, children, and old people, healthy and ill, strong and weak, who stretched out their hands toward the villagers at their births, weddings, and funerals. He felt what a waste every day spent outside of this country would be if he had to leave to be "resettled" to the east, to a place more different than far away. For the first time it occurred to him that land is eternal; that it didn't feel the loss of its people the way its people felt the loss of the land. People needed the land to make a go of it, but the land didn't need people; people needed the land more than the land needed them. Like every kind of love, it was inexpressible. It was the voice of his heart calling vainly to his sense of reason, because reason doesn't understand love and because from the point of view of others, love is silly. Was there only room for kindness, not hatred or contempt, in love? Who knew?

A train passed behind the hill in an arch; it was about ten cars long. It was a country local with old, long outdated cars. The train reminded him of the public notices, but it did not displace this strange feeling he had not known before. It was a feeling of lamentation and pain, but at the same time, joy for which he had no words, an escaping and returning dream, voice and echo, something deeper or larger than just memory. He found it unpleasant and isolating because someone was rending him from something he was already a part of, that he wanted to remain a part of, and to which his children certainly belonged. In the sound and scent of the forest and the wind and the very soft brass music, he was glad to be by himself, not to be seen by Anna and the children. Here he was without witnesses. In his hour of weakness, man doesn't seek witnesses. In his moment of defeat, a man prefers to be alone.

The music of the village funeral was like the air that he inhaled, like a heartbeat. Again, in his mind, he saw the familiar relay of his ancestors (some of whom had certainly sold, and maybe had even stolen, horses), for whom the goal of everything was a home. No one had to remind him what it had cost them to realize that goal. For the first time something he'd disregarded before occurred to him. He thought about Mr. Utitz from Podebradove Street who'd sold everything one day and with the money departed for land near the Mediterranean Sea in order to achieve whatever it was he couldn't accomplish for himself where he was living. It was only a fleeting thought. Maybe Mr. Utitz had been trying to catch hold of life as it passed him by like sand funneling through an hourglass.

The wind blew the grasses and the reeds around the pond, which rippled and splashed the water into waves. Here and there a fish flapped on the surface, a frog croaked, a pigeon or a dog took a drink. An orange cat sat down by the water. It looked at the water level with the wariness of a predator. An eagle flew high in the sky. The forests loomed on the horizon. The sun shone. Then a bird threw itself into the water from a height. It sounded like a little fist that hits the surface, and the chest of the water accepts the blow, deflects it, and smooths out to a calm. Everything is life—the truth and the echo of truth, which includes a lie, death, and pain.

The waltz faded. Somewhere in the back, at the end of the village from which some of Emil Ludvig's ancestors had originated, there lay a small cemetery. At this moment, when he wanted to change something that belonged to the past and was separated by two hundred years, some villager with a good and pure family tree was being buried in the raw earth who had a birth certificate he would no longer need that might benefit someone else. Emil Ludvig waited for another hour. He was glad for the wait. He'd resigned himself to the constant hustle of the past months and to the disillusionment he now knew, hardened by many defeats of which he was no longer fearful. He remembered one of his ancestors—he'd told Richard about him—who once drank up all his profits from the cows he'd sold on his trips to America. He'd fallen asleep in a ditch dreaming about fatigue and freshness, about his mother, and about the moments he had been conceived and born. He never woke up again. One accepts death if it isn't violent, even if it's unfair, so long as it's not an unjust act against one's fellow creatures.

He thought about Susanna: What good did it do her to be beautiful? No one escapes what's coming to them. When would they get retribution? How? With whom? Without whom? He thought about Anna, Helena, and Richard. What was due them? What would they all get? What is my own fate? Emil Ludvig pondered. Am I being responsible enough? I've got everyone else to worry about. There wasn't much for him to sort out. The air fanned him.

Finally the parish priest walked in, tall, old, alone. The will to pursue what he'd come here for returned to Emil Ludvig. He got up and stood waiting. He made an effort to look carefree, to rid himself of any visible outside eagerness along with that on the inside, which seemed grubby, unsuitable, and undignified to him. He didn't want to let himself be humiliated more deeply than he had already allowed himself to be humbled by his own thoughts. He tried to stand upright, to feel upright. He would ask but not beg. He struggled with himself; it was more profound than he could comprehend. He was ashamed about his purpose for coming; it seemed unjust that he had been forced into trying to free himself from a snare into which he never would have thrown anyone himself. He had come prepared to cheat and lie. He had come with a lie already prepared. Already it was worse than when he'd once had to borrow money. He'd sensed how it diminished him—even beforehand. He knew, just as at the notary's, that he would feel ashamed to talk about it, but that's why he had come.

"Some things happen only once," the old priest said, instead of a greeting. Perhaps he'd been thinking about the funeral, the dead person in the fresh grave, or of life. He had a deep, mature voice, full of surrender as well as kindliness. That encouraged Emil, but he cautioned himself, *Be careful.*

The priest continued, "That which nobody has for anybody and which everyone desires. We know only what it is, but we can't have it.

"Good day," the priest finally said.

I wish it was good, Emil thought to himself. "I am Emil Ludvig," he said out loud.

"I welcome you. What brings you to me? What can I do for you?"

"I am the son of Ferdinand Ludvig."

"Only some people know how to pronounce a 'w,'" the old man said, almost satisfied, like the teacher at the elementary school. (He didn't have to add that people learn that only in German schools, so he did not say it.) He invited Emil Ludvig in. He wore high, dust-covered boots and black cloth pants with bedraggled trouser legs. He was a dried-out villager, about seventy years old; he could have been a blacksmith, lumberjack, or carpenter with his large, overworked hands and bright blue, childlike eyes. He did not examine Emil Ludvig with long, drawn glances, and Emil did not dare scrutinize him. On the contrary, both avoided such glances. The old man took time with his words; he probably had already figured out what this man from the city, of whom he'd heard before but had just set eyes on for the first time, was looking for. Ferdinand Ludvig's son? The air was dry; there was something in it Emil Ludvig was hesitant to name.

The room was furnished with only a table and spartan country chairs with straight backs, a cherry bench, and an open metal-tipped trunk; on the inside, freely arranged prayer books lay inactively. Some of them had mountings and buckles on their canvas or black paper covers and appeared several hundred years old. Emil Ludvig thought about his father, Ferdinand, and about his father and many fathers before him, as many as could be fitted into a four-thousand-year-old stream, if he wanted to go all the way to the beginning or, perhaps, all the way to the end. When is a beginning an end, and when does an end become a beginning? They were new questions—secret and maybe not so mysterious. He had already noticed that the invasion of the Germans into the country had changed not only what he thought about it, but the way in which he thought about it. Where were his old carefree ways? He did not have to look too hard for an answer to that; as an old Jewish saying declares, "A person experiencing misfortune or one in need begins to trust nonsense." For the first time in a long while, he remembered that his mother had died blind. Had it been a blessing or a curse that she hadn't seen what those still living could still see until the last moment?

The old man had gravity in his face and eyes. His eyes asked: Are we weak? Are we strong? Are we able to sacrifice or do we just sacrifice the others? Are we pampered? Do we believe that all is in vain? Why are we really here? He reminded Emil of his father, who had believed that people commit two mistakes at once: either they believe they are stronger than they are and then they feel weak, or they feel weak from the beginning and never recognize how strong they are. Emil Ludvig then thought about what he was going to tell Anna. He collected the excusable and acceptable reasons why he had been first to the notary and now here, why he had taken the train trip in direct defiance of the strict bans (even to sit on a train without permission) on travel.

The tall priest waited patiently. With his sharp-cut facial features, he slightly resembled the wood out of which the furniture was made, blackened with age. Something in Emil might have told the man not to hurry. He allowed thoughts to resound in Emil, which (as when he'd sat alone in the garden) didn't seem obtrusive or irritating, but more prudent, deliberate, and secretive.

Emil Ludvig read the old man's eyes. Did he perhaps want to ask why every generation thought that those gone by were the last to bear the burden of human existence? His eyes flickered with the wisdom of people who care more about the affairs of others than about themselves.

Emil Ludvig did not immediately explain to him why he had come, although everything suggested that the old man already knew without ever having been spoken to. Would it be ridiculous to tell the old man to his face that he was here to find, if possible, a grandmother in his family tree who had converted to the tall man's faith or, in contrast, had converted from it? He could imagine such a woman— perhaps she had looked like an older issue of the tall old man facing

Emil. Perhaps she used to stand with her legs a bit apart, in her tall, laced-up shoes, as if she were confronting the steep slope of an invisible hill on her strong legs, with a pair of eyes that knew how to wait, and in which there would be an occasional flash of goodwill, trust with distrust, curiosity with indifference. Maybe she'd been blind, like Emil's mother, because of old age—not just because of all she had seen. He might have been concerned about telling the old man to be grateful for proof that one of his ancestors had had a child out of wedlock. He sensed how his dignity was disappearing; he stooped unwittingly before realizing it and straightening himself up to stand erect as the old man, although he was shorter. All the thoughts about escape from the disadvantageous position in which he'd found himself weighed on him like the pressure under which he was involuntarily bowed. Suddenly he realized it was the times that had reduced his dignity and made him feel humiliated, not only because of what was happening on the outside (thanks to the public notices and prohibitions), but from the inside as well—how he accepted it. The test of his dignity came up in every encounter with someone who was not in a similar predicament. He thought about Arthur's woman friend and about what Mr. Kantner had told her: that not every "yes" or "no" applied equally to everyone.

A cross hung on the wall; the martyr bowed his head under a wreath with a crown of thorns. Hadn't he been an older brother of Emil's ancestors, same as the tall old man's? Didn't that make him and his people and the tall old man and his people brothers? In the final analysis, weren't their two peoples just like two branches on the same tree? Hadn't both of them—the tall man and himself, just like all their peoples, come from one invisible, indivisible God? Did that mean they'd all have to end up the same way just because he had? Did the tall, old man believe that—or was it that he didn't believe it? There was no space in Emil's mind for any more questions. On a small table under the cross stood a wooden Saint Catherine. It was not the most perfect wood carving; perhaps that's what made it beautiful. There were few pieces of furniture; the wood smelled of pitch, old pine needles impregnated with oil.

The tall man did not rush to speak. It was easy for him to remain quiet while Emil Ludvig was silent. What caused them both to hesitate? Would haste have seemed insulting? For a moment, the priest looked past Emil Ludvig as the blind do—or did it just seem that way? What did he see?

The priest opened the cover on a small organ. He put his fingers on the wood, then closed it again. Perhaps this was the hour he normally played his organ. Now in his eyes was something that might have been a secret desire—other accounts—who knows? Emil Ludvig felt bashful. He tried to guess what was going on inside the tall man's head. There were so many books; he must have been an educated man, despite the small village conditions. There were worn-out volumes in Latin, German, and Czech. The tall man looked at Emil Ludvig as if to extend his hand and withdraw it at the same time, so that he might, before hearing what had brought Emil Ludvig or what he could do for him, touch upon the mystery brought by the man with the smart coat, gold wire-rimmed glasses, and confused eyes. It was a mystery incorporating questions dating back some two thousand years. Who knows what was going through the old man's head? Was it a kind of envy? Was it loss? A deep wrinkle formed above the old man's eyebrows. The tall, old man knew better than Emil Ludvig why thinking about people like the newcomer evoked emotions from sympathy to hate or even anger—what caused people, when they saw a man or woman like him or his children, to stop against their will. It had no meaning if they didn't stop to take into account what kind of man the one whom they all worshiped had been. What kind of truth demanded conquering and abandoning people? He avoided glancing at the cross; he looked at the organ lid. There was a line between admiration and contempt that went along with everything and everybody.

Who was the right person to ask why? Something occurred to him and he took a broader view on things. He didn't want to go that deeply into such matters in his mind, but he kept thinking despite himself, and it brought him closer to what he wanted to know.

Emil Ludvig thought of a prayer he hadn't heard for a long time. They used to hear it on Saturday when Anna asked him to at least go with her to the synagogue. It was a prayer welcoming Saturday, the Jewish Sabbath—the queen. Usually Emil wasn't wild for prayers and praying but he didn't want to deny it to Anna. He saw how the prayer, even the single visit to the holy ark, endowed her with beauty and filled her spirit with hope. Rabbi Kraus allowed them to read silently, each to himself, the portion on reflections appropriate for a holy day—the Sabbath—so that each would remember what humility means, how faith uplifts a person with hope. The experience taught a person to straighten his back when he feels humiliated, to raise himself from defeat when he feels on the bottom. Wasn't it a man's primary duty to learn to recover from defeat just like remembering to be humble when he was the victor?

Emil Ludvig sensed that murder stood between him and the tall, old priest. It brought them closer and made them more distant at the same time. They didn't have to speak about it. Both were already steeped in the understanding about the rationale for killing, with or without reason, people, individuals, groups, and nations. The eyes of the old man said, "We are not omnipotent. We're helpless, aren't we?" Emil Ludvig felt he would do well here. He steeled his mind to come to the point. He sensed that everything that had taken place so far created a barrier behind which existed the unpredictability of what would happen. Now was the time to jump that barrier and concentrate on what is, what will or what might happen.

"I'm from this region," Emil Ludvig said.

"Yes, I remember you. You were a boy when your father first brought you here," the tall man answered.

"I've already been to study my papers at the notary. You know how these administrative things matter now. I never thought that we would be needing to do it."

Emil Ludvig tried to keep his voice soft so as not to burden the priest with the weight that was stuck in his throat even before words ran from his lips. He wanted to break the wave of helplessness the tall man kept sending toward him like a signal.

"Yes," the tall man asserted understandingly.

"Once the local cabinetmaker came to make me a bed. The wood stayed beautiful—it never dried out," Emil Ludvig said.

The tall man nodded. He had furniture from the same cabinetmaker as Emil. If the cabinetmaker was to be a connecting link, an emergency net between them, it was only netting woven from a thin fabric, long ago disintegrated. Thanks to the war, all his yesterdays had begun running farther and farther backward and away. Where there was light, there was now darkness. Where there had been relief, there was now insecurity. Where there had once been rest, now there was only restlessness.

"I'm sorry to have come here without prior notice, but I heard that a German censor sits in the post offices, and I don't want to cause anyone any trouble. I went first to the notary. He's the same one who worked for my father. I'm glad he has not been replaced. It is a relief to be able to greet somebody in an old place who has always been there. They have appointed many of their own people everywhere. It's a pity."

"Yes."

"The conditions have changed a lot, and sometimes the people too."

"Yes."

"This is an old region. One can't even trace how long our people have lived here."

Emil Ludvig's hand slid unconsciously to the spot on his coat where he usually would wear his identification. He noticed that the priest's eyes also moved across his coat and stopped on the spot where he usually had the yellow star. He sensed that the old man was looking for contact points—his ear caught a hint of it from the threefold "yes," the nod, and the way the old man listened. Still, he felt them both hesitating, as though they were on a country footbridge too narrow for two people to cross at one time.

"Yes, they've lived here for a long time," the tall man said.

Emil Ludvig was pleased but at the same time just a little unnerved by the priest's patience. Suddenly, he had the feeling of throwing small stones into water and making a couple of small circles that spread and disappeared until the surface grew silent. He had to continue talking to pursue what he'd come for—had he begun correctly? The priest finally turned his eyes away from Emil Ludvig's chest.

The wood carving of the saint had an awestruck face with large, dead eyes that looked nowhere. It also smelled of oil. It looked as if termites had gotten it; there were lots of little scalelike scars and black openings in which oil glistened.

"That's reputed to be a thousand years old," Emil Ludvig said. "Kind of difficult to believe without written proof."

Was Emil ashamed to tell the tall man exactly what he was after because it contained a lie in advance? Why couldn't the priest comprehend this by himself? He waited for the old man to meet him halfway. He couldn't accept powerlessness or defenselessness from a man from whom he'd expected help. He searched for something to connect them. Unfortunately, the most important thing that connected them separated them as well.

The tall man's palm still caressed the lid of the organ as if it were a person. If the old man understood him, why had he kept his guard up for so long? Nothing Emil could say or do could harm him. Without the star, he had exposed himself; he was defenseless. Emil Ludvig felt humiliated once again. After all, it would have been enough for the old priest to report to the nearest police station that an intruder, who did not belong here in accordance to the official decrees, was in the region. Should he talk about his relatives? Should he tell about his ninety-year-old grandfather who'd sat himself down in a ditch somewhere near here and left the world the way he had always done things—his way? Why was he so bothered by the priest's restrained manner? After all, he had not said what he wanted—why he had come. He also sensed humiliation in the tall man. Was there some hidden reason for it on his part?

"In a thousand years, many things will trickle out of our memories and what is not written down will become lost," Emil Ludvig said. "Nobody remembers a lot of previously adjudicated matters anymore, yet there are entries in the records about them to which someone could hold on to and get relief for himself." Then he added, "These days the difference between the guilty and the innocent appears only between the powerful and the helpless."

"Nobody is innocent," the priest said.

"How do you mean?" Emil asked.

The priest remained silent. Was he giving Emil a chance to be more detailed and tell him what was on his mind?

The priest thought about the funeral he'd just come from. He mused about the final essence of a man's life; maybe the pettiness of life seemed secondary and unimportant to him. He wrapped himself in his silence. In the end, would all roads not end up in a single place when the slow waltz is heard only by the ears of the survivors? He must have known that the newcomer had not come just for idle chatter—that was in his blue eyes, behind the lenses of his glasses, in his drooping shoulders, the way he stooped and straightened up quickly, and in the way he clearly struggled with something inside. Were they already connected by the mutual humiliation? Was it just bashfulness? Was he ashamed of anything within himself? Outside of himself? Did he, in actuality, want to say something that he did not want to say, and did he need to tell something that he did not want to tell? Would the younger man seem different if the older man had just come from a wedding or a child's birth rather than a funeral? He cast his glance down toward his shoes.

"We've been at home here for a thousand years," Emil Ludvig added. "It's impossible to just glaze over it and not think about it."

"Yes, I think about it," the parish priest said. "I think about when man fails. I think about what is above and below and what we mean by that."

"We may not know where we came from, where we have been, but we lived here for a thousand years. We dropped our anchors here just like others who came from other places. A few people would like us to get used to some other place."

"It is not necessary to become accustomed to another place," the priest said as though someone had accused him of something. "It's not only a question of belief."

The echo about the failing of man reverberated between them. Emil Ludvig looked inquisitively at the tall, old man to understand all that his answer contained: what it denied him, what it confirmed and offered. He wanted to win the tall man's confidence, the result of which would be understanding and then—what then? Was he asking the old man to lie on his behalf? He sensed the thing he should be ashamed about.

Was it possible, he thought for a fraction of a second, that everything that had transpired up to now would be declared null and void? Would everything then be rescinded by some high-authority German office and then vanish, soon to be forgotten, like a bad dream?

"I think, sometimes, about what would happen if all people had a day of atonement like that which my wife and children celebrate."

"Yes, I know your liturgy," the priest said. "Yom Kippur."

"Some of it is religion, some customs, the rest tradition. Many a thing has been hung around our necks which we have not done and cannot do anything about. It was like that long ago; it's worse now. We each search for some way out of it, if not for ourselves, then for our wives and children; for the place which we came from; for those we've mixed with who have mixed with us."

Emil Ludvig couldn't imagine the priest spreading hate among his congregation. The call for revenge, the squeeze of retribution for something that had nothing to do with being inferior. It was something that would lead to results that wouldn't be looked at closely. What did they want them to do? Pour salt in their eyes only because they had been born from different mothers than the priest and his believers? It wasn't a religious war, was it? It's a massacre of souls. Emil looked the tall man straight in the eyes; he had to stand straight with his head lifted. He tried to put as much goodwill as possible in his voice. That wasn't difficult; it was in his nature. It would not be good for him to lose his patience now, he chided himself.

"You've got a nice place here," he added. "The autumn has come to stay. Everything is ripening; the colors, the fruits, the leaves. I'd like to be as tranquil as the water in your pond—as the eagle in the air. This is eagle country—I just saw one. They've got so much freedom—such a lack of attachment. There are so many animals of prey, like eagles and hawks, here. It's a beautiful land—and it doesn't look poor," Emil said.

"Yes, we're content," the priest said patiently. "As long as we're allowed to be self-satisfied."

The tall man looked like a saint on a wooden cross, even though his hands were at his sides. Something weighed on him—a vision in which he wanted to meet Emil Ludvig halfway and which distanced him from Emil at the same time, like a being from another planet, and with which perhaps he talked to his conscience.

Emil Ludvig looked out the window into the garden. The tall man belonged to everything here, like the trees in the garden, like the soil out of which they grew, as a person's skin becomes the picture of his years, like the circles in the trunk of a tree.

"I can feel the way in which I belong to all of this," Emil Ludvig said suddenly.

"Yes, we belong to ourselves, to the earth, to God."

The tall man smelled of fresh soil and incense. He had a strict mouth, a complexion beaten by the wind, and for a moment resembled Cousin Frantisek. He was tall and squinted his eyes as if to be able to see farther or better.

"Have you ever thought about your origins?" Emil Ludvig asked.

"Every day from morning till evening, and from dusk till dawn, I think about my origin, about the origin and destiny of all people—about truth, about justice, about good and evil, and about holy things and about the devil. It is a sin to be ashamed of one's origins. It is an enormous sin. I think about what we discussed—it's better to keep silent what nobody else wants to hear."

"That's what I wanted to hear," Emil said.

"Why?"

"Why?"

"Yes, why?"

"That's the reason for my coming here."

"I'm afraid that I don't understand you, Mr. Ludvig."

Why had he said that? Would he now refer to laws and public notices and rules? Emil Ludvig did not compare the peacefulness in the window and the desolateness of the village to the city where he felt more like a fish in water than here, regardless of his admiration for the serenity of nature and the countryside. Looking at their dust-covered shoes, he recalled the soap factory on Lord Mayor Avenue.

"I have been to the notary because of the regulations that now have been following one after the other," Emil Ludvig said. "When you ask me why, I shall answer you why."

The tall man waited for what Emil Ludvig would add. His eyes suggested that he was a man capable of freeing himself from himself.

"I come from a Jewish family and have a Jewish family, but from remarks I heard my father, Ferdinand, and his father, the senior Ferdinand, make, I overheard something that could be like an unexpectedly lucky card coming to someone in a pinch—something like a small miracle. It is a game in which everyone cheats. I have come to take a look at the old papers, whether I might find such a card. Perhaps you understand. I don't want to offend anyone or ask for anything that doesn't belong to me. I never cheated anyone, either an individual or the authorities. I'm not lying—or, I don't want to lie—that's not my kind of game, but I don't want to reproach myself for having missed out on something I might reproach myself for in an hour of distress. It would be easier to exist if one lived alone, but nobody lives alone, and I don't want to blaspheme. I have a good family. I'm doing it for them as well."

The tall man listened to him and spoke with his eyes. Emil sensed his emphasis on certain words; everything that was and wasn't apparent to everyone was written in his face—the power of patience, the way people do and don't know one another and what does or doesn't change them and their relationships with one another.

"We are all Jews a little bit," the parish priest said suddenly. "It's not guilt. It's not a sin. It is human. It must not be considered a sin, under any circumstances." Then he added, "I have one soul."

That knocked the breath out of Emil Ludvig. What did the tall man mean by that? Did it sound like understanding, like a promise, like a lead-in to a desirable outcome? Wasn't it obvious to people what was good and what was evil without having to have it shoved in front of their eyes each day? Wasn't it a basic tenet of the world that what was good must be good for everyone and not just for certain people, and the same with evil? Where would the earth be (and where was it getting to now because of how the Nazis wanted it to be?) if what was evil for some could be good for others? Weren't words, thoughts, deeds, satisfaction, fortune, and hope either good for all or bad for all? Wasn't there just one single face, one pair of eyes, one voice of just one man? A weary haze surrounded the terms "good" and "bad" as if they were falling asleep or were already sleeping. It would look like an unpleasant fairy tale that never ended if it wasn't the most authentic reality. Fear also had many faces, like courage or decisiveness or clear judgment, or judgment at all. What did a person have power and weakness and a clear conscience—or the ability to lie through his teeth—for? There was violence, lies, a false peace in the air. There was a lot of apathy and false silence—and there was also a lot of false preaching too, Emil thought to himself.

What did a person have power and weakness and a clear conscience for? All of a sudden, Emil understood what the outcome would actually be. Evasion fell from the tall man's mouth. Was he again demonstrating his helpless disengagement from Emil's problems? (Was it possible that even in the spirits of those very best or most honorable and most selfless, truth and lies were so commingled that no one could choose between the two anymore? It occurred to Emil Ludvig that his brother-in-law, Arthur Pick, had already given up smashing his head against the wall over the state of the earth. For Arthur, everything had gotten so discombobulated that there were no longer any borders between good and evil or yesterday and tomorrow, let alone today. He accepted the confusion of existence as though he'd never known anything besides it and had gotten used to it a long time ago. He was already proudly making his way around the earth without borders, without unnecessary efforts to distinguish good from bad. Arthur had been the first of those around Emil who had reconciled himself to the fact that what had applied yesterday for everyone no longer applied today, at least, not for everybody—and in some cases, no longer applied at all. "Come what may" was Arthur's philosophy so that he could hold on to at least some type of judgment and not go completely crazy when everything around him already had. Suddenly, Arthur's shadow reached up to Emil. The world was only what it was, not what someone wanted it to be, needed it to be, or would like it to be.) Did he want to settle with him as he would with a debtor or a beggar? In the priest's eyes there was hesitation, anxiety, rebuke. He glanced into the trunk containing the books. There were many records of many events, but there was nothing there that would have prepared him for Emil Ludvig's visit. The tall man knew that others before the Germans had marched into the country and declared their laws, their regulations. The Germans were not the first—only the latest. At other times before them, the Jews had not been allowed to eat at a table with non-Jews, had been chased into the streets during the Passion plays, had not been allowed to live with the non-Jews in the same houses or to be treated by the same doctors. Jews had been forced to live in the closed-off parts of towns and villages. They had been forced to bear identification. They had not been allowed to study. They had been converted to another faith, expelled from the country, killed. The old priest knew that what the Germans were now doing was even worse than these things he'd read about in history; the way it multiplies. It lurked painfully in his eyes and threw him off balance.

"No, we all aren't," Emil Ludvig said. "We may have been a long time ago, but we aren't anymore. A little? A lot? Probably we don't have only one soul; the Germans figure it differently. I am not concerned that not all of us are. Not officially, according to the papers. It wouldn't even be as good as it sounds."

"Maybe we had the same father?"

"That was so long ago that it's no longer the truth. I fear that for us even these bad affairs will get worse."

"Perhaps not," the priest said.

Emil Ludvig met with the old man's dry glance; he had searched for a common denominator which did not exist to link his fate with their own. If the priest walked out into the streets and stated openly what he'd just said privately to Emil, he would be taken to a concentration camp and the Gestapo would knock his teeth out, regardless of his position. If everyone went out into the streets and said that they were, even an iota, Jewish, there would be more people in the streets than soldiers. The Germans would then send tanks against them, but it would be better than all this silence and fear everywhere. Emil Ludvig talked about the cards and the rules by which to play. He could picture all the people in the streets and how they referred to justice. It hadn't yet come to that and maybe it wouldn't now. To cheat a swindler cannot be a sin or a crime. Emil wanted to return the conversation to what he'd said about the papers. The tall man digressed from it by speaking in generalities about people such as himself feeling "a little like the Jews"—but only from within and very secretly. The wood-carver hadn't depicted the man on the cross with overly Jewish features. But it would be nonsense to reproach anyone for it; it would be like reproaching the Chinese missionaries who distributed pictures of the saint with slanted eyes. It occurred to Emil Ludvig that the good times had gone. Perhaps they might come again, but for now, they'd fallen from every higher goal to become a pile of horse droppings for the sparrows to peck at.

The tall man's eyes spoke about sympathy, but they also spoke about sin, guilt, and innocence. The dignity in the old man gave off intelligence about life, injustice, and the need for balance. Perhaps I'm too impatient with him—maybe that's unfair, Emil thought. It would be beautiful, though, if mere intelligence were sufficient participation in a conversation. Grandpa Ferdinand once had told Martha and Emil that this man's ancestors in the village had demanded crucifixion so loudly, so eagerly, that stones flew. All the men, women—children too—were made to pay for the broken windows. False enthusiasm against false accusations, Emil thought. It must have been very distasteful to profess the sanctity of the Jewish religion while at the same time wishing that there was none so that the "Jewish situation" could be settled more easily. Father Ferdinand used to laugh at that. Doesn't everyone get what they deserve? Certainly not. Many generations came to learn that at the cost of their own skins. Furthermore, what looks like a sin isn't always a sin, and vice versa. In the very marrow of his bones, Emil Ludvig believed that all people were connected by something called understanding or brotherly love, but his notion of brotherly love stalled at the question of where so much hate had come from.

He hadn't just come here to ease his mind about what might have been impossible to square while still living, but the deeper reason rose to the surface with each second that he stood opposite the tall man and with every word that they exchanged. Grandfather Ferdinand used to tell him how alone they had been in the village. Sometimes they had not been able to defend themselves against the village boys. Perhaps that had been an aberration, perhaps not. Emil suspected that the tall priest was trying to read his thoughts. Emil Ludvig sensed that he hadn't succeeded in achieving the purpose for which he'd come.

"It isn't good to be a Jew in Germany," Emil said. "To quote the German minister of the Air Force, Mr. Hermann Göring, a person can't decide for himself who is or isn't a Jew—it's Mr. Minister who decides."

"God's mill grinds slowly but surely," the priest said. "We used to know what man is, and what is or isn't human. Sometimes we don't anymore. I am troubled by that."

He did not smile, although Emil tried to.

"According to the Nuremberg laws of the year 1935, one exception in a family is enough to delay matters—at least, until they can be investigated," Emil said.

The priest shuffled his feet once. His face was calm, motionless, his voice still patient. He did not invite Emil to sit down.

"I'm not asking for a lot. What I am asking for is important for my family. I'm not asking for anything illegal. I am looking for an exception of record. You are the last hope, Father."

Emil Ludvig did not smile now either; he disliked begging. It reminded him of Anna's having gone in the worst of times to call on the richest man in Prague for financial aid, by virtue of their mutual religious identity. She'd received the charity of twenty crowns. (He'd reproached her cautiously that they weren't so bad off for her to have to go begging, though she probably knew what she was doing.) All the while Emil felt humiliated and he knew why—it was the pride and the defiance of the generations of horse thieves who had been his ancestors. Why would such traits go back that far? Emil had asked himself that the first time he'd spent a sleepless night reflecting on what dignity was, what deprived one of it, and what caused someone to let himself be humiliated. He knew that Anna would not go to outsiders to beg for money again; he thought about begging—he was about to beg a second time—though he hadn't yet finished doing it for the first time, yet.

"I have no fear about anything from your side or from anyone else," the tall man replied, guessing Emil's thoughts and worries. "I am not deaf, dumb, or blind."

"Maybe there's something in your books?"

"Unfortunately, I know my books," the tall man answered kindly. "I have read them many, many times."

Now Emil was alarmed at the man's kindness that hid his fear, or cowardice—the fear a person could fence himself in with so that he could build a wall between himself and someone else and not be touched by anything he didn't want to. Was it the truth? A lie? Evil? Good? Justice? Injustice?

Suddenly whatever it was was too little. The division between the good and the bad was lost. But the tall man had not turned cold. He remained the same: dry, attentive, patient, and constant. In his eyes was self-denial and helplessness despite his power and jurisdiction. There were obstacles beyond which he could not go. He *was* blind, deaf, and dumb. He had renounced the understanding of the need for action. He did not recognize what was at stake. It occurred to Emil that he had not wanted to be intrusive; he was ashamed of the urgency and insistence with which he had come, along with the consequences of the simple fact that he'd been born of a Jewish mother. He did not say that very fact was sufficient to complicate a person's world more than if it had not been so. Confusion pounded in his temples. He kept referring back to the courage of the parish priest, losing his own. Courage? Who is his own master in this life? Perhaps the tall, dry man understood that but only in the way a person understands talk about somebody else's fever or illness, not the fever and illness itself. The parish priest had refused him all the same, even with all his "yes, yes, yes." After each successive indication, Emil's shame, which had a single motive, grew.

The parish priest kept silent now, as did Emil Ludvig. They knew that there were no words for the contention running between them now. Surely the priest had heard rumors about how some families had wrenched themselves free of the officials' claws in this manner? What was more important? To respect oneself or to do for the family what his conscience had whispered for him to do? The parish priest had so many books—some ancient. He could not know them all by heart. Why is it so hard to convince someone who can help someone else that he must do it even if it won't benefit him? Anna had probably felt the same way when she'd asked the coal baron for the twenty crowns. He who gives without hesitation gives twice.

The tall man noted that the shyness in Emil Ludvig's eyes had turned to anger. That left only one small step to despair—and in despair, a person descends to the bottom of his soul. For a moment the tall man wanted to shield himself with a lack of sympathy for Emil, but he did not allow himself to do so. He hesitated about how to defend himself. He knew that Emil Ludvig was in the right amid lawlessness; that he was right though surrounded by lies. The news about Germany had traveled to the tall man. First, people are rejected from society, then condemned as people not worthy of living, *leben-sunwerte Leben*. He'd heard about the castle where the German physicians had displaced the nuns and in their places had put Germans (most of whom were Christians) who were incurably sick, invalids, or senile old men to death.

"I'm afraid you don't understand me, or else I have been unable to explain myself," Emil Ludvig finally said.

"I would never be able to lie," the parish priest said. "It is a deadly sin to me."

"Perhaps," Emil Ludvig replied. "But even in the light of the news that has come from Germany and Poland where the murdering may be going on?"

The tall man did not actually speak of falsifying documents—he spoke only about lying and sin. Emil Ludvig understood that their interpretation of what was a sin and what wasn't differed. He kept trying to outguess the priest. What had led him to refuse?

The priest also didn't say that even though he was against imprisoning and murdering, the church was not. He sensed why saying it would not have been enough. He was a wise man who had buried many old men and brides and young men at the brink of adulthood and witnessed enough births and weddings to see under the surface of the cycle in which life does not offer everyone the same gifts. He felt his own helplessness, but not the helplessness of God. Man passes, God is eternal. He knew, too, that behind all the "yes's" and the kind nodding, the man before him faced a single, all-encompassing "no." It was that "no" that Emil would carry away with him. The parish priest felt that he had failed, but he did not want Emil Ludvig to sense that too. He did not say that he was just a small limb on the body that directed the fates of the world, nor anything about the divine's intention to test his sheep's endurance. Was it possible that the error that had lasted for many generations was coming to a scandalous climax? Was it only a test or was it going to be the next stain on the mantle of the church? In that moment, the dry old man would not like to be the gardener who'd planted and cared for trees and flowers, the tiller who'd made the land more fertile, the man who'd begged but had not received. In his mind, he compared his own will with the highest.

"I am looking ahead," the parish priest said. "I am looking above. I am with those who hope."

Emil Ludvig felt like telling the priest that he was only one of the many who'd lost courage, even if only in comparison to their not leading others into danger. What was the priest thinking right now?

"They are your books," Emil spurted out, but he thought, We are below—above is far away. Hope is also disappearing like steam over a pot. It occurred to him that the life they'd been used to had been taken away from them, though they themselves hadn't changed. He had done everything he could to hold on to that old life which had seemed to him safe, dependable, and good even if sometimes (and definitely, in the long haul) it hadn't turned out that way. Life had changed on him right under his feet, like sand or water running through his fingers.

"It is not in the books and it would be a lie, Mr. Ludvig."

"They are lying more than all the lies of the world that anybody has ever committed. They raised up the lie to rest the principle of their empire upon. I would defend myself against them with the truth if they'd let me, but for them, my truth is less than the lie of the last of their people. They mandated malicious rules against which one cannot protest but only acquiesce. They abolished what had been the truth that people like you, me, and my family believe. Clinging to old principles and goodwill won't help us. They are lying even when they tell us what time it is, what the weather will be like, which day, week, or year it is. For them, my truth is a lie and a curse. We're just trees here." Then Emil fell silent. Didn't this make insects out of those who were declaring him an insect? No one could call his neighbor an insect without making an insect out of everyone. It made the old man an insect; everyone was returning to their insect origins—or to their insect ends.

The priest looked at Emil. It took him a second to comprehend what he was saying.

"Yes, we are all like a tree, roots deep, invisibly deep."

Now Emil Ludvig knew that he had failed. Even the failures of others were falling on their heads. All the betrayals and lies of Germany had been thrown against them. He looked at the floor. It was fashioned of heavy, polished planks. Each plank was scrubbed as clean as a table. The floor was so clean, one could eat off it.

"We live like chickens," said Emil. Then he said, "You can't save everybody, but maybe, if you could save just one person—one family." He didn't expect the old man to reply; it was beyond answering.

He felt the way the German emigrant, Mr. Luxemburg, must have when he'd come for lunch. It was true—everything that he'd said about Kristallnacht, the night of the broken glass—how the Germans had decimated their Jewish population, how they'd beaten, brought to trial, and imprisoned people. All of it had once seemed as if Mr. Luxemburg had been exaggerating to get something from them, but it had not been a lie by the speaker—only by the one listening and not hearing, not understanding, or not believing, as if knowing it better than the person already afflicted by it. What is sin? What is a lie? And where was the truth? Where is love? Understanding? Solidarity?

"Yes, there are a lot of lies around us," the priest said, his voice evasive for the first time. Should he save one family of many? Lie? Perhaps he felt that Emil Ludvig viewed things more sadly and darkly and his prospects more gloomily than what really awaited him.

Slowly and with emphasis, he added, "I knew your people—your father and your grandfather and even your great-grandfather who died before you were born. He used to sell horses. They were honest people. Death pays all debts. They lived their lives well. They held on to their honor unyieldingly and on to their religion unswervingly. Their spirit lives in our region. They were modest and proud, as the books commanded them to be."

The priest said nothing about the horse thieves who were among Emil's descendants. Was he afraid, in a way, of his guest? Had he allowed the history of religion to pass through his head?

Finally, he said, "Even the thousand years in our country are merely a quarter of the centuries which support their tenacity. They deserve all the honor."

"Do you remember my mother?"

"Yes. She died blind."

Now the priest was neither lying nor silent.

It seemed to Emil Ludvig that the priest had something resembling forgiveness in his eyes. It was forgiveness only in his own mind since he was the one who'd accused himself. Wasn't it a silly sentence from the Talmud that Anna had called on so many times before when Mr. Joachym Luxemburg visited them? "Whoever saves the life of one person saves the entire world." It would be good if that were really true. Didn't the Talmud distinguish between human sacrifice and killing as murder? Murder was forbidden by God and by sacred law. The Bible didn't draw a distinction between killing on purpose and killing by accident; murder was unforgivable under any circumstances. To take the life of someone was unpardonable; killing is the biggest sin. Maybe a bigger sin would be to kill the innocent. Didn't the priest sense that was what things were coming to?

"It may have been easier to obey the law when the law still applied," Emil said, "or to hang onto illusions that still looked like the truth, but then weren't remembered as truth any longer, not even a shadow or an echo of it. That's already water under the dam for us. It's a new era."

It was obvious to the priest that Emil Ludvig felt humiliated. The priest didn't say that he wouldn't want someone to be wronged by somebody refusing to defy the law, because then he would also have to say that he was just an old man in a small parish barely able to pray daily for the victory of truth, hope, and love, and that he did not have to help Emil Ludvig because even the Holy Father was praying for that. Responsibility had been divided disproportionately, although it was being measured by the German Reich, its armies, police, crowds of denouncers.

Apparently this is the way it is, Emil said to himself. Helena had brought home from school a quotation that "deceiving a tyrant is not lying." It is not enough just to raise one's voice against weapons (although Emil would have liked to hear at least a whisper).

Emil glanced at the cross, at the carving of the man who had spoken Hebrew, had prayed in Hebrew, and who had been circumcised on the eighth day after his birth. In two thousand years it had not gone that far, but that is what Adolf Hitler was using as an excuse too.

The parish priest looked harried and fatigued; only his patience remained. He was a man on the bottom of the hierarchy—a man who, outside of his kindness, could do nothing; nobody could jump over his own shadow.

Emil put his hands in his coat pocket. He felt the presence of his two savings books. He would leave both of them here. He had never been after money just for itself. He merely wanted to live in a better way—not to feel like a makeshift workshop worker. He also had pictures of both of his children. He carried them like a talisman. He looked at the old priest, like someone he had already forgiven. After all, they feared destitution along with loss of their lives. The way Emil Ludvig saw it, the Nazis wanted to cast them into the greatest possible poverty. First they would alarm the people, then drive them from their jobs, from the better apartments, and eventually from all the apartments. Then they would take everything away from people and threaten them with banishment so that they wouldn't know whether to cling to what was or to what would be, as if it could not be worse. The nicest thing in the world might be knowing not only what was, but also what was to come. Without that, everything lost its sense, even the most beautiful thing. One looks into the mirror in the morning and is unsure about seeing what one sees, preferring to see something other than a face, one's own and a stranger's face at the same time, Emil thought to himself. It is ridiculous, but this is how it is. One cannot give up his pride and exist as before.

He felt a little sorry for the priest and a little angry. The tall, dry man had preserved his dignity but had not supported Emil's. That, Emil would have to deal with by himself. Despite everything, he now felt closer to the old man but also that they still remained strangers to each other. Suddenly, he knew that Arthur had been right; Arthur, the cynic, the man with no illusions. What did a hundred and fifty grandmothers back mean anyway? Nobody would sacrifice himself for anybody else that quickly. It might be easier to talk about things in hindsight. Much of it might have been an error but, at the same time, an error that lasts for two thousand years is more than just any error. It was easier to ridicule it than to take it seriously. What had been an error was now a lie.

"Sometimes I wish that all people were the same color, the same race, and the same religion so that no one would have any prejudices against anyone else," Emil said. It was not necessary to say, "I am leaving now."

"I'd like that too," the priest replied. He lifted the organ lid. He sat down on the bench. He sank his fingers into the keys. He played "Closer to God." Emil Ludvig picked up his hat and left without waiting or saying a word of good-bye. Would the priest perhaps stop him and call him back? Nothing happened. Only the hymn sounded melodiously. It drifted from the house, into the trees, across the pond, into the meadows, and faded away at the edge of the forest. The music still sounded distinct after a hundred, two hundred steps, even after Emil passed by the long garden from the outside, around the pond and the footbridge for fishermen at the end, and then to the little railway station where he would wait for the train back. He felt the kind of serenity only depleted people do. Perhaps no one at home would find out about the trip. He knew that at home everyone relied on him; he would try to return to 137 Royal Avenue in good spirits. He had neither won nor lost; he was just back where he'd started. He was filled with apprehension about what it would all boil down to.

How had he gotten the idea to ask for something from the notary and the priest they might not have been able to give him? Would he have done it for someone else had he been in their shoes? For whom is his skin not closer than his shirt, after all? Among the trees on the field path, it did not seem that anyone waited for someone else to wring his neck.

Thoughts forced themselves upon him. He loathed begging, but circumstances seemed to force him to beg all the time; first from Arthur Pick and now from the notary and the parish priest. Perhaps at every second of one's existence it was necessary for a person to be ready to desert, betray, or disappoint someone and at the same time willing to rely on someone, trust him, and expect things from him. What was happening with the world, with people, with himself? Was it the end of the world? The end of man? He sensed that whatever happened would involve everyone so that it would not be just his personal shame. At the same time, he resisted the thought that from this moment on the common fate would be his fate as well.

On the road behind the pond, he asked a man in a hunter's jacket, without a rifle, whether he was on the correct path to the railway station, even though he'd already seen the station. In a resigned voice the man told him he was going the right direction, and then asked: "Have you seen a couple of my dogs along the way?"

Emil Ludvig did not get a look at the man's face; he overheard sorrow blending with expectation in the depths of his voice.

"No," he answered the man.

"Pity," the man said. "I would hate to lose them."

"Perhaps they'll come back," Emil Ludvig said.

He had not seen the dogs along the way. The question did not leave his mind: *Have you seen a couple of my dogs along the way?* How does it happen that the sadness is always the same, even if the causes are not? He looked at the trees. There was no grandmother in his family tree, no bastard or in-law, no married-into-the-family black sheep, no weed that his, as every good field, absorbed easily. He smiled. Wasn't it all ridiculous?

He noticed a tree trunk near the railway station that reminded him of a naked woman or child. Lightning had peeled the bark away, and the crown had died away along with the roots, perhaps, but the tree would stand until the next gale came to uproot it. When he was little and Grandpa Ferdinand and his father were still alive, they took him into the hills with horses and harnessed them onto a sled to prove to the merchants how healthy, young, and strong the horses were. There were jingling bells on the sleds. The horses, so sweaty that steam rose from them, stopped in the freezing cold at a tree scorched by the wind and weather. It was only a post with the bark peeled away; at the end of the stump a little twig grew. The tree had reminded him of a naked person in the wind and icy frost. Grandpa had torn the twig from the stump and stuck it behind his hat. Eventually, Grandpa and Father sold the horses. Emil knew he shouldn't compare himself to a naked tree or think about what makes trees better off than people. He never thought that he would remember the old tree. He should not blaspheme. Soon, he'd have only the rocks, stars, birds, and rats to envy.

The thought came back to him that he had tainted something that he was now unable to set right, as when Anna broke the first coffee cup from her wedding china, and she was correct—she never forgot about it. What would he try now? The Gestapo issued a notice that those who had money might request emigration, as long as a country that would accept them could be found; Shanghai had been mentioned. He walked along a stone-edged path full of thistles, cornflowers, and dandelions; the parish was far behind him now.

Emil Ludvig was alone at the small train station except for a single train dispatcher, the telegraph operator, and the stationmaster who sold the tickets. Except for the front entranceway, the building resembled a rabbit hut and a vegetable garden. The train dispatcher lived here. He liked to talk with the occasional passengers, but he did not dare address Emil Ludvig, as if he already knew that those who had been to the notary and the parish had other worries than those known to train dispatchers on the railroad. Emil Ludvig greeted him and let himself be greeted. "Hello, good afternoon." It would be nice if the day had been a true reflection of those words.

Everything that he had known from his childhood was here: meadows, apple trees, pine forests, the wind with the smell of heather, the sky, and the fresh autumn earth. He did not want to give in to the disintegrated echo of wistful happiness that could seem like happiness only in hindsight. If only his life's greatest worry were Helena's whooping cough and Richard's anemia or tapeworms. He thought of the things in their apartment at 137 Royal Avenue: an armoire, a tin cup for gargling that all of them shared, the green linoleum, a heater, the beds, a table at which they all ate, and everything that accumulated in the wardrobe closet for Anna, Helena, and Richard, since they never threw out clothes. Then he thought about the money he had earned with the German firm Mr. Kantner represented. Pity that there were no more of such earnings. Could they live here? Perhaps if he had a different set of papers, and then only for as long as they absolutely had to. Maybe they could do it temporarily—if it became absolutely necessary.

He looked at the train dispatcher. He felt ashamed of envying the man's fate without even knowing him; a person who had nothing to be afraid of besides what the majority feared.

The old man was still playing the organ; every now and then, the wind wafted strains of the melody from the parish to the station. It might not have been, but it seemed that he played the same melody over and over again.

The train arrived. The train dispatcher went through the usual motions; he waved his baton to Emil Ludvig: "A happy journey. You look like old Ferdinand Ludvig's son. He used to go with my granddad to school in a house where there had been a pub named Modesty; we've got his pictures at home."

Emil had no time to answer back except for "Good day, good afternoon." The words sounded lovely: "Good day, good afternoon."

The train pulled in. It was nearly empty; only a couple of villagers, taking provisions to their relatives. Sometimes the Germans put officers of the former Czechoslovakian Army in charge on the freight trains to prove their discipline, courage, discretion (but primarily, their allegiance), but seldom on local and passenger trains. They acted as if the war would last forever.

Emil Ludvig waited in the compartment until just before the last stop. Perhaps he should have taken at least a small suitcase with him so as not to appear conspicuous. For a while he rode alone, then a passenger who made him uneasy took the seat beside him—a soldier with a skull and crossbones on his hat (the so-called *Schutz-Staffel,* an

SS abbreviation, *Fallschirmjaeger*) on a furlough. He seemed not three years older than Richard. Emil Ludvig soon stood up and went out into the corridor, glad that he did not have a suitcase, so that the young SS wouldn't take his leaving as an offense or provocation. Emil Ludvig stood by the window watching the passing countryside. It struck him that the soldier might become insulted; perhaps it would be good for him to return to his seat facing the young SS man. The thought was echoed by a feeling of humiliation. He realized that he had blue eyes and fair hair like the soldier—but when the soldier began reading some handbook, Emil Ludvig decided to stay in the corridor. He now sensed what the parish priest had been afraid of: the world had not changed on the outside; it had changed from the inside. Everything had become gravely dangerous all of a sudden, at least for some people, maybe for all. He looked forward to seeing his family again. He thought about what had changed. Perhaps he had expected something from the family that a family, although it provides so much, could never guarantee.

Home, he repeated to himself. And in the echo he heard: cage, trap, danger. He would simply not permit that—not the part he could control, at least. There are things the husband, the head of the family, must not allow if he does not want to be untrue to the trust of the people who depend upon him. He wished he were back at 137 Royal Avenue. Where would he put on the star? He reached into the little pocket on his vest where he'd put the safety pin. The star was there too. Putting it back on would not be difficult if he was lucky. So far, he had been having good luck even in misfortune. I am already like Arthur, he said to himself. It is just a stupid card game. It seemed to him that what he had the others had too; what he didn't have— what he couldn't have—nobody could. He thought about his family as if it were a fortress which no one could penetrate, and, at the same time, he knew that was not how it was or could be. The family is the mirror of an era and of its people at a certain time. Once, as a child, he was in a hall of mirrors with hundreds of mirrors; he saw himself in infinity, but he knew just one image was being reflected.

In every train car there was a familiar public notice. Emil didn't read it; he didn't have to. These days, he opted not to notice anything in print; the notices assaulted his eyes: "Summons. A second repeat. It has been ordered . . ." and so on and so forth.

Cruelty was the Gestapo's totality: even when it wasn't as cruel, each directive that followed was worse than all the others that had preceded it. Whether it was the Gestapo, the SS, or the army protectorate giving the orders, they were all acts against citizens, unarmed civilians. The orders only made sense when taken together as a whole. It was a blitzkrieg of terror. It was a shame that only those directly involved and not the entire population managed to see it.

The return trip seemed longer than the ride out had been. At one time, the return trip had seemed shorter; now it was the other way around. It might be a long time before I'll go through this countryside again, he thought. The autumn sky was darker blue than around noon. It grew a little grayer near Prague; then stars sprang up in the sky.

The SS man got ready to get off the train: he rearranged things (gifts perhaps) in a small suitcase. According to his identification, he belonged to the Waffen SS division of Gren Bohemia und Mahren. Only then did Emil Ludvig notice that both his hands were bandaged under the sleeves. Maybe nobody had it easy.

In the lavatory at the railway station, he affixed the star on his chest at his heart and told himself that if he walked fast on the left sidewalk by the building portals and stooped a little, the star would not be conspicuous and he would be home quickly. Walking so fast made him breathe hard. In the final analysis, he thought to himself, a person is glad to end up in the evening where he started out in the morning. Everything was a circle similar to a snake that bites its own tail. The circle in which everything ends at the same time it is beginning. The unintentional movement from the beginning to the end before the circle closed was what summoned forth hope in a person, before every crumb of hope turned into despair. There wasn't any sense in complaining; he just didn't know what he should do.

He hurried as fast as before so that, if nothing else, he would at least make it home a little bit sooner.

From Helena's notes:

I had a dream about Alfred Flexner. We were on an outing. We stayed behind in the woods, alone. Then he took me home. He asked me why I was sad. Everything seemed beautiful to him, in spite of the circumstances.

I was looking at the sky at night. I saw the roofs of Prague, the castle, the hundred towers and smaller turrets, the thousand years the city took to grow so when I was grown up and old enough for it to fuse into what they call the human memory, all I have to do is raise my chin and I have stars in front of me whose weightlessness sometimes makes me blissful and other times frightens me to death in the same way infinity does, though I don't know why. What is man in the vastness and never-ending world, under the light of galaxies that are like a mirror which does not reflect anything, nothing, nothing but himself? I feel the triviality like the endless number of arrows piercing my heart inside and out, that which they call the soul, I do and don't understand. How did the earth come to be? How did man? Where did everything begin, and where will it end? If not everything, at least some things will and certainly I will, like those closest to me, my friends and foes. Why do I search for something destructive if I have already had to yield to an enormous superiority, even those who are destroying us? Was the idea of Samson that Mama told us about when we were small, like Rabbi Kraus did, born from hopelessness, from the desire for revenge, which destroys the others when we already have to surrender as well? The starry sky is above me, as if we belonged to each other, an infinite ocean similar to the never-ending number of other oceans. Someone said that in the beginning the earth was only water, frozen to the depths of three hundred meters under the surface of water, from which life was born. The sun had to warm up the ice in order for it to soften and melt before something could happen. Other people claim that life began by the nearing of the sun and the earth, that were so far away that it sentenced the earth to eternal coldness, lifelessness. I don't know if I really want to know how life started, what made the huge meteorites strike that maybe then fell again on the earth as if the German Luftwaffe were bombarding London with the hardest-hitting bombs. Or why do I want to know? Why? Some astrologers speak about some enormous, unimaginable universal catastrophe that started everything, as if catastrophes were the forewarning of everything. Is it possible that somewhere about me, in the dark of the universe, some icy oceans are dissolving, wrapping an unknown star like an apple peel, so that in a billion years something similar to the inhabited earth will evolve? And if people come into being, will they be the same people on earth — like Hanna and Dita, the Mautnerova twin sisters, like Mr. Janourek, the jeweler, the first Czech Nazi on Primatorska Avenue and organizer of anti-Semitic activities? I read somewhere that life as we imagine it takes roughly ten million years to evolve. Is the disturbance that I sense, the noise, that comes to me from the silence above me, only the echo of huge collisions, by which everything started? The echo of an echo?

I stare at the window for an hour. It would be better if I would go to lie down.

What will I dream?

✿

5

Emil put on his best clothes, shoes, and tie once more. He did not put a handkerchief into his small breast pocket. He cleaned his glasses. Wasn't it laughable? There was a slight possibility—as with everything in Germany—of getting to Shanghai. Why Shanghai?

"Shanghai." The word rang with the sound of distance, safety, of something almost unreal. Of course, anything far away would sound inviting: to be far away from this place would be a comfort. Distance was a quality of the stars, the deep seas, of the wide-open arms of unknown continents; it breathed safety, while the message of the nearby uniforms was a threat, each marked with a skull and two strikes of lightning. Many office workers now wore the badge with the iron crosses on their uniforms.

He was already in line at the Zentralstelle fur jüdische Auswanderung. Two people confirmed that Bolivia had closed its borders, with a list of those who were to be excluded: the Chinese, blacks, cripples, half-breeds, those ill with tuberculosis, degenerates, people treated for mental illness, criminals, Communists, and Eastern Jews. Emil no longer had a reason to envy those people as he had the week before along with the train dispatcher at the little railway station, the fields and forests, the weeds, the flowers, the eagle that had soared so high it had nearly disappeared above the clouds, the sun and sky. The world is full of people one doesn't have any cause to envy. It was enough to have simply been born a Jew for a person to be different. Suddenly, it occurred to him what kept envy alive—could it be the things that some people had been born with that others would never have? Could there be something more to it than that? Something hidden for a long time, like a submerged river before it makes its way to the surface? He felt an invisible solidarity with those whom he probably would never meet. Someone had become agitated over a rumor about the "definition" of an "Eastern Jew." Was there a difference between an "Eastern Jew" and a "Western, Middle Eastern, Oriental, or Polar Jew"? It may not have been as much of a sense of solidarity as if someone—also invisible—took a giant broomstick in his hands and swept all those who did not come in handy into one pile in a small and continuously diminishing corner. Somebody else chided the man who had whispered about the term "Eastern Jew." He was asked if he was a maniac. Emil Ludvig shuddered; he did not like his thought comparing people to rubbish. The Germans did not think about the worst. They wondered if they had left any other possibilities open for individual families to emigrate. Just thinking about what the word "family" meant made him happier. It was enough for him just to merely think about the word for an image to grow in front of his eyes which he couldn't describe to anyone else. The only thing that bothered him were the other images that constantly got in the way.

The room was packed. If the emigration office granted everyone's requests, none of them would remain here. Of course, that is what the Germans wanted—to get the Jews outside of Europe—and they wanted it now. The goals were exactly the same—only the motives differed. A less ludicrous idea was contemplating relocation to Shanghai—a city that yesterday he'd heard of only from songs. All he really knew about China was from having read an occasional article about Canton, about the Japanese occupation, the rape of Nanking, and the massacres that had not seemed nearly so terrible from a distance (since there were so many Chinese). If someone had told him a year ago that he would now be attempting to emigrate to Shanghai, Emil Ludvig would have made a circle around his temple with his index finger. Wasn't it absurd to try so hard to get somewhere one did not even really desire to go? In spite of everything, he would still prefer to stay at home at 137 Royal Avenue—to take off his coat, take off his shoes (his best, although they were like his shirt and tie, three years old), and loosen his belt above his expanding waistline.

At home he'd play the mandolin—the Italian melodies, "Dinah." He realized he was thinking these thoughts so that he would not have to focus on where he actually was. It was a Gestapo office. The chief, Adolf Eichmann, was called an "angel of death." That was also said about Sturmbannführer Guenther, though to tell the truth, neither of them looked the part, and both had walked through the office several times seeming in no way deadly, except for the skull-and-crossbones sign on their green caps and their membership identification of the Waffen SS. They were soaped, scrubbed, washed, and ironed from head (with their short military haircuts) to toe. Neither shouted; they behaved properly, which could not be said about the Jewish aide who, in contrast, yelled more than he had to. The office did not look like a cage full of beasts, although the German uniforms and those who wore them were horrifying in another way. Everyone here needed a *durchlasschein.*

From what was said and from the long line of people, Emil Ludvig was unable to conjure up any other picture for himself than the one with which he had come here to apply for emigration to Shanghai and to pay for it with his savings books. Someone in line said he presumed that it was already too late, but he did not say for what; another one answered him, "After all, it doesn't rest in our hands."

The Jewish aide interrupted their conversation to educate them on how they should act and proceed when they got into the office. He told them to answer immediately, even to the most humiliating names. If they were told to state the name "Israel" or "Dirty Jew," it would be better to just say it. They had all heard the words said many times already. Emil couldn't react to them anymore: *Dirty Jew. Israel.* The constant repetition had made the words lose their importance, their impact, as they would have had being heard for the first time. Should they slap their own faces? Insult themselves? What had happened was even worse than Mr. Joachym Luxemburg from Germany had once told them—it was and it wasn't. It was probably the actual experience itself that most got under people's skin. They had to repeat everything the aide said to show that they understood—and when the man said *everything,* that's what he meant. You couldn't act like you heard something wrong. It was just these phrases, like "Israel" or "Dirty Jew." In Germany, every Jew was a dirty Jew. Not only did every insult to a Jew go unpunished, it was considered praiseworthy, merely additional proof that anyone who carried Nordic blood in his veins had nothing to be ashamed of for traditions that had gone on for hundreds of years. Whoever had been born of a Jewish mother to a Jewish father never lost his racial, if no longer religious, tattoo. A Jew was a Jew was a Jew. A *dirty Jew. Israel.* The terms "dirt," "Israel," and "Jew" went hand in hand. They were the same, like white and red blood cells, the stars and stardust, light and dark, night and day. Once a Jew, always a Jew (even if by chance he didn't have flat feet, dog ears, or a crooked nose).

The room was stifling hot, yet no one dared loosen even a button. The villa was administered by the army; everything reeked of warfare; the doors were white, the chandeliers richly decorated, and the parquet floors shone like ice. It had once been a Jewish villa, but it did not matter who had lived here or where they were now. The Reich leader's picture on the wall reminded everyone of where and who he was and who the current owners were. Emil Ludvig sensed everyone's fear. It hung in the air like a perfume that clung to their nostrils and skin. A person who was interested in emigrating could turn in an application all week, from ten to half past twelve, Monday through Friday. Individuals as well as families came: each interested person received his or her "file" with the clerk's documents and remarks. The files for New York and Australia had, according to the Jewish Religious Community's communication, all been given out by now, but Shanghai still remained an option. No one yet knew who would be permitted to use his money and last opportunity for Shanghai. By now, no one needed any convincing that people lived and worked in Shanghai as they did here. The people would be a little different, but didn't people differ here? Nothing was forever. Wherever one could survive the war was good. Who would not want to desert an endangered territory? Except for the American citizens who would embark collectively on a ship from Hamburg by the end of the year, it was not possible to get outside of the Reich's territory anymore.

The Jewish aide kept order without break so that the line to the door would be straight and no one would step out of it. He was a youth with black hair in a buttoned-up sports suit like a uniform, a wide-shouldered former gym teacher from Berlin, Hans Joseph, with a Jewish star on his black jacket.

Emil Ludvig had both of his savings books in the breast pocket of his coat of fine English tweed fabric. He had visited a few travel agencies with Arthur; they'd been accepted courteously but with reserve—as if even talking with them was a waste of working time. In some places they had been accepted kindly and the agents had sat down with them in a semicircle, like a meeting, but in the end, the results shrank to mere lip service on both sides. In some places they were even asked for payment in advance before a finger had been lifted and without any guarantee of the outcome (which was, of course, impossible). Arthur stated seriously, "To live or to die, Emil—that is my question. I can see nothing in between." Finally, only the Gestapo's offer to emigrate was left.

Emil Ludvig thought about emigration the way children play the "Heaven, Hell, Paradise" version of hopscotch. He thought about what he would do if he got the permit and what he would do if he did not. Anna's brother, Frantisek, had met a German woman, Fräulein Glass, a month ago. She had settled in Prague and had brought precious news that Frantisek passed on: The Ecuadorian Republic was looking among the emigrants for paper production experts, and in the Dominican Republic and Cuba they tried to get mechanical engineers, electrical engineers, and agricultural experts. From her, Frantisek brought the news that the Germans intended to move the Jewish population out to Madagascar and make them into farmers, just as Europe had once changed them from farmers into something else. Frantisek's German friend, Fräulein Glass, talked about the way the Germans in Prague entertained themselves with the Jewish question like someone betting on horses or playing a lottery or as when a child in a forest steps on an anthill and then amuses himself by watching what happens. There were more and more Germans in Prague all the time. The Germans intended to colonize Prague with three hundred thousand German families. They did not take it *quite* seriously: Why would they be concerned about the most serious aspect of it? Did they consider the Jewish question recreation? Had they dug the Jewish question from the trash and sharpened their wits on it, as when adolescent children play social games . . . half seriously, half for fun? The Germans reproached the Jewish population for its cosmopolitanism. Why? What was wrong with it? A fish swims in all rivers and seas, and nobody thinks unkindly of it for that.

According to Fräulein Glass, the topic of Jews and jellyfish had come up at a social function in the German House. They spoke about the poisonous, burning jellyfish sting; it was better to handle the Jewish population with kid gloves. She also told Frantisek that the news about the German victories was not as contrived as the population believed. They had fought in Africa more successfully than before and had taken the coast from Benghazi to Tobruk, and from there, all the way to the Atlas Mountains in Morocco. They had their people in Casablanca as well. They had no difficulties in sharing power with the French authorities. One good turn deserves another, and Europe, from Poland to Denmark, from Yugoslavia to Belgium, already belonged to them. Food, goods, raw materials, and cheap labor were flowing into Germany from all the occupied countries.

Many people had not come in to arrange for their papers because of their fear of direct contact with the Gestapo. That created an advantage for those who dared to. Nothing ventured, nothing gained, Emil repeated to himself to chase away the fear. He couldn't say why, but the word "Madagascar" sent an unpleasant chill up and down his spine. Madagascar. What if the entire world became German? In such a world, he would have no place to emigrate.

The Jewish aide filled the white-tiled Dutch stove in the corner with coal. The heat here was really too intense because he kept the fire up so eagerly. When the aide opened the stove door, the scattering flames reminded Emil of hell.

Emil Ludvig thought in retrospect about all his attempted actions: nothing had come of sending Helena's and Richard's photographs through the British Affairs Offices to the English queen at the last minute. Yesterday he'd filled out his emigration file. In each of the sections and at the answer to each question there was a postscript about volunteerism, which he signed freely. The peculiar thing was that his idea about it involved, besides money, the back porch, the building, the young landlord's budgie cages, the view of the spherical gas holder, and what they would play at the World, Co-Operation, and Humanity cinemas. Money was the main item, however. But he did not hesitate; he sensed his advantage in that he had some. All of his money was good money. It was his to give out. Money had always made the world go around.

He held his file under his arm and waited for his turn, the letter "L." The *Aryan Struggle* again had written about him that he wanted to look like a bank owner in order to confuse the population. The way he dressed wouldn't confuse anyone; the informed places knew who was who. Yesterday a stone broke their window on Royal Avenue.

The longer he stood here, the more progressively doubtful being granted permission to emigrate to Shanghai appeared, although more attractive at the same time. It was a strange change of quantity into quality and back again, everything condensing and then dissolving. All at once, Emil had a strange thought: Am I still what I am—what I once was? Haven't I already become somebody else? Emil Ludvig and Shanghai, Shanghai and his family. It was a confused goal or rather a confused means composed of still tinier aims and means. Certainly, as Mr. Sternkopf stated at the Ascherman café while they were playing cards, the main thing was not to confuse the causes with the consequences, the symptoms with the disease. It was important not to lose one's head just because so many people had already lost theirs. Pity that it had all come together differently than what it had pointed to at the beginning. How else should one measure the world if not with oneself, with what one felt, with what one thought and did, how one saw things? Hans Joseph, the Jewish aide from Berlin, instructed them again on how to proceed when they were in the office.

"Most important, stand at attention like soldiers."

I won't have any problems doing that, Emil Ludvig thought to himself.

"Take off your hat in front of every German uniform. Cast your glance down and bow your head. Even the civilians you see are Gestapo officers. Is that clear? Even the lowest rank, the adjutants, and military servants are the *army*." He pointed out that it was important to answer exclusively in German.

I won't have any trouble with that, either, Emil thought, nor to the inquiries that will be raised by the German officers and clerks.

"Do not speak among yourselves for any reason, even if it seems necessary. In all instances, wait for questions before answering, before stating anything."

Some people tried to bribe Hans Joseph. They pressed rolls of banknotes into his hands. He refused them with a disdainful glance. He probably did not want to commit himself to anyone or anything. Things were fair and unfair. Corruption was unfair. The aide was cautious; nothing escaped him. Some of those who wanted to bribe him wore ashamed faces, but only for a moment; others only shrugged their shoulders and put their money back into their pockets.

Emil Ludvig saw how people had been changed just by the fact that they had come here; they were different from the way they'd been before and how they would be afterward. It was as though something immediately alerted the soul and pulled something away from them or, on the contrary, gave them something so that they differed from the beings who entered here without anything registering on the surface. Had their souls been crippled? Taken from them? Emil had the sense that an invisible, relentless hand had touched him, had dug into his insides, and had ripped something out so that he would never again be what he had been when he'd first come here. Could he somehow have defended himself? He felt helpless and then guilty about his helplessness. (Unintentionally, he thought again about Joachym Luxemburg. He had been the harbinger of what was coming toward them and would happen without their realization of it. Was Mr. Luxemburg in Prague the same person he'd been in Berlin or elsewhere in Germany?) Emil couldn't just wave his hand and rid himself of the thought that all those present here—on the Jewish side—were now different, having been stripped of their spirit or part of their inner selves. Something forced him to compare it to a pea pod that is green on the outside but has lost its color on the inside. It was a silly and a terrifying thought at the same time.

The Jewish aide spoke perfect German with a Berlin accent. He was a well-developed young man. (Somebody said he was a homosexual and had therefore emigrated from Germany.) He appeared to have a good handle on the military manners of his employers.

"In any case, do not discuss anything—God, human rights, civilization." The aide's voice grew softer: "One gets shot for that." And then: "The officers have no time for that." Finally, he said, "The first thing they'll ask you is if you are Jewish. You must answer immediately. Hesitation means denial. Denial is punishable. Is that clear?"

The door on the first floor opened. The melody of a record player emerged. It was the well-known melody "O donna Klara, Ich habe Dich tanzen gesehen." Emil smiled in his mind. The American song about Shanghai would be more fitting. Who wanted to discuss God, human rights, or the roots of civilization with anyone? I want to go to Shanghai, he thought.

But from the inside, from himself alone, Emil heard many words addressed to the German officers and clerks about God, human rights, and the roots of civilization. In fact, the entire time he had not spoken about anything else in his mind. He spoke German. If I want to get to Shanghai, it would be better to keep my mouth shut about it, he thought. Even if the German officer said that—as Richard once brought home from school—Jews killed their children and sacrificed them to the devil, I must keep silent and only answer questions, as the Jewish aide emphasized every five minutes. What would I get out of it if I persuaded a German officer, for example, Mr. Guenther or Mr. Eichmann, that I would not sacrifice so much as a squirrel to the devil even if he promised me Aryan papers, reliable grandmothers on both sides and sixteen generations back, to negotiate a mutually more advantageous contract? He played with it in his mind for a while. This is valid, he would say. This is, this is not. This is valid. Madagascar. That is not. Shanghai. That is valid. The devil? The Jewish aide demonstrated the interval at which a person had to keep distant from a German uniform, even as he stoked the stove with more coal.

At least I know who Richard takes after in this regard, Emil said to himself. Pity that he had not taken Richard with him. At least the presence of Richard helped him figuratively. Perhaps it was better if no one saw him here. That was what he'd told himself the week before, on the train, wasn't it?

The letter "I" had been attended to and the letters "J" and "K" as well. The man in a fur coat who had spoken about Bolivia earlier whispered that he had not admitted to all of his money, that he would have to be a lunatic to do so. But now he looked at the aide to ask whether he could postpone his hearing. Again the word "maniac" was heard. "Hold your place in line, please," the aide repeated, sticking his chest and shoulders out. "You are not permitted to leave until your turn has come."

Hans Joseph, the aide with the military bearing, was shouting again. In reality, he communicated to them—including the man who had spoken about Bolivia—that everything took an expected course, that the number of men in the line must correspond, nothing could be postponed or switched, and each should remember his instructions in his own interest.

A German soldier, Waffen SS with the *Panzergrenadiers truppen* insignia, descended the red-carpeted marble stairs. He had no cap. He had straw-blond hair parted on the side. The black-haired aide stretched himself to attention immediately.

"The letter 'L' has properly fallen in line," he reported. "They are waiting to be presented."

"*Schon gut, schon gut,*" the soldier said. He had an extraordinarily high voice.

The door upstairs was slammed shut and "O donna Klara" faded away. Mario Schapira's son-in-law stood in place about ten "L's" ahead of him in the row. The son-in-law, a chemist, wasn't Jewish, but he'd converted to Judaism when he'd fallen in love with the religion teacher's daughter. The couple had a little girl. It was said that there was a need for chemists in China. Schapira's son-in-law was prematurely gray with childish eyes and a rounded forehead. He looked somewhat hapless, as if he didn't know how to count to ten. Some said he was a mathematical genius. If his papers didn't specifically state that he was not racially stained for sixteen generations back, he might not, like Emil Ludvig, be able to prove it. He stretched himself to attention and looked ludicrous. He had a large coat, and a shabby shirt collar, yellow tie hanging askew. What would he say if they asked him if he was a dirty Jew? Would he say that he wasn't?

Emil Ludvig shuffled after the aide shouted "at ease." The emigration file he held under his arm seemed like a splinter that had to be pulled from the skin for the pain to subside, and not like a raft on which he could float across the Pacific Ocean from Prague to Shanghai.

Emil's figurativeness reached only both banks of the Vltava. Luckily, the Germans weren't lords of the entire world yet—not even of all of Europe. They hadn't gotten to the British Isles, except for a few of the smaller islands; the islands were too small potatoes for them. The world was still bigger than they were, and after all, the Germans had short arms for many things, even if they seemed to be giants. They'd never lay their fishhooks on America (to Emil, America had once been the place for many people who'd gotten fed up with living on the old continent for one reason or another, for those who hadn't liked it here or who hadn't prospered) unless they could send their agents, spies, ships, and submarines to South America first. They'd have to be satisfied with what they had, for a while at least, and allow their desires to go unfulfilled on certain things. It was only here that they could force people to say "Israel" and "Dirty Jew" about themselves.

Every day they would broadcast "Good night and a firm hope" from England. Arthur had then suggested another greeting, a saying from the Ascherman café: What is the difference between an optimist and a pessimist? The pessimists have moved out and the optimists are dead.

It wasn't appropriate to say another word about that. Then Emil told a tasteless joke to lighten things up: How did a man know his wife was dead? Sex was the same, only dishes were piling up to the ceiling in the sink. Arthur had said that it probably didn't thrill the Germans that according to world statistics, four-fifths of the world's inhabitants were dark haired, so fair-haired ones were in the minority, and that according to a German philosopher Susanna was reading now, white men and blonds were only pale black men; the ideal color of human skin was somewhere between olive and black. That Arthur certainly was a big joker.

Whenever Emil Ludvig stood at attention, the thought that he had once wanted to become a professional soldier returned to him. It would not have been a bad way of earning his daily bread: regular pay, a roof over his head, proud looks. The aide repeated how and when to address a German official: to add "Israel" to each male name, "Sarah" for the women. The aide recommended that they bow and recite their requests and replies in a soft, respectful, and humble voice. Any other tone would be considered impertinent and provocative. Then they were to again stand at attention.

Anna had relatives in Shanghai; that's what had convinced him they should go there. Many were said to have left Shanghai for Honolulu and then San Francisco. Who knows? Only a white door now stood in front of him. The letter "L." Zentralstelle fur jüdische Auswanderung in Prague. Deutsche Geheimestatspolizei. In the thick, brown paper file were his savings books, certificates of engagement rings that everyone had to turn over to the Reichsbank's Prague branch, a gold bracelet, and a gold wristwatch that he had bought with his earnings from his business with Mr. Kantner. He had been told he could keep any other things he had as long as they were made out of inferior or undesirable metals.

What had been on Arthur's mind when he said that his question was to live or die? Could he see nothing in between? He thought of Mrs. Ohrensteinova who used to buy thread at their store. She faced the same question after dinner one night while Mr. Ohrenstein put both children to bed. When Mr. Ohrenstein returned to the kitchen, he found his wife strangled on the wire of a standing lamp. He ran for Doctor Mautner, even though it was past eight by then and he was not allowed in the streets. Her forehead was resting on the table, as if she had fallen asleep, but her tongue hung out. He resisted the thought that a dead woman could scare the living.

The aide, Hans Joseph, instructed from the side, "Knock once, wait to hear a 'come in,' enter, and remain by the door before being called to approach the table with your file."

Bolivia must have fallen through by now, Emil thought. The British are still defending themselves, shooting down airplanes, even losing their own. Still, at least someone is defending himself against Germany and the Nazis. Shanghai still might be a possibility. Stick with it, little man, he steeled himself. He knocked.

Emil Ludvig figured out what was all going on in the first second before the German official had even batted an eyelash at him. It was the blue-eyed, fair-haired Mr. Ernst Kantner, still wearing the same gold wire-rimmed glasses as Emil. Emil Ludvig pulled himself to attention.

"Jewish?"

"Jewish," Emil answered.

"Dirty Jew . . . Israel . . ."

"Dirty Jew," Emil said, repeating the instructions he'd gotten in the hallway. He felt blood rushing to his temples. He was ashamed. Should he not have said it? He wasn't here just for himself, after all. He was here as the head of his family. In his sleep, night after night, it would beat in his blood: *Dirty Jew. Israel.* He wasn't able to cope with it inside. He felt a shame so strong that he had the sense it had knocked him over like a tornado. Neither was he able to deal with the fact that the administrator in the uniform with the army cross and on the left side the *Ehrenblatt — Spange Des Heeres* was his old business partner, Ernst Kantner. A five-leaf silver button on his sleeve indicated he belonged to the administration section of the Waffen SS. Emil hadn't recognized his own voice: how he'd spoken, leaving an echo trailing off in his mind. Wasn't he spitting out his words too quickly? Wouldn't it give him more confidence to force the words out slowly? All at once, everything he'd thought about on the way over here came together. The result was fear: fear of everything German, Gestapo, Waffen SS—their black uniforms, symbols, the color of secrecy, the night, cold, and stone. And dying away was the echo of what he'd just said about himself to Mr. Kantner: "Dirty Jew . . ." What would happen now?

"Name?" the official asked without glancing from his papers on the desk. He did not say it roughly. Everything he said was part of his office duties. He pushed aside the previous file. The people entered through one door and exited through another. Mr. Kantner looked nearly the same as he did when purchasing Prague goods with the help of Jewish traveling salesmen for his Munich central office at Ungelt. Had it been difficult for him to exchange his civilian clothes for a uniform? Had he been forced to do it? Had he wanted to or had he been playing an orchestrated game from the very start? A flash of elation to see that the man at the desk was in fact an acquaintance, and that this could accrue to his benefit (or could it be just the opposite?) immediately ran through Emil Ludvig.

"Emil Israel Ludvig."

Mr. Kantner compared the name with the list that he had handy. There was a number next to each name. What would happen when Mr. Kantner finally raised his eyes?

Mr. Kantner was still using his old American fountain pen. He checked the left side by the name. Apparently, it meant the beginning of the negotiation; he did not look up. Did it dawn on him who was standing before him? Had perhaps Mr. Kantner forgotten him? Many people had passed through this room.

"Do you know anyone in Shanghai?"

"Maybe. It is far away, and we have not had any news for a long time. My wife Anna's relatives."

"But look here," Mr. Kantner said all of a sudden. "It's you. Isn't it a coincidence the way people meet up with one another?" He coughed. He put his palm in front of his mouth.

Mr. Kantner smiled with closed lips and raised his eyes to meet Emil's. His uniform was scented with either French or German perfume. It reminded Emil Ludvig of perfume he remembered Mrs. Hannalore Kantner having worn at their business meeting.

"So, it's you," Mr. Kantner said again. "How people meet up with one another—such a small world! How are you doing?" Without waiting for an answer, he added, "Shanghai is a modern city, but it has its drawbacks. There could be a crowd of a dozen or so people waiting for a telephone booth. Some products can't be found even if you offer to pay a hundred times more for them than they're worth. The ways of the Orient are foreign to us, sometimes even repulsive. One should be well prepared before he undertakes such a journey."

Even then, Emil Ludvig didn't answer. He struggled to breathe for a little bit, or had he perhaps wanted to say something but had changed his mind, thinking it would be better just to swallow the words?

"Something must be done about this, that's true," Mr. Kantner added. But he did not say what.

"In some ways it will be good for us, too, if many people leave. Not, of course, because they won't be able to take everything with them, but because they will destroy the propaganda that has been levied against the Reich that everything on our continent is inhuman. Every one of you who reaches foreign shores will destroy those horrible, mostly fabricated, and totally abstract ideas about what the Gestapo does to people. They will see you, alive and healthy, with your families. You'll help the Reich more than you perhaps think you will," Mr. Kantner added.

Emil Ludvig noticed both interest and an icy watchfulness in Ernst Kantner's eyes. It reminded him of the interest, zeal, or bitterness of the Mr. Kantner he'd known from Ungelt.

Mr. Kantner looked at his watch to see how much time he had left to give to Emil Ludvig's case. "You're looking good. You haven't changed," he noted.

The newcomer's eyes contradicted that.

Emil Ludvig did not expect Mr. Kantner to stand up and stretch out his hand for a greeting. That would have been too much. He had already uttered the statement "Israel," "Dirty Jew." He had mixed feelings. Mr. Kantner got up. He gave Emil, his onetime commercial traveling salesman, a friendly handshake. Everything in Emil Ludvig rejoiced, although cautiously. Mr. Kantner continued smiling in his dry manner; he stood in front of his large writing desk. The office took the largest space in the former Jewish villa.

The first thing that occurred to Emil to do was to take out one or both savings books and give them to Mr. Kantner. As a gift, a bribe, as a contribution; to utter the password and give up something that could return to him later in any form. Of course, he did not dare do that. But it was the only thing that he had learned well—giving. To give means strength, more strength than joy, it seemed, an advance for something for which one waits, and confidence, self-confidence that things will be better. Something told him to do it. He followed his impulse, which had already advised him many times; he did it.

"Oh, that's for me?" Mr. Kantner asked. "Thank you. You've always been accommodating." He looked at the inserted slip with the passwords. "I had wanted to ask you whether there was a password for the account. There is. What nice passwords: 'the First One' and 'the Second One.'" He was silent for a while. He put the books on the edge of the table so that he could put them in his pocket after a while. What was he going to do? He returned behind his desk; he sat down. He thought about the further procedure in light of the gift. He smiled.

Emil Ludvig could only guess what Mr. Kantner's smile suggested. He sensed a trap: he did not believe Mr. Kantner, or at least felt cautious about him without being able to explain more than a few primitive "why's" and "because's."

Ernst Kantner also knew that the regulations directing their lives had changed them into different beings. Every directive brought something new that always made those involved reevaluate their situation thoroughly. They were no longer able to imagine what would follow because the past had taught them that circumstances are unpredictable. Once it had been possible to guess what would happen on the basis of what had already been. That had been ripped from their grasps. Even the most trustworthy Jewish prophets had become pathetic figures, if not complete liars. What had worked yesterday as wisdom today became ignorance, absurdity, and delusion. Reality had played with them for too long. They were not prepared for the tricks and masks of that which tomorrow would be history but today was still only a riddle of how to survive until the next morning. Every uniform created panic in them. Mr. Kantner looked over Emil's papers.

"I have my duties here," Mr. Kantner said. "My responsibility is to weigh and assess each case, individually and together as a whole, judge the pros and cons for each side, such as—what is involved financially, and how to reach the designated goal."

Emil Ludvig had to restrain himself from unconsciously nodding. He did not say a word.

"I am always searching for an understanding with anyone who

shows goodwill," Mr. Kantner said. "We are not giving up our efforts in this area. Anyone—wherever on the earth—who has the ability to understand us is not too distant from us. We will join with anyone who can add to our endeavors and peace-loving tendencies, if not a full peaceful organization of world affairs. We must all begin with ourselves, those near to us, those people we live with. That way we'll destroy what cannot be missed—what cannot be left unanswered."

The window was covered with paper tape so that if a bomb dropped nearby, it wouldn't cave in from the air pressure.

Finally, Mr. Kantner concluded, "You're doing the right thing. Even if you may lose, at least you have the courage to gamble. I know what hope means to a person. I can see that you live normally. Lots of people try to keep clear heads—perhaps because there's a war going on. There's no point in being needlessly fearful ahead of time. Something always happens—it always leads to something—and today there is hardly anything one can do without risk. Risk is an unfamiliar quality, just like fantasy. Is there—when one looks at the whole picture—no hope made from the same materials as risk and fantasy, sometimes painful and sometimes painless? While I'm on the subject, a lot of what people think and say is provocation against our dignity, against the foundations of our national, state, and spiritual existence, and against everything sacred to us. It serves no purpose save for confirming the motives of our provocateurs. They force us to protect our principles, which are legitimate and permanent. We want to be the masters of our own fate, that's all. Unfortunately, it is too late for certain kinds of knowledge. It's not only who and where they sit. The old ways of doing business no longer work. Every bad step created ten even worse ones."

Suddenly, Mr. Kantner interrupted himself. He fell silent for a moment.

"They are safe with me," Mr. Kantner said.

He had now confused Emil for the third time: the first time was his presence in the office, the second time was by mentioning the cinema, and now, what was he thinking? At least two or three possibilities occurred to Emil Ludvig about what he had said. Had he perhaps been referring to the savings books?

Mr. Kantner then returned his glance to the savings books. He took his time. He inspected his neatly arranged desk. His complexion was pallid the way it is with people who shuffle paper to stretch out their days into the night and sleep little. He had gotten a little thinner; did he perhaps not have time to eat three regular meals a day? One could not say that he seemed to fit any less in this Gestapo office than he once had fit in the commercial central office at the Ungelt. He smiled. His smile said two things: first and foremost, that happenstance had provided him with an opportunity, but also that the way people met up with one another was both amusing and interesting.

"We're meeting at a difficult time, Mr. Ludvig. Yes, yes. I'll do what can be done. I would like for us to meet not only as businessmen, but as decent people. You look good. I'm glad to find you in a good condition." (Perhaps it seemed a bit puzzling to Mr. Kantner as well.)

"Has Shanghai captivated you?" he asked.

"You could say that," Emil confirmed.

"They want younger people there, but we can 'cast a blind eye.' You're not looking too bad. You haven't aged at all. Like I said, you look the same—you haven't changed at all. Have you discovered a formula for permanent youth? Some people know all the secrets of living well."

"Thank you," Emil answered, still standing at attention.

"Well, very well," Mr. Kantner said. "At ease, friend. Make yourself comfortable."

Emil did not answer. The instructions of the aide rang in his ears: he wasn't sure he'd acted as he'd been directed to—he'd said "thank you." That had seemed to be the most suitable thing. In his mind, he could hear the words connected with his name: "Emil Israel Ludvig. . . . Dirty Jew."

Without looking at Emil Ludvig, Mr. Kantner said, "I often wondered during my previous stay in Prague about what would happen if the Germans, with their sense for orderliness and cleanliness, were a small nation—like the Danes, for instance. Do you think that the war would have broken out—not just armed disagreement, but a large, all-encompassing war? Why does every decade or every other decade see a war erupt? What do people as clever as you—I don't mean just you, but your fellowship—think about it?"

Mr. Kantner's voice had a certain haughtiness despite the friendly tone. Emil did not say a word. Mr. Kantner responded to his own questions; he had not presumed that Emil Ludvig really would follow or try to answer his complex sentences.

After a while, Mr. Kantner added, "For the present, I have been working at the registration and emigration section in view of my experience with the knowledge of local mentality."

Emil kept the realization to himself that Mr. Kantner had probably been a high-ranking member of the Gestapo back when they'd done business together, keeping silent and waiting. It was almost unreal.

"My business tasks are now being fulfilled by younger, and perhaps more efficient, successors," Mr. Kantner continued. "We must not talk ourselves into believing we are irreplaceable. Pity that you aren't working for us anymore. I remember what we had in common. What does not become the past in time? Once you taught me the good Czech sentence, if you remember, when I wanted to say that something happened a long time ago: 'That was around the year of the tobacco when those hairy winds blew.' Had you not explained it to me in German, I might not have understood it even today. You have a gift for language; that could come in handy in Shanghai. I don't envy anyone who must learn Chinese. One will need the gift for drawing as well. As I say, you look good—well dressed."

Emil's reply was a mute consent, a bowing of the head and eyes. When they had seen each other the last time, Emil had left the remainder of his provisions as a bribe and Mr. Ernst Kantner had accepted it. Would he take a diamond necklace now, too, if Emil had one to offer? Even if he had one, caution would probably not allow the man to take it. Mr. Kantner stood up again.

"How did your wife enjoy the German candy?" he asked. "What about the children? Are they in good shape?" (Back then, the Munich central office furnished its employees with lots of inexpensive German sweets and foodstuffs, and Mr. Kantner had been generous.) Then he noted, "They recalled me when the bank, with its calculating machines, easily replaced both my hands and head. Our heads we have only once."

That was the moment when Emil was struck that, though he couldn't say why, during the words about his hands and head, Mr. Kantner could suddenly slug him in the teeth and sit back down again.

What Mr. Kantner actually did was stand up and open the door to the adjacent room. He took a chair from the corner and offered it to Emil at the side of the desk where the savings books with the slip and the passwords sat (right next to the horsewhip). It was only perturbing that he left open the door to the other room, which may not have been empty, as one could hear from it a sigh and the shuffling of shoes.

"How is your health?"

"Thank you," Emil Ludvig answered.

"Won't you sit down?"

"Thank you."

"You may."

"Thank you." (He didn't know what else he was supposed to do to fulfill the orderly's command.)

"May I have your file?"

Still standing, Emil passed it to him without a word. Mr. Kantner took the folder and glanced into it. Emil sat down on the very edge of the chair. In a way, it negated something, after all. He felt a little more comfortable now that Mr. Kantner had acknowledged their acquaintance. The humiliation he'd felt from saying the words "Dirty Jew" and "Israel" eased a little. He felt as though he was the gardener in the film Mr. Kantner had talked about, and the duke had invited him to sit down in his study.

"That should do it," Mr. Kantner said. "By the way, everything that's going on, including your registration today, is merely another term for normalization; an effort to set things and conditions right, to assure the definitive place of each individual in the whole. After all, your people have been trying to do this themselves, either by assimilation or by emigration into a single country, and I am convinced that the normalization must take place so that we can attain the Final Solution and put an end to exclusions, bans, unpleasantries."

Mr. Kantner read the writs and documents in Emil's file. "Some things are, I think, a bit uncomfortable to all sides involved, even to those who have merely been observing, because they are so close. Everyone will welcome a Final Solution, I am convinced. All present attempts at a solution have failed because we found ourselves in the end where we had been in the beginning. We all must lend a helping hand, that's what I think. As I say, you look good; I am satisfied you are in good shape."

Then he said, "I would like to inform you about everything before you decide. Everything that is going on today is temporary, as regards the war, therefore a bit more strict at first glance. The military masters have the leading word before the cannon will grow silent. I have heard—you must have heard as well—rumors that have nothing to do with the truth. It is enough to tune in to a foreign radio for one to be deafened by the propaganda, fabrications, and mudslinging that the enemies hurl on Germany with the awareness that there is not so much as a pinch of truth in them. They are outright distortions, exaggerations, and overstatements emphasizing negative aspects, raising inaccuracies and mistakes to an art. It would be too easy to talk about it as a breach of agreements, contracts, or the understanding among decent people that had before been connected by business, I would say, with the same intensity with which the war divides them presently. Now we're all working toward the time when bread, butter, fresh eggs, and cream will be of higher quality. I am not reproaching you for wanting to temporarily escape this period which has not favored you, for a Chinese seashore city. It is far, but it is not Africa. I do not rule out that you may want to return. The certain thing is that your children will not become Chinese; not even your grandchildren will; although I heard about a Chinese town where your people have existed for six hundred years. I approve of you, I'm trying to put myself in your shoes." He knew that an applicant tries to anticipate what awaits him, what gives and takes away his strength and courage, and what he probably already knew and perhaps preferred that he didn't know. It was better to let them stew in their own juices so that maybe they would just open right up—even here at the Gestapo office— and let all the schmaltz in their hearts out—what perhaps they even believed in.

For a little while, Emil Ludvig had the same feeling he'd had in the foyer, that something was actually happening that was at once both too real and unreal. He caught himself looking at Mr. Kantner's hands and counting how many fingers he had, or he avoided looking at him straight in the eyes, as though he'd lose his will if he did that or perhaps that Mr. Kantner had somehow already taken his will away by hypnotizing him. The gaps in the doors that led to the neighboring room filled him with terror as if someone could walk through matter, through the wood and metal doors and take him over or do something else to him. They weren't hallucinations because the whole time he knew exactly where he was, why he was there, and who he was with. At the same time, he couldn't get rid of the feeling that he was in a dream. The light burned his eyes a little, but it wasn't as strong as before, and everything seemed normal. He recalled the first time he'd gone with Arthur to visit Mr. Kantner at the man's former place of work. Emil had been close to death then, too, judged but not executed. He had learned to believe that from the time he was little, some miracle would always save him when push came to shove. (Hadn't he come here today because of that?) But he quickly opened his eyes because for a fraction of a second, a white, orange, blue, and yellow light overpowered him. When he opened his eyes up again, it was gone. He felt his entire body shaking. Of course it was fear. He looked at Mr. Kantner's shoes. The man's personality certainly exuded strength, power, and confidence, incomparable to anything. Emil suspected what it all meant, though he hadn't learned anything new from what he'd first heard in the foyer. It crossed his mind that he would keep his little visit here to himself, as long as everything went well. He wouldn't say a word about it to anyone. He was ashamed of something he didn't yet understand. It was the deepest shame he'd felt that pervaded his entire being, like the fear he sensed when he looked at those doors to the next room, as if someone were invisibly passing through them to take control of him and beat him and torture him or to immediately order him somewhere from which no one had ever returned.

Meanwhile Ernst Kantner leafed through and examined the documents, signatures, records, and codes which only he himself understood and which Emil had had to secure at the German and protectorate offices. He repeated several times that Emil Ludvig was in good shape and that, eventually, the Final Solution of the Jewish question would be advantageous for all.

It was the only one of his points that he continually repeated: a solution for everyone, primarily, one which was final. No one would have to search for another solution again. It was like death. He smiled because it seemed clever and the right thing to do. Nothing ever comes after death. Death is the end. Period. There's no halfway of anything like that, unlike virginity, which was possible to fake. Death was either final or it wasn't death; a solution, and nothing ever again after that. Period. The end.

Emil tried to listen without giving Mr. Kantner justification to ponder his distraction, lack of participation, or indifference. He looked for continuities. Mr. Kantner added that the German military authorities had the town of Tabor in southern Bohemia or Terezin in northern Bohemia in mind for the normalization of the Jewish population which didn't emigrate. He also tossed around the possibility of moving the Jewish population to Madagascar, the onetime French colony. He smiled. How funny a word it was.

"Mada-gas-car."

Didn't it sound like three codes? Mada-gas-car? He also referred to it in connection with the Final Solution. He laughed to himself about something; that was evident by his expression and by the slightly uplifted corners of his mouth.

"We would be happy if there was a sieve that just separated those who deserved to go from those who didn't."

He spoke like a man who, along with the highest authorities, had been made privy to all the plans of his country, and it lent him not only the awareness and knowledge of the importance of the task, but self-confidence as well. On invisible scales, Mr. Ernst Kantner's side had tipped the balance of Emil's side, which had risen like foam, like a light fog, like soot.

In the corner of the office was an aquarium; Emil's attention was caught by the little fish that swam near the bottom.

"Thank you," Emil Ludvig said.

"Let us bite into that sour apple."

In Emil's emigration file there were photographs, each in triplicate. Mr. Kantner looked at the pictures of Richard, Helena, and Anna. "They won't be children much longer," he remarked. "Time is flying. The boy has really grown up. I read that he is working now in our mutual trade, leather; that he makes leather cases for soldiers' military tags. Excellent. Your little daughter reminds me of my own little dancing partner. *Meine damalige polonaise Dame.*" Then he added, "Some applications cannot be accepted or are refused." He continued, "I hope you aren't feeling dizzy. Occasionally some people do. Out of nowhere, their heads begin to spin and their knees buckle under them. Usually, luckily, it's only temporary. Lengthy spells, as the doctors say, are the result of brain tumors, not to mention other things, of course. You don't look as if you have one of those. Quite the opposite—you look very healthy."

"Thank you," Emil Ludvig said.

"It begins with problems in the ear," Mr. Kantner said, sounding neither worried nor accommodating.

Emil waited to hear what he would say next.

"The worst is getting sick before a trip—that changes one's plans. But that, I hope, will not happen to you," Mr. Kantner added.

Then he said, "As Quarrel von Clausewitz teaches us, as long as we deal with a well-armed enemy, it's almost impossible to change his mind unless you let him wait for a better opportunity than the present one. It's a so-called foolproof method. As long as one side is interested in negotiating, the other side must be interested in waiting."

And then he said, "You know for yourself how painstakingly our country pushes for peaceful negotiation—for understanding between all sides—for compromises that are not only advantageous, but peaceful. When was the last time you had a medical checkup?"

"I don't even remember anymore," Emil Ludvig admitted. "But if it's necessary . . ."

"Are you sure you're all right? Who likes having their knee tapped by a physician's hammer to see how he twitches or kicks, like a small child? As I say and hope, you look as if you don't need it."

"Thank you," Emil Ludvig said. He caught the sound of bashfulness, shame, objection, in his voice. "They have grown up fast." He also caught the sound of humbleness in his voice for which he had no liking.

Emil Ludvig felt, sitting here like a young pupil, that he was being punished, perhaps for not ever bothering to go ask about how good his children's grades were, or the other way around, for what he had let Anna do from the first grade to the seventh, in Helena's case. Without trying, Mr. Kantner had succeeded in bewildering him beyond expectation. It was his voice along with the uniform (not to mention the little horsewhip), the writing desk, and his two savings books that confused Emil, in addition to what Mr. Kantner had said about finding him in good condition as if he were a thing, about the Final Solution, by letting him sit and not closing the door behind him to the adjacent room, with his summary of some country's geography and history and the lesson German scientists, politicians, and soldiers, like Mr. Kantner himself, had learned from past mistakes or deficiencies. It was a voice within a voice, a tune with a different self-satisfaction besides the self-confidence and courteousness that had captivated him when they had met for the first time as business partners. All that was yesterday's news. Ernst Kantner held Emil Ludvig's file and read his cards, throwing them like dice.

"I must acquaint you with the conditions that have not been presented to you in writing yet," Mr. Kantner said. "With respect to the war which has been drawing out, the authorities require a certain sum of money for the emigration file and the passport with an exit permit. It is necessary to remit for it at once. It is also an approximate, not the complete, compensation for the procedures that society is expending for you. It may seem somewhat anachronistic, but I do not have the ability to change that. We are all subordinates and there are regulations, for which there are no exceptions. You know German thoroughness," he said with a smirk. "Even though a positive outcome can be neither promised nor guaranteed, the file and the emigration passport presume the voluntary sale of your estate—movable and real, and of savings, stocks, shares, or obligations, into our hands. Please pay attention to that condition: it is completely binding and it is not overly advantageous, as I am obligated to state and as I dislike to note. Of course, I shall do everything that depends on me, but my hands, just like yours in a certain sense, are tied. No solution can be final, as long as the authorities allow exceptions. It outrages even the rank-and-file men, not just our bosses. The movement that has taken such a long time coming to power is touchy about exceptions. I must also concede openly that I am just one of the links in the settlement of your request. If you are selected, you will be expected to have paid all the fees, given up everything you have, and gotten a file—which means that you will have sold all your property to us, you will have made the apartment free, let it be sealed along with the furniture, dishes, and that which you are not going to be wearing, including fur coats and forbidden articles, of course. You will then pay the appropriate additional amount in cash, and even then, you may still not get a positive answer. Also, it's bothersome that there is no appeal. Everyone's case is considered just once, on principle. At the same time, there have been cases to the contrary where people have gotten off all right and the deal is concluded obligingly. That is the law. The law's public notices are accessible everywhere. Only a few people have not become familiar with them in detail. The law does not ask what you or I say about it. Neither your consent nor mine is contained within them; therefore, it would make no sense to ask me to alter things. I would not be able to do so even if I wanted to—I must and have to confess that freely. That is the mode of my assistance out of old acquaintanceship—you are not my only acquaintance in Prague. I hope you understand."

"Yes," Emil Ludvig replied.

"Before you inform me of your decision . . . we have just a couple of minutes for that, unfortunately . . . I shall look into our confidential documents to see whether you are recorded there."

"Thank you," Emil said.

While Ernst Kantner read in the confidential folder that Emil Ludvig had been nearly a regular guest at the Christmas distributions of gifts for the poor or people in temporary distress at the Prague German House and that he had sent the photographs of his two children to London to the office of the queen and to an emigrants' organization, there broke forth from Mr. Kantner's mouth the words which were to the clerk similar to liqueur for good digestion after lunch or a rich dinner: "Good, good . . . correct . . . outstanding . . . aha . . . well, then, I see, see. . . . We keep getting closer to the Final Solution. . . . That we should do. . . . Yes, yes, yes . . ." and so on and so forth. He noticed that the man opposite him sat at the edge of the chair in the manner with which inexperienced girls, rather than adult men who are heads of families, would sit and that Emil Ludvig appeared to lean—perhaps out of respect, perhaps out of caution, maybe out of fear.

"You're feeling well, I hope?" Mr. Kantner asked.

"Thank you," Emil answered.

"Only sometimes do people feel like eagles, so high that the land disappears from sight," Mr. Kantner said.

He did not sound coaxing anymore, nor was there a cajoling tone to his voice as he'd had while still doing business for the Munich firm at the Ungelt.

Again, Emil Ludvig did not respond. He felt as though he were getting progressively smaller, rather like a mouse spotted by an eagle from the greatest height and descended upon, with both knowing how the encounter would end. He felt that if he had to be here for much longer he would change into a tiny grain of sand, mute forever in the stormiest sea (and not just for the words "Israel" and "Dirty Jew"). What Mr. Kantner had said to him was comprehensible, and he did not ponder any longer the modulations in his voice, the trebles and basses between which Mr. Kantner let his voice sail through like a fish, a bird, or a beast. For the first time, it occurred to Emil Ludvig that Mr. Ernst Kantner had never addressed him by name, perhaps as though he did not have a name anymore. Perhaps he did not want to use the added name Israel? That would be putting the best spin on the explanation, Emil admitted to himself.

"I read in your papers that you visited our German House at Christmas every once so often to present gifts. I did not know that you like singing so much and that you know how to sing in German although it is written here that you sing in Italian, too, along with dirty ditties every once in a while—I have a note here: *common songs.* What all and everything do people not notice? You wouldn't believe what people bring in here about their neighbors and friends. We are said to have gotten the tradition of the December tree from your people, although by now it's all forgotten pagan history. Still, instinct and experiences return us to many things in paganism—the holidays of the sun and light, harvests and crops, the holidays of dusk and darkness and stars, the moon and mainland and water and flowers. Your son attended a German kindergarten for a season? You refused to enroll him in the German first grade, I read. Did you want him to learn German? Your wife is from Moravia, from the border zone, born Loewy. I almost think it's a pity they did not grant your request in London and so did not invite your children to sojourn for a couple of years—though the air raids are unpleasant. After all, what can we expect from the aristocracy, am I not right? They would learn English; that cannot hurt. . . . Here is your yearly income deficit for the past five years. The war has not impoverished you—on the contrary,

I see. I like to follow such a curve as yours; it went up a great deal. Here, one of your female relatives is written to have spent several years in an Italian monastery. An interesting family. Are the pictures of your children the same as the ones you sent to England?"

"Yes," Emil Ludvig blushed.

"Sometimes it is difficult to explain things with words," Mr. Kantner said. "They don't look shy; I have no doubts they will endure the trip."

He let Emil Ludvig remain silent. "You know how it is. We believe that some countries are good, some are worse."

Emil Ludvig did not understand right away. He felt guilty about everything he had ever done or undertaken without Mr. Kantner actually accusing him. It occurred to him: They take what they want. They stop at nothing. They are only concerned with getting power from everything and over everyone. Certainly, there was a degree of avarice about it, but after all, wasn't there a limit to everything?

"Many people share language, culture, history, and religion with us, though not within the same boundaries or with the same interests," Mr. Kantner said. "You should be grateful to us for destroying the prison of nations. We are canceling unfair boundaries. We are uniting what once seemed to be at odds. We are returning law and rule where inequity and anarchy reigned. Do we not have long arms? We can reach far behind the boundaries. Even ruin and destruction is a triumph for some countries, considering they have been struggling for hundreds of years. There's no point in kidding ourselves, the old world is dying. We are beginning with Europe. It reminds me of the song the German army sings: 'Today Germany belongs to us, and tomorrow, the whole world.' The world should be grateful to us. We have defeated the Balkanization of Europe. Where would Europe be without us? What was independence for most of the little countries that we unified? They were afraid of war. They only printed more money. They acted weak, as if they had grown together like Siamese twins."

Suddenly, he paused. He realized what time it was. Time had passed quickly; he was glad to have it over with. Noise and voices from next door filtered through the room.

Emil Ludvig had the feeling he'd had many times before: that not only did the world around him humiliate him but something inside him did it as well—as if he'd somehow caused it. He didn't know how he'd caused it because, subconsciously or not, he had done nothing of which he could accuse himself. Besides, was there anything here he should feel guilty about? It was impossible to understand. It was intangible. It existed like a seed from which a poisonous flower grew—like an egg which hatched an embryo.

He was not the only one who had neglected his own protection. He was not the only one who had not defended himself in time either; he could recall in his mind countries—both great and small—that had not protected themselves. How many countries had already let themselves be brought to their knees by the Germans, and how many would there still be? How many people? Yes, down on one's knees a person feels deeply humiliated. How to get out of it? How to straighten up again? It was beyond guilt and guiltlessness—for the moment. He could hear his own words ringing in his ears again: *Israel* and *Dirty Jew.* From the corner of his eye he caught sight of the slightly open door. Had he caught a glimpse of a shadow? Had he sensed a noiseless rush of air? Terror oozed from that door. Why? All he could do was hazard a guess: he didn't really know why.

"Your people are more sensitive sometimes than a jilted lover," Mr. Kantner said. "They immediately see a catastrophe in everything. Perhaps it's residue from the past when they would repeat to one another everything that had gone badly. There's no sense in caving in to panic after the smallest of directives—that wouldn't get anyone ahead. You won't be setting off by yourselves on that longest of journeys: one group travels while another prepares for the journey. You have no idea of the amount of people involved behind the scenes. With the endurance of bees, they do everything possible so that you can set off; planners, architects, psychologists, and lawyers—not to mention the strategists. We should be giving them respect and thanks instead of overlooking them."

He must mean himself, Emil Ludvig thought.

Mr. Kantner's voice had the tone of an informal acquaintance, nearly a friend, but there was an evil eye inside him, just as there was in his expression. Emil thought about Saint Tib's Eve at the German House when they'd served sponge cake and hot chocolate and the children had sung *"Stille Nacht."* He'd gone there to boast to Arthur about everything he was still able to do, as when they had been boys.

Anna had been nearly tormented by it. Some things are the last we need, of course, dear Anna. Had someone always been watching them? If so, then they must have also peered into their bedrooms while they made their children. Had they looked into the kitchen, under the lids into the pots? He felt like a fly under a microscope when its wings or legs had been torn off—when they stabbed at its eyes. Wasn't it impossible, after all, to have each and every person watched? They could not have had that many people, or could they? His thoughts followed through, after a long time, to a picture of a German captain in Poland: how they'd shot the Russian captives holding a white flag.

Mr. Kantner, it seemed, did not wait for any answer or for anything else. Suddenly, he smiled, perhaps to encourage Emil Ludvig.

"I shall register you preferentially, then," he added. "Revealing to you more than I should, it is very late for registration, but I can do something about that. Many people were here before you, more desirable in regard to property, for the higher authorities. It pays to have money in all times, as your countrymen say. But as I repeat, something can still be done for you. I hope I will read your records as positive entries next time. I know that you would like to know the deadline—until when, and so on. Unfortunately, I am unable to inform you of that. We must wait and see. Why, in fact, didn't you make application for Shanghai earlier?" Then he added contemplatively, "Even if I am able to advance you as if you'd come in this morning, or yesterday, or at the beginning of the week, it is not certain that you will receive your emigration passport. I would be lying to you if I said differently. In any case, I must request the appropriate amount from you, signatures in all frames of the questionnaire. As I see from the savings books, there is just enough for you to deposit the required amount. That is good and bad, but not the worst. Can I write in here, then, that you agree and will give me your signature?"

"Gladly," Emil Ludvig lied; he tried hard to make it sound convincing and respectful. "Yes," he added. "Certainly."

"Your 'yes' is sufficient," Mr. Kantner said. "For me, everything concise suffices."

Emil thought of Anna for a second time; all her predictions were coming true. Once again, they would be back where they started. He shuddered with the thought (who knew why?) of the room next door.

Could it possibly have been a torture room? The Final Solution? As long as a person was alive, Anna might say, no solution was final. He looked at Mr. Kantner.

"I'm afraid that you will remain without savings," Mr. Kantner said, "but I hope that it will be that way for only a short while. You have an emergency reserve which will provide you with relief?"

"Not really," Emil Ludvig answered.

"Who does not have something in their emergency reserve?" Mr. Kantner smiled. "I can tell from your papers that you are not a bad sort of fellow—a person's nature can help him just like it can harm him—it all depends on the circumstances."

That Mr. Kantner could get all of that out in one breath confused Emil a little bit once again.

"At the end will come every success. War does cause some small inconveniences. What are they in comparison to the effort of our Deutsche Reichbahn, which has to secure the routes of thousands of trains every day to get people like you to the point of their final destination?"

"This is all we have," Emil Ludvig repeated.

"Hopefully you will overcome that quickly."

"Yes."

"There is vitality in you. You're in good condition."

"Thank you."

"By the way, people who go to our camps near our borders here or in the East have no cause to worry. They will get an opportunity to earn satisfaction through hard work."

"You know," Mr. Kantner added, "a lot of your people are drawing dangerous conclusions about our entire movement and nation based on a small group of extremists who are only a fleeting phenomenon. The people who journey into our camps in the East have no reason to fear. They get a chance to work. They earn their eventual reward with hard work."

At that moment, Emil remembered the toothless man, Joachym Luxemburg. They filled out the emigration file, each frame, every question, added to the answers consent or denial to the appropriate questions so "the file could be passed on higher," as Mr. Kantner put it. They went through an entire tangle of regulations issued by the German secret police, the Central Office for Registration of Jewish

Inhabitants, the Reich's imperial government, individual ministries, the Reich Protector, the governor, and other authorities. Mr. Kantner went across the individual frames, items, and sections with his blue eyes in which lay sympathy or the lack of sympathy, interest, indifference, wonder, resignation. Did he do so much work with everyone? He may have been doing that same thing many times now, while it was the first time for Emil Ludvig and, he hoped, the last time.

"Do you see it is thorough? What one misses, the second makes an effort to come up with or pick up—the third one, infinitely. It is a sieve, a funnel, a ladle—as the terms can be applied to people. Many dogs, hare's death, as they say. I am glad I found you in good condition."

He ruffled through his papers and listened to the noise from next door.

"As I say," Mr. Ernst Kantner added, but then he didn't say precisely what he'd intended to say. "In some ways I can only praise your scheme. It cannot hurt to close one chapter and start another; to let go of the past and look into the future."

Emil Ludvig knew before they got to the column "sewing machine," which they'd now have to turn over, what the voyage to Shanghai meant: he was reduced to poverty, the same as Arthur Pick, Messrs. Neuman, Winternitz, and Tanzer. He felt uselessly proud of his courage to have come here and applied. He hadn't defended himself for what he wanted; he felt just as humiliated as he had felt on his way here. It wouldn't have been any different if someone else behind the table had yelled at him from start to finish—at least he would have saved himself from Mr. Kantner's discourses about German enlightenment and their "Final Solution."

"You can be content; I am also satisfied," Mr. Kantner said.

"Thank you," Emil Ludvig said.

"My pleasure," Mr. Kantner answered. "As you know, I love to be correct."

Emil Ludvig waited instruction according to the information of Hans Joseph, the Jewish aide who continued barking orders persistently in the corridor (perhaps from the impatience of the people who had had to wait that much longer because of the time Mr. Kantner used up with him as a result of their acquaintance). How would Mr. Ernst Kantner indicate to him that he was allowed to get up? His legs were going stiff from sitting at the very edge of the chair; he did not dare do anything. Just for a moment, it seemed as if he looked at Emil as if he was a unique sort of dying man—as though he was someone who was still alive but not really living anymore, or did not have long—kind of as though he was an interesting but nearly useless animal. Or not?

Two pairs of eyes, virtually the same, looked at each other. Their eyes, behind the lenses of two pairs of glasses, mirrored everybody's thoughts.

All at once, a German voice came through from the room next door. "Now, just once," the voice said, "say, 'My father is a pig' . . . then, maybe you'll get authorization." The silence lasted only a second: "My father is a pig," said another voice (it was obvious that the person had a speech impediment). "My mother is a pig"; then the person repeated it. The sound of a stamp could be heard.

"We saved ourselves from that," Mr. Kantner said, visibly shaken. He'd heard the voices from the room next door, same as Emil. His chest with the iron cross on the scarlet and the white badge on the wide, red lapel heaved. He had probably caught his breath and then had to exhale hard.

"So we have met again," Mr. Kantner said and got up without having told Emil Ludvig to stand. "I'm sorry that we weren't able to lead a more pleasant debate, or one about more pleasant matters, at least. Dealing with you has always been pleasant. That has not changed. One cannot claim that you would belong to the ugly type of business entrepreneurs the newspapers and readers' letters have been writing about. I have not even asked about what undertaking you followed after our firm had no more . . . you know what I want to say, don't you?" and his gaze, fixed inward, at the same time asked, "What is the worth of a member of a race which nobody, or just a few people, care about, either here or abroad? As long as people can serve as hostages, without knowing about it, how long does their domestic or international value hold? What will be with them when they become worthless?" And then, when he caught the blue-eyed glance behind the virtually identical glasses, Mr. Kantner found pleasure in his own words for the last time, perhaps so that Emil Ludvig would take them all the way to the Final Solution.

It involved discovering that he had to speak like an inspector for war in a civilian sector, not like a businessman. As in the previous times, they were surrounded by plenty of papers, although different ones than the supply slips, orders, purchase authorizations, and the like. Even so, it had been mainly business. Something for something. Not only goods for goods or goods for money—a new country for an old country, the old known risks for unknown ones. Maybe. Certainly, the negotiations would have taken a different course if they had not met as old acquaintances. Mr. Kantner did not miss out on noting that both were imperceptible cogs in an immense machine of war. Under the circumstances of people serving as fuel, it made no sense to rack one's brain with metaphysics. It is in both sides' interest to come out and welcome the Final Solution; Emil should believe him in that, at least. He also added that he was glad Emil spoke German so well. Many people from his circles reported to the German cultural circuit. It did not make sense to whine and weep for the past either; we do not stand above ruins, like Jeremiah. A war is not a light matter, when Germany has against itself the greatest barbarians since the fall of Rome.

It was half past twelve, the end of the office hours. Mr. Ernst Kantner did not mention Shanghai anymore. He glanced out of the window, remarked dreamily that it was raining, but not too badly—did Emil have an umbrella? In the distance, clearer sky had already broken through the clouds and was extending itself.

"You can exit through the entrance through which you came," Mr. Kantner said finally. "Make it clear that no one is to enter anymore, will you please?"

"Thank you. Yes, I shall." Emil Ludvig got up.

Ernst Kantner's blue eyes smiled behind the gold rims of his glasses. Emil Ludvig sensed that he was forever altered from how he'd been when he'd come here. Bravery changed a person, just like humiliation did. But the same could be applied to Mr. Kantner: he had completely changed from what he'd been like when Emil knew and remembered him from before. He seemed content. His fair hair had thinned out a bit since his previous stay in Prague. He followed the other pair of blue eyes, retreating because Emil backed away and did not want to turn his back to Mr. Kantner. He backed off with a moderate bow. Mr. Ernst Kantner was the Gestapo. Many things could still happen. Wasn't it terrible what the person in the next room had

had to say about his mother and father, that they were pigs, just to get an authorization to leave the country? It was one step more degrading than what he'd had to say in the words "Israel" and "Dirty Jew." What would a person stop at for the chance to exchange an impossibility for a possibility, hopelessness for hope, shame and self-humiliation for dignity? Was that the last thing? Could it go even further, even lower—closer to what Mr. Kantner had kept calling "the Final Solution"?

Mr. Kantner took the chair that Emil had been sitting on and carried it into the next room. He put it in a corner and closed the door. The shadow cast by the chair disappeared. Emil then saw how the movement of the shadow edged backward. When someone told him something about a lion's den, he would tell them about this. Or maybe he would tell them nothing. He sensed his shame and what would no longer be different; what would never fade away in time and would never heal either. It was a shame that perhaps he could continue to live with, with difficulty, as though it were an incurable illness.

The entrance to the villa was guarded by two different Waffen SS men than before. Emil Ludvig took off his hat and then held it in his hands until he passed the slope by the gas sphere. *Israel. Dirty Jew. My mother is a pig. My father is a swine. Thank you for the stamp — for the German Durchlasschein. . . .*

Permission to go? No—just the application. A Final Solution? They were strange words. He prepared for the manner in which he would announce at home who had been his registration official in Stresovice at the Aryanized Jewish villa with a Jewish aide. He would tell them only that he paid for it with their entire property, to the last nickel. So, everything that he had made from the Germans, they'd taken back again. It seemed a little bit to him like shadowboxing— a strange kind of gymnastics. I own only what I have on my back, he thought. He caught himself, as many times before, praying that nothing bad would come of what he had done. At the same time he felt old. He saw himself in the shop display windows. His early morning elegance suddenly seemed shabby, wrinkled. What had happened that morning was now the past. Everything happens only once, doesn't it? Everything changes so much that it doesn't change at all. In reality, he was still elegant. Only his face was frowning, his forehead. He had gotten old but he'd aged backward in time, not forward. He returned to where his ancestors had once been before they became scattered all over the earth. What was a person supposed to do if everything that was better became worse, and what had been merely bad became the very worst—if every day, life's darker side revealed itself to him?

From Helena's notes:

Papa acts like in the final analysis, there'll be nothing worse ahead for us than having to move. The Germans have promised that families won't be torn apart, so we shouldn't worry. If Papa does, he doesn't let it show. He thinks that a father's duty is to keep the family together — to be the pillar everyone leans on. None of us want to spoil his pleasure. We indulge him in the illusion that he's the strongest and there's nothing to fear as long as we're together. Then I looked at him and saw something I'd never seen before: he'd shrunk. All at once, he didn't seem as tough, or as firm, with his head up straight as a ruler, like when the tailor was showing a suit on him to his assistants, how to walk right in a new coat. His head was bent, his eyes bleary. I went to the window and pretended I was interested in what was going on in the street.

I dreamed about my father, who had been assigned by the Jewish Community to build a garrison for the Waffen SS with a group of masons. He had been going there for a whole month when one of the Wehrmacht soldiers, assigned to guard duty so that the Waffen SS can pursue other tasks, pulls him off and makes him take care of rabbits. In my dream my father is building a palace from whose terrace you can overlook the whole world. I hadn't known my father was such a magician.

6

It's going to rain again," the guard, Thornten Godemke, said.
Emil Ludvig looked at the sky without answering.

The rabbits that Emil cared for looked at him with their pink eyes from behind the grating of their cages. He now worked at the construction site of the Smichov barracks for the Waffen SS; eventually he'd been put in charge of the rabbits.

Thornten Godemke surveyed the training field, the meadow, the sky, and the rabbits. The males urinated on the females before engaging in sexual intercourse. Godemke watched them for quite a while. Somewhere, a long time ago, he'd read that the smell is supposed to bond them.

"What kind are they?" he asked.

"An Angoran breed," Emil Ludvig answered.

"Angoran?" Godemke repeated after Emil; he probably neither wanted nor expected a response. "You know who eats them, don't you?"

"No," Emil replied cautiously.

"There's always someone who enjoys eating that kind—are you thinking who?"

"I'd rather not," Emil said.

"Why?"

"If I may be allowed to say, my wife played with chickens when she was a child and never could eat them later on."

"That's not what I was thinking," the guard stated. "Is your wife from the country?"

"She's from Moravska Trebova," Emil Ludvig answered.

"What breed, or race, let us say, were the chickens?" barked the guard, more to himself than at the rabbit feeder.

The Waffen SS flag with two black thunderbolts outlined in silver fluttered from the pole on the training ground; it flapped in the wind, heavy with rain. Waving on poles in front of the headquarters were three black flags lined in black and white on three edges with a black, crooked cross in the middle of a light silver circle. The tracks were close; a train could be heard rumbling nearby.

"These are going to the SS kitchen," Thornten Godemke remarked when the train had passed. He probably didn't know for certain what unit it belonged to—he'd come to guard the construction for the Waffen SS because the headquarters had its own building with its own people patrolling the training area—presumably so that it wouldn't vanish into thin air—who knew? To the devil with it! He was here, and he was on guard duty. Prague headquarters had its own singular objectives and ways of doing things. It wasn't any of his business: It was, and it wasn't, he thought to himself.

"Angoran, you say?" Godemke repeated. "But a Jew is feeding and taking care of them. That doesn't figure, like one plus one, to me."

It occurred to him that to some extent they were Jewish rabbits if Emil Ludvig, with his yellow star sewn onto his chest, was looking after them. Then he said, "I would like to believe that rabbits are only rabbits, as they were in the beginning and will be again at the end of time."

He didn't say what he envisioned in the in-between or here and now. He tore off a switch from a bush next to the cages and waved it in the air at them so that it whistled. It was a good switch: supple and strong enough to give off a clear sound. He whipped the air with it a couple of times.

"How do you come to speak German so well?" he asked.

"I went to a few German schools," Emil Ludvig replied.

"Did a lot of people speak German here before the war too?"

"It's always been the second language."

Thornten Godemke sliced through the air a few more times. "Well, well," he said, "now it's the first, if I'm not mistaken."

Some parts of the construction were called the "Jewish Wall." No one was allowed to work on a German construction without supervision; each labor unit was guarded by a soldier. Some soldiers belonged to the Wehrmacht rather than to the units of the SS; Emil Ludvig and the rabbits were guarded by Thornten Godemke, a Wehrmacht infantryman from the town of Spyer.

"Shit," Godemke said suddenly.

Emil Ludvig didn't even respond to that.

The unfinished building now rose to a height of seven meters. They had called about three times as many Jewish bricklayers to the project as they could use; there were many on-the-job injuries, and the chief liked having substitutes on hand to put in two or three new workers for each one missing. The skies were cloudy and threatening rain. The autumn had been a wet one; the earth was already soaked and had become mushy. It exuded the stench of grass mixed with slime permeated with animal smells—a warm odor, calling to mind life, mud, and carrion. The grass covered an expansive meadow and was even more lush than it had been in the summer or the beginning of fall. It glistened. The combination of smells irritated the guard's nose. The layered clouds neared the fenced-in ground and cages covered by a wooden awning. There was an aloofness about Godemke, the guard, that was the eerie opposite of a scream.

The guard gazed at the fence and then across it at the buildings farther away as if they were unclear, unexplained spots. There was something in him, as with all prison guards, that evoked suspicion and calmness. He stood as if leaning on something invisible. He followed the sky—the large glittering openings between the layers of clouds. At the same time, his eyes held something lost, an unarticulated or unexplainable image. He looked at Emil Ludvig as if he was trying to tell whether he really came from planet Earth or had flown here from Mars in the form of stardust and had acquired human form only once he was here below, among earthlings, though it was not internal—only external and a sham—equipped with a spirit set out by German military doctrine the Nazi inspector had trained the guards to exhibit in their duties. Even if this man, Emil Ludvig, didn't appear as an angel in Thornten Godemke's eyes, it was hard for him to believe that he could be the devil: he was too small for his pants, his jacket, and his shirt at the collar and wrists because in the last few months he had obviously lost weight. For a little while, it seemed from the expression in the guard's eyes as if he might be testing whether or not he was a part of a dream himself, and the field, the cages, and the buildings beyond the fence were also part of some live dream or reality. He had to wipe his nose; that presumably made him look like he was concentrating more. He missed the opportunity to talk with someone—to chat a bit—if for nothing more than that it makes a fellow feel like he isn't on some deserted border watch all alone, even if he's in the presence of other people. Thornten Godemke perceived the enormous silence of the world; the harder he thought about it, the less he understood it. From morning to night he kept order, but he comprehended the confusion swarming below the surface; he could imagine a world of worms and insects under the thin layer of grass and mud which wouldn't harden until winter (but by then, he hoped he wouldn't be here). He understood the order and disorder to be one of the world's incomprehensible faces. The army decided most aspects of things for him, perhaps inborn or impressed into every German soldier, so that he would have duty, obedience, and discipline in his veins the way others had music in their blood. That helped him untangle things a little, but it also left a lot of room for doubt. Secretly to himself, without telling anyone else, he sensed an unknown anxiety that perhaps one is born with and that terrified him. Where did he get it from? What did it mean? They had conquered Prague, Bohemia, and the surrounding lands—why didn't he feel all the safer for it?

Godemke wiped his nose and predicted to himself when the heavens would start pouring. He followed his charge, the feeder of the rabbits, the Jew, Emil Ludvig. Even if he couldn't discern Jewish features on the man, the star of yellow work cloth lined in black identified him as a Jew.

"It's almost raining already," he remarked. At the same time, it occurred to him that even though it wasn't raining yet, the rabbit feeder would still have to go along with it: if a German says it's raining, a Jew cannot do anything else but agree.

Emil Ludvig hadn't responded this time either.

Over at the cages, Emil Ludvig was thinking about Arthur Pick. When he had to stay with the rabbits late into the night, he imagined Arthur's theory about the wonderful light that reflected from the eyes of wild animals. The rabbits reflected electrified lights in their eyes at night too. If he looked at the rabbits from a distance when he was bringing them grass, their eyes were green. As soon as he got close up, their eyes were red. Even far away their enormous leaps told him that the animals he was looking at were rabbits. They didn't have tigers' orange eyes or, camouflaged as leaves of the same color, the green eyes of a squirrel preparing to capture a butterfly. The rabbit was a domesticated animal; Emil Ludvig wished that the world was more like rabbits than like ocelots, tigers, or crocodiles. There was no fierceness or defiance or inflexibility in them like that of the men he heard from the training ground of the young SS men, out for their nightly exercises.

He sensed Godemke was thinking about something that was far from him, like the giant from the flatlands before the Flood, lacking judgment, the gift of reason, maybe even the gift of fear. Emil Ludvig had not understood Germans for some time now. He had quickly become reluctant to consider them as equal to himself or, to the contrary, himself as equal to them. As Helena had learned, it made no sense to appeal to something that someone already knew about another person. It embarrassed him whenever he thought of it, and he didn't intend to test the guard in order to possibly disprove it. The more carefully he measured Germans by his own values (where good was just good and bad was just bad and there was nothing in between, because a person would lose his spiritual footing by what was in between), the less he understood them. The guard's silence didn't bother him; perhaps just the opposite. Wound throughout his thoughts on Germany and Nazism, he felt the rabble and the rot hidden by the uproar and the gloss, the propaganda, and the abuse of the gift of speech and truth which had been transformed into lies. Unlike Joachym Luxemburg, the Jewish emigrant from Germany (about whom he thought more and more—he probably wasn't the only one in the family who did either), he still hadn't made an adjustment to it. All of them continued to bide their time because there was nothing else left for them to do. He felt like an animal that wants to hibernate, but because he was a man, he couldn't know what the spring would bring. It didn't matter to him, except for how it might be disagreeable, whether it rained or didn't rain. The barracks radiated order to him, as they did to the guard, but he sensed the German in everything—the rot of death—without being able to express it inside other than by boundless contempt. He had learned to pretend. Everyone had learned to close their eyes, to lie their heads off, and to fake it, otherwise they likely wouldn't be able to bear their lots. Feeding and caring for the rabbits was far from being the worst fate he could face: he might end up in the quarries, the brickworks, or at the cemetery—neither was it the worst to have a guard who stared at the moon or who looked like he might fall asleep while awake and stay awake when he slept standing up, leaning on his German rifle. In the meantime, there was an ocean between them—except that Emil Ludvig already knew how even a negligible trifle could have far-reaching consequences for a person working for Germans. He thought about how Helena had learned in school about mankind in the Ice Age, the Stone Age, and the Bronze Age and about how man had evolved from the apes.

He stood a bit to the side of the concrete mixers and the mountains of red bricks, sacks of cement, and building timber. Beyond the construction site, a meadow spread out until streets and old work buildings close to the railroad car and a motorcycle factory reappeared. Emil Ludvig had found a source of grass in the meadow. He didn't complain that the wet grass cut his hands like sharp scissors and that his palms and the back of his hands were covered with gashes; he carried salve in his pocket. He didn't want to look like the incompetent Jewish workers handing one another bricks on the construction, saying, "Thank you doctor sir, thank you doctor sir." He had attained the position of rabbit feeder by chance, without any connections looking out for him: the clerk at the Jewish Community had granted the position to him. He often thought how his destiny was sure to be acquiring more Jewish traits daily and resisted allowing his thoughts about himself to become in advance like a memory of the dead. As long as a person lived on hope, who knew what might happen? Some kind of resolution (along with catastrophes for Germany) was in the air. He did not cause too many worries for the soldier who guarded him throughout the entire shift. They had an unexpressed agreement: their own private pact. At certain times, Emil Ludvig felt like a real-life illustration of the biblical coexistence of the lion and the lamb. He knew to the last drop of marrow in his bones which one of them was the lion and which the lamb—and he didn't try to reverse the order. He had also accepted that he could get to know Thornten Godemke. Did he want to? To tell the truth, not really. The soldier was glad that Emil Ludvig spoke good German. It decreased misunderstandings. As far as order was concerned, Emil understood that not even the slightest excuse was acceptable, but there were sometimes exceptions, depending on Thornten Godemke's mood—he endeavored to lighten his workload by every possible means. Every now and then, he and Emil talked, presumably because it was unbearably boring for the guard, but only about those things a slave and a master or a lord and his servant could talk about when no one was around—mostly about the weather, signs of the stars and wishes arising from dreams, about trees and food, how sometimes one wished for old times and places, about teeth (when the guard had toothaches), about the milk, butter, baked goods, and bread that had been sold years ago in Prague and Berlin and Hamburg, about how not long ago there had been a wilderness where today's construction site now stood, and about how rapidly a seven-story building grew when, as the guard said, "everyone did his part."

Sometimes Thornten Godemke would tell Emil Ludvig about his father-in-law's house in Spyer that the most distant members of his family had helped build—brothers, brothers-in-law, and the oldest relatives—and so Emil found out about the guard's wife, his past, his likes, and finally his nature. Godemke had clung to his mother. In the evening he would watch the stars for a long time. The dew on the grass in the early morning fascinated him, and it had to have lifted his spirits because it caused something resembling a preoccupied smile in the corners of his mouth. When it came close to raining, Godemke would stand for a little while with his fists clenched and his head fixed on the clouds. Other times, when the sun was shining and the sky was a clear blue, he would put his palm on his chest, perhaps pleased by the beats of his own heart, and when the wind blew in his face, he would crouch like a cat; at certain moments he looked like he was getting ready to jump or crawl on all fours. But most of the time he appeared reserved and insecure, like someone who doesn't know what the future holds for him a year, or maybe two, ahead, and the insecurity of everything that perturbed him, especially those things which made the most powerful impressions—perhaps like an ant not getting distressed by the size of a boulder. His face sometimes held the speculation of a person who knew there was an unpleasant surprise waiting for him somewhere, too, and didn't know how to stop it from coming. Most likely, he was happy for each day that he was wrong about that, and if ever he truly laughed at something, his smile still was as mischievous as a boy's. He was probably thirty years old, maybe thirty-five. From the shadows of his reserve, certain features, prejudices, or hobbies would emerge from time to time, because in front of Emil Ludvig he must have felt like a naked woman in front of a blind man. There was nothing to cause the heavens to fall down, no big discoveries or disclosures. There were only little ripples from him, the foam of some secret and mysterious ocean that had arrived at the shore already in its mildest form.

Godemke had a passion for interpreting dreams. He racked his brain about what influence the moon really had on people—what it did to them, how it changed their moods—when there was a full moon or a new one, and when the moon disappeared like it had never existed—what effects the far side of a full moon had. The stars, the sun, moon, stardust, and unknown rays from the stars certainly have an effect on people—or the storms on the sun written about in scientific magazines—the constellations of the stars, perhaps constellations of the galaxies and of entire universes, which only appear endless and chaotic to people but in their entirety are something that exceeds human perception and man's limited reason. He knew that they would probably never be known either. Godemke wondered whether folk medicine in the Dark and Middle Ages wasn't perhaps a better means of healing than modern medicine. His eyes were melancholy, blue, full of dark and light and unanswered questions and something that either had no words or could not be expressed. In certain instances his face, eyes, and mouth seemed gloomy or even simpleminded, or filled with resignation and silence that washes over a person as in a completely devastating flood or fire. There were no storms brewing in Thornten Godemke's spirit; it was obscured by invisible clouds and brightened, if not by the sun, by invisible stars.

He was familiar with how clocks worked. For extra money, he collected old timepieces the way some people collect stamps. He had already bought three antique clocks in Prague. Most of the time antiques went for a song here, including German cuckoo clocks—he'd already seen the astronomical clock on Old Town Square with the calendar, zodiac, the apostles, Death, and the rooster at least a hundred times. He knew the legend about the master clock maker, Hanus, whom the town officials had blinded so he couldn't re-create the same clock for other cities like Nuremberg or Dresden.

In time, Emil and the guard had gotten used to each other. The guard knew that the rabbits were doing well: they looked clean and they were gaining weight. They stared out with their impassive, evasive eyes, eating and reproducing ceaselessly. There was never any mess around the cages. Godemke also had realized early on that Emil Ludvig would never think of causing him trouble.

"If ants pile their hills up high, it's going to rain," Thornten Godemke said. "And if worms lie on top, the winter won't be bad." He had already been dreaming about the spring since the fall. He didn't like the winter. He had noticed that Emil Ludvig was cleanly dressed, even if his uniform looked funny on him; he'd never yet seen him either unshaved or dirty. In his mind, Emil got high marks for liking cleanliness the way he himself liked order.

Emil Ludvig waited until no one was around anywhere. Then he slipped the soldier a handbag made of alligator skin that he had once bought for Anna—*Aligator France.* It was intended as a bribe, but he could not say that directly. He neither was, nor could be, on such good terms with the soldier. Between everyone, including the two of them, there was a chasm and unanswered questions. In his soul, Emil Ludvig always trusted that in the end, things would turn out better than they might. He viewed hope as does a tightrope walker who toils away on the high wire and as an invisible net which, at the same time, would catch him if he stumbled, upset the rope, and fell, so that it wouldn't mean the ultimate—death—something from which there was no return. Emil Ludvig often thought about hope: hope, fortune, and bad luck were terms that people couldn't help thinking about in such times as they were living in now. Hope was something that united people as if they were all children of the same mother. Besides that, Emil Ludvig trusted that he had gotten to know people, at the very least from the time that he had served on the Austrian side in the First War, in the most substantial way—whether they were good for him or not. With Thornten Godemke, it was more complicated and dangerous because Godemke was a guard and a German and Emil was only a rabbit feeder with a yellow Jewish star on his chest. When Emil wanted something from the soldier, he had the feeling that they became joined and separated at the same time. The apathy in Godemke's eyes confused him. He didn't want to lightly take it for goodness. He knew that he was searching for a German in the nature of the German guard, maybe for something that he needed instead of what was really there, or something he would much prefer besides what was actually part of Godemke's nature. He weighed it in his mind and knew that he was taking a risk. But he had thought about this exchange (it was an exchange, of course) for a long time and considered every movement a hundred times. He had also thought about what could happen if Godemke became insulted. Breathlessly, Emil Ludvig waited for what would now come. What would happen? He was afraid to look at Thornten Godemke's face.

"What am I supposed to do with this?" asked the guard. "Do you want to sell it to me?"

It was still a beautiful bag. Anna had not used it often—only on select occasions, like to Helena's dancing lessons or to synagogue— but even then rarely, so people wouldn't stare. In his mind Emil Ludvig again told himself that he would buy Anna a new one after the war if everything turned out well. What good are luxuries—pleasure and an eye toward the future—if you lack the necessities or if security and a sense of everything flowing no longer exists? By autumn's end in Germany, the protectorate, and the occupied territories, people like himself were forced to concentrate on making it through the winter like hamsters or bears. Not only was it impossible to tell how long the winter would be, it wasn't even definite they'd be remaining here. Emil no longer relished winter as he once had either.

Thornten Godemke was embarrassed; it took him a while before he took the bag in the hand that wasn't holding the rifle. He noticed immediately that it was a lovely piece of work; perhaps the nicest thing Emil Ludvig still possessed. The thought crossed Thornten Godemke's mind that these people had only been required to turn into live animals.

"Hmm . . ." the guard grumbled. He didn't expect an answer to his question whether Emil wanted to sell him the purse or not. He didn't have a wife or children, only a mother. Most probably, she'd only seen a bag like this one carried by other women, or perhaps in a display window.

A cold autumn wind blew. The recently constructed building

looked muddy, like after a rain. A large German truck brought in more new bricks, beams, and window frames. A crowd of Jewish workers gathered at the freight truck. The construction would be ending soon. A couple more carloads and then it would be time to start worrying about where the Germans would or wouldn't be sending them. The workers could've killed themselves with their eagerness: no one was a slacker. Everyone wanted to look good under the eye of guards and the SS construction chiefs.

"Tomorrow, they're going to bring the doors; then they'll do the floors, fix the bathrooms, kitchens, and guard room," Godemke added.

The wooden sheds were crammed with cement. Military construction had preference over everything, and in military construction, the Waffen SS building had first priority.

The rabbits' area was an extension of the fence. The wind didn't blow in there so much. In three months Emil Ludvig had got used to it, just as Thornten Godemke had gotten used to him. Rabbits were born and matured. The soldier saw that in Emil's Jewish hands they prospered as well as if they'd been in German ones—and neither one of them knew what was going to happen after the barracks were finished.

"I thought this might come in handy for you—to give to someone as a gift," Emil Ludvig said. "It's genuine crocodile. French skins—the *Aligator France.* The French have got access to raw materials in Africa, Indochina, and somewhere on the islands of Central America. It's real leather, almost new—a superb piece of work. I know about that stuff a little—I used to work in the field."

"When?"

"First I worked in textiles, then in leather—when we used to be allowed to work for the public."

"And what do you want? You're going to want something. That much I know for sure," said the guard.

He glanced behind his shoulder. No one was around to see them. Anyone who didn't absolutely have to be outside in this weather had abandoned the site for the sheds and trailers of the construction managers. The bricks, fixtures, and window frames had already been stacked and carried away.

"Listen," Godemke added. "Do you seriously believe that a rabbit would breed with a rat? Your books—like the Talmud—say that.

That's got to mean a domestic rabbit—but you were thinking of a wild rabbit, huh? It's forbidden for you to eat rabbits, while for me, baked rabbit or rabbit in cream is a Sunday meal—even without cream. No one has explained why this started the war to me yet. My mother probably wouldn't believe that anyone would refuse to eat rabbit meat. I also heard that you measure the months and years according to the lunar calendar. According to you Jews, God was supposed to have created the heavens with his right hand but the world with his left. But back to those rabbits—you Jews meant the wild rabbit, right?"

"Yeah, a wild rabbit," Emil Ludvig answered.

"So talk."

"I'd like to come back at noon."

He had finally gotten it out: he glimpsed the same thought in Thornten Godemke's eyes. The soldier had a rough voice and even, gray eyes. They filled with their own sort of relief. Godemke had once been a pewter craftsman but hadn't practiced his trade for a long time; he'd learned a new one, soldiering. Serving in Prague wasn't the worst post. Here, he was out of harm's way. Some officers claimed that Prague was an old German city: it certainly had been a nice one, with a good outlook on life too. Maybe it wouldn't even be good if every city, country, and continent was only German. Where would it end? Too much of anything is bad, he thought, but no one who valued his own hide would say that out loud. Still, sometimes it almost already looked that way—that the world maybe wasn't, but would be, German from the center to every corner. The city had definitely been built by German builders and according to the designs of German architects even if the bricklayers and stonecutters had been local. Czechs had long supplied the Germans with labor like Italians had stone. Old Europe had always been largely German, but never as much as now.

"I need a couple of hours," Emil Ludvig said. "For my family."

The animals could be heard running around in the small space of their cages, their little paws and backs beating against the thin wood, covered with straw and leftover hay.

Godemke hid the bag between two piles of planks. He did it carefully so that he would not scratch the leather. That means he liked the handbag—he could tell it was quality, Emil thought. Now he waited for the guard to give or not give his consent. The Germans definitely shot day and night everything and anyone—even their own people—who did anything against their orders.

Emil's eyes were red from lack of sleep. He had stopped expecting clearance for their trip to Shanghai; he had also never caught up with Mr. Kantner at the Stresovice villa in the Jewish emigration office in Prague; he hadn't even gone (it would be unthinkable without an order number that had to be requested at the Jewish religious center on Maislova Street). He'd made just a single visit, and in the final analysis, Emil was just as glad not to have to deal with the Gestapo a second time. He had been quite lucky with Mr. Kantner (except that now they found themselves completely broke). If he hadn't taken a job doing masonry, he would have had to go begging. A lot of families had found themselves on the street. They got evicted from their apartments, which were then given to German clerks. Being out of work had always been, was, and would be the worst thing that could happen to a man. It made one feel useless and unneeded to oneself and to others, not only today and tomorrow but also for the entire time one had still been working. Being unemployed caused people to suffer and even to hang themselves. Three reports of suicide by people who had lost their jobs and been thrown out of their apartments had come to the Jewish Community Center yesterday. These families had to go on charity from the Jewish Community, which placed them temporarily in the synagogues before kicking them out again because the space was needed for horses, or to store furniture, books, or carpets. Emil Ludvig wasn't alone. How a person holds himself together when he finds himself broke depends on his nature, doubly so. Arthur Pick hadn't taken it so well; to him, it was like a tunnel drilled from two sides or a candle burning at both ends. Still, they'd probably both made up their minds not to complain, most of all, to anyone else—and they refused to blame themselves for what they hadn't done, either, since they'd done everything possible not to have anything to regret and feel even more miserable about.

Over his work clothes, Emil Ludvig wore his old coat that had acquired a thin sheen from the war but at least was clean and not falling to pieces underneath. The wind added to Emil's blearyeyedness: he looked like he hadn't slept at all. His eyes teared from the wind. He was thinking about the three unknown people who had committed suicide.

Yesterday Anna had found out what had happened to Charlotte and Karel Munk. The prettiest of their four daughters, twenty-four-year-old Olga, had jumped into the air shaft and killed herself. She'd done it one hour after they received the summons for a transport. Olga had been a small, gentle girl with golden hair and green eyes. The people from the ground floor came to her father and said, "Mr. Director, your daughter has jumped down the air shaft." They didn't mean it unkindly. Many people have only one thing in life to get excited about—what happens to other people. They probably also thought that the longtime head of the Jachymova Street Jewish School might allow them to take his belongings before he left on the transport or before the people from the Jewish Community came to take them away. Would the Germans devour everything in the end? He went to fetch his daughter. He brought her back upstairs to their apartment, dead. In the meantime people took away what they could carry in their hands. After all, the family couldn't hold what she'd done against her: she hadn't known what was in store for her. For some people not knowing is worse than telling them. . . . Olga had been the cleverest of the four Munk girls.

It was a blow for Anna. She had considered all of the Munks to be exceptional people. They weren't only middle class but people with unpretentious dignity, humble and proud, with an unassuming kindness. They bore their humility as an honor or privilege. For Anna, the Munks—the entire family—were like a people that had, perhaps, come from far away but had settled here, learned the language of the people among whom they lived, and proved their usefulness. In her eyes, the Munks had crossed many rivers, mountains, and valleys to establish themselves where they were now. Their lives had seemed to her like answered prayers and wishes fulfilled. They weren't her closest relatives, but neither were they the most distant. They weren't overly delicate, nor were they crude. The head of the family, the patriarch, Uncle Munk, the director of the Jewish School in Jachymova Street on Old Town Square, was a figure that represented security for her. Looking at him inspired her: she held him up as an example to her children. Uncle Munk was both the flagpole and the flag for

Anna—the figurehead of the family—a man who, in her view, had at least come close to flawlessness in his life. His words and aims were thoughtful and, from a distance, affectionate and enviable. In comparison, it seemed to Anna that among many lackluster people, Uncle Munk was most like the sun and the moon—or truth and lies, justice and injustice. He was graced with virtues that no longer graced others and, as Anna had to admit, probably no longer could. Olga's death discredited all her beliefs down to the core. Her death, and the image of Uncle Munk carrying her lifeless body back upstairs, brought sundown to Anna, the reign of night and dark, of a desolate cry, a lament, a bleakness engulfing everything and everyone. It was a still-moist wound, festering and unhealable. It left her frightened, horrified, transformed, like a piece of bread turned to stone; she ran to hide herself in her work, sewing several hours longer each day and into the night.

"Have they already been fed?" Godemke asked.

The soldier's voice also held the desire to end their conversation before someone caught them.

"As always, yes, Mr. Godemke," answered Emil.

"Master Sergeant" was always on the tip of his tongue, like how they used to address him in the army—"Sergeant, here, Master Sergeant, there"—except that Thornten Godemke wasn't a master sergeant. Who knew what kind of military ambitions he had? (In spite of their order and duty, sometimes the German soldiers seemed to Emil like wild men who emerged from ancient forests to transform the rest of the world into a jungle according to their designs.) He hadn't felt so guilty since he'd accepted work as a representative at Mr. Kantner's German firm. He'd done so in part because that was his business and he knew that a man had to work in order to have a clean conscience and in part because at a time when there was so little to choose from, he'd opted to work for a German firm rather than loaf around and fall into hunger and need.

"Why do you have to go?" Godemke asked.

"My sister is leaving with my brother-in-law and my niece."

"Where are they going?"

"To Lodz, they were told. They have built factories there and they want to cultivate the new territory—it's in what was formerly Poland—now it's called Litzmanstadt."

"Poland for the winter?" They'd better dress like they're going to the North Pole. I know it—I've been there," the soldier said. "Is your brother-in-law a farmer?"

"No. He used to sell wine and shoe polish. For a while, more recently, he built roads and cleaned snow at the Ruzyne Airport like I did."

"How old is your niece?" the former pewter worker asked. "Is she pretty?" He winked his right eye.

"She's twenty and she is very pretty."

"Black haired?"

"No, a brunette."

Thornten Godemke looked like a villager in uniform at work or on vacation in a foreign city. He was cold too. But it would have been worse in the East for him. He was still able to tell good from bad and better from worse. Like everyone else, he had no guarantee that they wouldn't send him to the eastern front to fill in the empty spaces constantly on the rise left by those who died or had been injured. Few soldiers had such a guarantee. It would be nice if they would send him to Italy—to Corsica or Sicily if not straight to the Italian Riviera, or to Greece—to somewhere warm, but not to Africa. When he thought of the German troops there—the Africa Corps—he often imagined the sand deserts like the Sahara and the jungles and ancient forests with people whom Germany had long tried to colonize and civilize according to its ideas. He couldn't imagine himself among headhunters or maybe cannibals. He only thought of the overpowering sun beating on their helmets twelve hours a day until soldiers went mad from it. He imagined avalanches and columns of dark-complexioned and black naked bodies. Rivers and swamps, satiated crocodiles, and snakes as thick as the trunks of cedar, olive, or pine trees. But how far was that from here—from his post as the Jewish rabbit feeder's guard? The image of his mother's mangy cat surfaced in some connection when he thought about Africa, but he admitted that it was an image from childish, unknown, and unsought regions, like certain places, streets, and lanes in Prague. It didn't conjure up any uplifting feelings—on the contrary, he thought to himself. A lot of what he had discovered in his military service had been simple imitations and fabrication, a uniformed life not blessed by luck but without massacres to have to bear witness to. Still, he certainly needed a lot of patience for everything. He sensed that what was fighting in his soul was an echo between false praise and repentance that no one had ever forced him to make. But why wouldn't he hope for some minor gain, which he hadn't even tried to have in the end? He even practiced his defense in his mind in case by chance someone in the future accused him of something. He could list the most respectable from all of his motives. Could he? He would have to.

Thornten Godemke sighed, swallowed the saliva in his mouth, and then collected whatever moisture there still was on his tongue and spat. He rubbed his hands together. He was particular about his fingernails even when wearing gloves. In the meantime he rested his rifle between his knees. He glanced across his shoulder again. Emil Ludvig was saying that he had attended a local German school.

"Have any of your relatives left already?" the soldier asked.

It seemed like he was asking questions just to keep the conversation going. But would something else follow that?

"My wife's relatives, Charlotte and Karel Munk. He is a former school principal. He had four daughters, three unmarried. One jumped into an air shaft."

"She killed herself?"

"She killed herself."

"It's all just a bunch of shit," the soldier said suddenly and spat again off to the side. "It's full of *scheisse*. I'll tell you something. If someone thinks that there's nothing more to be done, that everything has reached its end, then whatever he's got ahead of him doesn't make sense anymore either. But that is always his mistake. The biggest fault he can have is to think that he can't do anything more because everything is lost. By doing that he not only spoils things for himself, but for everyone and everything around him—that doesn't apply just to your niece jumping into the air shaft."

He recalled the harlots in the German cabaret before the war. Luckily he hadn't taken part in those dirty doings. What was it that holds people together throughout life which they suddenly relinquish as if their spirits had died inside? Shouldn't each person do everything that is in his or her earthly powers to do?

Something snapped in him. That always happened when he didn't understand something and then the more he racked his brains to get it, he ended up not understanding anything. He sensed how existence was without shame and could trouble a person until it came crashing down like an avalanche of rocks, dust, mud, and slime, rendering even the most powerful powerless. I haven't fixed myself on any big ideas, Thornten Godemke thought to himself. I don't have what it takes to rebel or to make peace—what?—with people like myself? There are all kinds of instincts in people, and it doesn't take much for cruelty to emerge out of nowhere in a person—even when the cruelty is to oneself. Then he said, "Some women think from the top down and from the bottom up. A person will do what he wants despite everything and no matter what the cost."

"There were three bulletins about people who killed themselves just yesterday," Emil said.

"Like I said," the soldier repeated. "Who did she help by doing that—herself? You?"

Emil Ludvig said nothing. It had surprised him that some of the German soldiers didn't like the life they'd never dreamed they'd be living—as masters of a foreign land with nearly all of Europe under their thumbs, having access to raw materials from the Atlantic Ocean all the way to the Urals. At the very least, there were some things about such a life they didn't like.

The soldier rubbed his hands. Earlier that morning they'd talked about fishing. Thornten Godemke hailed from the Spreva River and was fond of the sport. He knew the best fishing places and nooks of the river to catch eels, bream, and carp, but he wasn't able to fish much anymore because he had to care for his rifle instead of his rod and reel; he had to keep the barrel and chamber and everything else about it in order (he kept the barrel clean by sharpshooting, as did all the soldiers), but he still enjoyed talking about fishing. While he didn't have any other willing ears, he had to content himself with Emil Ludvig's Jewish ones. He wondered about how it was possible that even though this man didn't look very Jewish and was an outcast of mankind, he took such good care of the rabbits. He didn't seem like a demon or devil or stardust incarnated—neither did he have long ears like a dog or a nose like a rabbit or flat feet. The soldier didn't like hearing that someone had committed suicide: it profoundly aroused so much conflict and dismal disgust in him that he could not be sure whether it was only discord or aversion he felt. He didn't know why and he refused to scrutinize it in himself—that's just the way it was. A person probably had to accept violent death the same way he'd already accepted the war. But how could an all-out war declared by one country against another be equated with the war a person wages inside himself? Thornten Godemke collected fear within the shadowy regions of his soul as if in a maze where he'd been left to his own mercy. There was no brightness anywhere: defenses had been ruled out. He gazed at the grass, moist from dew and the first drops of rain. Though likely he had only a murky conception of the family whose father carried his daughter out of the air shaft, the thought washed over him like an unknown, black wave. He felt his own heart beating. What was fated and to whom? Was it some people's fate to end up like that? It would certainly be nicer to lie down on his cot and snooze away until after his shift, knowing that he wouldn't wake up until dawn—until five o'clock when his alarm rang. Why did he have to allow himself to have nightmares in advance just because someone killed herself? He imagined the leap into the air shaft. He turned his eyes away to look at the rabbits—his gaze went over the meadow and the fence. To voluntarily take one's own life was something that the guard, Thornten Godemke, could not accept.

There were some good things about talking with the guard for Emil Ludvig too. Through him, Emil had learned many secrets about fish: how much fat, iodine, calories, and protein fish could provide to people with heart or stomach ailments—Godemke often spoke about how healthy it was to eat fish. Once he had also declared that one advantage of fish was that they couldn't speak—but they were not deaf.

It occurred to Emil Ludvig that it went against the soldier's grain to decide something of his own free will—to shoulder the responsibility of letting him leave for a couple of hours. Was that why he'd rather not let him go? It would be distressing, but there wasn't anything he'd be able to do about that either. He would just have to accept that he wouldn't be able to see his sister—maybe forever. He'd already risked a lot with the handbag—that had already been made clear. He had learned to lose. He had come to have the feeling that nothing he possessed would be his again until Judgment Day—and anyway, the day would soon come when they wouldn't be his any longer—don't they say that a coffin has no pockets? It's not written anywhere that that's the way it is or has to be or that it isn't that way and shouldn't be. Simply put, that was the way it was for him too. A person loses a person—a brother, his sister, brother-in-law, and niece. That's how Olga had disappeared from Anna's life. The living turned into the dead. Like Thornten Godemke, Emil Ludvig began imagining the head of the family carrying the dead girl out of the air shaft.

The barracks building about five hundred meters from the rabbit hutch was already finished. Sometimes the shouted military orders wafted over in the wind. The very young men of the Waffen SS Voluntary Fen Division of Bohemia and Moravia drilled there. They'd shot one of their own men to death by accident while practicing with live ammunition. They'd dug a grave for him, leaving a low mound, three-quarters of a meter high, with his helmet hung on a hooked cross. They decorated the grave with fresh roses every day. Next to the cross they'd stuck the division's shield into the ground—a two-tailed lion with a double cross. Even from far away the orders sounded stern—like a whip cracking.

"A soldier in the rear gets bored," Thornten Godemke said. "Death seems far away from here—far from the heroic adventure which others have the good fortune to experience—as if each death wasn't final. Half the world is watching and waiting for us to fight ourselves to death until there's no blood left to be spilled on either side."

The soldier wasn't expecting a reply: he sounded as if he were talking just to himself.

"I once wanted to become a professional soldier," Emil said. Godemke's words had surprised him—but then again, not that much.

"Hasn't it crossed your mind that you never should have been born at all?" Godemke asked, half joking, half seriously. "One must do the thinking for animals since they don't know how to make themselves understood."

Godemke looked over his shoulder again; he took a pack of cigarettes out of his coat pocket and lit one up.

"They've been given the best grass," Emil said. Maybe since Godemke had already disobeyed one prohibition he'd be more likely to disobey a bigger one and let Emil Ludvig leave the rabbits for a couple of hours.

"Is the bag from the sister leaving for Lodz?"

"No, my wife, Anna, used to use it—but not very often," Emil answered.

"I can see that," Thornten Godemke acknowledged.

Emil looked tired. In truth, he hadn't lied about, diminished, or exaggerated anything.

The soldier threw the half-smoked cigarette to a relatively dry spot on the ground and glanced at Emil; he did that occasionally because he knew that Emil would pick it up. When he did, the guard asked: "How many cigarettes did you smoke a day?"

"I started with twenty and worked up to sixty."

"You damn near got smoke cured, didn't you?"

"I used to cough day and night—that's true—but I cough even when I'm not smoking."

"You see, you stopped smoking, which I can't say for myself. You only smoke now and again when you poach one—if yes, then yes. If no, then no. Soldiers are in the same situation as that with women—poachers. If yes, then yes. If no, then no way." He smiled with crooked but healthy teeth. He thought to himself that he and Emil could have been fellow countrymen ten years ago. They could have easily worked in the same factory, in the same city. They wouldn't have differed much—one a German, the other Czech, or first German, then a Jew or a Jewish Czech—but the party and the war had changed all that. The Germans had built a wall between races and people, nationality and religion, but had they separated the wheat from the chaff? Neither of them—neither he nor the keeper and caretaker of the rabbits—had grasped it yet. Jews were no longer allowed on the street (unless they were going to the synagogue—and then, only to the few that hadn't been made into stables or warehouses) or to go to the hospital. Before the war it had been different; he and Emil Ludvig had been equals before the war (Long before the war, he added to himself). By the time they understood, it would probably be too late. Hitler was right. There was something worse than democracy—that which came after it. And what they were saying in the army was that it would become yet another hundred—even thousand—times worse for people like the rabbit keeper until it couldn't get any worse—it wouldn't, they wouldn't, be. He wanted to say that madness was contagious, but he kept the thought to himself. These days, a fellow was afraid to tell even his own mother the truth. If Germany would only not flex its own muscle in the meantime—if it would only not stick out its own back and arms, Godemke thought. They had already been splattered by mud and jeopardized the future in the past. There was nothing to envy them for—*Aligator France.*

Thornten Godemke watched how enthusiastically Emil Ludvig smoked the cigarette, sheltering it in his hands and exhaling into his coat until not even the butt remained.

"You're like a flame swallower," Godemke said. "I believe you could live off tobacco."

Emil Ludvig didn't answer.

"Are you afraid?" Godemke asked.

"I am afraid," Emil admitted, and to himself he added, *There's no bliss or joy living in German Europe.* Aloud he said, "Either I'm afraid or I'm ashamed." He thought, as he often had before, about humility and the line between it and humiliation, about what erased the feeling of usefulness, the sense for beauty and the endurable, in life. That which wipes dignity out of life like dusk withdraws the light from the day before it is transformed into night—something that makes ugliness from beauty and turns truth into lies.

"We're all afraid or ashamed," Thornten Godemke said.

Emil felt uncomfortable. He had no doubt that Thornten Godemke meant it sincerely—he could tell from the way it was said, the expression he had on his face, and how it had sounded. It took a while before the expression faded. Thornten Godemke didn't have to say anything else. All at once, the tables had turned. Emil Ludvig didn't want to make it harder or more dangerous for the soldier. They both knew what they had to do. Germans shot even their own people, and not everybody got his own small monument with fresh roses on his grave every day.

"I've got only my conscience too," the guard said. "Even though they say your people's hellish invention was warping a person's soul the way you maim the body by circumcision. No one wants to get himself done away with, if you know what I mean." He shot a glance in the direction of the playground where the young SS officers were sweating.

"There's a war on," Emil said.

"And it's taking its time," Thornten Godemke added. "Who

knows how long it'll drag on? It's not the lightning crusade they promised."

"We are innocent," Emil stated.

"Innocent or not," the soldier said, "nobody admits to being innocent when they don't have to. You know how it is yourself. Someone's innocence is always another's guilt. Somebody's always got it worse."

"It wasn't always that way."

"No."

"You know yourself what Germany gained with this war—and what they'll probably still gain even if they actually lose."

Emil Ludvig decided to stay quiet.

"What do you mean by that?" the soldier asked. "The truth, now—you don't have to be afraid."

"Weapons can't break a man's soul," Emil replied after a while.

He thought about dignity, fire, and the days when suddenly he'd been happy for no reason—when the sun, or the whiteness of the clouds, or a voice, or a song had enchanted him—days when he could be carefree and it wasn't at anybody's expense. He thought about times when he'd understood that nothing in the world, including people, could be without fault or blemish because a certain amount of fortune and misfortune falls on every age—when just summing up things or being able to see ghosts and phantoms wasn't enough for anything. As if he were looking at the world through two different sets of glasses, he thought about the days when he felt happiness and life, which nothing could shake or ruin. What he'd said to the soldier was all he could say without sounding ridiculous or pompous.

Emil Ludvig looked at the barbed wire atop the watchtowers. At the bending trees, the spirals of the branches swayed in the wind. He was surprised at his own words. He'd felt this way when he'd been at the notary and the priest in his hometown. He hadn't been able to express it, but it had been inside him like oxygen is in the air, water flows in the rivers, and scent is in flowers, except that it was also like the stinger of a wasp—its defense, but that which also causes it to die when used to inflict force.

"If only it were your way," Godemke added. "I don't want to argue. If it were to take a month or even a year. But what if the war goes on for five, six years? You don't think so?" Then he added, "In the world today there are a lot of pitfalls, but that's not the primary danger." He didn't say anything else, but there were many questions in Thornten Godemke's eyes: What would happen tomorrow, the day after tomorrow, in a year? He probably had a better idea than Emil Ludvig did, and perhaps he wasn't referring only to Emil either. He wondered what his mother had already seen in her lifetime.

"What other choice do we have but to wait?" Emil asked. "Some things we knew were coming, but a lot of it we didn't expect. A lot of it was kept hidden from us—they slammed the door in our faces. It's almost better to put blinders on our eyes. Who today isn't afraid of what is yet to come?"

Emil realized that he'd never expected support from a German soldier, but he'd already been wrong about so many people, why not misjudge a German guard? It could be a trap or bait, and then again, maybe not. The worst thing was that the result would stay the same. It would be unpleasant not to see his sister—maybe ever—again. His eyes wandered off to the grass and mud. He thought about Arthur Pick, about his sister, Martha, about his niece, Susanna. He knew that his brother-in-law had opened his daughter's letters. Now it would not make her angry: they'd be together and she'd never write to anyone again.

"It means nothing else," Thornten Godemke said. "It doesn't depend on what they say to you—whether you'll go to the East or somewhere else. You're the only ones who are confused. The people upstairs know what they're doing—to where and to what war they're sending you. I realize that it's difficult not to let yourselves be terrified and jump into air shafts like your twenty-four-year-old niece did, but at the same time, maybe nothing had been prepared yet—they're still cooking up some stuff upstairs. They still haven't solved all their own problems—what isn't, can't be, and maybe someday will be, if you understand what I'm saying."

"I'm trying," Emil Ludvig said.

"Nobody's taking any actions alone. It's not better than what I've experienced in the past—and I've seen my friends become enemies, 'the king's killers' turned into innocents; and innocent people turned into death traders. They're selling gas for bombs. They're making ovens like pots for potatoes, like washtubs or fishnets. They can make ersatz—substitutions and imitations—out of anything. I don't want to even know what they're fertilizing fields with in Germany and in the occupied territories these days or what they're making soldiers' jackets out of. But that's high politics for you and me," he added in resignation. "I heard from your people about the fortress on the rocks in the old country where they began to realize that they had nowhere to go, surrounded up there in the rocks, outnumbered, sure to be defeated. They chose to commit suicide rather than hand themselves over to people who'd kill every last one of them. But I wouldn't have done that in your niece's place. I don't like that kind of thing. Are you a part of as many countries and peoples as it's said you are?"

"Some fellow countrymen don't know what to do," Emil Ludvig said. "Misfortune is in the air for everyone, no matter what anyone does."

"Maybe," Thornten Godemke replied, "and then again, maybe not. You ought to stick together."

"Who can defeat the entire world?" Emil Ludvig asked suddenly, as if he were interrogating himself. "That, for certain, can't be changed. How is it possible to starve people and chase them into an abandoned place without food, water, or clothing? That would even be a bit too much for today's world. And at the same time, none of us wants to ruin what he's trying to save at the same time." It came out a little confused and incomprehensible, but Thornten Godemke understood.

"All that remains in the long run is ashes," the soldier said. "Probably not even fire."

"I need to go now, Mr. Godemke," Emil Ludvig finally said.

"Are you sure the rabbits have what they need?" Godemke asked again. He was probably still hesitating. "We're talking like two lunatics."

"They've been fed." Emil Ludvig looked at the rabbits.

"All two hundred and fifty?"

"All two hundred and fifty," Emil replied.

"They can't speak and they're in our hands. Don't spend time any place you don't have to. You won't be much help to them anyway."

The soldier wrote Emil Ludvig a pass on a slip of paper, which might not turn out to be very helpful to Emil, but who could be sure? It might be enough that the pass was written in German or pointed out where Emil Ludvig worked, reciting the SS phrasing with a garrison address. For many people, that would be more than enough to let him go on his way. Emil looked at the soldier, expressing as much devotion and gratitude as he could muster.

"Wednesday is a good day for everything," Godemke said. "You should carry a pair of ears from a black cat in your pocket and when you're in danger, burn them and feed the ashes to a witch."

"I'll be back in just a couple of hours—you have nothing to fear, sir."

Thornten Godemke floundered in his knapsack and pulled out a long soldier's loaf of bread and a piece of waterproof canvas. He wrapped the loaf in the canvas and handed it to Emil. "As they say on the Spreva, chicken in July isn't worth a fly," the soldier said. "Go—and see that you're back soon. Tell your sister that it's cold in Lodz and they should take their warmest underwear, and tell that pretty niece of yours to take along her high boots—it's muddy or full of snowdrifts there most of the year too. Get a move on!" He spat. Then he added, "Decency is dead. We Germans killed it."

"Not all of it—not everyone," Emil Ludvig replied, but in his thoughts he was already at his sister's.

"We started a war that will never end. It will last a thousand—ten thousand years, and not until then will its echo run clear. When every child that has yet to be born begins to reason, he will have to come to terms with the killing that we started and introduced to mankind. You don't have to wait long or travel far to see that I am right." And then the soldier added, "War is like a pendulum. From victory to defeat and from defeat to victory. What you sow, also shall you reap. What you steal will be stolen from you in return. We'll have to resurrect decency in ourselves if we want to survive as a nation."

"Doesn't that apply to everyone?" Emil Ludvig asked hesitantly.

"I don't know anymore," Godemke said. "I used to know, but not now. Don't ask the dry wells where the water is, or overflowing rivers why they rose, or the sea where it sprung from."

Again he asked, "Isn't it true that you measure the days, months, and years by the moon instead of the sun? And that your day starts at dusk when the first three stars appear?" And he thought, That's when the night falls, not day, which starts at dawn—so he didn't wait for an answer. He had also heard that Jews prayed to demons as well as spirits, and he'd been planning to ask Emil Ludvig about that for a while now, but for some reason he had been embarrassed to. The keeper of the tavern his father frequented and his father's father, old man Godemke, believed in the occult and also that sometimes the devil entered the body of a crippled person in the form of a prayer. He couldn't say himself whether or not that was true, but certainly some malevolent spirits existed. Here and there he'd heard about the Talmud and Jewish mysticism, but Emil Ludvig seemed too worldly and cosmopolitan for the sort of thing that old man Godemke had been interested in—such as the Book of Creation, what was connected with the number ten and numerology in general, the composition of numbers and sums, and all bodily and spiritual existence related to them and to their God, like a flame is related to everything that burns and what it was said Jews separate into spirits of the water, fire, and air, and why they consider the universe to be an animate entity with a life of its own. He remembered that they'd learned similar things in school about Pythagoras in Greece, who also promoted numbers—number four, for instance—as the founding principle of the cosmos and who was of the same opinion on spiritual manifestations as he was on numbers and matter. It had probably taken root in people long ago, Godemke thought. One true thing for sure that the German political doctrine proclaimed was that Jews actually liked to stray from the established customs; they believe if their God could do so, they could too. It was even said there was a famous rabbi in Prague who had, according to some mysterious lore, created the Golem, an artificial man who could be brought to life and returned to stone again by the mere mention of the name of God.

"I feel as if I'm battering myself with every word, and you too," the soldier said, almost to himself. In his eyes was inconsolable sadness and anger that couldn't break free. It resembled both a cry and an accusation. Surrender and reconciliation. Provocation and exhaustion. It was often in his expression as if he were whipping his German heart and his German soul and would be willing to tear his soul apart and pry open his chest to let the light in and chase away the dark. He turned to watch the young SS officers drilling from a spot where the wind clearly brought the shouting, orders, and the men's responses.

"It would be better if you stayed here, but go."

"Thank you. I'll return as quickly as I can."

"I hope you don't get run over—be careful," the soldier said.

The cries of the young SS men on the training grounds reminded Thornten Godemke of Hitler and made him recollect fragments of what his father and the eldest Godemke had understood about the occult sciences Hitler had a weakness for. Most likely a lot of it was based on faulty logic, but it wasn't smart to say so very loudly—every insult to his majesty, to the offices of the Reich and of the premier of the Nazi Party was tantamount to a ticket to prison, if not straight-out execution. The occult sciences say that everything that exists and occurs has been preordained by the Creator. Everything? Even that which is poorly ordained and corrupt? Even a rifle bullet, no matter who is shooting whom, a gun's bayonet, fire, and prison? A wound inflicted from behind? Leg balls and chains? As good as his mother was, she believed that "whatever God permits is good," Thornten Godemke thought. The throes of war had stirred up things in him that chafed him like old pants that had been worn a long time. He didn't want to fall as far as his Jewish rabbit feeder had, ending up envying the rabbits—their indifference, thickheadedness, and feedings—but for the past two nights, he'd had unsettling dreams. He dreamed about his mother: she'd warned him against prostitutes and lechery; but every dream ended with murder, robbery, and trains carrying booty away to Berlin. Luckily he forgot most of his dreams right after he woke. Once, in a pub, the oldest Godemke had been frightened by what he'd heard occultists believed: that the sins of the fathers are punished for four generations. One didn't have to be an occultist for that—it was enough to be German.

"Yeah," he said into thin air.

✿

7

An hour later, Emil Ludvig was at 428 Royal Avenue. He entered the house with the stone cherubs on the front. He didn't notice if the faces were smiling or weeping. He ran up to the second floor and rang the bell. Martha, Arthur, and Susanna were preparing to relinquish the apartment to an aide from the Jewish Community Organization who would seal it up and hand the keys to officials of the Zentralstelle fur jüdische Auswanderung Prag in Stresovice. The procedure probably was nothing more out of the ordinary for the Pick family, or for Ernst Kantner, than it was when someone got sent to Shanghai or Madagascar, or to Lodz or Theresienstadt, or wherever. The main thing was to get rid of all of them and to make Prague, Copenhagen, or Paris *Judenrein*—pure, free of Jewish inhabitants. An Aryan city in an Aryan country in an Aryan Europe. Arthur wore the expression of someone happy to have "at least that" behind him. The Final Solution—for this moment, this place? There wasn't one for them already, anyway. Nothing here could upset him further, not even that they were already being kicked out—in the name of the law—of the country where they had been born, had worked, and lived in peace with everyone else.

Arthur Pick was covered with bruises as if he'd fallen down, perhaps on the house stairs, after having had too much to drink, or had been hit by a car and barely survived—or had he been beaten? Why had Godemke told him to be careful not to let himself get run over? Did the Nazis now have a new sport—hitting pedestrians with their trucks or ambulances—the way they'd murdered the young Jewish poet at the National Theater?

The speakers on the street had been reporting the top story since the morning—German troops were deep into Russia; its capital was within arm's reach. The enemy's leadership had already fled the town. They'd taken to their heels like rats. The announcer's tone of voice didn't change when he spoke about the tank units, the air force, artillery, or rats; it was somewhere between matter-of-fact and enthusiastic. It was just a matter of days, perhaps only even hours, until the German army would cross the city's borders into its residential outskirts. Unfortunately, the announcer said, they might not find the primary criminals there—most likely, they'd escaped to beyond the Ural Mountains . . . and then immediately after the voice came the sound of the powerful army marching. It sent a cold shiver down the spine.

Emil Ludvig's nose had filled with a foul smell on the way past the soap factory; he couldn't get rid of it. The walk past the train station no longer delighted him the way it once did when he used to go with Richard to watch the trains. Martha, Arthur, and Susanna had gotten their summons for the transport on Saturday; was it a coincidence that it fell on the October Holiday of the Tents? They were among the first to be called. Had the German authorities wanted to make it easier on them by making them recall how their ancestors in the desert had acted during this same time of year? (In the Moravian farmhouses where Anna had come from, the Holiday of the Tents was celebrated with a partially primitive zeal that probably still existed in every farmer and people connected with the land.)

Emil had come with Anna earlier to help them pack. Martha had insisted that they take a few dishes with them before someone else carried them away; Arthur had wanted to give Emil a letter opener to remember him by. Emil had kept refusing; Anna had not felt good about it either. What would they do with more dishes—or a letter opener? Let the Germans have them. ("For so long we didn't have such things and we managed without them . . . we are going to manage without them now," Anna had declared.) It was the sixteenth of October: it would have been worse in the heat of the summer or the cold of the deep winter. Was it possible that whoever at the emigration office had been preparing the transports knew something of Jewish rituals and took that into consideration? How was it—come to think of it—that no Jewish generation (let anyone say what they will)—had not escaped some kind of catastrophe? Emil Ludvig would have laughed in the face of anyone who'd told him that ten years ago, before Mr. Luxemburg, the Jewish man who had been deported from Germany, had come. He would also have laughed if he'd been told that one day he'd be forced to pack his bags and leave Bohemia.

"We look good, don't we?" Arthur said to Emil.

"What happened to you?" Emil asked.

"You can figure that out," Arthur replied, evading the question. "What do you think is going on everywhere?"

Martha looked like someone recently released from an institution for the partially blind. Emil Ludvig knew where he was in spite of the chaos and things littered about; the flat had its own characteristic smell.

"What about my turtledoves, canaries, cats, and my dogs?" Martha asked, as if the pets had not been in German hands for a long time already. She asked about the animals the way old people ask about their relatives who have been dead for years and can barely recognize their grown-up children whom they can remember only as being small.

Arthur was getting drunk on the dregs of the rum they were not allowed to take along with them: alcohol was *strengstens verboten.*

"He's been drunk all during these last days and making scandals for me as well as Susanna," Martha stated.

"The world is divided into two kinds," Arthur said, as if he hadn't heard her, and he rubbed his bruises. "The beautiful and the ugly. The first kind sees themselves as beautiful so that everyone else seems ugly to them for a long time before they kill them—they are the countries that are able to defend themselves through wars, and the countries that can't."

He didn't have to tell Emil where he himself fell, or Emil, or the Jews and individuals scattered all over Europe.

"There has to be some higher principle, a higher power," Emil protested. "Some kind of justice." He thought about how Thornten Godemke had let him come here.

"How is a higher justice supposed to exist when you can't find even the commonest, simplest fairness in people?" Arthur retorted, smiling.

With his slick, greased, black hair, for a moment he looked like a devil laughing at what resembled that which was now, and how in all diverse shapes and forms it would always be both old and new to kill or let oneself be killed, to be capable of making war or not, to defend oneself or capitulate. There was no other choice. Before it had gone hand in hand with standing or relinquishing one's ground. That didn't require any big plans or begging for some sort of limitless faith. It reverted to ancient instincts when the only one who could hold his ground was the person who was able to defend himself, not once and for all, but again and again and again, endlessly, for as long as the person could have meaning or remember some sort of endlessness. Waiting for even the slightest inspiration or for a dazzling lightning strike had already been ruled out. Arthur appeared as though that which contained the gift of speech had gone dumb and that which contained the gift of hearing had gone deaf—and the impression he made didn't matter to him; his eyes testified to that. A kernel of madness had already become implanted in everyone, and the only question that remained was how quickly or how slowly it would grow before it engulfed everything. No one could rely any longer on anything that once maybe had or could have had meaning; not even the echo one might want to or could hear remained. There was no sense in appealing to something or labeling it, be it truth, fairness, virtue, or fair play—from the most ridiculous to the most heinous—because it already meant something different for everyone. Even the mildest of appellations inspired terror and the most terrible no longer seemed that different from everything that could still look normal. The soul was already in pieces and reverberated in the word, the concept, and the title and transformed into the name of the city Lodz (now called Litzmanstadt after a German general from the First World War), where they were being taken, in cattle cars, like all the rest (twelve horses or one hundred people to a railcar). Even in his inebriation, Arthur Pick's lively, dark eyes with their shaggy brows noted what was happening around him. He had the expression of a person who'd stripped the people around him, including himself, of their masks. He followed every movement and sound of what was going on beyond the windows, outside on the streets, and he smiled: they hadn't prevented any of it—everything that had happened happened right in front of their noses. The world wasn't merely a maze in which one could only get lost. It was too late to worry anymore about whether the Germans were just bluffing: the suitcases were at the door. As Emil had once said earlier (in regard to money, of course), he was nervous but not afraid. Now everyone was nervous and afraid—they had a reason to be. And no one believed anyone—even oneself—anymore.

"You're not alone, Emil," Arthur said with a smile. "I think about how Napoleon had hemorrhoids and how that affected the battle at Waterloo. I think about what is festering in Hitler. Or what's gnawing at Himmler. Did you hear that before he started to organize the SS, he took care of chickens and hens? It's too bad he didn't keep doing that. What is it that makes them twaddle and blither (gets them so full of hot air)? Where do they get the energy to constantly be preaching to someone? Where does their pretension and haughtiness come from to move the border of Germany west to the Atlantic and east to the Urals? Are they thinking they'll harness all of us to their services? They must assume we're even bigger bastards than they thought in the first place."

Emil Ludvig remembered that Arthur Pick had not always spoken like this. He hadn't talked this way when they visited Ernst Kantner at Ungelt. But a lot had changed since then, and that applied to both of them.

"If I ever had any doubts where this all was leading to, whatever we did, the work clearing away snow at the airport and the people responsible for it have chased away even the slightest doubt, Emil. It's all downhill for us. And don't think that I'm just confusing my situation with the destruction of the world. Not even a beginner is that naive. If the Germans ever had any difficulties with their plans, those times are behind them and us too. If someone protested, do you think that would stop them? If it came to—let's just say—some international outrage, for example, would any countries refuse to import and buy German goods out of principle or on moral grounds? Probably not. They're hardheaded. They're going for what they want. And that entails getting rid of me and you. You know how clean their theaters and cinemas and parks will be now? And the air around them? Their backsides won't be tainted anymore by sitting in a place your or my butt rested on a train or a tram somewhere. But as soon as they didn't meet with even the slightest objection, not to mention that we would possibly dare to raise a voice against anything ourselves here, it must've given them a big kick in the pants. Who knows if they expected that things would go so smoothly for them. In the war with me and you, they are already on their victory march, in which nothing can no longer deter them, except final and complete conquest. As far as the moral side of things is concerned, we're already dead, before they murder us for real. What else is the humiliation of mankind than the murder of the spirit, Emil? To torture the body, like they torture people in Petschkov Palace in Bredovska, is one thing, but to torture the soul by humiliation is another, yet both of them together form the perfect murder, the ultimate defeat of the enemy. You have to acknowledge that they have now already forced you, like me, to accept a violent death as something tremendously fair, and whatever didn't match that would be a deviation from the duty, truth, and Nazi German vision of the world. Mr. Hitler and his people cannot afford that. That would demoralize us once again, and someone would have to come after them to repair and finish what the Nazis started. Period. Convincing themselves they don't have enough railcars to take us where they want, maybe even to the North Pole, is like saying that the moon is the sun and the sun is the moon."

"Believe only half of it, Emil," Martha said.

Susanna threw a scornful look at her father. Why did he talk about murder when they were only moving, forced out of the country and resettling in the East, at the new Lodz, Litzmanstadt?

Arthur had been earning little money, and in the last little while, almost nothing. Because they were so angry at him, Susanna and Martha would not give Arthur anything to eat, although he knew that they did not have enough themselves. Jewish rations bordered on starvation. He had to steal in his own household. He had complained to Emil. It wasn't anything personal anymore. That wouldn't make sense either.

"I'm glad I made it here on time," Emil said.

"We're ready, Emil," Arthur said.

"Do you need help with anything?" Emil asked.

"Do you have any food?" Arthur wanted to know.

"A loaf of bread, a pack of sugar. It's in the canvas so it won't get soaked, and Anna is sending a small bottle." He pulled out of the bag the long loaf of bread wrapped in waterproof canvas. "That's just for the road, before you all get food at the place. But that can take time. I work with a soldier who served in Poland. Some would prefer if things were not like this. If you are lucky, and I hope you are, you'll meet such people. I still can't believe that all Germans, just because they were born of German mothers, are bad from day one. The bad ones are just playing first fiddle. The railroad there doesn't work exactly on the dot, but the military transports probably have preference. That would be good. You'll probably get there soon. But even so, I'm sorry not to bring you more."

He knew that in their household he would not find a single whole loaf of bread. Perhaps they still had a few potatoes, but they would not be much help on the road unless they ate them raw, like rabbits.

Arthur looked at him distrustfully. His wife and daughter had refused him food in the past weeks because he had not been trying, as they thought he should, to work for the German constructions as a bricklayer or a bricklayer's helper, as Emil had done. Anna still took in sewing by hand (on the side, by needle and thimble, when she had to turn in her sewing machine). If Arthur didn't do that and he swore that he wouldn't, where was Martha supposed to come by food beyond rations?

Where had he gotten so beaten up, for God's sake? How had he come by that? Emil Ludvig looked at the shut suitcases, ready to be taken away.

Susanna had been teaching languages on the side, and for that she at least deserved to eat. She did not want money from the pupils—it was better if they brought bread, margarine, sardines, as long as they were available. She taught Italian, English, German, and French. She had discovered something to use she had learned in the cloister when she needed to. Arthur smirked. (Not long ago, Emil had glimpsed Martha bringing in a glass tray with thinly sliced bread and ersatz coffee with chicory to Susanna during one of her lessons in the living room; a grand piano used to stand there. Arthur had hid himself in the curtains in the anteroom; when the nearsighted Martha walked out of the kitchen, he grabbed the bread and ate it before Martha even realized that she was carrying a tray only with coffee. Susanna didn't say anything. After the Italian lesson, she shouted at Arthur that she would not want to be a father who had been cursed as a thief and a good-for-nothing by his children—a parasite living off his wife and daughter.) She never made enough money from the language lessons to feed all of them, and Martha hadn't wanted Susanna to go to sleep, get up, and have to work on an empty stomach.

"You look different, Emil," Susanna said.

"Are you taking your best with you?" Emil asked. (Don't we all already look different? Emil thought to himself.)

"I will take my favorites," Martha said.

Once, Martha explained the meaning of her charm necklace to Helena. They were made mostly of porcelain, mosaic, and tin so she hadn't had to turn them in to the Germans. In the first place, the china animals and coral beads were beautiful, and second, wearing the right charm around one's neck helped ward off evil spirits and could even keep one healthy. It did her good to know that she had something like this that was hers—something she had long enough to know that tomorrow, when she opened up the wooden box where it was resting, she would again find it there.

Aunt Martha had already surrendered her cats, dogs, and birds; only the charm necklace remained to her. From his own personal things, Arthur had kept only the letter opener; he had stopped offering it to Emil as a memento.

"Shouldn't we cut that loaf up into three parts before we leave here?" Arthur proposed.

"No," Susanna replied decisively. "I'll take it."

Arthur had not been happy when Emil entered, but in his voice was the cheerfulness of drunkards to whom (or so they think) nothing can happen. Arthur smiled with his thin lips above which he used to sport a dapper moustache à la Adolphe Menjou (reputedly a big anti-Semite). He looked like a phony fortune-teller with his thickly pomaded hair, sharp nose, swarthy complexion, and bushy, tousled eyebrows almost as thick as two moustaches above his eyes. His fixed look was like that of a soothsayer who had predicted a long time ago what would happen—what everything would lead to. Four hundred years ago he would have been a Nostradamus, the Jewish-Christian half-breed *Mischling des erstern Grades,* who knew before anyone else that the twentieth century was going to be the century of submarines and that the Germans would never get onto the British Isles even if all hundred million Germans sang and rang their bells to the song *"Denn wir fahren, denn wir fahren, denn wir fahren gegen Engeland."* Nostradamus, of course, had spoken of "the eye of the sea." What else could an eye of the sea be if not the periscope on a submarine? Who foretold that Paris would fall? Who described the first German blitzkrieg? Arthur felt like he was in the shoes of the onetime half-Jew, Nostradamus.

He gazed into the mirror they would have to leave behind. He saw himself as though he were a stage actor writing his exit in an unfinished play before it ends. "Don't I look like the eternal Jew? I hope that no one expects me to take on all the sins of all the people and carry them away with me to Lodz—Litzmanstadt. How does it suit me to curse those who have cursed me and who are going to keep on cursing me? Why should they have it better, only because they'll get rid of me someplace to the east? How come nobody asks why it's happening to me in the first place? Only I have the appetite and the passion to play, to have what belongs to me? I should caress the hand which brought me the papers for our transport—the same hand which is going to come for my mirror, for my wardrobe, for the chairs and dishes which I bought for myself with honestly earned money? It took me a good thirty years to do it all."

Then he asked, "Can a man expect some understanding from his daughter or his wife in his hour of need, Emil? What do you think? But don't strain yourself to answer, I'm not counting on any—it's too late for that."

Arthur said it drunkenly, probably so that it wouldn't sound cruel. But the cruelty was there, through and through. Then he said, "I'm not sorry for anything—and not at all for myself. That would give the Germans too much satisfaction. Let them know that an incorrigible sinner is leaving inside me, a merry fellow. I won't be bothered by anything. They won't live to see me give my consent. And don't let them anticipate that my goods and effects I'm going to leave for them here in the apartment will save their souls."

He smiled, probably at something in his mind that he had turned topsy-turvy, also courtesy of the rum. "If they want me to be immortal, I'll do it, but I won't live forever." Then he belched.

Susanna turned away.

"That's disgusting, Arthur—haven't you got any shame?" Martha said.

"Uncle Emil, I can guarantee you that we're the only family leaving with a drunken head of the family."

"Evil had an advantage over good: people would rather shut their eyes so they won't have to look—so they can't see it," Arthur stated suddenly. "When Martha was still allowed to have cats, I used to watch them when they went hunting at dusk and brought home mice. Then I couldn't think of them as nice and friendly cats anymore; in one moment they had changed into what they always really were— wild animals—each one out for himself. They'd prowl around as if walking on air and then carry the mice off in their mouths. I chose to close my eyes and shoo them away. A person hates to look evil directly in the face. He prefers to pretend that it doesn't exist."

"Perhaps," Emil said.

"You don't see the biggest evil of all. First, because you don't want to, and second, because evil doesn't always leave calling cards. Sometimes, it seems quite friendly, like a best friend giving some useful advice."

"I'd rather think about nicer things too," Emil admitted.

"One day we'll learn to see what we don't want to. We will have no choice."

Emil did not respond to that.

There were still last-minute details to attend to. Arthur had left an unfinished letter on the table. Was it instructions for Emil and Anna or for someone Arthur wanted Emil to deliver it to?

It was a letter Emil could read before he put it into an envelope with a stamp with Adolf Hitler's portrait on it. It was weighted down with the bronze letter opener that Arthur used on all his correspondence, including those that weren't addressed to him.

Luisa, wrote Arthur. *I have been hoping all this time and have been consoling myself constantly, and it's here already, all the same. We are leaving in less than two days. The seconds fly by with enormous speed. They grow and make up the minutes, the hours, and the days. Every second is a tiny step which brings us closer to uncertainty, a stride into darkness. We're allowed fifty pounds of belongings each, as long as it fits into one suitcase. They told us today that any other baggage we might have would get lost. Amazing perceptions, aren't they? I hope that you won't get summoned—I wish with all my heart that you won't. I am sending you the last verse: I see two glowing white stars, I am searching who to ask why they glow the whole night long and for whom they send light. . . . Oh, Luisa . . .*

Arthur didn't notice Emil reading the first page.

"They're first-rate horse traders—I don't even say businessmen anymore, Emil. Mr. Kantner is probably no exception. They're only changes of clothing, a myriad of disguises for the most diverse of opportunities. It wasn't so long ago that Mr. Chamberlain was waving the paper in London with Hitler's signature on the Munich Treaty, declaring that peace was secured, not just now but for future generations. I, too, admired how cleverly they outwitted Hitler and denied him his tidy little war for the Sudetenland. They handed it over to him without a war anyway, just like they handed over Prague. It didn't cost him a single bullet. That's a sort of broader view of things, but from up close and personal, I can't see it any clearer. Just imagine, they let you pay rent for the whole year in advance and then run you right out the second week after the quarter. When we close the door behind ourselves and step out and disappear behind the Powder Tower, it'll settle a lot of people's guilty consciences—if they've got any left, that is. They won't have to feel ashamed—that's if they've got an iota of shame left in their bodies—that one Mr. Arthur Pick doesn't even have a handcart to carry his few things in—his property up to fifty pounds, as long as it can all fit in one suitcase. Who'd still give me the eye when I'm not allowed to walk in the center of the sidewalk? Putting on a *borsalino* or carrying an umbrella would be provocation enough. I don't have the heart to act like an aristocrat anymore either. No one will have to stand up for me anymore, even should they be disposed to—and frankly, I reckon, most would not. Who'd want to get beat up for being a Jew lover, a white Jew? Where are the days when all we had to surrender was our crystal and gramophones so we couldn't listen to Aryan music such as Mr. Wagner or Liszt? In the final analysis, I'll be just as happy to bid farewell to all this here. The neighbors will breathe a sigh of relief too." He took a breath. "And the Germans can rub their little hands. *It* had cost them nothing. Everything we're leaving behind is pure gain." He licked his lips. He had no more than a drop of rum left.

Arthur did not have to speak about the machine that had set all this in motion. He had been the first to dismiss it when it began. At first the humiliations had been too subtle to make a mountain out of a molehill about them, but their sum total, from restriction to restriction, was less petty than the restrictions by themselves—for instance, the ban on raising white mice, canaries, cats, or turtledoves; the surrendering of the radio set, the fur coat, skis, sleds, a rabbinical grandfather's wristwatches or gold chains; or being banned from shopping, except for potatoes during specified times, or from concert halls and schools. He stood in front of the mirror to convince himself that what he saw was still Arthur Pick—that he still existed. He searched himself for traits that were identical to Hitler. Dark hair. Demonic eyes. Hypnotic gaze. Moustache. Striking eyebrows. The art of speaking to the masses in simple, convincing images, as if a hundred thousand people were one person and one person a million people. It wasn't only not being permitted to go to a dry cleaner's, or to a barber, or to eat onions, garlic, or raisins, because that could be seen as ridiculous even though it was a fact. He recalled how, long ago, Emil wasn't able to laugh until he was sore at Hitler pontificating; he'd enjoyed Charlie Chaplin movies more. (Probably those two, the little man on the screen and the figure on the podium, were identical.) People buzzed when Hitler announced in the Reichstag that if the world's Jewry (including Emil Ludvig, Arthur Pick, and Messrs. Tanzer, Neuman, and Winternitz and Co.) was successful in yanking Germany and the world into war, at the very least, it would mean the end of European circumcisions. From the way things looked, Hitler had played fortune-teller a few times, and a lot of what he'd said had turned out to be true. Nothing was changed by the fact that to him and Emil, it all seemed hilarious. He'd have plenty of time to ruminate about it on his way to Lodz—and what he couldn't finish during the trip, he'd be able to catch up on when they got there. Some of the laws had seemed so petty and didn't really concern him, but they'd had unforeseeable results. Turn in skis? Come on. The Germans had to be kidding if they believed that Jews would arm their own units with them. Turn in skates? Was the SS planning to participate in the winter Olympics? The order requiring him to turn his gold cuff links into the Prague branch of the Reichsbank did distress him, though— and now, at the end of all the pettiness and prohibitions, he was waiting to leave his own apartment to the unknown for somewhere in the East and comprehending the deeper meaning of it all. He would fade away like an unpleasant stain on the coat of the population, from the face of the country where he'd been born and where, he thought though there hadn't been much time to think about it, he would also die.

Arthur wrinkled his forehead and moved his thick, black eyebrows, which were, for the first time, threaded with gray like his once raven hair. The triviality and the progression of the bans took away their edge, which his body had accepted in name only, weakened and incapable of resistance. He would go and everyone would surely breathe a sigh of relief.

"Isn't it ridiculous that everyone, including us, is keeping silent?" Arthur suddenly said. Probably he just wanted to speak one more time in his own apartment. "They forbade us to speak—and the rest of the world is quiet out of shame. But if anyone should say that the Germans are idiots, he ought to have his head examined—no one could be cleverer than the Germans. They have made silence and impassiveness, fear, terror, and informants their servants—who else has ever been able to do that?"

Emil Ludvig continued reading: *With this letter, I say good-bye. I am only sorry that we have never met. Should you want to write me once more, then do so immediately to the Radio Market of the Great Exhibition Palace in Holesovice. Yours — Irving Egon Kahn, formerly of rubber and chemical cements.*

Martha squinted with her light blue, nearsighted eyes. She rested her hand on the empty white mice cage. Susanna paused near her brass bed for a moment. Martha stumbled against the cabinet that still held her good dishes.

Out of nowhere Arthur said, "Now we're going to learn how to grow old in a different way. From the realm of phantoms we're stepping straight into the realm of the East."

He caught his daughter's gaze; she stared at him as though he were crazy—as though she'd once been able to take him seriously only by mistake.

"In one way or another all of us resemble one another, like each egg looks like any other egg," Arthur concluded. Then he rhetorically asked Emil if he could guess how many nights he hadn't slept a wink. He gazed into the light of the room as if he were looking into the twilight, into the maze of shadows where everyone had already been abandoned, betrayed, and left to fend for himself. He chuckled, as if he wanted to pooh-pooh a thought that still worried him.

Hector-Hugo wasn't there: they'd handed him over a long time ago, even though they knew that such an old dog would only be destroyed by the Germans. He had been barely breathing; Arthur had literally carried him to the dog assembly area.

The crown molding was as beautiful as it ever was, with flowers, grape clusters, apples, and bananas pouring out of stuccoed cornucopias—only everything was covered with cobwebs.

Arthur looked at Susanna and Martha: the past and the future had been turned upside down, the legs of one placed on the head of the other. "I don't expect things ever to go back to how they were. What is—was—mine no longer completely is; know what I mean?"

Susanna stood stiff as a pillar for a moment. She was beautiful, filled with bitterness. She was disgusted with her father—with herself, too, and by Germany, Germans—by everything that her life had become, but she also knew that it hadn't happened all at once. She didn't even have the heart to yell at Arthur to stop him from everything he was saying, implied, or revealed in his face. She felt his deterioration: his surrender to cynicism, to self-pity, to drunkenness, to becoming a ridiculous clown nobody wants, making his last exit involuntarily, but who, it seemed patently clear to her, still took himself seriously. She knew that the Germans let their murdering madmen advise doctors about how to handle the sick and infirm, like letting a drunk advise the sober. Now, before the journey, she felt her stomach was becoming heavy as if she were pregnant. She was wearing hiking clothing as if she were going to the Brenner, with lace-up boots and a white wool skiing hat.

Arthur began merrily singing something to himself about how everything that was no longer is, the fleetingness of youth. He irritated Susanna, but she did not want to say anything more to her father in front of Emil. Arthur put on a flat workman's cap made out of fancy checkered fabric, which he used to wear at work on the road or clearing snow. "Forget that we're saying good-bye," he hummed. And then he finished with, "I am an oyster with a pearl in my entrails." He probably wasn't having any more dreams about his face bleeding after a woman touched it, who blamed him afterward that even after the most incredible tender moment, he looked like he'd committed a murder, or about the one-quarter-Aryan sweetshop keeper at the Ascherman café on Dlouha Street at the Bristol Hour Hotel who claimed that the white milk he fed her was blood. The last dream he'd had was that he bought a ticket for the lottery and won sixteen bowls of soup and sixteen plates of food but the person who paid out the winnings was a friend and offered him money instead of the plates. In the dream Arthur got seventy marks; when he woke up with a parched throat and thirsty, dry lips, he realized that he was smiling. Winning pleases a person even in a dream—and who knew what it meant? Susanna glanced into the mirror for the last time and saw herself and Arthur looking at each other standing next to each other. She bent down and rechecked the strap on the duffel bag again.

"Shall we go?" she asked. Her head ached. She could feel her emptiness. She scanned the apartment. Arthur's funereal *borsalino* remained on the coatrack. In the corner was the aquarium. The fish were the only pets they hadn't had to surrender. Perhaps the Germans forgot about the aquarium, but besides that, they hadn't omitted a thing. Of the birds, turtledoves, canaries, white mice, dogs, and cats, only bowls and cages remained. There was nothing to be done; the fish would die. It didn't make sense to ask Emil to do something either. The apartment would be sealed shut.

"I feel guilty—even for things I haven't done, Emil," Susanna said. "Don't try to explain why to me. I'm critical of the wrong people— but these same people are already vanishing in the fog. It's probably true that we aren't worth as much as we thought. Chosen? By whom? Just turn it upside down and see what happens."

She looked at Arthur, first with contempt and then with pity and perhaps also a shadow of disgust. She glanced in the mirror and at her mother.

"I feel crippled. I still have legs and arms and a head on my neck. But they have amputated my spirit. They have cut off from me what could have been—from what I wanted to be, prepared for, and from what never had time to happen. What did I study and work for? Why did I wish and dream? It's probably possible to amputate dreams, the past, the present, and the future. I am no longer looking forward, only backward—but there is no actual life behind, only a memory of reality. The last remnant of my life is already waving to me from behind." She cast her beautiful eyes downward.

Emil Ludvig wasn't sure if he understood what his niece had, or perhaps still, expected from her father, from Martha, or from herself. "No one is faultless," he said.

"No. Nobody," Susanna agreed. "It's just that some of us are also without common sense." For her, it was an hour of shame. "We have been consumed like a fire that burns itself out, Emil. That's all. Now I have to leave."

She felt denigrated, humiliated, eradicated from her own existence. Her father's cynicism could no longer bother her. She wasn't even mortified by his self-deprecation any longer; she'd ridiculed herself already for an even longer time. The cynicism filled the atmosphere of the room like air. One only had to breathe to feel it.

"Don't try to shoulder more than your share of the guilt," Emil said.

"I must say good-bye to all of this," Martha said. "God knows when I'll see it again."

She looked around with her nearsighted eyes, although she could actually see no more than a few feet in front of her. She had been having hallucinations since Saturday; she saw her little pets and was talking with them. She realized how forgetful she had become. Her head was spinning; she could no longer concentrate on anything. She had either hallucinations or vertigo.

Arthur left greasy fingerprints on the once white doors. With a glance he caressed the velvet curtains. Martha wiped away her tears.

"Chin up," Arthur said mockingly to her. "We're going to the East because somebody doesn't like my hairy fingers." Then to Emil, "By the way, Emil, if they send me my retirement, collect it for me." He had paid up to the last little while. That was all he could know about his retirement fund that he had paid into for twenty-five years. It had disappeared into thin air along with everything else.

Children were playing and loud shouting came from the apartment above. Judging from the noise, people were trying to dance. Someone overturned a chair or a basket; elsewhere a gramophone played.

"Our lives weren't so great that we have to feel bad," Susanna said.

Arthur smiled. "True. They say that children try to remember what the parents try to forget."

"Well, Arthur," Emil said, bidding him good-bye.

"There is an excuse for every crime," Arthur said. "I don't want to—and I won't meet my future murderers on the street. Not I, nor my wife and child." Then he said, "They beat me up in the café because I was saying something about human rights. They were agents of the Flag, who were wearing stars so that no one could tell them from us. They told me that I should be grateful to leave for the East with my head still on my shoulders along with fifty pounds of belongings, if, as I have to repeat to myself, I can fit them in one suitcase. But I daresay I'll now experience the cheating and abundance of the life most people lead, according to them, who weren't born into a cushy home. They kicked me in the gut and head when I was already lying under the pool table. I can be grateful they didn't kick my eye out."

"I'm ashamed," Emil said. "I didn't think about that." It seemed to him as though everything was taking an impossibly long time.

"Everybody for himself, Emil. From this moment on, everyone only for himself," Arthur said. "If, by any chance, you never see me again, you don't even have to act like I was ever alive. Treat me like I never lived. I have learned to act that way with myself. It's true, that not long ago I believed that we were in our best years. I beg of you, don't try to talk me into taking it back."

"It's already happened, Emil. We have no choice," Martha said.

That was the last thing they said to each other.

Emil Ludvig helped Susanna and Martha with the suitcases. They were allowed only fifty pounds in each suitcase; one hundred fifty in all three. It had also been said that it was permissible to have forty pounds in a suitcase and ten in a carry-on, but there'd been no guarantee about that. What if the forty-pound suitcase was lost? They recommended only one piece of luggage at the Jewish Community—to make sure.

On the stairs Arthur Pick had to hold on to the railing; Martha held on to her brother. Susanna went first. She didn't want to hear her father talking about who would probably clean the sidewalk when he was gone. Emil thought how Arthur probably would never take Richard to the Prague Zoo, or any other zoo, at night to show him the green eyes of the deer, the yellow or red eyes of all the different kinds of foxes, and the jaguar's eyes, orange, when he pointed a flashlight at them. He thought about the rabbits' eyes. Emil could still see them. All of a sudden he wondered what kind of eyes a rat would have and he shuddered.

Emil could sense how the fabric that weaves and holds families together was soundlessly disintegrating. He imagined Susanna as a girl departing for the Catholic cloister where she would be raised. It certainly was not nice, good, or correct that she was leaving now without trying to hide the fact that she hated her father. Arthur asked her whether or not he looked like a traveler—he didn't expect an answer. He laughed in the street as if he wanted everyone watching him through a window or from the sidewalk to see how easily he took it all. Emil went with them to the streetcar. They all embraced. They each took their own luggage and left on the rear platform.

And now I must go quickly to meet Anna, Emil said to himself. The need for haste helped him. From the speaker, the supreme command announced the names of the Russian cities occupied by the German troops; it was on good authority that they were at the Volga River. Then the music started . . . the drums, the pipes, and fanfare. Emil was grateful that at the very least, Anna had her God to turn to. He took a shortcut to the synagogue to rendezvous with Anna, as they had agreed to if she got permission to say good-bye to Martha, Arthur, and Susanna and he had enough time.

Long flags with brown-and-red sun insignias and a huge broken cross flew from the German kindergarten and the school on Primatorska Avenue. Next door the soap factory smokestack fumed and belched its stench all up and down the street. The main entrance to the synagogue from Primatorska was closed. The entrance to Rupa, the store with the sweetshop right next to it, was decorated with garlands and long colorful ribbons, and the display window was filled with colorful little pictures for the customers' children. The large shop on the other side of the synagogue with an entertainment and shooting grounds, table soccer, hockey, and game machines and Ping-Pong was also full. Children were already out of school for the day. Emil Ludvig walked around the entire synagogue. Synagogues had been closed since the fifteenth of September, but Anna told him that if he wanted to find her, the back entrance was already open. Was it possible that the Germans weren't going to ransack the synagogue because some people still worshiped here?

Cantor Mario Schapira's son-in-law guarded the back entrance. He and Emil greeted each other. They had both wanted to go to Shanghai but had remained in Prague. After all, what could unite people like having Jewish relatives and paying a visit to the Gestapo in a Stresovice villa, for heaven's sake? They smiled at each other; for some people, words aren't necessary for understanding. Neither of them had gone far.

"Have you got yours?" Mr. Schapira's son-in-law asked.

"No, my sister, her husband, and their daughter have," Emil answered. "And you?"

Mr. Schapira's son-in-law smiled. "Go inside, I'll close it again."

Emil Ludvig had not been in the synagogue since his wedding, August 23, 1923. The scent of a tinge of lemon, old perfume, and oak furniture hit his nose. He searched for Anna in the balcony, but she was not there. He found her downstairs where, as a matter of course, women did not generally go. A German firm had long since acquired Mr. Neuman's store, adjacent to the entertainment and shooting grounds and opposite the German kindergarten and school, although it sported the same floating doll, baby, and bride's outfits in the display window as it had many years before: WHATEVER YOUR DARLING'S AGE, USE NEUMAN'S. WAITING FOR THE STORK? HAS DIANA, THE LOVE GODDESS, PAID YOUR DAUGHTER A VISIT? NO NEED TO TEAR YOUR HAIR OUT OVER IT. MAKE IT NEUMAN'S PROBLEM. One mannequin had a white dress, the second a blue one, the third a pink one. Sometimes all three dresses were floating in the display window together. People want a change, Mr. Neuman insisted. There were outfits for nursing babies, outfits for brides, outfits in general. The children detained their mothers at the display window so that they could see one or maybe all three floating dresses. A white week. A blue week. Then a pink week.

Emptiness loomed from most of the benches. The rug in the middle of the little passageway was worn through. Many feet had passed back and forth this way. Now many of those feet would tramp down longer passageways.

The little altar step and the large gold crown with a red border were made out of olive wood, imported from the Promised Land or from Turkey, after the synagogue had been completed. Children's singing floated in from outside in the main street where the German kindergarten was. *"Fuchs, du hast die Ganz gestohlen; gib'sie wieder hier."* And mixed in with it, the speaker announced the latest news: *"Das Oberkommando der Wehrmacht gibt bekannt."* The march into the enemy's capital might be a question of hours. Nothing stood in Germany's way to the Urals, to Germany from the Atlantic, to the Pacific Ocean, to a Germany above which the sun would not set. The Final Solution. Again the marches and the news, and the news and the marches. "*Deutschlandslied. Ich habe einen Kamaraden. Kaiser Friedrich Marsch. Kurassier-Marsch.*"

Anna was nearly startled by Emil. She was concentrating on Mario Schapira's religious service. It was cold inside. Outside it threatened rain again. Emil tiptoed in.

"You should have put on something warmer," Emil said, sitting down next to Anna. "There's a draft in here. I guess they wanted to give it a quick airing out."

"It's been a long time since they heated in here," Anna said. She looked sickly. She had not been sleeping at night. She thought about Arthur, Martha, and Susanna on the transport, about Martha's hallucinations, about Susanna's dejection and the way she'd converted to Catholicism at the last moment to no avail. Was it a sin to want to remain at home alive? She thought about her relatives. How Uncle Munk had carried his daughter who'd jumped into the air shaft in his arms. She thought about other years at this time: when she'd gotten married, when Emil had taught her modern dancing and explained to her about social customs among businessmen and business representatives, when she'd been pregnant for the first and second times— Helena had been so difficult to bear and Richard had almost shot out. She merged her most blissful memories with Cantor Schapira's prayers. She had expected to find relief in the synagogue, but it hadn't come. She felt tired; it was a new, different exhaustion than sewing for long hours into the night and then again at dawn. Time, the world, worries, the future, weighed her down. She felt the coarse and relentless chest of the world pressing into her. All suggestions of regret suddenly hung close to her; she did not see anything uplifting, or light, anywhere. She sensed the shadows enshrouding her spirit, burdening her, without her having done anything wrong. She couldn't recall any visible sin, but she—all of them—had to have done something wrong which did not serve anyone, not even themselves, and there was nothing positive to which she could appeal in her mind. She felt something weighing down on the bottom of her being, as if her foundations were caving in, as if she were losing faith in herself, in her work, the conviction that if she just would work diligently, everything would be solved, even if not easily. Moving around her throat she felt invisible hands strangling her, and she couldn't defend herself because she didn't know well enough what she was up against. She suspected that she stood on the threshold of unforeseen circumstances and that this was only the beginning, before the threats and warnings and terrors turned into direct danger. It mesmerized her so thoroughly that even her prayers couldn't break the spell. She had never experienced such monstrousness before, and she feared that she would go mad from it. She urged herself to remain calm. She wasn't alone in the world. Today, just like every other day in the week, she'd gotten up at five and sewed to make up the time she'd lose in coming here.

She tried to maintain what she called her "working rounds" at all costs. She sensed that soon Arthur, Martha, and Susanna would meet the fate that was waiting for them as it waited for everyone. It wasn't just a hallucination; she felt it stabbing her heart. The feeling hadn't always been there: she'd begun to feel it only recently, including most of the time she prayed earnestly, pleading to God. The relationship between Anna Ludvigova (maiden name Loewyova) and God was not equal: hers was the feeble song of a suffering spirit whose dreams remained unheard. Today, in the synagogue, where until now she'd felt more peace than in any place built by human hands, it seemed to her she had passed the borders of her own existence—past that which had been permissible yesterday and that which she only partially comprehended from afar. Her blood ran cold whenever she dwelled on the future. For Anna, it was an unknown and indeterminate anguish because that which wasn't clear and simple was unbearable. Her lips became slightly distorted by the prayer. She suspended her litany to God almost as in surrender; she found herself debating or quarreling with God. It startled her as though it was something even more horrifying than horrible. Her rheumatism flared, causing pain in her joints and aching muscles, cutting her speech with God short. She was afraid she was suppressing a premonition of bad things to come. She had never confided what really pained her, physically or spiritually, to anyone. Everyone had enough worries. She thought about Helena, Richard, and her husband. She remembered her father's recounting of the pogroms in Russia, Poland, and Moravia—how kindhearted Catholic and Protestant families had saved Jewish babies so that many newborns never knew who their real parents were or whether they were killed or sent God knows where. Those stories had never left her. With Emil she was inclined to forget such things, as if yesterday's world had been erased, and everything today and tomorrow held the promise of the future. Beside him, the world sometimes seemed rosier, even when it wasn't. His carefree ways were like a sun in which she warmed herself, even though she reproached him for them to his face (just in case). When their children were born and started growing up, responsibility forced him to take care of things; he stopped being so hopelessly lighthearted. Both of them had to buckle down a lot—but that was the least of what they'd had to do.

All of a sudden Anna Ludvig had the sensation that the heavens were collapsing and the end of the world was waiting for them, as though that were the embodiment of everything that had happened up to now. She'd never had such a premonition before: was her husband attempting to view the war lightheartedly now too? Wasn't it good that the soldier, Godemke, had let him leave the rabbits? Before all this, she had been unable to get him to come to the synagogue for anything—she hadn't even tried; he had his own agreement with heaven. Some things are only good when they are done with free will and not just because somebody else wants them done, and besides, God wasn't her property to hand out to him. If God was everything good in mankind and in the universe, then there was more of God in Emil than in some people who prayed from morning until night. But what if God were really the worst and most evil in people, and it's a person's job to separate the right and just from the evil and unjust?

Anna listened only halfheartedly to Mario Schapira's sermon, supplying the other half by herself. If there were a God, wouldn't the good be rewarded and the bad punished? If God existed, how could he let things get as bad as the Nazis threatened they would, day and night? What became of people for whom things suddenly had taken such a bad turn—but had it really been so sudden?

Anna felt cornered; she had more questions than answers. In the final analysis, only God and her family remained for her, and the hope that something would happen to prevent the worst from occurring, just as Emil believed that nothing worse than what he was capable of doing to his worst enemy could happen. I have a good, kindhearted husband—I have good, healthy children, what else could I ask for? I am healthy, I can work; why don't I get up at four in the morning? Instead of going to bed at midnight, I could go at one or two, so that we'd have more bread and margarine and no one will be hungrier today than long ago when we were bad off and it seemed the store might go under?

Suddenly even these worst months didn't seem so terrifying.

Only a few people sat at the dust-covered altar. Mario Schapira wasn't wearing his religious robes. His suit was too large for him now; he had lost weight.

"You might be better off at home," Emil said.

"I don't want the Schapiras to be here alone."

"They aren't here alone."

"How did you get here?" Anna asked.

"I've got a written pass with a signature. Don't be scared about anything. Do you want to see it?"

"When are you supposed to be back?"

"I can still stay for a while. I can walk you home."

"The clouds will gather until the hail falls," Mario Schapira said.

"We shall see," Anna replied.

She was different in the synagogue than at home with the children, once near the sewing machine and now on her bench with only a needle and orders for alterations beside her. There was something uplifting and desperate about her at the same time: there was the dignity of a countrywoman, like the dignity of trees that grow long and straight even when they bend to the wind or with age or to unforgiving nature, and there was the dignity of the flatlands and rolling hills, of massive rivers, the silent snowfall, the rustling of water, the rhythm of rain lulling one to sleep. It was made up of the weakness and the strength of everything that comes, lasts, and then passes away. She had large, tired, deep eyes. She bore the strength and wretchedness that only man knows, but perhaps animals too, which is inexpressible, shaped by man into the concept of fate's inscrutability with which no one, not even Anna, can cope without guidance from above.

Cantor Schapira had been waiting for the moment when the sun would begin to set, but nevertheless he began the ceremony with the usual words—a little early to be sure and a little confusedly—about a silent prayer, which reminded one of the doors shut just now, for the mixture of the joy and fears, the accomplishments and the fear of the week that was now behind them. It was a prayer for what had happened just a little while ago and now was behind them, committed to memory, whatever it had been, because the past swallows every present like every tomorrow engulfs all the yesterdays, and what remains of everything is only that which is what we are.

"This day," he said, "is one in which we will not do, but be. On this day, in this moment, we only are, since being is more than to be. And to be is equal with God."

He certainly had started early, Anna thought to herself along with the others, but he probably had had some reason for doing so. He spoke about the path—the course of the world that we travel upon seen and unseen, that which we touch and which remains untouched, the sense of which we perceive only approximately because there are moments that arise necessarily and unmistakably when we are one with the world which is and which was and which will be, since at the present time it was that moment when we could tear the world into the smallest pieces in order to fathom its spiritual essence before it returned to a whole in our soul. It was Saturday, the Sabbath, the moment of quiet and warmth and light that can come from us alone. He spoke about what the Sabbath was: the day of rest. For the men and women who came before him, the Sabbath was a sign of the agreement with God and the universe. For those who kept the Sabbath ordinances faithfully, if life and existence wore at them, the Sabbath would restore them to wholeness. When life was bitter to them, the present moment relieved them. Then Cantor Schapira asked how and why the lives of all those present were different from those of their ancestors, but he didn't offer an answer, stating, "Beloved, go and meet your bride; beloved, come and greet the Sabbath." It rang in the space of the synagogue as if in an empty chamber, a little like it was in a barrel. Those words about abundance and the well—about the song and light—could the age-old words encompass what is and what is not? How many truths were they missing? How much truth equals the past?

Then came the prayer for the dead: *Blessed be his name from the ages to ages. Amen. Praised be his immortal name, above all songs, above all praise. Amen.*

Cantor Schapira nodded for those present to stand; they stood up.

There is only one life, one reality. Only that which is purely just is always just, and the purely unjust is always unjust. Now he tells us: There are many truths, much of which are just, much of which are unjust. But today what is unjust and bad and evil for one can be just and good for another. Someone says, what is good for you is bad for me. And still, certain acts and words must be bad for everyone. Beyond all the half-truths, false truths, and lies there is a simple and clear truth that one day we will be able to understand. *Blessed be his name. Amen.*

The cantor spoke about what Emil Ludvig had remembered: about the necessity of strength, courage, and patience, and the strength to overcome; about the humility by which a person measures his worth and the courage to rise above defeat; about the patience to purify oneself and rid oneself of everything one knew well enough was imperfect inside.

He prayed to the things that should never end: the sand and the sea, the life-giving waters, the formation of clouds, the prayer rising from a clean heart. Then he repeated himself: *Blessed be the name of God, teacher of peace. Amen. Let God visit peace on all the children of Israel, on the entire world. Amen.*

The air in the synagogue was damp, and the cantor rasped a little bit; he'd probably caught a cold. His words really resounded a little emptily.

The children's singing and the fanfares and reports from the supreme command of the Reich's imperial armed forces outside repeated ad nauseam. Mr. Mario Schapira spoke about the Ten Commandments, that the world had been different before them and would be different when they were gone. It would not be their world because they could not accept it. They had to reject the bloodless world where people had pretensions about their stature because of the title of their birth, their class, or their race, when in fact, at birth, just as in race or death, people were the same. The Germans took the word "killing" in its original meaning. They murdered without reason. They put injustice over law. They could not accept the world in which a lie was passed on as a truth and a wrong as justice. The history of the world and man on the earth would begin anew, Mr. Schapira told the few people who were there, including his wife and daughter (who was pregnant again by her non-Jewish husband who had converted and was now guarding the rear entrance). The world as they knew it was dying; for many people, it was already dead. It would have a different rebirth, because that would occur only when people stopped killing one another. They would not need it to prove their greatness, pride, self-sacrifice. The only sacrifice in the world to come would be self-sacrifice in which no blood would be spilled. Then, nobody would miss the old world, which might not have been as good as it seemed to so many people, only because they had done nothing to make it worse.

"What's he talking about?" Emil Ludvig whispered.

"He's talking about you and me," Anna said. (She had wanted to say at first that she didn't know.) "About our children, Helena and Richard."

Emil Ludvig nodded in greeting to the cantor; perhaps Mr. Schapira did not even recognize him. He could not see well. They had met each other for the first time at the synagogue. Did the Ten Commandments really strip people of the privilege to lie, steal, kill, plunder, and bear false witness, and rape women and abuse children and raise oneself over another? Was it still criminal to let one set of people worship you and reject others? Mr. Schapira gave the impression of a person who wanted to stifle some words by using others, to stop the acts which words could not stop.

The Wehrmacht high commander's voice interrupted him again: the advanced units of the heroic German army stood in front of the capital city of the satanic enemy, of the bulwark of barbarity, of the chief danger of the civilized world. The executioners and demons of Europe stood before the most difficult, most complete defeat. Beethoven's "Yorkscher Marsch" began thundering at the end of the short announcement.

"It's an icebox in here—there aren't enough people," Emil whispered.

"Where do you think they are now? At the Great Exposition Palace?" Anna asked him.

"It wasn't right for them to let Arthur feel resented."

"I doubt he was able to eat for the road."

"You're tired. Go home and rest. I'm going to go back again. So far, we've been lucky."

"After you left today they came to old Kubr's to search," Anna said. "They asked him which railroad workers he knew from the gang they arrested, which was delaying trains, got shot on the shooting grounds in Kobylisy—like they shot General Elias and Dr. Vancura. They wanted to trip him up with the pretext that he could present mitigating circumstances which might save their necks. He defended himself: he told them he'd been retired long ago and didn't know any members of the underground—in fact, he didn't even know that such sabotage groups existed—he'd assumed the German Reich had everything firmly in hand. They slapped him around, said he was a provocateur despite his seventy years, and took him away with them. They barged into his apartment with Dvorak, the grocery store owner, who spoke to the plainclothes policemen in bad German. Old Kubr pretended he did not know German. They screamed at him that he was an instigator; they would deal with him at a different place and in another way. Right now, they're probably cleaning his ears and eyes out for him, but not with boric acid."

"Why him?"

"They were searching for a worker who was believed to have been visiting Lida. Old Kubr said that they were out of luck, and that it might be lucky for her—she'd been dead for a long time. He told them to keep looking—that he isn't always completely with it, and can't remember in the morning where he put his shoes the night before. They told him, and Mr. Dvorak translated, that they would help him remember, but they didn't guarantee it wouldn't make him dizzy."

Emil and Anna's conversation shifted from Martha, Arthur, and Susanna to the Ten Commandments. "Man is not a fly that someone can get rid of only by waving his hand," Mr. Schapira quoted. Then he talked about how, one hundred and fifty grandmothers back, their people had helped the Egyptians build the pyramids and the Assyrians build their large temples; they had been there when the Babylonians and Hittites engraved cuneiform into clay bricks; they had fought with all of them, and also with the Ammonites, Midianites, Jebusites, and Aramites, with the Greeks as well as the Romans. Not even the Romans had succeeded in killing them off or ridding them of their faith. Mr. Schapira searched for hidden meanings in what had happened in the past and might happen again, but which he couldn't see now. He searched in the maze of puzzles, defeats, and victories of the past for a truth applicable today, the sixteenth of October 1942, at two in the afternoon in the dark synagogue on Primatorska Avenue, with the rain clouds continually gathering. What was it that bound them together and enabled them to carry on after the fall of Babylon and many empires from Nineveh all the way to the proud and seemingly unconquerable Rome? What are the centripetal and centrifugal forces that create and destroy great empires? What has kept them from the edge of destruction, so that they might perpetuate themselves?

"Four thousand years stand in front of us like a column," Mr. Schapira said, though it was plain to see that he hadn't a clue as to what would happen even in the next hour.

"I have to feed the rabbits," Emil Ludvig quietly said. "Godemke is probably already getting nervous."

"I'm scared," Anna said. "But don't tell me that I don't know why. Did you give him my bag to let you go? What did he say?"

"He let me go with a pass. That's enough, isn't it?"

That morning Anna had begged Emil to buy her sewing supplies; she had a purchase voucher worth only two crowns to last for three months, and they were allowed to buy clothes only from secondhand dealers.

Mr. Schapira talked about the hope which lasted as long as their hearts beat. It seemed like he was singing. Emil Ludvig looked around the temple nave at the chandeliers from which Richard had wanted to swing when he was little.

"Karla came over too," Anna said. "She brought a box of roasted almonds for the children from the amusement park at the Meteor VIII. I could have given it to you for your sister, Arthur, and Susanna to take with them. She gave it to me very unobtrusively; she hadn't even heard what had happened at old Kubr's."

"Haven't you heard?" the man next to Anna asked. "Once we were sitting in here, praying, and they drove pigs right inside."

Somebody opened the front door; the stench from the soap factory permeated the room. Emil Ludvig looked around the synagogue: a warehouse or stables could be made out of it, it was roomy enough. All of a sudden, it all came together—his sister's departure, everything that had happened with Mr. Ernst Kantner, and what Mr. Schapira, with his belly dangling through his old clothes, was saying.

It was now raining outside. The *Aryan Struggle* knew what it was writing about when its biggest headline had stated yesterday that the fighters against the Jews would unite even more solidly. Nobody would allow the Jewish storm troops to thrust the Trojan horse of their perversities into the closed ranks of the Aryan fighters. For the purity of the race! Away with the Jewish well poisoners! Long live the Central Committee and the leadership of the Aryan Flag Organization! Long live the members of the rank and file—the front guard of the fighters for progress!

Let them close tight enough, Emil thought, so that they choke themselves. They wrote about a clock whose hands could not be stopped even by the strongest Jewish hand. Did Mr. Schapira want to build a barricade in here? A human shield? A wall made out of old people's, women's, and children's bodies? From his son-in-law's body and the body of his newly pregnant wife? From Anna and a few people like Emil and the rest of them who came for the Holiday of the Tents?

Outside, a downpour had started. The flags on the German schools went limp. The speaker squealed in the rain. Mr. Schapira quoted by heart: *I am concluding a contract with you today, by which I declare that I shall never again bring a flood to the world.* The sky darkened even more.

"What Napoleon did not accomplish, Hitler has been successful at," the speaker outside blared. "Great, great, three times great is the Germany of this moment."

Emil Ludvig's nostrils filled with the scent of the temple nave. Thornten Godemke had brought him flour, sugar, and soldier's rations because the rabbits were gaining weight. He told Emil that he had guarded the gate of an institution where people's genitals, heads, and other body parts were being measured to classify the ideal Aryan. They also forced men and women to breed like rabbits, he said—he felt more comfortable guarding rabbits. It seemed to Anna that rabbits had strange eyes, fearful, even if nothing was happening to them. Why? Sometimes their eyes seemed so clear, yet in spite of that, they watched things as if they were dead.

"I've been expecting you."

Mr. Mario Schapira went pale; he gazed toward the front entrance at the very end of the aisle with the worn-out carpet. Large, thick raindrops ran down the synagogue windows. The speakers played a series of three marches: "Hoch Heidechsburg," a "Hessischen Fannen

Marsch," and the "Alexander Marsch." He grabbed for the prayer book that was on the chest-high table in front of him.

Two German policemen in boots and riding breeches walked toward him, striding briskly. With them was Mr. Dvorak, the seller of imported goods and spices from their building at 137 Royal Avenue, and behind him, Slavomir Mayer, the dance master, to serve as translators, along with boys in Hitler Youth uniforms from the school opposite on Primatorska Avenue. No one was going to get away with violating the protectorate's laws as they were doing by being in the synagogue.

They came all the way up to the acacia wood Torah case: Mr. Schapira's son-in-law was inside now too. The door stood ajar behind him, and behind it stood another small group of Hitler Youth. Mr. Schapira took two steps back toward the Torah case, which contained the religious constitution binding all those living as well as the dead and yet unborn—laws about individuals and the community to whose word and glory the invisible God granted his authority. The cantor held the prayer book on his belly, but he wasn't reading. Above his head was a huge, slightly cracked, golden crown with a crimson border. He opened his mouth to say something to the policemen or to Messrs. Dvorak and Mayer, but before he could utter a word, one of the Hitler Youth put a fist in it, splitting his lower teeth against the upper teeth. Blood ran down the cantor's chin and neck. Mrs. Schapirova shrieked; her scream filled the temple and dissipated.

Mr. Schapira stated, "No stable or warehouse—this is a sanctuary." He got slugged a second time from the same Hitler Youth and kept silent.

"*Schweigen, todschweigen,*" the Hitler Youth said, and he flailed away with his crop at the golden crown above the altar, and then also with his other hand when at first nothing happened. *Todschweigen* was a German word that had come to Prague with the army, with the Gestapo, and with the Hitler Youth. It meant to quiet—to silence to death. But Mr. Schapira was still living. They hadn't come to kill him (there were other places for that, here and in the East) but only to beat him and drive him out of the building he called a sanctuary which, depending on what the captain of the cavalry, who'd taken command at the former police stables not far from the synagogue, decided, would become a stable or warehouse within a week.

"*Alles heraus,*" the Hitler Youth said. Everyone rushed toward the rear exit where the littler Hitler Youths were standing. Some of the Youths were surprised at the power they had. Others spat at people, while still others just laughed.

The younger boys in little brown shirts, shivering in black corduroy shorts, kicked the first people to leave out the back. They spat at Anna and Emil Ludvig, who got goosebumps on their thighs.

"Everyone out," Mr. Dvorak translated. Mr. Mayer complemented him amiably as if giving instructions to young dance students: "First the back benches through the rear entrance, please, then the middle benches, then the benches in the front. No confusion, please. If there are any women sitting in the balcony, then also exit to the rear, please! Through the back entrance, I repeat, through the back entrance, ladies and gentlemen!"

Mr. Mayer clapped the palms of his hands together. "You shouldn't have been here for as long as you already have been. The building has been taken under the protection of the army and the authorities. Who'd like to tangle with the German army—with the authorities, ladies and gentlemen? I hope you're here by mistake. Even for that— and I'm certainly not exaggerating—you could be shot."

"*Was sagt er?*" a Hitler Youth asked.

The grocer translated for him in his bad German. The policemen eyed the new army property. It seemed that no one had harmed anything by praying. Somebody kicked the golden crown. It flew under a bench; it was lighter than it seemed. They could hear footsteps, words about bad luck, pain, and horror, but no one said anything— they just hurried outside. Then, they could only hear the shuffling of feet.

The smallest Hitler Youths in their clean uniforms with daggers at their waists still looked around, puzzled. Apparently this was the first time they'd ever been in a synagogue. They laughed progressively louder; as they summoned their courage, they passed remarks about individual people—that they limped or stank like animals.

"All Jews are war criminals," their leader, the highest-ranking Hitler Youth, said. Outside, the speakers reported how deep into Russia the German armies were now fighting, and then bells started ringing—from the way it sounded, perhaps all the bells of all the churches in Europe—bells of thanksgiving.

The smallest Hitler Youths drowned one another out shouting that the synagogue reeked like a disinfection or a delousing station. What would be here tomorrow? A warehouse? Stables? For how many horses?

Mr. Mayer didn't stop hustling them out: "So, go on, go on," he added politely and energetically. Of course, it hadn't been decided for certain by the German cavalry captain, but if he was satisfied with the former police stables, perhaps it might be possible to get him to alter the decision to make the synagogue into a warehouse just a little bit and instead try for something different like the large, barnlike dance halls in France. The authorities could clear the way for him. But then, Mr. Jandourek, the jewelry store owner, would have the final word, and he might perhaps prefer to make the synagogue into a cinema, cabaret, theater, or covered ice-skating rink—in short, something a broad range of the neighborhood's population could benefit from. Of course, Mr. Dvorak would probably prefer the warehouse, especially if he knew he'd get a fair piece of it to store his herring and potatoes in. We shall see, we shall see, Mr. Mayer said to himself, and added aloud, "That's the way to do it, boys, that's the way." He knew many a person among them. He clapped as if to a lively country dance rhythm.

"This isn't a tango, nor the English slow waltz, ladies and gentlemen—well then, please. Right. Excellent. Let us say a foxtrot, a polka—something faster—a mazurka, but so that your legs don't get tangled in the rhythm. A gavotte, maybe?" He smiled broadly. "Yes, a gavotte. A Jewish gavotte. A little Jewish dance in the new Europe. To the East, in the rhythm of a gavotte."

Emil Ludvig got his pass ready; he held Anna's hand. They were almost outside. Only when he turned around did he see that the policemen and the bigger Hitler Youth had surrounded Mr. Mario Schapira, his wife, his pregnant daughter, and his son-in-law. They formed a circle around them. He couldn't see it very clearly because they kept heading for the street, and it was raining heavily. Mr. Schapira still held the prayer book against his chest with one hand; he wiped his lips off with the other.

"Pity I did not recognize them earlier," Emil Ludvig said.

"What would you have done?" Anna asked.

"Yeah, what would I have done?"

Everyone moved as quickly as they could, ready to raise their hands up, but nobody ordered them to. Two of the bigger Hitler Youths were Mr. Dvorak's sons; the third, smaller son tiptoed with the little ones at the rear entrance, as their leader. They were proud of their father; they wanted him to be proud of them. Before they came here, they'd caught part of a conversation between Mr. Jandourek, their father, and the dance master, Mayer, about what a Jewish lie it was to profess that man was born free or good if he was not born as an Aryan or to German parents—that it was just one of the artful lies and pretensions of the inferior race, and even if they painted themselves over a hundred times, they'd never get among the members of the pure race. They were like rats: they were numerous and gobbled down whatever they found. They were like lice: they leeched onto everyone and everything, soiling and infecting it. They were disgusting even to look at. They claimed that all people were equal because they were weak themselves. Thank heavens there weren't more of them or they'd strangle and suck the blood out of everyone like vampires. They should be exterminated—gotten rid of—but really mercilessly. This time it wouldn't do to throw them out the door just so they could come back in by the window, like they've been doing a thousand and maybe even two thousand years already. They only look like people— like everyone else. They didn't even like horses well enough to give up the synagogue voluntarily for German stables. Liberty was not for everyone, not even the majority, but only for the leaders in a plurality.

The oldest Hitler Youth said that the Torah, the summary of the Jewish teachings, the five books of Moses, was understandable only to the Jewish initiates as a guide for war crimes against which gas on the French and German battleground of the First World War was merely child's play. A secret sixth, seventh, and eighth book even existed about how to rule the world by conspiracy, but an ordinary mortal would never find out about it. They were going to put an end to that. The leader of the Hitler Youth waved a book from the synagogue's archives where the history of the building since 1858 was, the date the cornerstone had been laid. It had taken ten years to build. The edifice had lasted up to now. Everyone felt this was how it would end. Heil Hitler! It sounded equally as emphatic in Czech as it did in German: Hail Hitler! Even words like "freedom," "honor," and "victory" became poisoned in the mouth of a Jew. They were afraid of the word "race"; they didn't want to admit, even to themselves, that they were a race—that there was a difference between their religion and their race. It was twilight in the synagogue; rain poured into the street.

A covered truck stopped in front of the main entrance of the synagogue. The young men in Hitler Youth uniforms, who in the presence of both policemen, Mr. Dvorak, and Mr. Mayer had pulled down the acacia wood altar and for amusement had kicked the scrolls wrapped in velvet with decorative buckles for want of anything better to do, looked out from the entrance. The wind had let in the rain, and the smell of the soap factory wafted in again. From a distance, none of the youths appeared to be older than Richard, Emil thought. The policemen led Mr. Schapira with his wife, his pregnant daughter, and his son-in-law away to the car. They said something to the women— probably that they could go home—but they had refused; they both wanted to remain with their husbands. "You should reconsider that," the first policeman said. Why? Because Mr. Schapira had disobeyed the injunction on using synagogues and then had not wanted the building to become a stable or a warehouse. They'd settle that with him elsewhere. The Gestapo always had a few people under its thumbs at the Great Exposition Palace; it would be no problem to add a couple of new souls to a transport, even after it had been dispatched. The luggage could be sent for afterward. Mario Schapira was having trouble getting over the sideboard (which they hadn't taken down); he was still quite heavy, though he had lost weight. The truck had a gas cylinder instead of a fuel tank in the back. Mario Schapira held on to his prayer book until he finally dropped it trying to swing over the side. Mr. Schapira's son-in-law picked it up and climbed over the sideboard with it. Mrs. Schapirova had to be thrown into the body of a wagon because she had her hands clasped and couldn't get in herself. They also helped the daughter in so she wouldn't hold up traffic. At the worst, she'd have her child somewhere besides at home.

"That's the end of the false worries about the individual," Mr. Dvorak told Mr. Mayer, so Mr. Jandourek would hear them. The important thing now was what would become of the synagogue: a stables or a warehouse? Which of them would get his way? Enough, now, of Jewish heresies about the dignity of human life—that everyone's value equals another's.

Because of the rain, the incident caused little commotion. On an ordinary day people also had other worries. The truck had an awning. The place was full of German policemen and Hitler Youth. The speakers shouted out victory, fanfares, drums and tambourines, pipes, flutes. The amusement shooting grounds were full; perhaps people had sought shelter from the rain there.

Emil Ludvig left Anna at home; that was one place they were still allowed to be. He was unable to console her by saying that sooner or later they would all be together again—Arthur, Martha, Susanna, and the Schapiras. He'd been gone for a long time; he took off his star so that he could ride in a taxi to the Waffen SS barracks construction site.

Thornten Godemke asked him where he'd been for so long. The downpour had stopped. By Emil Ludvig's look, he didn't wait to get an answer. It wasn't raining anymore and they were alone (the young volunteer SS exercises had already ended); Godemke polished the crocodile skin of the back of the purse with a white cotton cloth to shine up the skin a bit.

"What's going on?" Thornten Godemke asked.

"The same as usual," Emil Ludvig answered.

"Better not to ask, I know," the soldier said.

"No," Emil Ludvig agreed.

Emil set out to feed the rabbits right away, as if it were the most important thing in the world. The grass had gotten soaked. He saw that Thornten Godemke had done some of it for him.

"You look like the shepherd for a school of fish," the soldier said. "What happened? Have they left for Lodz-Litzmanstadt? Have you lost your tongue?" Then he added, "They've been fed. I took the task over for you. Where's your pass?"

"I feel like a toddler," Emil Ludvig said. "I'm constantly in the arms of others, either at their mercy or not." He gave the soldier the pass as if it were an expired pawn ticket.

"They want that," Thornten Godemke said. And then he asked quietly, but with military brevity, "What're you going to do?"

"What should I do?"

"I would know what to do."

Thornten Godemke tore up the pass. He lit up a cigarette and smoked. Then he passed Emil the remaining half. He did not want to throw it on the ground after the rain; there was plenty of mud and lots of puddles around. Emil Ludvig stared into the rabbits' eyes. Nothing reflected back in them.

"I don't know if I understand what you're saying."

"Somebody could offer you sanctuary, don't you think?"

"Everyone's terrified to do that."

"Maybe my mother could."

"Your mother?"

"My mother is a widow in Berlin."

"In Berlin?"

"I can give you the address."

"They'd kill anyone who lends us a hand," Emil Ludvig said.

He didn't say what he had just seen: how they'd beaten Cantor Schapira and taken him away along with his entire family. It was the whole chain of experience, from the German Jewish immigrant, Joachym Luxemburg, to now. In his mind, he added what he had heard. It was probably only a fraction of what was being said. He'd seen enough prior to that to imagine what was awaiting them. Or could it have been, even so, just an aberration? A passing frenzy? Granted, an enormous one, but still only an unusual craze that would subside like a flood does, or a fire dies down, or an earthquake rumbles itself out? Was it only a storm, that is destructive but blows over, as all storms in nature and in history have done so far? After all, they couldn't shut everyone away in concentration camps, could they? He imagined a huge sea and the tides. He sensed that which was more terrible than terrible because it was more terrible only for him.

"You can't think about that. And if you do think about it, you mustn't pay any attention to it. A person is only a person when he does what he must do, regardless of everyone else. How many of you are there?"

"Four."

"My mother only has a basement room, but hopefully, she'd know of someone."

"It's far away from here."

"Yes. It's far. You don't know anyone to help you here?"

"I know a lot of people, but no one I could turn to for help."

"That's a shame," Thornten Godemke said. "Think about it. If you don't come, I'll know what's happening. I'll give you time. I'm not going to just let them rub you out."

"Thanks," Emil Ludvig said.

"I'd do it if I were in your shoes."

Their eyes met. They stared at each other for about five seconds. Emil Ludvig looked to the ground. He wondered whom one could trust or not trust these days, and how trust crossed barriers, uniforms, and people as if it were dividing the good from the bad, and the revolting from the comforting. Whom could one trust? Was it impossible to know? Would he believe the most humble? It was probably like trying to count the stars. Evidently, infinity came in many things; it was in the starry night above, in an individual, and in people. He felt how the borders of everything that had held the world together up to now had shifted, so that it was possible to see even through its obscurity. Emil Ludvig also sensed what his wife Anna had felt before he had come to her to the synagogue—how all the supports that had held the heavens together so that it wouldn't collapse in on itself were giving way, and how the end of the world was coming. Yes and no. Thornten Godemke's mother? Suddenly he imagined a woman in a dark basement apartment in Berlin and felt sorry that it was so far away that he'd never be able to get there. One thing he was sure of, as Mr. Godemke said, a person does something no matter what—whatever the cost. He looked into Thornten Godemke's blue eyes and then into the impassive, red eyes of the rabbits. He gave them the softened, wet grass. The rabbits didn't have the wild eyes alligators have. They were the carefree, reddened, inflamed eyes of animals who'd surrendered to the care of his hand, before they went under the care of another human hand. Only the world that existed now reflected in their eyes, not the world that had been or the one to come.

THE ECHO

From Helena's notes:

I feel like I had been swimming the whole night under the sea and I knew that there was still another day and night left, and then some. Despite what is yet before me, I expect I will make it to the other shore, across the unknown dark sea, as long as my breath and strength hold out.

I read that monarch butterflies have a built-in navigation system in their brains, smaller than the eye of a needle, which they pass on. One generation sets out on its journey with a system ten times stronger than the nine generations that came before it and the nine generations that will follow. They make the trip from the south to the north and then north to south, two thousand five hundred miles at a height of a thousand meters or, like it said, three thousand feet above the earth. There are thirty-five to a hundred million of them, and they fly in the sunlight for five months. They look like an orange carpet. They take off at dawn with the first glow of light. At night they roost in trees, and natives claim that they look like they're praying. Their milk glands contain something that protects them if birds swallow them. If a bird does swallow one, it spits it back out because it's inedible. In the end it saves their lives, from generation to generation.

✤

8

During the entire time the prisoners left the trucks, the crowd kept tearing them apart. The trucks were confiscated, Renaults or the Opelblitz like the one that had arrived in front of the synagogue on Lord Mayor Avenue. With German military license plates and with the battered field gray and the cracked masking paint, the paunchy Renaults looked condemned. Only the SS guard commander's car was nearly new: a black Daimler with armor-plated sides and with bullet-proof glass and headlights painted over blue, with a clear rectangle the size of two razor blades placed next to each other for the high beams. The road was lit with reflectors that were not dimmed with anything. It had been over a month already since the American bombers from the base in Foggia had flown above— the area of the camp with its five crematoria and eight pits where the dead were burned when the firm of Topf at Wiesbaden could not cope. The eastern front had been quiet for several months, and nothing disturbed the partial operations of the comprehensive plan for the extinction of all members of the Jewish race, a plan named Night and Fog.

In front of them were the walls of the underground undressing room and a gradual concrete slope as if for an immense empty warehouse of potatoes or into catacombs for growing mushrooms. There were gray and black smoke-stained walls made of bricks manufactured in a brickyard not far away and a bit larger than those used to build the original cavalry barracks at Auschwitz-Birkenau to serve the Polish army, then the Austro-Hungarian troops, and eventually the Waffen SS units. There was plenty of soot and ashes mixed with dust on the ground. In places, puddles formed around the hydrants, and mud formed as the layers of dust ate through.

In the middle of the night, it was dark and the reflectors broke the darkness up only in a few places. The invisible dust and soot with ashes irritated their noses, mouths, and throats. They had to work to keep together. That now was the main goal: working to stay together.

Somebody asked, "What is it?"

"A waiting room," an eighteen-year-old SS soldier answered.

"A waiting room for what?" the voice wanted to know.

"For the Messiah," the young SS soldier answered; he had been told these Jews did not believe anybody and yet were preposterously trusting at the same time. Indeed, that was the last time they'd ask. They wouldn't bother anyone the next time.

The SS soldier saw a repeated image: the empty, frightened, or uncomprehending expressions of people who had only twenty or thirty minutes of life left before them. The drawn-in, hunger-stricken faces, expressions of the sick. Without a doubt, along with their unfinished accounts and their customs, they took dangerous bacteria into the crematorium with them: maybe typhus, maybe even cholera, various illnesses they might spread across the world. Luckily, all of it would burn away with them in twenty, thirty, or forty minutes, depending on how many cans of zyklon-B were used on them. It's better that we keep the required distance of at least five feet between us and them, he thought to himself. Let them take their diseases with them to the crematorium to burn without infecting him. He pondered about the danger of his post.

Hanging over the gate next to the camp was a sign written in Hebrew—which meant that one of them must have translated it, written it, and taken care of it in the wind, snow, and rain—THIS IS THE GATE OF GOD THROUGH WHICH ONLY THE JUST CAN ENTER. Next to that were written JEDEM DAS SEINE and ARBEIT MACHT FREI, just above the main gate. It was not the only sign on the only gate in Auschwitz-Birkenau, but no one was surprised anymore by the German, or rather Nazi, sense of humor. Who knew who had the idea first? Emil Ludvig thought about how many people would lose their lives in a revolt, and he came to the conclusion that even if the last one of them were to fall to the ground, it would not be more than the number of victims that had yet to pass through both sides of the ramp from the endless transports that arrived from within the remains of Europe. He no longer wasted his energy being surprised at the work the Germans put into creating a facade of normalcy within the Jewish ghettos and temporary camps, like Theresienstadt in northern Bohemia, only so that the Jews and non-Jews of Europe would think how far removed the Nazis were from the cruel treatment of human beings. In this the Germans had succeeded. They created the perception that, in comparison to war and the anxieties that war causes, they were more accommodating than could have been expected. Then, in their bigheartedness, they fed their prisoners two hundred and fifty calories a day, once every twenty-four hours, and some days not even that much. They didn't come here to recover, as to a sanitorium, but to die. Those whom illnesses and hunger, beatings and punishments did not finish off were guaranteed a solution—the ovens. Everyone ended up as ashes. No one would again experience the arrival of the sun, the following dusk, the first star, a moment of prayer, the next night, the next spring, summer, or fall, the first or last snow, rain, wind, the flight of birds. No one would again see the one they wished most to catch sight of—even for one last time. The Germans had obliterated the border between the first moment and the last. Between good and evil, between the just and the crooked, between that which a person had wanted to do right, even if no one saw him, and that which he was afraid to do wrong. This the Germans drowned in a pool of water which they called a race—Germany—the German calling. That was lost in a camp of no return.

Emil thought about what he'd heard—that death is lighter than a bird's feather. It would seem ridiculous not to agree. The burden of life is heavier. Words. Thoughts. We all want to live, even though it be under the worst circumstances, because at the end of every thought is the invisible hope. Maybe. Perhaps. Who knows? All that time they had stood close to death. They had become used to death. It was with them like a constant companion, day and night, like a sister or brother, when they stood up or lay down on the bunks, or when they were forced to carry stones. In the meantime, in spite of everything, they were still living. He once saw a person here crouched down on the ground near the barbed wire, saying to someone, "It's high time—Monday afternoon—they should come for me. I've already waited for an hour." As if it were yesterday and he was only waiting somewhere in Kraków or Antwerp for the bus, for the share of a crust of bread, but knew that he was waiting as if he were trying to shorten the wait by letting them throw him on the truck so he wouldn't have to go on foot. People were collected like that three times a day—they no longer wished to go on living. It changed them. The line between the value and worthlessness of life disappeared. A second in the concentration camp was enough to make them different, and if they had not ended up here or managed to get out of here, they would have been different anywhere else they had gone. None of them got out of here. The most immense moment of all was still ahead of them: the unknown—death—that which all have in common. Somewhere amid them were the weaker ones. They took sticks away from them so they couldn't use them as weapons. In the darkness that surrounded them, there was no longer any difference between the blind and the seeing, just as there would be no difference between the mute and the deaf and those who could still speak and hear. One broken thought still flashed through his mind—that once they killed him, as they killed all those before him and would kill all those after him, it would haunt history like an echo of all humanity. The reverberation would never end; it would remain like an open crack—red, like the color of blood, and black, like ash. Maybe. Who knows?

Maybe it was no longer important. Finally the question How could this have happened? stopped bothering Emil Ludvig. How could they and those around them have allowed this? But now it only was—pure existence. He felt like a grain of sand, like the last drop of water before it dries up from the heat coming from the center of the earth.

Rolf Tuepe, the young SS man, had distrustful blue eyes and flaxen hair. He perceived everything as if he had distanced himself from it while at the same time was proud of his activity and participation. He was a part of the greatest undertaking that Germany had ever attempted. He could feel how he had surpassed everything around him, including the war—at least the war as his parents and grandparents knew it.

The young SS man had already formed a picture of the people and families that came but never left. He tried to avoid them as individuals whenever he could, but it was not always possible. He faced only the darkness but appealed to the safety of searchlights. This was sort of a slaughterhouse, but that wasn't his affair. Sometimes Rolf Tuepe would turn away. He would look into the darkness or up to the sky or to the stars, away from the crowd that shuffled in only one direction. There were the things the young SS officer could not have imagined, before he'd come here. The sure thing was that the Final Solution was the best one.

To the young SS officer, Rolf Tuepe, it seemed almost funny that they, naked, everything taken away from them, still believed in their own dignity as firmly as in their rocks and deserts two or three thousand years ago. Here they would lose the pride, self-assurance, or conceit; here all their transgressions would be burned and swept away from the earth. Besides, in a war, everybody deserved the same, at least on the side of the vanquished. For the time being, there were voices and sighs and shouts and groans, shuffling of feet, sights, words. They had it all behind them now. Everything would be solved inside. It was better to leave them in the fresh air, in the darkness, to tell them nothing, not even to imply anything. It occurred to the young SS officer that this was the time when everyone behaved like a child, even the wise and old, experienced and accomplished. He had seen it several times. In fifteen minutes they all would meet the same fate. Subconsciously, the young SS officer, Rolf Tuepe, wanted to find something good on both sides—something they could have in common. But except for the air, there was nothing.

While alive, they believed in too many myths. He pondered over what else would burn with them along with their secret loves and hates. Who knew how many experts were there, knowledgeable in God knew what; no longer would they live by their wits. They would not live. Period. The Final Solution. They'd find it was like the inside of a gymnasium, a hall of celebrations. Only it is a celebration for us, he corrected himself in his mind, not for them. There was not much difference between people and cattle being led to the slaughterhouse. Even the bravest and the most courageous had a lump in their throats, shit in their pants, and tears in their eyes. It might be a consolation for them, the young SS man thought. They would be rid of their sheds, their bunk beds without mattresses, the neutral zones by the fences where they were shot without warning, the wet rags that they wore day and night, the roll calls in front of the barracks where they sometimes had to stand all day and even at night. Those who could not bear it went to the chimney a long time before those who were here now. At least they were together with their families, what they always wanted more than anything else.

In a short while they would begin to beg for mercy, for a bit of life, for a gulp of air. A lot of them would pray unintelligible prayers to their God. He spat into the darkness.

"What's here?" an old man asked him.

"The beet warehouse, don't you know that?" the young SS man answered.

"What's going to happen to us?" he heard the old man ask.

"Nothing," Rolf Tuepe answered. And he thought: In fifteen minutes you won't have to worry about it anymore. "Should I record it, since you all ask the same question all the time? Now, go, go, go."

"Are we going to die? Like the fish in Harmenz?"

"Fish in Harmenz?" the young SS man wondered aloud, but the old man was gone. The crowd had pushed him away. Good, the young, slim, and tall Rolf Tuepe thought.

"What's going to happen?" asked the next one, a young woman.

"What should happen? You'll have a bath to get rid of lice, fleas, and all that filth. Look at yourself—how repulsively you sweat. You need to be disinfected. You'd look like spooks if not for the darkness. Shame on you, to smell this way! When did you last brush your teeth? When did you last change your clothes? Be happy that you've got a chance to get rid of these rags. Then they'll give you black pudding with sauerkraut and mashed potatoes."

Farther down somebody said, "Tailor? We need those like salt, come to me later."

And someone else hollered, "Hurry up while there is hot water. We only have one boiler."

Another SS man, perhaps a wise guy, shouted, "Who needs Alka-Seltzer after dinner?"

Rolf Tuepe thought, It's amazing. Nothing of interest ever happens. Every night and every day it's the same. Come on, forward, you filth, get a move on, hurry. The question of where they were going, what would happen, what was expected of them was repeated over and over like a broken record.

Now a serious ten-year-old boy with huge eyes asked the young SS man, "What do you want to do with us?"

"Ask those who were already there," the young SS man, Rolf Tuepe, snapped.

"I never met any of those who went to the showers," the ten-year-old answered.

"Too bad. Have your eyes and ears examined after you've had your shower," the young SS man said.

"You're lying," the child retorted.

"Do you want a thrashing? I told you to ask them inside. Hurry up."

"All of you have always lied to us," the boy answered.

It occurred to Rolf Tuepe that somebody goes to his death and all he has is his past; the Germans live and they have their future, clear as a sunny sky, as the brightest stars. It's a big night, it will be a big day. You will run away from your past, give yourselves fifteen—twenty, at the most, thirty—minutes, the young SS man thought, silently addressing the child and the unknown crowd. Everything will die with you—the past and the future. Body and soul. All that will remain will be rags, wooden shoes, and what you hid up your ass. It will be over for them. For him too. It could be more pleasant too. In some respects, they were better off than he was. He looked forward to playing the record, "*Wiener Blut*," that he'd received for Christmas from his parents in a couple of hours. The familiar melodies ran through his mind.

"You're a liar," the child said again and then disappeared before the young SS officer could bother with a slap.

It occurred to Rolf Tuepe that he wasn't sure which Strauss composed "*Wiener Blut. Grüss Gott, mein liebes Kind.*" And "*Du süsses Zuckertauberl mein.*" And "*Mir scheint, du willst spassen.*" Or "*Du lieber Schatz, lass dir gesteh'n.*" Silently, addressing everyone and yet no one, he hummed "*Auf Wiedersehen.*" There is also a finale, but without the polka or the polonaise. Without an overture. Or maybe, after all, with an overture.

"*Wiener Blut, Wiener Blut . . . lalala — la-Wiener Blut . . .*"

In a pub frequented by Rolf Tuepe's father on Saturdays they were probably sitting around a table at this very moment, singing, with well-chilled and foamy beer at their sides. When Rolf Tuepe departed from the railway station, his father had said to him, man to man, "You are going to the East where people are being killed day and night. One has to learn to stop being shy while killing. That's not easy. I remember how I had to overcome it in the First War when I thought that perhaps I wouldn't be able to kill like the rest of us. That passed. There is no need for pity. You are not doing anything bad when you kill. You are doing only what you have to do. Don't look back. Don't feel sorry. Don't apologize." His father would have been proud of him. Rolf Tuepe did not feel sorry about what was going on around him. He was proud of it. He did what they all had to do. Of course, everyone didn't get the same chance, he thought. Being outdoors helped his rheumatic heart. He did not handle himself—at the very least—any worse than any of the others. His father could only imagine what took place here; it was top secret. And probably a lot of time would pass before he could share what happened with him. In his family, there were eight members of the SS. They probably knew, he thought—Wolfram Axel, his mother's cousin, and Peter Hatesaul, his father's younger brother, Althious Freihers, a distant cousin. Maybe they were even up at the front lines.

It would be difficult for his mother, or the mother of her mother, or her father, his grandfather, who would also probably not believe it either. In his mind's eye, Rolf Tuepe saw his fourteen-year-old sister who wanted to become a nurse; he saw her forehead, her eyes and hair, and he heard her girlish alto voice. She always spoke as if she were singing to herself. Within her was the innocence of youth and the sympathy of a sister. He'd say to her—with the undisputed authority of an older brother—"We'll kill all those who deserve it. You no longer have to be afraid of them. You'll live in our world where they won't exist." And then he remembered his father: "Never worship the hand that you can bite. Never look back. Never pity. And never apologize to anyone. You are what you are. You will be what you will be. You're only what you make of yourself, what you do not allow others to make of you. 'Let bygones be bygones' should only be said when you toast your health, not as a denial of what you are."

"It's terrible, it's terrible," someone shouted so that Rolf Tuepe heard it.

"It is better to have an end with horror than a horror without an end," he recalled his father saying.

Rolf Tuepe suddenly felt that although he was far from his family, he was not alone. The person who had cried out with horror was gone.

As long as it could be done, Emil Ludvig endeavored to hold on to his wife, Anna, and the children, Helena and Richard. If the crowd tore them apart for a while, he needed to know that they were close by. Three times they got pulled away from one another and then back together again.

Next to the entrance to the underground undressing room, two German ambulances with a red cross on both sides and back were parked. They were reliable Mercedeses and BMWs with robust engines. When they came here last September, the ambulances nearly evoked trust. Now everyone knew that the cars with the German red cross delivered zyklon-B to the delousing station and to all five crematoria: little green crystals the size of small peas, used for killing insects before the war, just as they would be afterward. The painted red cross, even on the engine hood, did not calm or mystify anyone anymore. Many words had lost their meaning, and symbols had spoken more expressively and understandably than words. Already perhaps a thousand people had left before them, a thousand of them were still waiting, and seventeen hundred people would be brought by trucks from the family camp B 2B, right next to the Frauen Konzentrazions Lager B 2C, and the Gypsy Camp B 2E during the night.

All four of them had been in the family camp for six months, since September, and it appeared that the Germans would use them as proof of how decently people were being treated in German camps and that they had left the families that arrived from the Terezin fortress together. They worked and waited for what would be. Sometimes they worked at the Sola or Vistula River; a couple of people from the fisherman command caught fish at the pond on Harmenz, but most were left at the camp. In the meantime, hundreds of thousands of people vanished into the crematoria. Nobody actually would ever be able to count how many. The closer the war from the East came to the center of Europe and to Germany, from which it had started, the more efficient the killing became. It was the most massive slaughter man had ever achieved. But the Nazis did not touch them. They even increased their food allotments three days before. Only the night before, the order had come to prepare for a transfer to Heyderbreck. No one had heard that name yet. Around Auschwitz-Birkenau, there was a giant net of smaller camps attached to war factories for cars, weapons, and synthetic gasoline. It was in their own interest to suppress panicky voices among themselves. And, in the end, they boarded trucks and arrived here—no one willingly, but because there was no avoiding it.

At moments, Emil Ludvig satisfied himself by sensing the outlines of Anna's, Helena's, and Richard's heads. In the family camp, the Nazis even left them their hair and clothes, which in Auschwitz-Birkenau was a privilege the others had not had. It seemed that for a long time the Nazis had kept them there with extraordinary consideration. Sometimes Emil would search for them in the darkness by their shoulders, their movements, by the raised hands that fenced in the darkness. They advanced slowly. It was enough to feel that they were close by.

It was March. In Poland, the early spring was cool. The snow still fell, though sometimes with rain, and sometimes it only rained. They became accustomed to the local raw weather with the morning and night frosts, and, as time went on, they even stopped missing the warm stove, privacy, and rooms where they could be by themselves. Somewhere far ahead was Katovice. And not so far away the rivers Sola and Vistula, and Kraków and Warsaw still farther out into the darkness. Near the Sola and the Vistula grew clumps of birches, willows, and alders, and poplars which the first German commandant had ordered planted around the camp. And not far from the camp larger chestnuts grew. Then there lay ponds, fields, forests, and swamps around the camp. But now they were faced just with walls. Throughout the night, storks and crows flew over them. In the birds' voices was a distance that separated them here from everything and everyone. The trucks had stirred up dust that had settled. It fell on them like a gray sandy cloud, and it was unpleasant to breathe. In a while they would be thirsty, and there would not be anything to drink. Besides that, the air was full of ashes and soot and smoke which contained the taste of burned bones and soap boiled to mush and glue.

The things that Emil Ludvig's family had saved and retained for six months were left behind in the carriage. They had been told that they would still return to the truck, to leave their possessions in one place and remember the license plates of the vehicles. It was in their interest so that everyone would be able to sit down again where they had before. They wore the worn-out spare shirts that had gone through the delousing station many times, shoelaces and straps and knapsacks—everyone had a knapsack—tin knives, which also were forbidden outside the family camp, and pieces of wood such as forks or Chinese chopsticks that could be utilized for diverse purposes. But nobody among them clung to things, except for the objects that reminded them of what they had meant outside. They were glad not to have to take care of anything. Even so, keeping together employed them completely. In addition, they'd had a special allotment of food for the journey, but because no one who had stepped over the doorstep of Auschwitz-Birkenau believed the Germans anymore, they all ate it immediately. Who knew when they would eat the next time?

Emil Ludvig fixed his glasses on his nose. He protected his head near the temples and forehead so that nobody would accidentally break them. He was no longer happy about his gold wire rims with which, together with a smart suit, he would look like a bank official. He constantly held the palms of his hands flat near his eyes, like horse blinders. Earlier, while he climbed down from the truck over the closed sideboards, he spoke with Richard and whispered to him to attempt an escape at the first opportunity. Should he get to Prague, he gave him two reliable names of people who would give him money and something to wear: Landa and Kucirek. There are still decent people in the world. There are not many—but these two are. But now, a wall was in front of them; one could not run away from here— the reflector lights not only illuminated the way to the underground but also created a dam of light that would uncover even a mouse flashing by, a bird who would fly through, a shadow that would betray itself. Except for the violent light of the reflectors, they were engulfed and surrounded by darkness.

Just for a fraction of a second, while they advanced, Emil Ludvig imagined Richard succeeding. He let the crowd drag and push him very slowly, knowing that they were not together anymore, but he did not expect that they would get together again, as he certainly knew all four of them wanted. In a deeper sense, they were together; yet he wanted it differently. Every possibility was always the first and the last. Being together until the last moment meant something. Nothing meant more, and nothing meant anything but that. What were the last thoughts of a father, the last thoughts of a man, the last moments when he still has a family? The family is a crib, a wedding as well as a grave. The family is that which is first as well as last; the family is an inalienable, intangible, indissolvable bond, which can be eroded only from the inside. A family is more than the riches into which one is born, more than glory with which one dies. A man cannot achieve anything that can surpass or overshadow his family. A man can sin or be guilty, but it must never touch his family. During the whole time he did all he could for them to remain together. He would be ready to pray, even to swallow his own excrement, not to betray them. It was the only comprehensibility in the incomprehensible bustle of the world which in the past six months had been limited to the camps, the barracks, the crematoria, the constant presence of the Waffen SS and the kapos and the block elders, the famous Jewish leaders from Prague, Berlin, and Vienna who had become cowards, the leading athletes who had become teachers and officials and kapos of the family camp here. The last one of them, a twenty-five-year-old German Jewish educator from Berlin, at being told what was coming, swallowed a cyanide pill, unable to put himself in the forefront of an uprising which, in this case, had to include the children for whom he cared as well. It was no longer a choice between cowardice and bravery, being silent or uttering a cry, guilt or innocence. Emil knew that he was at the end of the road, the milestones of which were marked by incessant humiliation. The camps that the Third Reich had erected, thanks to its brightest and most devoted and diligent brains, were not just death factories but human workshops for humiliation as well. The Germans wanted each of them to grasp before letting out the soul (in which the Germans did not believe—as if the soul were only a speck of soot to remain on the smokestack wall before being replaced by another speck) that what had happened was a historical necessity undertaken by the Germans in the name of the racially chosen nations.

The Germans served as a mirror to show them their vulnerability. What had happened to their God? Were they not the chosen? In the mirror they discovered their own silence. It was their silence and the guiltlessness, fright, repressed screams, indrawn breath. The mirror reflected silence instead of shouts, not only their silence but the silence of the surrounding world. The Germans crippled them with their own helplessness, securing themselves against a possible uprising by cleverly moving them endlessly from place to place. There was an overwhelming silence that swallowed their last breath. Silence had embraced, enclosed, and swallowed, and in time it had digested everything and everybody. The German world was strong, and strength defeats weakness.

Within Emil Ludvig, the shout directed at the young SS man—"You are even killing the children!"—still echoed. As if it were something new—the children, the old, the healthy, and the sick. The young SS man did not even bother to answer the shout, let alone strike the one who was responsible for it. And now the shout remained like an echo: You are even killing the children! You are even killing the children! You are even killing the children! Emil Ludvig moved forward with the crowd, step-by-step.

Sometimes, if he overcame the torture of hunger and the hopelessness of their situation, he considered the myth which Arthur, in spite of his insensitivity, had perceived within the maze of life. From here the maze of life resembled neither a river nor a pond, neither a mountain nor the deepest abyss, only a hall, as Helena had imagined it when she was young. There was a saying that the devil waits to take something back from everyone for services he has performed in their names. It was a myth that time heals all wounds or that everybody gets what he deserves. It was useless to believe that it was or was not so, or was, or never was—at least not for people like them. Perhaps time would separate somebody from the immediacy of the shot, from the burning sensation it caused, but one would doubt that someone would forget about the concentration camp and Germany in this generation, or forget the torture of hunger, hope, hopelessness, cruelty that would be hard to equal. The myth that silence is golden also vanished. The camp resembled a stone thrown into a human pond, with ripples that spread like a disappearing silence, returning as nothing but a stillness. They never heard an echo from the outside. It was an uncomfortable silence. The stone could have destroyed the myth that what one doesn't know can't hurt one. Everything that will happen behind a man's back, in his absence, will in some way and at some point in time catch up with him. You cannot run away from anything in the world. But the greatest myth was the idea or belief that civilization and law epitomize the good and bad experiences of many generations with the intention of protecting everyone from the first to the last better than he could defend himself. Civilization is only a thin and shabby coat on the surface of the world inhabited by man. It's enough to scratch a little on the surface to show what man is, what he is capable of doing to other men.

Emil Ludvig did not have to put together the things and events about which he would only have laughed on the back porch of the building at 137 Royal Avenue as if they were not possible, just because he could never condemn them to anybody. A long time ago he understood the value of man: how he looks at others, what he agrees to share. He knew far more than he ever wanted to know. Only he did not know all the details about his relatives, his sister Martha, and her husband Arthur and daughter Susanna. It sufficed to see all five smokestacks emitting smoke day and night, the smoke from eight pits where the remainder of the dead were burned and rose to the heavens. They could guess. It was more than knowing or not knowing, beside stillness and shouts, memory and images of the future. He returned to Anna's relatives from the Loewy family, Charlotte and Karel Munk, whose daughter Olga had jumped down an air shaft before the transport and whose only married daughter had come here with her new family. The Ludvigs found out that they were not living anymore, not a single one of them. Three months after the Ludvigs' arrival to Theresienstadt, where they had not managed to catch up with them, their youngest daughter, Henrietta, while cleaning the personal effects of the dead or of the people who had left for the East, stumbled upon something hard in the lining. When she unstitched the lining, she found a gold bracelet. She put it in her pocket; for gold she could get a couple loaves of bread. An SS officer who surveyed the workplace with a telescope saw her. He called her to him and took the bracelet. At the Little Fortress, Henrietta was shot to death. Charlotte and Karel Munk with two daughters, Martha and Eliska, who had been a hunchback, had arrived here. The latter went to the chimney right away; except for twins, hunchbacks scarcely interested the German doctors.

Once Emil Ludvig asked some prisoners in the locksmith Kommando if they hadn't, perhaps, heard of Cantor Schapira. They looked at him as if he were from another world: where had Emil arrived from that he was even asking? By the year 1941, most rabbis had been burned inside the synagogues with their flocks. Didn't he know about Lithuania? About the burned prayer rooms in Riga, Talin, and Vilnius, where the only-too-willing local inhabitants had set the fires before letting the Germans take over? Everything had been burned— from Berlin all the way to the Baltic states. What the Latvians, Lithuanians, and Estonians didn't burn, the Germans did. Very few managed to avoid the flames. Those who managed to survive all of that were now here—we know about them—right? Emil Ludvig stopped asking about Cantor Mario Schapira, and about Martha, Arthur, and Susanna. Searching for one's people inside the concentration camps was the same as searching for a needle in a haystack. And, besides, the Germans didn't allow them an hour's rest, day or night. During all the time they were here, the Nazis did everything to insure that they could not recover from the shock. They had split their families apart as well as any other ties a person might still try to hold on to; they had moved them from one place to another—they had torn them from their roots again and again—and finally, exhausted, confused, starved, and sick, they arrived here.

What had seemed impossible or unacceptable only the day before now struck people as normal and maybe the model of the "good old times" of tomorrow. Not only did nobody count on the world ever returning to its rutted tracks; nobody wanted it anymore. The hope for such a world had perished within him, because it would probably end in smokestacks, humiliation, barbed wires, the manufacture of soap from human bones, of military blankets from human hair, with experiments to change the black Jewish hair into fair hair and the brown Jewish eyes into blue ones. The Germans knew what they were saying when they talked about the Final Solution. Eventually, the soldiers and the officers of the SS said in their moments of openness, everybody's turn would come. In the meantime, they could live—because others perished in the chimneys instead of them. Everybody who still breathed was living on account of someone else whose turn had already come before his own. Why not save the pure wine for oneself? A person could get used to everything—to furnish skin to replace the burned skin of the German soldiers, to be submerged in ice-cold water to test their resistance, to indirectly help German fliers who had been fished out of the English Channel. Everybody knew about it. The officers assured some of the prisoners how futile it would be to hope that someone from the hundreds of thousands and millions of prisoners would become a *Geheimnistrager*, a carrier of a secret, a knowing person who would carry out what he had seen. After the war, not even the wisest, the most prudent, and the most experienced people will be willing to take at face value what a confused and desperate survivor will maintain had happened. The witnesses will not stop dying out just because there is no more war. They will become wrecks before they become extinct, aging prattlers with suicidal tendencies because they will not get over the impossibility of communicating what they still remember, and even that is not, nor can it be, everything. The SS officers knew what they talked about. The only thing that even they had not known was the inability to express one's own humiliation by the most courageous and hardiest witnesses. The whole truth would eventually never come out. Even those who would survive the camps would not, after a while, want to believe what they had lived through. Those who had caused it would not feel like getting themselves to the gallows and so would prefer holding their tongues before the grave could swallow them up. And, because the humiliated were unable to express the depth and the entire scope of their humiliation to their children, or their acquaintances, the story would never be known. The SS officers were not encumbered by twinges of conscience or shame for even a fraction of a second. If things had been different, they would have called aloud from the very beginning. They knew that the truth was dead before it could be born and kept alive. They knew that a lie would continue to triumph in their cause, all the way until the end of the world and of time.

The prisoners struggled hard to cling like barnacles to what still had made sense the day before, but they were pictures growing dim, faint, and progressively fainter, a haze that faded away with every hour in the camp. The Nazis wanted them to think about themselves with their last flash of a thought, stripped, in rags, physically and spiritually, that they were inferior, junk flesh and blood. The trains had brought people from Bohemia and Moravia, Austria, Germany, Poland, Greece, Italy, France, Norway, Holland, and Belgium. These same trains carried away gold, artificial limbs, clothes, and the ground-up bones of the dead from which they would manufacture fertilizer for the spring plowing and planting. There would be more and better flour for biscuits, bread, and salt sticks. Slaughtered children and old women and men were closely related to German pancakes from spring to the harvest and from the harvest to the bakers, confectioners, and cooks, from Auschwitz-Birkenau to the nearest railway station.

Where should Richard escape to? Germany was everywhere. No one would be allowed to pass a piece of bread to him without the danger of being shot to death or hanged and humiliated on top of that. Europe was German. It was a German house, an invisible but palpable lattice that no one could penetrate. Even now the SS units combed through Europe from west to east and from east to west, from south to north and north to the south, so that not even a single carrier of the Jewish star, even if he hid beyond seven mountain ranges and seven rivers, would escape his fate, the German fate. The Final Solution, from the solution after which only the crematorium has the word, and after the crematorium the chimney, and after the chimney the wind which would blow the ash around the entire wide Mother Earth, drown them in the sea, chase them into mountains, and cover the valleys and abysses. That which the Germans began, the wind, brother of man, would finish.

A lot of people realized already that this was the end and perhaps were even glad and would sooner have it behind them. It was a disease they got over without taking to bed; it was beyond a cure. Life had lost its value. They were worthless. They went toward death like freezing men toward their final sleep—when they desired to sleep only to escape pain. Then, the desire to escape pain becomes greater than the will to live. Only a few would fight to trade the worthlessness of their existence for the worthlessness of death.

"Quickly, quickly," the guards called out when they approached the gray walls, as soon as they left the trucks. "You are all so filthy that you can be glad nobody can see you at night. Who wants to get typhoid or smallpox, covered with this much dust? Do you want everyone to become infected? You must go under the water once again."

Those who had come here first refused to take off their clothes for the second time because they had bathed before they were loaded on the trucks and it had been before—surprisingly, in spite of panicky voices—really a hot and cold shower and disinfection. They did not even want to enter the underground undressing room, which meant work for the soldiers and kapos, who had cowhide whips and rifle butts to break up the crowds.

"We're not on a playing field. Move along, move along, and do what you're ordered. You will all be bathing. Is someone here against hygiene perhaps?"

From one ambulance with the red cross, the dog soldiers pulled out several German sheepdogs who multiplied among themselves, but they were dogs well trained for military purposes, and together with truncheons, cowhide whips, and rifle butts, they turned into a forcible and convincing device. The dogs were excited and made savage by the first blood trickling down the arms, faces, and bodies of the ones on the edges who pressed onto those who walked ahead of them, or onto those who had stopped and had not wanted to take so much as a step anymore. A few dogs had been set loose. Somewhere an irritated kapo shouted, "What do you idiots want? Everyone must die. Do you want it harder for your children and mothers?" (One SS officer reprimanded him and reminded him not to let his stupid mouth run loose.) And then, "Wise up, move along. Take off your clothes, so that everyone will fit in here. Or do you want us to beat you to death in front of the washrooms?" The dogs were freed from their leashes and chains. They barked, baring their teeth like animals that had tasted human blood and human flesh before and smelled a new feed.

Still dressed, the people began pressing themselves into the showers against those naked ones who had wanted to escape the fangs of the dogs and the blows.

Maxims which always proved themselves right in Auschwitz-Birkenau started to fly through the air. "Move along, you're going to bathe, keep orderliness, be sensible, don't believe rumors, for God's sake do what we tell you, nobody shall so much as touch a hair on your head, try to keep order, for God's sake, and don't complicate our work—we're all just people."

People in the cloakroom escaped from the dogs but not from the cowhide whips.

It went on ad nauseam. The soldiers were continuously spurring them on to a greater speed so that no one would have time and so that they themselves would accelerate it. "Line up by forties. Haven't you heard? By forties. Eight lines by five makes forty. The ones on the sides start counting. Fast. Forty. Fast. You'll return, go take a bath. Don't be afraid, quickly but no flurry, don't panic, who told you that you're not going to take a bath? You are to be bathed. You are going to the showers. You have our commandant's word of honor. What else do you want?"

Many of them recognized the camp commandant's black Daimler. It was the truth then. Perhaps the Nazis had received an order from Berlin for some strange operation, for which they would use people from the family camp. Perhaps they would keep them here for six months for that purpose, and they had allowed them to exist almost beyond all reason. Maybe they wanted to convince the Americans, the Swiss, or the English? Maybe the Nazis intended to trade them for their captured generals? If that was the case, they would at least have goods to be exchanged.

"Dirtied up in this way we won't send you anywhere. The commandant won't let himself be scandalized. You won't go even a meter farther looking like this. Perhaps you think Germany is a dirty puddle? Quickly, inside to the showers."

The trucks whirred with their engines running as if they waited for them to board again. The ambulances also had their engines running. There must have been double the number of dogs than in the beginning. Their lives were still worth inferior gasoline, running engines with which the soldiers wanted to deceive them, except for the dogs, cowhide whips and blows, roaring, and the customary sayings. By now the ears and heads and eyes of everyone ached from the roaring, the fear, the prospect of the showers and the green crystals of zyklon-B. The soldiers treated them like novices whom they brought to the showers easily. They promised them warm water to wash the dust from their bodies, hot tea or colder water to extinguish thirst, clean underwear, and work. Was it better knowing or not knowing what the showers really were? Since nine in the evening till midnight, they'd sat in the railcars. The trucks circled with them and jolted along the road leading to the town of Kraków and between the Sola and Vistula, but only in the distance of two—at the most, ten—kilometers, and on each car sat the SS men armed to their necks, so that jumping out would not even cross anyone's mind. One could not see in the darkness where they were. As long as they did not dismount and recognize the familiar buildings, the crematoria, the chimneys. Furnaces. The underground cloakroom. It was not Heyderbreck, then, the new camp where the people would demonstrate old experiences. At times, it would seem as if there were other furnaces, other underground cloakrooms, other chimneys. It was a starless, moonless night; a cold early spring. Only the dampness, the cold wind, the near aftertaste of the swamps, and the lowering night sky were the same. It was tomorrow already. They had set out yesterday; already it was the next day. Midnight had passed. It was not a road from somewhere to somewhere else. They did not ride into another camp, as the commandant had sworn solemnly when he came to calm them down, although originally he was going to have a concert of a Beethoven symphony, performed by a women's symphonic orchestra, composed of the Jewish as well as Aryan women prisoners from the occupied countries of Europe. Kraków, Katowitz, Heyderbreck— that was all outside the camp—some other place—only the underground cloakroom, brick walls, the smokestack, and the furnaces were *here and for them.* The wind grew colder as the night progressed, and the nearby swamp gave out an almost sweetish stench. How is this night different from all other nights? Anna asked. She could answer that herself. But she didn't answer. The answer was in the wind, in the darkness, in the pieces of ashes from the dead, already burned in the ovens.

"Quickly, quickly, faster yet. For God's sake, you have no time, you can't behave like slugs!"

They advanced into the darkness now like blind people led by the fire, whose flames skipped over water. They tripped, step after step, as if they were entering hell but were unable to turn around, only to advance as if they trusted their guides. Like a blind person with a cane, they did not want to lose their way, yet they were glad they could not see. They were in limbo from which the route led only to the flames, separated from water which would only come later and wash off their stuck-together bodies and separate them. They were together, though at the same time apart. In the gully, no flames burned yet. It was just a gently sloping entrance to the underground cloakroom where it was too late for everything, even the exchange of illusion for hope. There was no difference between hope and illusion.

"Whoever gets in first will get out again first," the kapo shouted.

The last wind to strike Emil Ludvig before reaching the underground slope reminded him of the Dolomites. The warm and cold wind made one feel cold, and one could smell the stench of human bodies in close proximity. When he was seventeen at the Piave, he had served with the Austro-Hungarian artillery; the noise had damaged his eardrum, and he could hardly hear on the left side. He thought of the sea in Trieste. Of the enormous silence which was so appealing and the humming of the sea. Of the countryside where he had been born, where he had met Anna. The vibration of those times rang in his veins, in the beating of his heart. He saw and heard his mind, but he was not hearing or seeing.

"Move along, move along quickly."

And the beating. He imagined the mountain pass in Italy, where a river skipped along the boulders at the bottom, where they had been forbidden to bathe; the water would have dragged them together with the equipment under the surface immediately. The boulders had been smoothed by the millennia of rushing water; they had the shapes of animals, human faces, mysterious signs. The rocks and the water embraced the boundlessness, the enormity and immeasurability of time, of life, the unbounded abyss of death.

Emil Ludvig dreaded that they would not be together again. It was an upside-down fear that signaled his desire for them all to be together again instead of dreading what lay ahead. He did not want to think about whom the soldiers and kapos beat, whom the dogs bit, who bled, who was in the cloakroom naked already, and how everyone would squeeze into that place. He was afraid of going mad with fear before reaching his destination into the darkness of the cloakroom. And then. He had already reached—as everyone—his infinite *after.* He had a headache, a different one than ever before.

The child next to him asked his mother where they were going. Why did everyone shout? It was fear of the dogs. The children, as everyone, knew that words would have been only a veil which should bring relief, but could not. The child reminded his parent that she was still a mother—nothing had changed that yet. The mother took the remark to herself. Blood ran down her temple, but it could not be seen in the darkness. The child asked why her head was wet and why it was sticky. The woman had her clothes pulled, half torn off. She made an effort to talk.

"You wanted to go to Grandma and Grandpa. That's where we're going, to them," she said in Czech.

She assured the child that they would be in the same place soon. They would see Grandma Janetta and Grandpa Viktor. The faster they would walk, the farther they would leave the dogs behind. "All our people are there, ahead." Her words encouraged the others; other names, words, shouts, and calls replied separate from the roaring, urging, and the physical blows.

"Richard," Emil Ludvig called out. "Helena. Anna."

The crowd pushed and shoved and dragged him, and it was enough for him to lift his feet and make short strides. He guarded himself so as not to stumble and not to fall so that the crowd in the darkness would not trample him.

"Where are they?" the child wanted to know. "Are they there? Why are we walking in the dark?"

"Just ahead," the woman said.

Many mothers lost their children and children their mothers before coming to the cloakroom. "All of them are there already. We know the way," the woman added. "Keep holding on to me."

"I'll keep holding on," the child answered.

They passed the young SS man, Rolf Tuepe. At that moment, the young German man in the uniform thought that if you asked any mother if she was willing to be saved if they killed only her child, or if they asked any son if he would sacrifice his mother to gain an hour of life, or if they asked a daughter if she wanted to live instead of her father, probably no one would hesitate—or only a few—so they could breathe for just a while longer the air filled with ashes in their prisoner's rags, without a shred of dignity or what they called pride, past or future. It was a truth that his friends had already confirmed for themselves more than once; he himself had not had the nerve to try it yet—perhaps next time. Even the concept of *next time* was only reserved for the select race. For mothers and daughters and sons and fathers and the old—whoever is given a chance to buy a piece of life for himself billed to one's nearest and dearest—there is no next time. It is a cruel game to ask, but didn't Adolf Hitler say that even nature is cruel, so that no German would blame himself for learning from nature?

"You are with me," said the young woman to the child.

"Don't run away from me," the child pleaded.

"Don't worry. I will never run away from you. We'll stay together like this, always."

"Keep holding each other, just move faster," Rolf Tuepe urged. "Quickly. That's right. Quickly. Quickly. So everybody can have his fair share of time." The little girl's voice calling out in the darkness reminded him of someone.

And again the young SS man remembered the melody of "*Wiener Blut*," by Strauss. No one can deny that in the world there are both the worst and the most beautiful occurrences. How much longer would his shift take? No longer than morning. By afternoon he'd have caught up on his sleep. The wind was mixed with a heavy rain. When the moon came out, would it be full? Sometimes the moon above Poland swung like a drunkard. He remembered how the spring rain, summer rainstorms, and fall winds made the poplars wave. They'd waved in the wind when he arrived. Soon it would be his second winter in Auschwitz-Birkenau. Here he had learned how to feel the cold.

Sometimes he heard them singing in the family camp. They probably sang so as not to think about anything. They hadn't known for the past few weeks whether they were dead or alive, coming or going, whether they were doing right or wrong—as if it mattered. Nobody from his unit knew why they'd kept them in the family camp for six months. What did it matter now? Why couldn't these people be more accommodating? He could imagine how they were going to bang on the door, trying to scratch their way out. But no one would find the door handle. They would burn like paper, like white butterflies in winter, like ancient rocks and dried-up rivers from long ago. They'd become their own grave markers.

They had already seen the sun set as they were driven here in the trucks. Now the wisest among them probably searched for the stars, but there were only clouds. Why don't they tell themselves they're going swimming? Or to the mountains? Or on an excursion? Emil Ludvig passed him by. Why don't they make it easier on themselves?

"Hurry up," the young SS man urged him. And it occurred to Rolf Tuepe why fish in Harmenz were dying at the fish pond only a few kilometers from here where they used to go fishing and where later the prisoners went to dispose of the ashes. The fish choked on the ashes. Of all things, the most prominent in this region were the ashes. Ashes, ashes, everywhere. His lungs were full of it here. Only ashes. Who could know when there might be fish swimming there again?

Rolf Tuepe felt something, something that one could not understand unless he was born and grew up a German, in this generation—the same and yet different from all other German generations preceding him and yet to come—supremely placed above all others, which, if not for the camaraderie among the sixty or ninety million fellow members of the tribe, could almost be called different, certainly unique. Each generation comes up with a way to differ from the last, just as the next will differ from the present. He knew who had already disappeared from this earth. They only needed to catch the other half and finish what they had started. It was rumored that even the thorough German organization had a difficult time counting them all. What does it matter if no one counts, ten hundred thousand dead here, ten hundred thousand or a million there? But the Jewish prisoners were at least the most valuable to them. Perhaps life meant as much for them, the young SS man thought to himself. They won't be bragging that they are one of the oldest nations. They won't be older. They won't be at all. It will be a big war, on a grand scale.

Emil Ludvig listened to the voices around him so that he would not miss his people.

Behind their backs, the engines still droned and the drivers had to rev up the engines at full throttle, yet for whatever reason? It no longer made sense to ask why about anything in Germany. Other trucks brought the remainder of the transports from last September. The road to Kraków was clear again. In the mother camp, Auschwitz I, the concert might have concluded, if it had not ended, without the commandant.

The young woman with the child vanished, but most likely the two of them only became lost in the darkness. The Germans have enough gasoline for everything, Emil Ludvig thought, otherwise they would not let the engines run continuously at full throttle. Out of four thousand people, at least half must have been in the cloakrooms and washrooms by now and the rest by the road. The Germans really had enough of everything: raw materials, gasoline, wire, concrete, trucks, trains, people. They did not miss them at the front. Why did they select such a night for their execution? How was this night different from any other? He had the same thoughts as Anna. Isn't it said that over time husbands and wives come to resemble each other like siblings? It was merely the night from the seventh to the eighth of March. They knew the Jewish calendar well. Did anyone in the crowd still believe that he would come through? It was like a relay. Even an uneducated person didn't have to tax himself to understand it from beginning to end. The Germans are most zealous. They do not want to commit the errors that others committed, halfhearted efforts, the false self-confidence and inconsistencies, while they beat up many and killed only some; the Germans would kill everyone. The Final Solution. They took it in their hands with German efficiency. They would avoid the mistakes of the predecessors. They would pour the baby out with the bathwater. The commandant explained to them yesterday that the period of the general quarantine in the family camp was over. They would have to get ready to depart right away. At dawn, the camp would have a new mission. The families would not be torn apart even at this time. That he could guarantee with his German officer's word of honor. "The families will remain together. Preserve the discipline, you will not be sorry. I have received the orders at the last moment." With the latest technology, with the world's silent indifference or with only feeble objections, the German commandant could lie because a lie can be justified only by another lie. It would last too long, until somebody broke through the vicious circle of lies. And yet under the blows, which might be the last ones, in the barking and under the teeth of the German sheepdogs and the German Dobermans grown wild, already bloodied in the darkness and dampness, people still might have believed in a miracle. "You're no novices," said the officer who spoke after the commandant. "You could not be taken for a ride by anybody." Two men with their calves bitten through limped along next to Emil. One was moaning with pain.

The Germans never had a lot of difficulty with them. To get them as far as here, they had actually allowed them to bathe once. They had given them soap and a towel and a cup full of a Lysol mixture for washing their hair. It was always the same delousing procedure. Water came down from the showers. They had only forgotten to warm it up, and the supervising SS apologized. It made a more trustworthy impression. After the bath, the door opened up. They walked out and put on their clothes. That put them at ease. Some of them beat the incredulous Jews among them who, despite having bathed and walked out into the open, warned others against a trick. Emil Ludvig joined those who wanted to believe, because he did not know how to exist with distrust. He was never up to believing in the worst. He had been born that way. It was human nature. Believing the worst means *calling* for the worst. The rich man who plays the beggar will become a beggar, his mother used to say. Why does man's most human element disarm rather than strengthen his resolve to defend himself? They should not have shouted down their basic instinct that protects man and forces him to defend himself and not to rely on anything, anybody, anywhere, under any circumstances.

It was late for many yes's or more no's. Certainly they, the prisoners, should have defended themselves, but a person must defend himself from the very first. Still, a thought crept into that—how should the children and babies defend themselves? And still, it was a concept in which remained a large void.

He had quieted Anna and the children before they climbed onto the trucks. They were only words, though they were grateful, just as Emil had appreciated their echo. The Germans killed people as a shoemaker made shoes, a baker baked bread, a watchmaker repaired broken clocks. Emil Ludvig understood Anna, Helena, and Richard's silence in the crowd. Like him, they had died in their minds a thousand times before they had gotten to this night so that it would not surprise them when it came. To that nobody needed any advice. That was the rule; everything else would be an exception. Someone might get ready to jump three times and then jump. It seemed to him that he had known that long ago. That it was something that he'd always wanted. Someone might hear about some city before getting there, yet when he finally arrived, he didn't have the feeling of being there for the first time.

We should have to defend ourselves, Emil Ludvig thought. To bite, to scratch. To choke. To hit them with our fists. To return to the time when we fought desert rats, similar, perhaps, to Bedouins, or to a time somewhere in Babylon or surrounded by Bohemian mountains, close to the earth and the sun. He felt it deeply in himself, filled with many thoughts and many illusions. We should have taken out knives or picked up stones, since we had no arms. To kill with a knife or a piece of iron. Certainly. We were born into a world where man either kills or is killed. Arthur had pegged it right—it was in the air. It had always been in the air. The body is naked underneath, though it is dressed up in various ways. Did the children learn that with their mothers' milk? Did babies breathe that in with their first gulp of air? These were just fragmentary thoughts. All he could do was reproach himself for not fighting back, for being helpless. At home, on the way, and here.

During the time he had spent here he had learned about many things that man was capable of doing to another man, things that before, he could never have dreamed of. But he tried to ignore them because otherwise he would not be able to exist even a moment longer. But they did exist, and they surrounded all of them. They learned not to see it, nor to hear it, nor to perceive it, and to live from morning until evening and night until dawn.

Again, that enormous mountain of reproach shrank to a yearning, a feeling of rebuke that he should have—they all should have—fought. Who does not defend himself in the end will perish worse and sooner than he should. The notion of self-defense buried him like a rock. It was filled with emptiness, which remained after some words. That was the only thing he was sure of, but it was too late.

He felt that he was getting a fever. It rang in his temples.

They make themselves believe that everyone is different, but they are not, Rolf Tuepe thought. They're all the same. There is no need to divide them into those who have plenty and those who have nothing, between winners and losers, those who will escape their fate and those whose fate is knocking at the door. What they managed to bring here they will leave behind, what they left at home is already in reliable German hands. They streamed in here from all corners of Europe, as if through a sieve or a funnel, the young SS smiled, thinking to himself—this is also night combat. Here we do for Germany what the tank brigades do in the African desert, the foot soldiers in Russia, the sky divers on Crete, or the mountain foresters in the Serbian mountains. Eventually the inner smile of the young SS was replaced by seriousness. They were perhaps doing more than all the other soldiers together. Except that this is top secret. We are forbidden—indeed, threatened—to blab about it because the enemy propaganda would misuse it for the next thousand years. It is a battle like in the bogs where a soldier with all his equipment can get lost without a trace;

like a battle in the endless spaces, in an immeasurable desert; like air raids in the enemy cities of London, Paris, Brussels, or Belgrade when the pilot dives toward them for the hill, to burn, to destroy everything underneath, everything alive or moving about. The SS professor in his lecture had warned the young SS men against those who were there in body but not in spirit. It is necessary to put one's heart into it, he said. German hearts. The hearts of soldiers. The heart of a European German.

Looking out into the darkness at the confused and perspiring bodies, he was reminded of German electricians who had installed the electric cables and then left. He did not have to envy them. Then he thought that tomorrow, after he had had enough sleep, he would need to get a haircut. In the town of Auschwitz, behind the tracks, he had his own Polish barber, an old soldier who had cut German soldiers' hair for years. Last time, the barber had even thinned out his eyebrows. He had a comfortable chair like a dentist's. Then the barber cut the hair in his nose, though the blond ones are not as visible as the dark ones, and the hairs in his ears, just like a proper barber should. Whenever he got his hair washed, the barber also gave him a massage—he liked that. Some younger officers sent the barber their wives, not to mention their children. The young SS remembered with pleasure the warmth and the smell of eau de cologne in the barber's tiny salon behind the tracks. Some soldiers and officers did not like how the Polish barber would look at their heads to guess what to cut off and how much and how to reshape it. They preferred to evaluate barbers' heads themselves. It's the same with me, the young SS man thought, smiling to himself. How does it happen that everything serious is also a little funny? Suddenly it occurred to him how many sins would disappear with those who had already passed him by and were now inside. Death is the most thorough sweeper.

The SS professor had told them, "Don't let yourselves be frightened or confused by the number of enemies who come here to be liquidated. Look at the trees—how many leaves they have—and then at the deciduous forest, however deep, and remember how it looked in the spring and the summer and what happened to it in the fall when the wind tore down the leaves one by one. No matter how many there were before winter arrived, all the trees standing there now are naked; all the leaves are dead. That has nothing to do with the number of leaves; it is determined by the will and order of nature."

"Will and order," the professor repeated. "In your case it is discipline, dedication to our ideal, courage in action—regardless of the nature of the action—self-assurance, and reliance on one's own strength. What did Hegel, one of the most famous German philosophers, say? War is a great cleanser. It guarantees the moral health of people corrupted by a long peace."

How is it inside? Rolf Tuepe wondered. They probably think that the skies are falling, he answered himself. They don't know the facts anymore, while we, outside, are just learning them. In the end, everything balances out. Things are normal every day, and at the same time, they are festive. It might appear like chaos, but it is not; they simply don't know. He thought how many unfulfilled promises would die with them. How many deceits. Death would engulf them all. Death for them, life for us—for my people at home, in Germany.

They were instructed, if at all possible, to calm the victims as long as possible in order to prevent any unforeseen confusion. Therefore, it was in their own interest to run things as smoothly as possible, to keep them as simple as possible. He mustn't lose either his nerve or his patience. They keep on asking; one has to accept that. His colleague, Christian Adolf Stoebele, claimed that it was better to give them answers—sometimes short ones, sometimes more detailed so they could not view it as just politeness—but that the very moment they protest, hit them as hard as possible. Only cooperation is acceptable. Disobedience has to be answered immediately, without complicated thoughts. Things must—as Commandant Kaltfleischer repeated over and over again—be crystal clear. Ambiguity only helps the enemy.

The SS instructor had stressed, "Three important things that cannot under any circumstances be taken lightly: irreconcilability, irreconcilability, and again, irreconcilability. Just remember: the Jew inside a Jew never dies. Jews use the past, protected by the Bible, as a stick with which they beat us. Now we turn them into sticks—with which we'll beat them. Nothing more, nothing less. Irreconcilability!"

The young SS man, Rolf Tuepe, added question marks to this precept and corrected the professor; the Jew inside a Jew never dies but burns. The Jew inside a Jew burns. Only ashes remain from the Jew within a Jew. Indeed, only the ashes will remain. You cannot determine race, nationality, and religion from ashes. Ashes are just ashes.

For a second, he considered the primitiveness of ashes. Then he concluded that even if he wished otherwise, he could not deny that the ashes falling down on them were Jewish. Wasn't that funny? They were always calling for attention. If in nothing else, then still in their ashes. How horrible, he thought, and winced.

The SS instructor said that Jews would like history to move backward so that they could return to where they had come from and from where they'd been chased away. Germany won't accept such games. History would move according to the German rhythm—forward, to the future, without even one Jew.

The instructor said, "War is an anvil on which the German character is being forged. What you are now—that's what the German nation will be for the next thousand years."

"Madmen, crazies," shouted a lunatic on the threshold to hell. Rolf Tuepe turned in the direction of the cry.

Rolf Tuepe felt how both the words of the Nazi instructor and his own words began to dissolve in his blood, like an energy that those who are not Germans would never understand. To be German meant perfection. The very edge of perfection. Nobody would ever again skin Germany as in the past war from which his father (a corporal and, later, a sergeant) returned with tears in his eyes. In opposition to perfection there can only be extinction, destruction, death. Here death has its generous days and nights, and every second in between. *Kaput. Vernichtigung.* Destruction. *Untergang.*

"One glance at them is enough. Maybe they once resembled human beings, but no longer," the instructor said. "The sooner we have this chore behind us, the sooner we'll have time for everything we want to accomplish during peace."

Rolf Tuepe tried to sense the will of the people who walked past him. Only some still held on to their will. From the others, it had vanished like steam drifting to meet the cold air, like a match lit and then extinguished by the wind at night.

At times, Rolf Tuepe had the impression that ghosts were brushing past him, some kind of demons, an echo. Only when they turned to look directly at him, questioningly, or with an expression of fear because they had no one else to take it out on except for this guard in uniform, almost alone, did they remind him of real people. One way or the other, they had to die; it was true that they resembled animals more than human beings.

The barking that changed into wailing, as if somebody tortured an animal, reached Emil Ludwig.

Rolf Tuepe tested himself to see how much he had hardened since he had first arrived as a novice. The novices had been gathered at the black wall in Auschwitz I to see how those who had been condemned to death were liquidated—a bullet in the back of the neck or a bullet in the head from the front, always from close range, face-to-face with the condemned. Rolf Tuepe had seen how they behaved, and how the soldiers let them bleed as if koshering cattle, and it was even more like the slaughter of cattle, for nobody chanted over the bodies. Once they brought in an imprisoned German priest who stuck up for his Jewish neighbor. He burst into tears while blessing the sentenced, then pleaded to be killed as well. The commandant did as he was asked. He invoked God and called for forgiveness, warning the commandant of a blackened Germany with an indelible guilt. Nobody pitied the Germans who were afraid of this. But sometimes it occurred to the young SS man that he heard another voice within himself, and he wondered what he would say to his mother or his father, or his grandparents, and he surprised himself that in the end he had prepared an explanation in his mind: how at the first before he got used to it, it almost disgusted him, and how he had to think about it at night, and how strict were the commands, and how he learned not to question, not even slightly, when he received an order, but to carry it out no matter what the command.

The young SS man, Rolf Tuepe, looked into the darkness at the anonymous crowd and was pleased that he managed to silence in himself his second voice. Nobody would have any use for excuses. No one would be left to accuse them, at least no one among the involved. They would be finished to the last one. He, just like all the other Germans who knew, would never have to answer to his conscience.

"Hurry, hurry," Rolf Tuepe urged, prodding the crowd without realizing it. They are going to the slaughter by themselves, he thought.

It's all so well organized; they are going to the slaughter by their own free will. All one has to do is stand here and hurry them along from time to time.

He did not know that the man he had just urged to move on was Emil Ludvig. Emil Ludvig lifted his eyes at the sound of the young, German voice.

"Faster, faster."

Emil Ludvig took two faster steps. One could hear weeping and shouting. He found himself again next to the woman with the child, although he wished that he had found Anna, Helena, and Richard in the darkness, in the crowd.

"Why did Grandma Janetta and Grandpa Viktor come all the way here?" the child asked. And yet another question, and then the woman's voice, "You've been a good girl, we all have been good, we're going to take a bath, we're dusty. You've heard the person in charge say it. We'll have warm water. You won't be cold."

A mother with a child in her arms whispered, "My baby, we'll stay together. I am not giving you to anybody. You are only mine. You won't be hungry or thirsty anymore. You won't feel the cold. We'll stay warm."

The child gurgled but did not cry and then became silent while the mother kept pressing it to her body. Tears fell from her eyes onto the child, and she kept on whispering how she would never give him up, how they would always stay together, how he would never be alone, not even for a moment, forever. She continued to whisper into the darkness and the night the one word: "always."

The young SS man, Rolf Tuepe, had had good teachers and hoped that eventually others would learn from him. His colleague, Joamin Achen, managed what some perhaps did not like but all appreciated. While burning the surplus from the transports in eight pits in which people burned in their own fat—of course with the help of wood logs and kerosene—Joamin Achen took a baby, perhaps only twenty days old, away from his young mother and promised to quiet him down. For a brief moment, he cradled the baby in the palms of his hands, and it stopped crying and twitched its mouth as if to smile. At the same moment, Joamin Achen lifted the baby in one hand and hurled it in a great arch straight into the big pit where it fried in a few seconds. The mother sighed and fainted, and Joamin Achen picked her up and threw her in too.

Rolf Tuepe remembered Horst Glatzer, who had served with the Einsatzgruppen commando when they were forcing the Jews in Warsaw behind the walls of the ghetto, which later burned down to its very last splinter, including all those inside. Standing in the cafeteria, he recalled how it had all been going well, one building after another, until they came upon the villa where the owner of the furniture fabric factory lived with his nine sons. It was June, and the heat in Poland was unbearable. They went into the villa with open shirts and jackets, but all the doors were locked. They knocked on the doors with their automatic pistols, with rifles, with whatever they had. At last, the head of the household appeared and then his wife. They were frightened by the sight of the armed men in uniform. Behind them stood their nine sons, in order of height. Horst described them as the kind of men who went to a synagogue in top hats so that nobody could take them for the *Ghettojuden.* No sidelocks, no beards, cleanly shaven. In two generations, they had climbed up to the top. The old man had come to Warsaw with nothing, without a penny. The first night he made a chair, and during the day he sold it. The following night he had enough material for two chairs, so he put them together and, again, he sold them, so that the third night he was able to make three chairs. Finally, he built himself a furniture factory. The family got used to success quickly. They surrounded themselves with only the most expensive things—silver candlesticks and crystal chandeliers, regal tables and chairs, three-inch-deep carpets as far as the eye could see. When they told the old woman to gather five suitcases of belongings, she announced that she could not because she had not packed for the summer. Packed for the summer? Horst Glatzer only understood it after a while; without being packed for the summer, she could not leave the house. She wasn't accustomed to sleeping in another bed. And so the soldiers locked them inside the villa, shooting into the windows when one of them dared look out, and they burned down the house. They all burned, along with their evening wear and silk hats and their villa and their fame, decked out for the first row of their synagogue, which now served the Einsatzgruppen as a garage.

Just as the Jews had helped themselves to everything in Germany, so Germany took it away again. From blood sucking to punishment, that was the first and the last step on their path which led through many centuries and countries directly to the crematorium and then higher, as high as possible, through the chimney into the heavens. What they had managed, in ten years, to catch up on, they would lose as quickly as if they still wore sidelocks. Sidelocks or no sidelocks, they had still been the same people for two thousand years. They thought they were tough and that the worst was behind them. As if clothes could cover up the vulnerability people have when their world is being pulled out from under their feet. It was just the same the other way around: a German in rags is still a German. The Jews spoke German, Czech, Spanish, or French, and they dressed like English, Americans, or Dutch, but they kept their Jewish traditions, and if not their traditions, they kept their Jewish souls, which danced when bills rustled or coins rattled. Even if they looked like German aristocracy or French courtesans, it was enough to nudge them, prod them, or kick them and everything they had ever been from the start came flooding back.

Africa and Asia were still in them, but very little Europe, even if they did dress with the help of a Parisian tailor and ordered their luggage from Frankfurt. This was where all their cunning and trickery ended—traps and illusions and magic. If they believed in the wheel of fortune, it had not served them well. It had spun fast enough for them, but it came to a stop here. They went like the blind, allowing themselves to be led and accusing one another. Nobody could deny Horst Glatzer's scathing sense of humor. Everything that a Jew exhales is only to multiply the Jews. When a Jew inhales, a Jew exhales. When a Jew does not hang himself, there is one more Jew than there should have been. Horst Glatzer never had to look for words. When a Jew marries a shiksa or a Jewess a gentile, it is only a Jewish snare to make one more Jew. A Jew molds the times, and the times mold a Jew. A Jewish hen lays a Jewish egg, and from a Jewish egg, a Jewish hen is born.

A Jew is a Jew forever. Even if they were to strip his skin off him, Jewish meat and Jewish blood would remain. The least that every German and Germany can come to terms with is Jewish ashes. There was no denying the truth: Jewish ashes would remain Jewish ashes. And one cannot do anything with them except, perhaps, fertilize German fields, because ashes cannot be removed from the earth, and if German hands did not do the job, the wind would.

SS Glatzer would relieve him, and then later they would meet in the cafeteria. Glatzer was fun to listen to. He could make a joke even out of a horror show.

Just as the SS professor said, where will Germany be when the Jews are dead and long forgotten? What did all the walking dead think when Hitler said that their final hour had struck? All the blows and scars and emotional battering of the German past fall to the bottom like a ship sunken with ghosts. The German will is victorious, halting before no one, unbreakable. The army and the SS and the SA are the pride of Germany. In every single German there beats the heart of all that is the best—that which is Germany.

The path to German greatness leads to the total destruction of the mob that comes from all corners of Europe into the camp, on the direct track from their house to the crematorium. From out of the Jewish ashes, the German phoenix takes flight into the world.

The SS professor's words and Horst Glatzer's sneers seemed to Rolf Tuepe soft as the stroke of a mother's or girlfriend's hand on the bare chest of a son or lover. He looked forward to the end of his shift and to sleep. There's little sleep, little rest. There is nothing one can do while the mission has yet to be accomplished. Then there would be mission number two: the colonization of the East, five hundred kilometers beyond the Urals. Germany would be everywhere.

Suddenly there was a child next to him, a boy, about eight years old. The boy lifted his head and asked, "Where's my daddy?" Before Rolf Tuepe could answer, the boy also asked where his brother was. He reminded Rolf Tuepe of someone. He thought that maybe he'd seen that face before: straight, black hair, a hooked nose, bright, green eyes. Maybe he had seen the boy's father?

There was fear in the child's voice.

"If you hurry, you can catch him," Rolf Tuepe said. "Run, he's up ahead!"

The child had gotten lost in the crowd. Rolf Tuepe didn't want to have to act as though he were some kind of missing persons bureau. Soon the little boy would be with his father and his brother. It was no lie when he said, "Run, run, run." Rolf Tuepe listened to the echo of his voice in his head. That afternoon the rumor had gone around that they had delivered a Jewish baby with two heads and two spines. Now that was something you didn't hear about every day! Could they hear the bell tolling for them? No need for candles, he thought to himself. Your father's up ahead. Or behind. Did they know yet? They didn't know what, but they knew why. They must have realized that they were the last. Every person has an instinct that tells him what's what. He felt in the mood for some hot tea. But he would have to wait.

The noise, which would only subside between transports, deafened and tired him. It was the opposite of Germany where, according to the law, it must be quiet enough by 9 P.M. to hear a pin drop. Germany is a quiet country. An orderly country. A country where people know how to behave, even in pubs. A country where mothers gave their children the best German names like Rolf, Gunther, Siegfried, Wilfried, and Dieter. They needed a wide choice: there were ninety million Germans, maybe even a hundred million. In Germany there was a law for everything. Nobody, even if they wanted to, could give a child some kind of Jewish or foreign-sounding name. It occurred to him that he liked to use "ty" with everyone who passed by. He called them what he liked, whether they were university professors, doctors, or any other formerly important person. There are two sides to everything, and nothing lasts forever. He could use "ty" with old men, five times older than he. It made him feel good. As he watched the men, women, children, and old people pass by, it seemed to him as if none of their faces showed any expression. It was as if they were already dead. Their future would be as their past: they would die.

Whenever the young SS man, Rolf Tuepe, passed those pits when nothing was burning inside of them because the technical installations worked according to plan, and the chimneys and ovens were in good repair, and everything went smoothly, he recalled Joamin Achen, the child, and the woman. If war means to force the enemy to submit its will under any circumstances, and with any means, then Joamin Achen was right and had managed not to eliminate any means of achieving his goal. According to him, the best and most reliable way to make the enemy submit its will was to kill him. How depended purely on circumstance. Sure, the young SS man thought, it depends on circumstance. First to make them notice you and then obey you;

that's the point. That's what we have to manage in any situation, with any people. It was easy to believe that it was also his war. It was his duty to participate. Not only because he was told to but because he wanted to. It was simple, just as God is simple. Just as the führer was simple. Just as the aims of Germany in Europe, in the world, were sensible and simple. War is good because it simplifies things. For him too. Yes, he assured himself, for him too. Here and now.

He remembered how he and his grandfather had gone to see the Busch circus and how he dreamed of becoming a lion tamer when he grew up. He could see himself commanding those big cats to sit on their high stools and then with his whip making them jump through burning hoops.

The Jews invented conscience, the SS instructor said, as a trick to help the weak rule the strong. They even invented the division between the sin and the sinner so that they could do the same thing over again. Reconciliation and forgiveness of the weak by the strong was also a Jewish deception. They really are *Judenschweine,* just like this one, who, according to his nearest and dearest, sacrificed himself for the others. Baloney. Here is the so-called solidarity; mothers give up their children, fathers their daughters, daughters their fathers, husbands their wives, wives their husbands—everyone for himself, everyone tries to save himself. It's the *Titanic* without the lifeboats. Everything would end up under the water. What wouldn't they give to go to the chimney just five minutes later than someone else?

The German soldier's heart is often too soft. That's a mistake. The instructor had encouraged them not to give in to their pity for the children. He mentioned lions as an example. A stronger lion chases away another lion from his mate and without pity kills his cubs, so that the lioness can have new ones—better, stronger, sturdier ones. The selected individuals that will take after the strongest male.

Emil Ludvig set his nearly dead eardrum to the pandemonium. It was not enough to scramble through the darkness blindfolded. The guards became thicker the closer they were. They beat the prisoners with sticks, canes, rifle butts. Some kapos brought cables and beat them with pieces of the cables. The crowd narrowed down among the strips of reflectors and became more yielding. It resembled a funnel through which they streamed into the neck of a flat bottle.

"It's a fraud, it's been a fraud since the beginning, they'll kill us, they can't be trusted," someone said. And then, "Do something—take them with you."

A shrieking woman's voice, before she was struck with a cable: "We will die, but you will lose."

"You are going to die first," the kapo roared, and struck her again with the cable.

And the young German SS officer for amusement said, "*Richtig, richtig. Schnell.*" And a bit farther they could hear: "*Hilfe, schnell, likvidieren.*"

The young SS man, Rolf Tuepe, felt what others who had entered the service with him had already confirmed for themselves: killing people is easier than one thinks, as long as one does not meet them face-to-face. The more killing that is going on around one, the easier it becomes. All those that were still within the grasp of illusion should come here for half an hour for one single guard shift. They would gain a totally different understanding of killing. They would see that it is like the way one bakes bread—one glimpses life in the oven. Killing is the most important thing in life. It is the compost that feeds man as long as he has strength. And not just man. All of society. In killing there comes a strength that drives the machinations of all mankind. Killing is the most primitive instinct. Killing brings everything to an equal level.

From the wilderness beyond the swamp, a strip of dawn approached. It brought with it thoughts of birches, alders, and chestnuts, willows and poplars which would hum even in a hundred years. Emil Ludvig dropped his hands for an instant, already near the underground cloakroom, and in the crush where they were being beaten and bawled at all the time, he lost his glasses.

"Faster," the soldier roared, one next to another, the kapos among them. "Don't make it harder for us or yourselves."

And then Emil Ludvig found himself next to Anna and wanted her to hold on to him, and it encouraged him, if that can be said, but shamed him at the same time. He felt guilty for what he had not done. He asked where the children were, and she told him they were behind them. He felt terror and resignation in his voice.

"Don't delay. Move along," the guards shouted.

They had reached the concrete slope. It led them through to where there were already people in the cloakroom packed tightly together. They squeezed in against those who were already packed tightly into the showers. There was still not enough room for all of them. The walls were rough: for years they had been painted over with lime. All around were iron benches and iron hooks for clothes and underwear. One could smell the stench of smoke, sweat, Lysol, excrement, and the bitter scent of almonds. At the same time one could smell the perfume with which the disinfectors sprayed the cloakroom and the showers from small hand pumps after each shift, as in a movie theater. The unprotected bulbs on the cloakroom ceiling were yellow. The wind, which brought the stench of the swamp, did not get in here anymore.

"Undress," the guards and kapos shouted. "Everyone leave everything where you are. It will be sorted out later."

"Murderers, revenge us!" somebody cried out, yet the cry was drowned in the noise and confusion.

In the underground cloakroom, they were watched by the Jewish men of all nationalities of the special detail, chosen to push them into the chambers and then, when everything was over and through, to drag them out, wash them off, and deliver them to the cremating furnaces. They were the most powerful Jewish men, among them Red Army members, selected captives who themselves alone, sometimes in six weeks, sometimes later, would undergo the same procedure, if they weren't shot to death before then. These men of the special detail also forced them to undress, shouting, whispering, persuading them. Perhaps some men from the Sonderkommando had acquaintances, relatives, or countrymen, mothers and fathers, sisters and brothers, and had to lie to them. They would see one another after the bath. They knew betrayal and what a man would do to survive. Others would continue to arrive, and others after them, on to infinity. Until their own turn came up. Until the last one disappeared from Europe. Even while they still lived, they in fact did not exist and lived no longer.

In some places the faint yellow bulbs shined so that they would not be in such a great darkness. The initiated could have thought about how long it would take in the showers, according to how many cans of zyklon-B the commandant would allow thrown inside through the ceiling. How quickly the heat radiating from the bodies pressed tightly together would shift the mercury to above seventy degrees centigrade. The small, green-gray crystals of clay infusion soaked in liquid hydrocyanide would start releasing the gas.

Anna Ludvig prayed: *Thy sun shall not set, thy moon shall not hide. . . .* Then she stopped.

Emil Ludvig started to unbutton himself. He still wore his Prague underwear and shoes and clothes. Where were Helena and Richard? Should he be sorry for not having bought cyanide vials for the entire family? Or, hand in hand, running against the barbed wires charged with high-voltage current? Yesterday, still in the family camp, they had been ordered to write stamped postal cards: *We are well, we are short of nothing here.* They added that they expected to be placed on a labor transport in Heyderbreck. They mentioned the new address: Neuberun bei Birkenau. They were recommended to date them the eighth of March. That was today. Once again, he came to think about Mr. Ernst Kantner, as if a coincidence had blown him to this place. Two words: Final Solution, yes. The echo of Mr. Kantner's words flew together into the echo of the only word. At first the Nazis had taken all their rights, then their homes, then their country, and eventually their names—they let them have only a number. Now they were going to wipe the last number off the surface of the earth.

Three brothers next to Emil threw themselves at the nearest guards. They wrestled the submachine guns away from the guards. But in a moment, the brothers lay in their blood in the darkness, and the other Jews stepped over them, farther on, into the cloakroom, deeper in. Two soldiers brought a flamethrower to the edge of the cloakroom. It was enough to let the flames lick a part of the crowd; the stench of burning flesh did its job. Then a lot of people roared, perhaps all of them. They were in a trap from which there was no escape. They were not dead yet, but they belonged among the living no longer. The concrete, the whitewashed ceiling, the massive concrete columns. The fungus on the walls, the sprinklers on the ceiling from which not so much as a drop of water ran. The door without a handle on the inside. One could not even turn around. They were naked and pressed tightly against one another. They could scarcely breathe. The floor was damp with puddles in which people stood. They had often heard that it was best to hold one's breath when the small crystals started falling down from the sprinklers, and then inhale once when there was more gas in the chamber. To inhale violently, deeply, once, twice, as quickly as possible. The door which could not be opened was where the thickest clusters of bodies, stuck together almost inseparably, would be found. And then, the strongest ones would want to climb over the bodies of the smaller and weaker ones, closer to the ceiling where the gas rose after only one minute, where they would scratch their own eyes and ears out, suffocate and choke on blood before everything would grow silent, and only the children, whom the gas had not reached in the press of the bodies, would be trampled down so that even this solution would remain in harmony with the last solution as well. They would not be in their right minds anymore, so that they would no longer be the fathers and the mothers and the daughters and the sons, but would only be vessels penetrated by gas. They would become something like inflated balloons. The people, as well as the pillars, would remain standing because they would not have a place to fall. The sprinklers near the bulbs in the iron mesh bars firmly fused into the concrete would withstand the brunt which the thinner layer of concrete on the ceiling would not, so that lines and scratches and torn-off chunks of skin would remain in it as a testimony of memory already long forgotten.

It is difficult to speak of individuals, of how they felt and behaved in the shower which was not a shower; and it is unjust, at the same time, because everyone was only one of whom there were so many that it causes dizziness. Every one of them had closed his eyes, covered himself up with sweat of the mortal terror, and might or might not have thought about life as an unbounded and indestructible river. Yet who knows what went through the heads of people in the gas chamber? Better almost not to ask what they thought about or what they felt, long enough, before unconsciousness visited them. Surely, without the moderation of sleep, everything covers only one word: "pain." What did they think about? What was first? What last? While it was still possible to breathe? Even before the faintest yellow bulbs went out, and the electric network faltered or they became bleary eyed. The fumes from people had outdone everything, before everything was taken over by the bitter smell of almonds. No one knew that it would take so much time before their souls evaporated. Everyone would have preferred being killed swiftly, at once by the Germans, but the Nazis did not give that to them—it would have been too magnanimous a gift—it would not have differentiated them from their predecessors, from the beginning until the end of the world.

Those killed from the family camp were said to have sung during the night from the seventh to the eighth of March. Maybe. It could be questioned, regarding how the guards drove and beat them, and that they had dogs on hand, and that it was a matter of concern to the commandant that the people who had spent six months in the family camp could not become *Geheimnistragers,* and that on order from Berlin, he liquidated them without endangering the camp's operation. Who would possibly be able to die by suffocating—endeavoring to avoid the blows by cables and canes, the teeth of trained dogs, and before the water swallowed them or the curtain was drawn behind them—still singing? Perhaps someone really did sing. No one will ever find out about it, just like many other things connected with the March night from the seventh to the eighth and everything that converged in Auschwitz-Birkenau. Perhaps someone sang to himself. Perhaps the sound of the flames sang from one of the many nights in Auschwitz-Birkenau. The world was dissolving in gas and fire, at least a piece of the world. That which was repeated here daily, in the night, without the slightest pause. According to some people, they sang the "Hatikva" and "Where Is My Home," the anthem of the country from where they hailed. Perhaps it sounded like that from afar. Maybe.

Perhaps this was how some wanted to hear about it afterward or it is needed by the survivors for future myths and legends. Perhaps they wanted to equalize or balance something through it: humiliation, pain, wrong, the death of the innocent, the greatest mass murder in the history of mankind, something that has no analogy, that cannot be compared to anything. Who knows?

What else is there left to say? On top of the underground cloakroom and the showers, bulldozers had piled tons of clay into corresponding rectangles. Several rains had been enough for the mound, which reminded one of a giant clump of potatoes, to become grown over with grass. On the grass sat the evening, then the morning, dew. A poet would say that on that grass the dew shone like the tears of the weeping earth. A turnoff from the street led toward one end of the mound where an ambulance of the German Red Cross stood. From the ambulance, an execution technician carried out a couple of tins of zyklon-B. He put on a gas mask as the disinfector slipped on gloves and gradually poured the contents of the tins into circular openings. From here, the small crystals got inside the sprinklers, from the sprinklers they would fall down to the naked bodies inside, emitting a sound similar to one dredging coarse sand and stone through a sieve.

Maybe the disinfector in the SS uniform whispered "Forgive us our trespasses," or it was he who sang that night. And then the disinfector covered up the opening in the grass again. He knew what was coming; he had done it many times. A cold wind blew. In the air and in the clouds rain waited. He wanted to have it behind him. The dawn progressed with a constantly widening stripe.

Dawn was like dusk. The light turned gray as the world stepped from night to morning, from compassion to the mundane, from remembrance to neglect. The dead were still inside. There were no shadows yet—there would be any moment. In the distance, the fog took over the darkness. The world was like waves in a dried-up sea. The sky fell to the earth, yet rose at the same time. Light was being born. Night and day still battled each other, and the darkness surrendered to the noiseless enemy. The earth—far and wide—was killed with weeds, mud, and stickiness. Somewhere far away birds tried to soothe the dawn. The dew was chilly. The day began.

Everything is maybe. Maybe Emil Ludvig knew that everyone would die alone. No one could know his feelings. Perhaps it is up to those who put words on paper about him to breathe souls into them, as though that were possible and preferable. They could have been together a thousand years. Even death could have visited them collectively, as it did visit them, like a pair of great hands which embraced and gripped them; but everyone dies alone in the end. He may have been glad that they were not together in the traditional manner, around the dinner table. Perhaps it was even a relief—as long as it can be put that way—in that it had been dark, that they had not seen one another, had not stood together. They had already gone so far that they doubted their value as human beings, their right to live. Their lives had changed from something to nothing. Something that is beyond value, value unto itself, and then—suddenly—nothingness. They almost began to believe that it was imperative that they perish. That was why so many people had accepted their fates, the German fate, from German hands. Emil Ludvig did not ponder over what made them guilty and what excused them for their actions. He only felt that which made him small like a windy storm lifting clouds of sand and scattering them into the distance, grain by grain, until not even a light dust remained. Surely he could think about this no longer. He had ceased to ponder what he had thought about so often before—that there were always more of them than of the guards, that it would be worth it to step out of line and rebel even if it were to cost him his life. He felt closer than ever to the laws of the jungle and to the jungle itself in order to accept the fact that they would perish because they were already weak. He felt that which he had already lost and which he was losing gradually until the moment when he himself would disappear, just as everyone eventually vanishes.

He felt exhaustion that was not due only to hunger, thirst, and physical fatigue. He did not feel fear. He felt both guilty and guilt-less. He searched inside himself for echoes of a not-so-distant tugging at his conscience which fed on the questions of whether to defend oneself or not, at whatever price, to defend oneself in time or even when it was too late. He felt himself much stronger than was his will, his struggle. Yet, soon it would even be too late for that. He couldn't reject reality any longer, as he had tried before, if only to appear stronger for the others, those closest to him, so as not to take away their hope which he himself had already relinquished. In a moment the gas would come. Then they would burn them in the crematorium as they had hundreds of thousands, and millions, of others. But still his mind was filled with the ugliness of the words "gas" and "crema-torium" so that it would have been better to hold on to his illusions. And it occurred to him again what had repeatedly occurred to so many people before him, whether it would not be better for everyone to commit suicide while there was still time, although inwardly, he would blame all those that had done so while at the same time under-standing why. Who knew how deep personal frustration could expand in relation to the hugeness of the military? And he felt a closeness to the naked bodies, the strangers who with their presence returned him to reality, and who, at the same time and until the last second, ex-changed undeniably human warmth and sweat and breath. They were still breathing. They were all still breathing. It was a horror which enveloped relief and a relief which fed the horror. He felt himself a part of a human crowd which would swallow him up even before that other thing had a chance to devour him. He felt the touch of naked bodies, hands, palms, legs, thighs, stomachs, and backs. He felt his heart pounding, wildly, as never before.

It occurred to him that his heart could burst and then he would be finished somewhat earlier than the rest. Or the heart of his people could burst? He knew how much better it would be, but even with this fleeting thought, his fear shrank and increased simultaneously or changed to a strength which made him hold his head up high. The thick crowd of people around him resembled the sea and waves of which he felt himself an indivisible part. He felt within his spirit that which we hold most dear. He wished to fall asleep but knew that he would not. A number of times he closed and opened his eyes. He was still breathing. They were all still breathing. And then he prayed he would faint as some already had in the undressing rooms before they were stuffed into the room like logs of firewood. But he did not faint. He only felt faint. It was indescribable because no one before him had lived through this. He reached out into a direction that had no boundaries. And at the same time he stood barefoot on the damp cement floor that was rough and cold. And then, still conscious, he felt how this too was slipping away. He felt a stranger's breath and a stranger's blood. Vomit. It was a sense of incredible silence in an even greater cacophony of cries, of light within a still darker night. It was a vastness that penetrated one with a silence more quiet than anything else, a dead silence. He felt his heart pounding. How many heartbeats still separated him from the dead?

Emil Ludvig lost the expression he'd carried in his eyes until the last moment, like someone who had tried while there was still time, and who had spun together dreams and hopes before he lost the strength even to dream, and hope turned into hopelessness. They had lived in the family camp like animals in the jungle, in the constant presence of fire and gas and beatings and hunger and cold, and each moment became precious, filled with the hope that they would at least survive until this moment. He knew he had resisted for as long as he could. He could not, with only the strength of his will, stop the machinelike deaths, but he could—and he knew that he could manage it perhaps with the proddings from his sense of futility—feel at one with his people; he held on to this like an imaginary yet firm point in the universe, so that nothing could pull him away from it. Everything was lost. His eyes were empty. The invisible thread that had held them together in the past held them together here too. In a moment, they would never see one another again. Maybe it's better this way. Maybe. Better and yet worse. It was already beyond good and evil—beyond judgment. It was altogether from a different world than he was able to comprehend. His world was only his conscience. He felt an awful emptiness. The injustice that had started somewhere, finished nowhere; it had touched everyone.

After fifteen or twenty minutes, it was quiet inside the gas chamber, just as it might have been before the sprinklers filled up and emptied out again. The people breathed loudly—they might have needed to hear themselves breathing, to show they still could. Together, and each of them separately.

Anna thought of her mother and father—of all who were close to her and had died and of all the dead whom she remembered. In a moment she would be with them. They were all being killed in a war declared by only one side. For a long time they couldn't understand why they were being killed. Just saying that they hadn't done anything wasn't enough.

And then she heard rustling, like a mouse running across a tin floor or a gutter pipe, or as if water would have streamed from the sprinklers. Or as if the old paint cracked around the sprinklers. A movement which took them like a river current away from life, from the realm of the living. Could someone taking in a breath of zyklon-B feel anything that would be uplifting, even for a fraction of a second? If only it were like that. Perhaps. Death, the sister of life, knows no one. Only the survivors, *Geheimnistragers,* remained. The SS officers knew by then that nobody would want to believe them, if anyone wanted to listen at all. Surely the people must have felt the small crystals fall through and the sprinkles hit their heads, shoulders, sliding down, if possible in the crush, through the arms and the trunks. The bitter smell of almonds. Surely someone shook his head to get rid of them because no one's arms could be moved anymore. The gas rose from the small crystals, the majority of which reached the bare concrete and the puddles. The waterproof bulbs, protected by the thick iron mesh, became lost. It must have been an immense burning pressure from the inside, as if someone poured melted, black asphalt inside a person. It penetrated Emil through all the openings in his skin. Through his nose and mouth. The gas. Everything that happens when a human being is killed by gas. Everything that pours out of a person; an effort to press out a giant plug from one's lungs with the last strength but still, the breathing in of even more gas. Enough. Death was only a few heartbeats away. Then, the end.

Does anyone want to hear about the saliva, how one's eyes and nose watered, or how one vomited, or about the blood? Words about the untiring voices inside the heart sound better. About the eyes that gaze ahead even in death. The stone burned by fire. A river bed in which the water dried out long ago. A hope that became hopelessness, just as an enormous continent becomes a deep sea. Or about the thoughts of the apartment at 137 Royal Avenue and how the landlord attempts to start the Ford with green mudguards, and how above the garage there stand cages for the budgies that the young landlord sold to France. About how Emil Ludvig convinced Anna, Helena, and Richard that the crucial things one needs in life are not just money and health because one needs both and, of course, good luck. He had been at the Piave campaign and had not had his leg torn off, only shrapnel in it which healed. He could reminisce about the pretty Italian nurse in the field hospital who would take him to the toilet and help him.

It can be hoped that the best thing in the shower was that when he lost consciousness and clawed his fingers into a stranger's body, he did not perceive who was next to him. Even in the last minutes, hate might not have come to him, which it would have for those who had murdered him. He was as far from them as Germany is from Prague, as far as the farthest stars, as distant as it is from one end of the universe to the other, from one end of infinity to another. He did not understand what was going on in the minds and souls of the German Nazis and their assistants. It was foreign to him—so foreign that it was as if it almost did not exist, even though it was murdering him, along with his people. It was only anxiety and pain. Embarrassment, insecurity, and fear, which he had hidden in life with his smile. He felt something that no person understands, yet must come to terms with at the moment of birth—an eternity that in a moment obscures how things will end; with humility or greatness, in pain or without. Only fractions of a second separated him from an unconsciousness with no return. It was a realm without words and without hope or hopelessness. It distanced him from the gas rising from the green crystals inside and from the black rain that had lost its translucence in the thick, black smoke emanating day and night from the chimney over Birkenau. Only the images of wild dogs tearing off pieces of flesh from the dead bodies passed quickly through his mind before disintegrating in the fire. In that moment an invisible sea of life and death opened its mouth and swallowed him as it had done all the rest. Emil Ludvig perished. He was two days short of fifty-two years old, and it was not the first death he thought about but the last one, and it disappeared through fulfillment.

It was his private share in the German Final Solution. There was nothing anymore. Nothing. Only the bitter smell of almonds. They were all together but everyone was alone. Everyone for himself; the best and the worst, the strongest and the weakest. They were like a tree with roots spread far and wide, a tree that had fallen down. They were like a dead tree, still alive a few minutes earlier. It is hard to imagine that history stopped that very minute, because it was no longer surrounded by other trees that would break its fall. They were like a tree burning in the forest, captured by fire, where first one catches fire, then the second, then the third, until they all burn down before anybody has tried to extinguish it from the very beginning. But history hovered above it all, the same history known and taught by the cantor in Liben's synagogue, from which the golden crown with purple edges probably ended up in the trash—unless somebody picked it up and took it home. It was the history of Sodom and Gomorrah, and of echoes of legends of Satan, who has no mercy on anyone. Gas ended all this just as it ended the fear that prevented them from fighting while they were not yet alone and while at least some of them still could fight. At that moment, only the echoes of echoes remained. They were disappearing fast, just as when the scream becomes a whisper and the whisper becomes silence. The stillness came after the cries, and widened like circles on the water, always wider, but at the same time weaker, so as to flood the entire world and dissolve in it as well.

All together, the disinfector used twelve cans at the price of sixty German marks. It was a larger dose of zyklon-B, let us hope. It caused a breakdown of the lungs, suffocation, and a violent decomposition of the blood corpuscles. The people in the concrete chamber became stuck to one another. Still, even here, families could be recognized in the dim light, as long as they succeeded in staying together. They had not been torn apart, as promised by the commandant the day before. The puddles on the concrete floor were fused into shallow depressions. The head of the crematorium had the fans switched on. If they kept part of their countenance, the victims had foam on their mouths. Their hair color, if they still had any, changed. Nothing remained the same.

"*Geendet,*" soldiers informed the commandant, who was already looking out the window of his black Daimler car. "Finished." Next to him, with loud yellow pigskin gloves in his lap, sat the inspector. Although he'd arrived directly from Berlin and had driven all night without stopping, he didn't show any traces of fatigue but rather of interest.

"I like punctuality," he said. And then he added, smilingly, "Don't they say that the most punctual of all is Death? He never misses a meeting. He keeps his word." He looked down at his watch.

"We work according to a precise plan," said the commandant.

"Gas?" asked the inspector general.

"It kills faster than chloroform," the commandant said.

The inspector looked at him.

"Without the danger of ingestion by others," the commandant added.

The inspector looked around. He noted the position of each guard, man, and driver, and it appeared that he was even counting the trucks.

The commandant had probably expected something different than what the inspector said next, but if he did, he didn't let it show.

"It is time to do away with the false solidarity among our people," he said. None of his men would have understood his meaning, but then none of them had heard it, and later it was not in the commandant's interest to explain it to the men himself.

For a while, the inspector watched everything that went on in silence. Then he asked, "It ends with this?"

"Yes, with this it is over," the commandant answered. "Except for the next time, of course."

"I am concerned with saving materials. What are the criteria for the individual phases?"

293

The commandant looked at him. For a second he wondered what kind of material the inspector might be thinking of. There were only two possibilities—human material and zyklon-B, or the German outfit.

He had no doubt that the inspector knew what he knew. "Do you perhaps mean the bonded hydrogen cyanide gas?" he asked politely but matter-of-factly.

"Could some of our people not know that they're wasting it?"

"Quite the opposite," the commandant said. "We don't waste a drop. Soon we'll visit the stores of materials and the spoils of war. As for zyklon-B, there are several considerations: I can add or take away several cans quite freely. It would mean shortening the state of consciousness to unconsciousness, if you understand me, Colonel. Death in each case comes later. We're speaking about fifteen, thirty minutes approximately."

"However," said the inspector. "Have you tested it on dogs?"

"On rats," corrected the commandant. "On rats," he repeated. "Then on undesirables—still on the territory of the old empire and with all the legal problems that it brought—until we brought the whole apparatus here to the Eastern lands where no obstacles exist for us; we crossed right over to the materials we use now. We took advantage of local resources, so to speak."

"Understandably," said the inspector. "You know how the leader feels about dogs."

"Certainly, Colonel."

"The first and last loyalty of our people must be uncompromising."

"You're in the right place, Inspector."

They both looked at the chimney.

"A slaughtered sheep doesn't suffer by being skinned," said the inspector.

"They are unable to die, just as they were unable to live," said the commandant.

"Yes," said the inspector. "Dying is also an art. Isn't it funny that those who boasted the most that breathing belongs to life as money belongs in one's pocket are, in the end, unable to breathe or to die?" He laughed.

The commandant did not laugh. "We'll help them. We don't begrudge the effort, intelligence, or financial burdens. Only some can leave as they were born; class distinction and other self-evident truths harden a man and educate him. This doesn't just concern children, if you know what I mean."

"Irreconcilability is the order of the day," said the inspector.

"I only know one kind of regret," answered the commandant. "I feel pity for everyone who hasn't gotten gassed yet. I feel sorry for every Jew who isn't here."

"It's war. The only rule which permanently stands when dealing with the enemy is that there are no rules. To the extent that someone wants to impose them on us, he must be sure that we know how to disregard them. I feel sick to my stomach when I think about international laws which do not make sense for us. The only thing that lasts is our honor. Honor for which we live and because of which we are living and will continue to live—not them."

"I know what war means," said the commandant.

"It's a remarkable place," said the inspector. "The place where strength changes into destitution and destitution into nothingness. There were a lot of them; not even one will remain. We put an end to the strangers on German soil. They won't share in German generosity or in German kindness. We changed the black scourge into a blessing. People no longer have to call in vain to their leaders to finally do something about it."

"It's the hardest to get them into the chambers," said the commandant. "For them, orders are not the same as for us. The rest is simple." For a moment the commandant smiled. "You can believe me that they would run over hot coals to escape their fate. We are the cooks, we know the recipe, and we know how to create a new dish."

"If everything continues to go as well as it has so far, we don't have to worry about the future," said the inspector. "No one has to test us about what is to be expected of the future, what is the thought behind man's greatest step in civilization. It is an ideal situation not to accomplish one, two, or three tasks, but to do it all at once. And in addition, you can even prove your loyalty, your ties, if you know what I'm talking about."

"A Final Solution," said the commandant. "Of course." It contained everything that was hanging in the air.

"My trade is war. Victory. The object of war is death."

The wind brought along clouds of ashes and the smell of burned meat and bones similar to the smells of a glue factory.

The inspector wiped his light-colored eyebrows under his glasses where the ashes fell, and he paused. He thought: Besides the clear goals that we wish to accomplish through the war and the reasons we now kill when before we negotiated, there are also subconscious reasons why man kills. There's a whole list of them from the most obvious to the almost unknown and completely invisible. But they are there. Nothing is more convincing than killing. Killing is beautiful. Only the circumstances are ugly, sometimes. But he kept this all to himself. Each has to discover this for himself.

"All is as it should be," the commandant said.

"No doubt about that," the inspector replied.

"Not in the least, Colonel. It is victory," the commandant said.

"It is more than victory."

He did not add that killing on a large scale, for anyone participating, provided he was on the side of those killing, is like a great poem, although perhaps no poem, even the greatest, can be compared to such killing.

"It is a victory that no defeat could ever erase," the inspector added. And when I say this—regardless of whether it was just a partial defeat in a military or civilian struggle or not—I know what I am saying."

His voice turned softer. He thought to himself: Fire, smoke, and at the end, odors, and if the wind comes, nothing. Nothing. Poetry and victory without a trace. Witnesses to their own defeat disappearing into the fire. In smoke. In the scent that dissipates in the wind. He had graying blond hair under his military cap, bright blue eyes, glasses with gold rims, and a round face. His belt felt a little too tight to be comfortable from the weight he'd gained. He had a nice, strong voice. And he must have enjoyed hearing it for he sometimes spoke like an actor.

"We are still here," he added, aloud after his thoughts.

"Of course," agreed the commandant. "*So ist es.* That's it."

"There are things which no one can do for us," the inspector said. "And for which no one but us would accept the responsibility. We will assume the responsibility. Every one of us. Not only that, but also strength combined with resolve and will to action. Responsibility and strength." Then he said, "That is not to say that it's in the public interest." Finally, he said, "The main battle of the war—the Jewish presence against the German will, the Jewish will against German time—here they meet, for the first and last time, the four dimensions of the world at the point of intersection, defined by German will, German action—the German solution." It was German time that defined the memory of the world. A German house which would be first in Europe, then the whole world. History could be deduced from German actions. And nothing would change that, not even ten thousand years into the future. He had finished his thought.

"Nobody would give a penny for them," the commandant stated.

"The Final Solution," the inspector said. "The end to their race, religion, conspiracy."

"Here we have a glass window—we can see inside," the commandant said.

"Who would want to look?" replied the inspector. "After all, it's no longer interesting."

"They look—to start with—like fish, caught up and writhing in the net, when the catch is good," said the commandant. "Like suffocating fish in a barrel."

What he saw was as fascinating as it was horrendous. The smell of ash and fire, burned flesh, fat, and hair saturated the air. It would be better for a person to look from behind a gas mask, thought the inspector, or to hold a handkerchief soaked in cologne over his mouth and nose. No, he thought to himself, what he could see from this distance was enough for him to form a picture. Nobody could accuse him of a lack of imagination. Reality outdid all expectations. Just a footnote about overrating the strength of one's enemy, about taking earlier advantage of opportunities; about inaccurate administrative work which led to combing Europe to get rid of the Jews. And still, some unanswered questions. Yes, it was true. A soldier should never go to a war that he does not fully believe in. Maybe it's a slow victory, bit by bit, but it would be total. And in passing, he remembered the words of the professor in the registration office in Prague who presented him with this question: If Germans and Germany are so good and Jews so bad, why do Germans and Germany see Jews as such a deadly threat? How can the most advanced, the most civilized nation be so unsure? Is it fear of a handful of Jews? In his mind, the inspector conjured up the professor to stand witness to what he saw.

"Some," said the commandant, "even take food inside with them." And he laughed. "*Guten Appetit. Wol zu speisen . . . Mahlzeit. Gute ver-richtung.*"

The inspector looked at the bitter expression on the commandant's lips. "Hate for one person means the deepest and the most devoted love for someone else. Is it clear to you, Herr Major?"

The commandant was silent for a moment before he said, "*Es ist klar, Herr General-Inspector.* It is clear."

The inspector felt that he had been denied only one thing: he saw nothing but fear in the face of his victims. Not admiration. Not envy. Probably not even hate. They're scared, he told himself. Scared. That's all. But surely, in juxtaposition to all the responsibilities and endeavors, energy and might, it was not enough. He was being denied the most important element—even right to the point of death—even in death and after death. It was only this that spoiled his sense of total victory—of complete superiority. And, he thought, our duty is to be both thorough and improvisational. We must plan and then attack when we have the opportunity—when the right time is here—and not back off when this race covers itself with a cloak of religion or religion takes off its cloak to reveal the race. It is preferable to exchange evidence for instruction according to the slogan "Night and Fog." The results are ashes. Once and forever. It is us or them. War is like a door we've opened out to the biological base of the enemy. Our day has arrived. If we miss it, the pendulum of history will return to where we don't want it to be.

He looked at the chimney, and then he moved his eyes to the barbed wire fence and to the administration building before he looked back at the place where he stood. The nucleus of German wisdom, all German knowledge from the first Teuton to the very last Prussian, Saxon, or Pomeranian, consisted of the knowledge that greatness could only bring forth extinction and only extinction could bring forth greatness. He stood face-to-face with an extinction as yet unknown to the mortals of this planet. The inspector's sense of being stunned gave way to fright, and fright gave way to shock, and at the end, after fright, there crouched greatness, a might in which he had participated but that also made him feel like a blade of grass in a storm. And that was the moment when he found the cold-blooded camp commandant's presence supportive and encouraging, although he would never let on. Germany is greater than man. It is the source of extinction that can no longer be denied. From all the roles he was forced to play, from all the masks one is forced to wear during one's life, this one was, he was sure, the most natural to him.

Compared to the inspector and his logic, the commandant was more down to earth. The final goal was the same, the means are just the flip side of the same coin; and he thought of the crew's chess competition, of the canary he had bought for his four-year-old boy, of his wife who was having a new dress made. One day the little one would wear a uniform like his father. The beloved uniform, he added to himself. If he had a choice, he would never take it off.

The commandant knew what would happen when the men from the Sonderkommando opened the gate and sprayed a stream of icy water onto the bodies stuck together with blood, sweat, and shit; bodies that reminded him of uprooted carrots, turnips, or beets.

"It cannot really be compared to anything; it overcomes any other achievement. It ignores the conditions that bound those who came before us and that would have limited those who'll come after us," the inspector added with a hardly suppressed excitement still deep in his thoughts.

"Not on our continent," said the commandant. "It will exceed the limits of our continent. It will spread from one continent to another; it will lead humanity from delirious raving to a yet unknown reality. It is a metamorphosis that will have more impact on the world than anything else up to now. It means re-creation of the world as we used to know it. It exceeds the passing of things past. It is the beginning; the beginning of the new, of our civilization. For now in Europe. But tomorrow?"

"True. We've showed the way. Now it'll be easy," the inspector said.

"We are learning," the commandant said. "We are trying. We are all doing our best."

They both looked at the chimney again. The first clouds of smoke would burst out of there at any moment, proof that the task, however incomplete, was being realized.

"Yes," said the inspector. "It's now or never."

They were enveloped by silence, disturbed only by the murmur of the dead. Silence was the only thing that remained of those killed. It spread like circles on the surface of the water as it swallows up a stone.

It's a shame that day and night do not have forty-eight hours. Twice as much time, so there'd be a faster pace than ten thousand per day and ten thousand per night. The inspector looked at the well-trodden path and thought to himself: The line of death. An abyss into which the greatest enemy of mankind was disappearing. An abyss into which, were it the other way around, they would only lead them. It is astounding, the inspector thought. Life goes on. He was drunk with the power of life and the helplessness of death. The inspector thought about choreography—ballet—and of how the dancers practice and then perform. Something between ballet and a march, he thought, and in his mind he imagined an infinite parade of people who were going to the ovens; sometimes they walked, sometimes they sauntered, and sometimes they had to be hurried along. Life is capable of creating a strange theater. He also thought about how the army, the police, including the secret police, reminded him of choreography, or maybe it was the other way around. Choreography and ballet reminded him of soldiers, police. Deep down he thought, I hope that they blame themselves. If it were not for what they are, and from where they came, and for what they want, they would not be here. What is happening to them is not what would have happened otherwise. What did they expect from their surroundings, that the world would protect them? How could anyone save them? They're not the first to have miscalculated. It is relatively easy to play tricks with their minds and torture their souls before they reach the Final Solution. This they have behind them. It occurred to him at ten thousand people a day, ten thousand people a night, that was more than eight hundred and thirty people an hour, thirteen per minute. Every hour, every minute, every second, in two twelve-hour shifts. He was still good at calculating. It was easy to multiply by seven, for the days of the week: one hundred and forty thousand people. It was even easier to multiply by fifty-two weeks. We'll see who will last longer, he thought to himself.

"The next train will arrive in twenty minutes," said the commandant.

"Yes, the transports here have priority. The focus of the war is here," said the inspector.

The commandant glanced at his watch. "In nineteen minutes, on the left side of the ramp. Do you want to have a look at the unloading?"

The inspector looked at his watch too.

The camp, which gave an impression of huge emptiness while also revealing an impressive fullness, had filled him with the wisdom that only war could bring. Something that does not even need an apology because it is so huge, almost indescribable in its size.

"In nineteen minutes on the left side of the ramp?" repeated the inspector for the commandant. It filled him with music, thought, feelings of glory, and satisfaction. "Won't you manage without me?" he said, smiling.

He felt how he had grown, thanks to the camp and to all that he had witnessed here; all that he had been until this moment was but a feeble effort, often a lie. This was the truth, the greatest extinction. It was like a fire in which rough iron is transformed into fine weapons. He felt both humiliation and arrogance as only doom can bring forth.

He felt as if he had an appointment with history. Destruction comes—he'd been a witness to that—a source of evil, the stem of all misfortunes, and chokes the expansion of a minority that wanted to take over the world. And just as a long time ago, in A.D. 331, when Alexander the Great introduced the new war techniques—among others, longbows and movable shooting platforms, the predecessors of artillery—so did the Third Reich institute unexpected war tactics and strategies to annihilate its enemy. He felt what progress they had made. It could not be compared to anything known before.

"Finally, here our men become men of steel," the commandant said. "Here we have the smithy, the anvil, and the hammer."

"It's a classic victory," said the inspector. "It's a perfect military operation from all angles—preparation, practice, and results."

"Yes," said the commandant.

That was the last thing they said to each other.

The earth around the crematorium appeared as if covered with a parched core. Aridity swept across the surface of the swamps.

The trucks had already driven away. The ambulances with the dogs too. Two men from the Sonderkommando installed rubber hoses. With a violent stream, they cleaned the bodies of the sweat, bloody foam, excrement, and the blood of women. They smelled as a result of their work. They reeked of it from their rags, even from their skin. The creaking of freight trains penetrated from the outside. It was more a factory than a funereal sound. Here and there, it seemed that some bodies jerked as in a spasm, but it was only caused by the jets of water. It almost seemed unbelievable that all had fit into the showers. They had all died standing up because there was no room to fall down. The night went away. The day arrived. Silence and wind and wind and stillness begat more silence.

9

On Royal Avenue there stands an apartment building with cracked stucco, number 137. Rain washes out the soil between the cobblestones. In the vacant site where the post office was to be erected, mud puddles lie. For a long time, there has not been such a rainy autumn or a creeping wet winter or spring. Perhaps not even the year the first Jewish transports left. People joke—it reminds them of that deluge when it reportedly rained for forty days and forty nights. A corner building with a closed store stares out from the largest puddle like a mirror.

The cutler's display window is being arranged with sharp cutting weapons of all types and sizes: hunting knives and small swords for the Hitler Youth and Luftwaffe officers, knives with circular openings, and daggers for the youth. The cutler never complained. In spite of the shortage of Swedish steel, he still received new orders from the military. Instead of the new material, he had willingly used the materials salvaged from raised English and American ships.

It is the coldest early spring in ten years. The large silver sphere on the hill opposite the public toilets, with entrances and exits shaped like snails surrounded with barbed wire, reflects the rain's glitter. The sphere looks like a cooled sun, painted over with three layers of field gray. For safety reasons, the military authorities emptied it long ago. Everything is secret. They will have to wait to fill it again until after the war.

The guards under the gas sphere, carrying rifles loaded with live ammunition, change after every four hours and wear capes against the rain. At night, the guards have dogs in position: shepherds or Dobermans who have proven themselves in the war. Earlier, just one gendarme would have sufficed here, but after the assassination of the police general Reinhard Heydrich, literally everything has been guarded, not only the gas sphere.

The tailor's enterprise already has its second company sign within the past two years. It offers first-rate cutwork for interested civilians, the last imperial fashion in the German tradition of officers' and generals' uniforms. Troops passing through the city from west to east and east to west and from south to north and vice versa sit at the barber's. The pork butcher sells to the soldiers for special food coupons. The former owner of the dry cleaning shop came from the German side of the Czech border region and serves only imperial German nationals. One can get any kind of paper flag with the swastika at the stationery store. On the kiosks and advertising fences and turrets, the main poster urges the populace: COLLECT REFUSE FOR THE REICH, YOU WILL STRENGTHEN THE WAR EFFORT. After the downpours and the wind, the corners of the posters come unstuck and twist. One can see from those underneath that they once used to show *Pancho Villa* and *Five Weeks in a Balloon.* On the inside as well as the outside of the toilet, there is an inscription in tar: ZILOPECK IS A GOOD BOY.

Above the rocks beyond the river, far from the train station where fog hovers, an institute for the mentally ill stands. Under it is the tower of the waterworks and the old cemetery. The graves are worn down, drowning in the rain. For more than a year, no one has been there, although someone wrote, in a primitive hand, *Thou art dust and shall return to dust: Where you are, we have been as well. Where we are now, you will also be.* It is an old expression, which has nearly become the fashion of the season. It is already on many a cemetery wall. In the wooden church near the Meteor VIII playground, the priest recites for people the prayer: *Forgive us our trespasses, as we forgive those who trespass against us. . . .* The believers brought in water to the church. The night from Friday to Saturday saw the heaviest rain. Between prayers, the people exchange the news from the battlegrounds limited by the view of distance and space. No one is able to explain why it has rained so persistently. In the hotel opposite the church, German soldiers and officers are being billeted. They are said to have arrived from the East where the Germans have been building huge camps for reeducation, where the participants work in twelve-hour shifts in the war industry and help Germany in this manner.

The department for disinformation may rub its hands. Wrath and distrust are being sown by the people who have changed into ash blown away by the wind, into the swamps, rivers, and the Arctic sea. This way they will be angry with them even after the war, however the war may turn out for Germany. Nobody talks about it unnecessarily, for in spreading *Greul* propaganda, slander on the account of Germany, there is capital punishment, and people would rather watch their tongues than talk unnecessarily. It will not even flash across their minds that they are sharing in something by being silent. Someone at the hotel has persistently been playing a record with the "Ciribiribin" waltz on the gramophone. In all three movie theaters, the World, Humanity, and Cooperation, and in the newly equipped cinema, On the Ship, German comedies and operettas are mainly being shown, such as "Woman of My Dreams" with Maryka Rokk. "Regiments Gruss Marsch" plays from the loudspeakers on the street.

The gasworks attendants have not received their new, coarse cotton uniforms since the time that the enterprise was taken over by the German Military Administration, as is true of all gasworks. The new fire station has been guarding the neighborhood on Royal and Lord Mayor Avenues, but fortunately, thanks to the alertness and vigilance of the civilian population, there have been only a few blazes.

Opposite the building number 137, where there is still a kindergarten, Czech children learn how to sing: "*Hanschen klein, ging allein.*"

The list of names posted downstairs in the corridors in front of the principal's office of the girls' and boys' schools has changed. There is not a single Jewish name here. Prague is *Judenrein.* The newspapers, which must be posted daily by the school's caretaker, repeat that it is a permanent change, for a thousand years. No more Dreyfus affair; no emphasizing and exaggerating trifles to make a camel out of a fly. Europe has become Fortress Europa: nobody will smuggle in heterogeneous elements here, as in the past. Germany has been waging a historical struggle for the Aryan culture, the Aryan civilization, even if it should be down to the last man. Who is not with us is against us. The parents are encouraged not to dirty the school with mud, since cleanliness is a fine life preserver. Preserve cleanliness, defend against epidemic; you are not barbarians. It is recommended that you clean your shoes on the doormat.

The bells are ringing again in the loudspeakers. Everything is as it was in the old days. Bells and fanfares.

It has been raining. New, plump, moist snowflakes fall as on March 15, 1939, when the Germans invaded the country and people wept in the streets, and everything fell under the snow and rain that covered the streets, the cobblestones, the city.

Still, many things are the way they were before. The flower shop, the iron hardware, the municipal authorities. The amusement enterprise Mahrer, Jandourek's jewelry store, the pubs, Express and Mercury, the toilets, the corner clock which has shown five minutes to twelve for a second year.

On the right corner of the house, number 137, the store with textiles and collar cleaning was discontinued. A branch office of the German Winter Aid, *Winterhilfe,* will be established here. A red-black poster, like the one that lists the names of the executed, asks for the help of the passersby with a quotation from the Bible. Help is needed for those survivors, the German men and women from Bromberg for whom Polish outlaws had prepared a bloody Sunday (says the pointy Gothic script on the poster) because Germany had to take possession of Poland. Also for the survivors, or the men killed in the East, where bandits have been constantly wreaking havoc in the rear. Also for the dead and the injured under the English and American terrorist carpet bombings in German cities. As well as for the soldiers who perished in the Yugoslav mountains and the Galicia forests. Winter aid is needed, not only in respect to clothing. The inhabitants of the Czech and Moravian lands, just like the inhabitants of Flanders, Denmark, and Belgium, as well as of other countries under the German administration, will get the opportunity to express their relation to the European fate of Germany.

For those who support the Third Reich, Germany holds firmly within her hands the threads that lead to all events. It's the end of the myth about Jewish innocence, of the Jews being chosen, of Jewish laws, according to which good is good and bad bad, for everyone under the stars. It's also the end of the Jews themselves. Finally.

The tin shutters are drawn on one of the stores. No one has thought about what all is going to be there or whether it fits on the shelves and into the empty boxes that remained from the original owner. The torn-down sign has been lying in the garage in the house courtyard with its lettering facing the wall. It reminds one of something that was, nothing of what is going to be.

Beyond the drawn shutters there is a dark space where only the mice, spiders, and cockroaches live. Twilight, dampness, and silence. Apparently it will need gassing out, first of all. The naked plaster dummies lean against the wall. The arms of some have fallen off. Others have holes in their bellies and in their chests or their sides.

Little is known about what happened to the former owners of the store and the apartment above it except for a postcard addressed to Mr. Husserle, in care of Karla: *We are well. We are short of nothing here. Everything is in the best order. We kiss you all. We are healthy and happy. Do not worry about us. Neuberun bei Birkenau. The General Government. Emil Ludvig and the family, Anna, Helena, and Richard.*

Finally it stops raining. The heavens clear up. A rainbow sails out into the sky. It looks like an aerial bridge between the corner building and the hill. Under it, the steel and iron sphere huddles. The air is damp. The sun falls weakly into the streets. Perhaps spring will come soon.

An alien, evaporated fragrance, a futile, inaudible echo. When the wind blows and it rains, just as in the faint, languid early spring sun that reflects off the tin shutters of the rolled-up blinds, it sounds as if someone invisible were singing, coughing, or choking.

❈

Notes

zu grund
bottom line

PAGE 47
aus guter burgerlichen Familie
from a good middle-class family

PAGE 102
Zentralstelle fur jüdische Auswanderung in Prag
Prague Central Office for Jewish Emigration

PAGE 139
durchlasschein
a pass

PAGE 145
Panzergrenadiers truppen
armored regiment troops

PAGE 146
"Schon gut, schon gut"
"OK, OK"

PAGE 147
Deutsche Geheimestatspolizei
German State Secret Police

PAGE 148
Ehrenblatt — Spange Des Heeres
Leaf of Honor

PAGE 166

Deutsche Reichbahn
German state railway

PAGE 205

strengstens verboten
strictly forbidden

PAGE 210

Mischling des erstern Grades
half-breed of the first degree

PAGE 213

borsalino
Italian black hat

PAGE 221

"Fuchs, du hast die Ganz gestohlen; gib'sie wieder hier."
"Fox, you have stolen everything; give it back again here."

PAGE 221

"Das Oberkommando der Wehrmacht gibt bekannt."
"The high commander of the Wehrmacht makes the following public announcement."

PAGE 222

"Deutschlandslied. Ich habe einen Kamaraden. Kaiser Friedrich Marsch. Kurassier-Marsch."
"Songs of Germany. I have a comrade. Kaiser Friedrich Marsch. Kurassier-Marsch."

PAGE 233

"Was sagt er?"
"What's he saying?"

PAGE 246

Jedem das seine
To each his due

PAGE 246

Arbeit macht frei
Work makes one free

PAGE 277

Ghettojuden
ghetto Jews

PAGE 281

Judenschweine
Jewish swine

PAGE 282

"Richtig, richtig. Schnell."
"Right, right. Quickly."

PAGE 282

"Hilfe, schnell, likvidieren."
"Help, quickly, and finish them off."

PAGE 298

"Guten Appetit. Wol zu speisen . . . Mahlzeit. Gute verrichtung."
"Bon appétit. Enjoy your food . . . meal. Good luck."

PAGE 305

Greul
horror

❖

About the Author

Arnošt Lustig was born in Czechoslovakia in 1926. After internment in Theresienstadt, Buchenwald, and Auschwitz, he escaped from a train of prisoners bound for Dachau. He returned to Prague to fight in the Czech resistance in 1945. When the USSR invaded Czechoslovakia in 1968, he was vacationing in Italy; thus began his life in exile. Lustig lives in the United States, where he teaches writing, literature, and the history of film at American University. He is the author of the collections *Indecent Dreams* and *Street of Lost Brothers* and the novel *Dita Saxova,* all published by Northwestern University Press.

❖

Jewish Lives

ISAIAH SPIEGEL
Ghetto Kingdom: Tales of the Łódź Ghetto

ARNON TAMIR
A Journey Back: Injustice and Restitution

JIŘI WEIL
Life with a Star
Mendelssohn Is on the Roof

BOGDAN WOJDOWSKI
Bread for the Departed